THE JIGSAW MAN

THE
JIGSAW
MAN

A Novel

NADINE
MATHESON

HANOVER
SQUARE
PRESS

HANOVER
SQUARE
PRESS™

Recycling programs
for this product may
not exist in your area.

ISBN-13: 978-1-335-49915-8

The Jigsaw Man

First published in the United Kingdom by HQ in 2021. This edition published in 2021.

This edition published by arrangement with Harlequin Books S.A.

Hanover Square Press
22 Adelaide St. West, 40th Floor
Toronto, Ontario M5H 4E3, Canada
HanoverSqPress.com
BookClubbish.com

Printed in U.S.A.

To Amber, Esther, Jem, Jonathan, Keri,
Luke, Patricia, Satu & Steph

THE
JIGSAW
MAN

THE
JIGSAW
MAN

PROLOGUE

6:44 a.m. Greenwich Pier, low tide, and Maxwell Perkins is walking his dog on the riverbank. He's not expecting to find pieces of a body. He walks on gray clay, wet pebbles and shards of glass, avoiding scraps of wood and discarded car tires. As he lets the dog, Petra, off the leash he notices the sunlight bouncing off something on the ground. He bends down and pulls at it carefully. Yesterday, he found a medieval pin and a Roman radiate coin. Today, it's nothing more than broken links from a bath plug chain. Disappointed, Maxwell stands up and sees that his dog is sniffing at something in the mud. It's late summer. The heat wave hasn't broken and the temperature is steadily rising. Maxwell wipes away the beads of sweat from his forehead as he walks. His T-shirt clings to the folds of fat on his stomach. At 6:48 a.m., he reaches the dog and sees what has caught her attention.

"Jesus fucking Christ."

He pulls the dog back by her collar. Adrenaline rushes through his body and his pulse beats in his ears. It's the same feeling he had yesterday when he discovered the Roman radiate coin. Inquisitiveness and excitement, which quickly disappears. Now he is overwhelmed as disgust, fear and nausea sweep over him. His free hand is shaking as he takes out his mobile phone. The phone falls among the wet pebbles. He wipes the screen against his jeans, checks that the camera is clean. He takes a picture of the severed arm.

One mile away, Heather Roszicky, an archaeology professor, is supervising a group of second-year students as they complete their fieldwork on the site of the old Deptford Dockyard. Heather leans against the riverside wall, checks her watch and sighs. It will be another four hours before the tide comes in, but she is eager to leave and return to her office. She needs to finish the final draft of her book on the decline of London river excavations before her editor makes good on her promise to kill her. She's missed her deadline twice and has already spent her advance.

A scream disturbs the calm air and Heather sees one of the students, a girl called Shui, running toward her. The rest of the students are backing away from the moss-covered rocks as Heather runs over to Shui, who has tripped over a piece of wood and fallen to the ground.

"What's wrong?" Heather asks.

Shui shakes her head and begins to cry as Heather pulls her to her feet. The students are talking loudly and all at once as they make their way toward Heather. Someone grabs her arm and pulls her toward the decaying ferry steps. Heather can feel the scream rising in her throat as she looks down into the murky pool of water and sees a headless torso among the black and green jagged pieces of wood.

Christian Matei, a kitchen fitter, is walking toward Nelson Mews, the last cul-de-sac on Watergate Street in Deptford. The river is not too far away, and he thinks that he hears the sound of a woman screaming but is then distracted by someone playing the trumpet, badly. As he approaches number 15, he opens the gate and throws his empty coffee cup toward the skip on the driveway.

"Shit," Christian says in his native Albanian as the cup bounces off the side of the skip and falls to the ground. As he bends to retrieve the cup something catches his eye. Half a meter away, a swarm of flies are dancing around an object on the ground. Coffee mixed with stomach acid is making its way up Christian's throat. His vomit covers the flies that are all over the ragged and decaying flesh of the severed leg.

1

The important thing was to stay calm. Not to let him see that he was getting to her. Again.

"Rob, I don't have time for this. I'm going to be late for work," Henley said, grabbing her car keys from the side table.

"That's the problem, you never—"

The sound of the front door slamming shut drowned out the rest of his words, but she knew what they were.

You never have time. Your work always comes first.

Detective Inspector Anjelica Henley looked back at the mid-terraced house with the freshly painted blue door. She wondered, not for the first time, what it said about her that she was happier dealing with rapists and murderers than her own husband. She checked her reflection in the rearview mirror. She had rushed out too quickly and hadn't had a chance to cover up the small scar on her right cheek and the dark circles under her eyes. Henley's phone cut off the latest road traffic reports from BBC London, and STEPHEN PELLACIA CALLING flashed across the screen.

"Where are you?" he said, by way of greeting.

"Good morning to you too. I'm on Deptford Broadway. I'll be about ten minutes," said Henley.

"Don't come in. I need you to make a detour. The bottom end of Watergate Street."

"Watergate Street? What for?"

"We've got a case. A bunch of body parts has been found scattered around the area. Too early to say if they belong to the same victim or if it's more than one. Ramouter's already en route. He'll meet you there."

Henley slammed the brakes as a moped cut in front of her. The tension returned, as quick as a click, twisting through her body. "What do you mean you're sending Ramouter?" She tried but failed to stop the anger from coating her words. "What makes you think that I—"

Pellacia ignored her. "I'm emailing the CAD details to you."

Henley smashed her hand against the steering wheel. The last thing she needed was an overenthusiastic and inexperienced detective snapping at her heels.

Watergate Street, just off the gridlocked Creek Road, was usually quiet, but now, at 7:40 a.m., front doors were open and the residents clustered outside, wondering why a stream of police cars had assembled on their road. The looming branches of the cherry trees created a canopy over the street, casting an eerie, twilight darkness despite the beating sun. Henley parked her car opposite the Admiral pub, just a few meters from the police cordon where a small crowd was gathered.

Trainee Detective Constable Salim Ramouter was standing on the other side of the tape, a short distance from the crowd. He was dressed in a navy suit, white shirt and tie, and Henley could see the shine bouncing off his black shoes. He was new to the team, though not new to the force, and he still looked "fresh" and untouched by the reality that would soon come with being a detective on the streets of London.

Pellacia had told her that Detective Sergeant Paul Stanford would be responsible for Ramouter. That he would be the one showing him the ropes, not her. Henley had been updating the information on the Crime Reporting Information System, known as a CRIS report, for another case when Pellacia had made the introductions. Ramouter seemed taller than she had remembered—almost six feet. He had a beard, which Henley thought he had probably grown in order to hide his youth.

Ramouter folded and unfolded his arms before settling on clasping his hands behind his back. She didn't like how eager and unprepared he looked, not that she was looking that authoritative. She was dressed in jeans, trainers, a Wonder Woman T-shirt and a blazer that had lain on the back seat of her car for a week. More suited to sitting in an office and not acting as the senior investigating officer on an active crime scene.

"Good morning, Inspector." Ramouter held out his hand. Henley ignored it.

"Where's DS Stanford?" Henley held up her warrant card to the uniformed police officer who lifted the tape.

"I'm not sure. I was only told to meet you here and to tell you that DC Eastwood is on her way to the Greenwich scene with Uniform and Forensics," Ramouter replied, pulling back his hand and following Henley. They paused briefly outside 15 Nelson Mews. A couple of crime scene investigators wearing blue oversuits were crouched on the ground retrieving evidence. A third stood taking photographs of the driveway.

"You do realize where we're going, right?" Henley asked as Ramouter put his hand on the gate.

"We're going to speak to Mr. Matei, aren't we?"

"Yes, and when we're done, I suggest that you ask one of the CSIs for some overshoes to put on when we get to the steps."

It was a short distance from 15 Nelson Mews to the Watergate Steps, where the road narrowed down to a cobblestoned alley.

They walked alongside a community park. An older woman and a Chinese girl were standing to the side talking to a policeman.

"That's Heather Roszicky," said Ramouter. "She found the—"

"I know what she found."

As they made their way down the alley, the smell of the river grew stronger. A mixture of stagnant drain water mixed with engine oil. Henley could hear the water breaking against the pebbled riverbank. A large terrace bordered Borthwick Wharf, converted from a meat processing and cold storage facility into a mixture of riverside apartments and commercial space.

Anthony Thomas, a senior crime scene investigator, appeared at the top of the terrace, pulling on a pair of purple latex gloves. Henley wouldn't trust anyone else to protect a crime scene. He was fastidious but, most importantly, he was loyal.

Henley hadn't worked with Anthony at a live crime scene for two years. A memory escaped one of the boxes in her mind: a hazy image of Anthony guiding her into a room to stand on a large plastic sheet. The goose bumps on her skin as the air-conditioning covered her in an icy chill. Not quite hearing the words that came out of Anthony's mouth as he scraped under her fingernails and combed through her hair, waiting for the evidence to fall at her feet. She felt exposed as the doctor examined her and recorded her cuts and bruises on a body map. The realization that she was the crime—it hit her in the gut with more fire than when the knife had pierced her stomach. They had trained her to be a detective, not a victim.

"I wasn't expecting to see you out and about," said Anthony. "Are you coming down to have a look, then?"

"It looks that way," Henley said. She was grateful that Anthony hadn't made more of a fuss that this was the first time he had seen her in the field in two years.

"Great, it will be like old times." Anthony pulled several pairs of blue overshoes out of a box by his feet and handed them to Henley. "Who's your friend?"

Henley made the introductions.

"Ah, a newbie. I've got one too." Anthony pointed to a young man who was standing stock-still behind him, holding a camera. He had already zipped his blue oversuit up to his neck. His eyes darted anxiously from Henley to Anthony. "Fun, isn't it?" Anthony said with a heavy sigh. "I'll see you down there."

"Come on," Henley said to Ramouter. "Let's see what we're dealing with."

Henley looked down at the tattooed torso, which was at least five feet from the muddy waters of the Thames. The torso had been severed at the neck and through the thighbones. Droplets of water glistened off the white skin. It had clearly been propped up between the moss-covered steps and the rotting, broken wood that was once part of the pier. The only thing that Henley could be certain about was that a white male, with a fondness for Manga anime tattoos, had had his legs cut off at the thighbone, his arms at the biceps. The cuts were not clean and surgical like the severed body parts Henley had seen a few years ago. She had been frozen to the spot the first time she'd seen the separated arms, legs, head and torso, dumped under a railway arch in Lewisham. She had learned to harden herself since then.

Her calves tightened as she squatted down. The head had been cut off just above the Adam's apple. Small hunks of bone were embedded in the ridged windpipe that jutted out among shredded muscle and clotted blood. Yellowing fat and connective tissue had the look of a raw, jointed chicken that had been left out in the air for too long. Henley stood up and breathed in deeply. The wind carried the briny, rotten scent of the river. She couldn't find the compartments in her brain that she used to separate the logical and hardened detective from the damaged and not quite healed woman who was standing at the water's edge.

She stepped away and made her way back up the Watergate Steps. She tried to shake off the sharp prickles of anxiety, but she couldn't get rid of the feeling that the torso had been staged for her.

2

"How long have we got until the tide comes in?" Henley was facing the river watching the small waves crashing against the derelict pier. She checked her watch. Nearly two hours had passed since the first 999 call.

"I checked online, and high tide is at 9:55 a.m.," Ramouter replied as he stepped around a half-submerged car tire, his eyes glazed with anxiety. "Low tide was at 3:15. Sunrise was at 6:32. A three-hour window for someone to dump whoever this is and hope that someone would find it before the tide comes in?"

"Maybe," Henley acknowledged. "But for all we know it could have been dumped after sunrise or was dumped earlier upstream before being washed up here." She inspected the glass facade of the Borthwick Wharf, empty commercial spaces and work units that opened to the terrace and lacked security cameras. Henley doubted that the local council would have extended their own CCTV cameras to this part of the street. They had been neglecting this part of Deptford for as long as she could remember.

"Has it been touched?" Henley asked Anthony, who had appeared at her side.

"As far as I'm aware, it's in situ. It wasn't touched by the woman who found it. Matei, your builder, said that he hadn't touched the leg but, unhelpfully, it's covered in his vomit. I had a quick look at the arms that were found downstream before I came here. From the looks of things, the treasure hunters may have prodded around a bit."

"There's always one."

The wind dropped and the air softly crackled with the electricity generated from the substation nearby.

"We're isolating the recovery of evidence to the direct path from the alleyway to the torso," said Anthony. "I doubt very much that whoever it was sat here and had a coffee afterward."

"They may not have had a coffee, but if we go with Ramouter's theory and the body parts have been dumped, then whoever it was certainly knows the river," Henley replied. "We'll let you get on. Ramouter and I are going to take a walk."

"Where are we going?" asked Ramouter.

"To meet Eastwood."

"And you want to walk it?"

Henley did her best to push aside her frustration when Ramouter pulled out his phone. "Google Maps says that Greenwich Pier is almost a mile away," he said.

"Your body-part dumper isn't the only one who knows the river," Anthony shouted out as Henley began to walk determinedly along the riverbank.

The gold scepters on the twin-domed roofs of the Old Royal Naval College pierced the cloudless sky. The bare masts of the restored *Cutty Sark* completed the historical panoramic view that Greenwich was known for. It was a resplendent, white-washed version of history that contrasted with the sewage that washed ashore. Henley stopped walking when she realized that she could no longer hear the sounds of Ramouter's leather soles slipping on wet pebbles.

"Where are you from?" Henley asked, waiting for Ramouter to take off his jacket and loosen his tie. She moved closer toward the moss-covered river wall as the tide began to encroach.

"Born in West Bromwich. Moved to Bradford when I was twelve." Ramouter tried to brush off the bits of mud that had stuck to his trousers, but they only smeared more. "Lots of moors, no rivers. Surely it would have been quicker in the car."

"This is quicker. Unless you fancy sitting in traffic for the next half hour while they raise the Creek Road Bridge."

"You know this area well?"

Henley ignored the question. She didn't see the point in telling him that she could have walked this path with her eyes closed. That this small part of southeast London was ingrained in her. "Whoever dumped the torso would have taken this route. It doesn't make any sense to come down here, go back up to the street level and then drive up to Watergate Street. Out of sight, below street level. Lighting would have been minimal."

"Body parts are heavy though." Ramouter tried to quicken his step to catch up with Henley. "The human head weighs at least eight pounds."

"I know." Henley pulled out her mobile phone, which had started to ring. She saw who it was and ignored the call.

"Head, torso, arms, legs. That's at least six individual body parts."

"I know that also. So, tell me, what point are you making?" Henley waited for Ramouter to reach her before maneuvering him toward the river wall as though she was chaperoning a child.

"I'm just saying that that's a lot of dead weight to be carrying around at three in the morning." Ramouter paused and placed his hand against the wall, trying to catch his breath.

Henley didn't openly express her agreement. She fished out a black hairband from her jacket pocket and pulled her thick black curls into a ponytail. She had forgotten how much energy it took to walk across the gradient slope of the riverbank.

Worse, she felt mentally unprepared for the job ahead, with a trainee struggling behind her who had no idea this was her first time as senior investigator in almost a year.

"It's a bit grim, isn't it?" DC Roxanne Eastwood shouted out as Henley finally reached the first crime scene. "Morning, Ramouter. Not a bad gig for your first day."

Henley had always thought that Eastwood actually looked and carried herself like a detective. Now, Eastwood was poised on the riverbank, the sleeves of her jacket rolled up with her notebook in her hand. She had come prepared for the river and was wearing a pair of jeans and trainers that had seen better days.

"Morning, Eastie. How does it feel to be out of the office?" Henley asked, her eyes drifting to a crime scene investigator who was putting an arm into a black bag.

"I should be asking you that," said Eastwood, with a look of concern.

Henley silently appreciated the empathy and placed her hand on Eastwood's shoulder.

"But since you asked, it's bloody terrible. I think I've got sunburn." Eastwood rubbed a hand over her reddening forehead. "Forensics are going to be wrapping up in a bit. Not that there's much for them to do. Bag it and tag it."

"Where's Mr. Perkins?"

"Ah, our illustrious treasure hunter. Last time I saw him, he was heading toward the shops. Said that he needed to get some water for his dog." Eastwood shook her head, obviously not believing a word of it. "I've got an officer keeping an eye on him. I wouldn't be surprised if he'd already uploaded pictures of his find onto Instagram."

"I want him taken back to the station. Ramouter can take another statement from him." Henley said it purposely so that Ramouter would sense she was in control. "If he's like most mudlarkers, he would have been out here first thing this morning waiting for the tide to go out. Where exactly were the arms found?"

"Just over there." Eastwood pulled down her sunglasses and pointed toward the foamed waves created by a passing river bus. The tide had already come in where X had once marked the spot. A sense of urgency filled the air as the river regained its territory.

"Did he say anything else?"

"Only that he found the second arm about three feet away from the first."

"It's a sick trail of bread crumbs," said Henley.

"You're telling me, and before you ask about CCTV, there're loads of cameras—"

"But none aimed at this part of the river."

"Exactly."

Henley's mobile phone began to ring. She pulled it out and answered. After a quick chat, she ended the call.

"That was Dr. Linh Choi. You wouldn't have met her yet but she's our go-to forensic pathologist. She's just arrived," Henley explained to Ramouter. She wiped away the sweat from the back of her neck.

"So, we've got two arms, both legs and a torso," said Ramouter. "Where's the head?"

Good question. Henley thought of the places between the two locations. A primary school, two nurseries and an adventure playground among the flats and houses. The last thing she needed was to find a head in the kids' sandpit.

"Can I have a quick look?" Henley asked the assistant from Anthony's CSI team who had just bagged up the arm and was scribbling in her notebook.

"Sure." The assistant unzipped the bag and pushed the plastic apart.

"Fuck," Henley said under her breath. Her heartbeat quickened, her stomach flipped.

"Oh," said Ramouter as he peered over Henley's shoulder. One arm was covered with gravel. Slivers of seaweed crisscrossed old scars. The second arm. Slender wrist, the ring finger slightly longer than the index, broken fingernails. Black skin. Henley could hear Pellacia's words from earlier ringing in her ears.

"Too early to say if it belongs to the same victim or if it's more than just one."

"Call DSI Pellacia," Henley told Ramouter. "Tell him that we've got two possible murder victims."

3

To anyone walking past, the natural assumption was that Greenwich police station was closed. The blue shutters at the front of the building hadn't been raised for three years, and two lonely orange traffic cones blocked the driveway, which led to a row of empty parking spaces. A faded poster redirected all prospective visitors to Lewisham police station or to call 101 if it was a nonemergency. The locals walked past wondering when the building would be knocked down and replaced with another overpriced, privately owned apartment block with a concierge service for the rich and a back door for the lucky few who had been allocated social housing. If the people had looked up, then they would have noticed that three windows on the fourth floor were open and a soft swirl of cigarette smoke was wafting out.

The Serial Crime Unit had been temporarily based on the fourth floor for six years. When the Metropolitan Police was a bit more flush, DCSI Harry Rhimes had been rewarded with the SCU after his team successfully apprehended a district nurse named Abigail Burnley, who had killed fifteen people under her care. Serial killers didn't pop up with great regularity, so the department busied itself with serial rapes, burglaries, kidnappings and cases considered too extreme for any of the twenty-six murder inquiry teams spread throughout London. Six years later, Burnley was serving a life sentence, Rhimes had been dead for eight months, Pellacia was in charge of an underfunded unit and Henley was heading toward him with a face like thunder.

"How dare you?" Henley didn't stop Pellacia's office door from slamming shut behind her.

"Don't you think a little bit of respect is due? How about, *How dare you, guv?*"

DSI Stephen Pellacia, who had been smoking out the window, stubbed out his cigarette. The strain of being in charge of the SCU was starting to show. There was more gray streaked through his brown hair and the circles under his creased eyes were darker. The euphoria of being the boss had worn off long ago and Rhimes's absence still hung heavily in the air.

"You could have given me some warning before putting me out there. Then to top that off, you dump a bloody trainee on me," said Henley.

"Why are you making this an issue? You've been on restrictive duties for six months. I thought that you would be—"

"There has never been an issue." Henley almost spat the last word out. "You're the one who told Rhimes that it would be best to stick me behind a desk."

"And you've been complaining about it every day since." Pellacia's green eyes narrowed and the small muscles in his jaw flexed with tension. "Look, we're going around in circles and I haven't got time to argue with you. I'm already late with this briefing. There's a lot to get through and I'm due at the Yard."

"Before we start—" Henley took a breath and counted to three. "Do you have any idea who the lead investigator is going to be on this case? The sooner I update the CRIS report and complete a handover, the better."

"Yeah, about that," said Pellacia as he stepped around Henley and reached for the door. "We're not handing it over."

★ ★ ★

"What do you mean we're keeping the case?"

The voice of dissent came from DC Eastwood. She pushed aside a loose strand of blond hair from her burned forehead. "I thought this was just a one-off."

"It's not," Pellacia said firmly, avoiding Henley's stare.

The SCU was housed in a room that was now far too big for their team. There was a time when the officers had hot-desked with CID and the Community Support Unit. The building used to shake with the sound of a suspect banging on the old pipes in his cell. Now the cells were more likely to contain Stanford having a snooze. The team at this point consisted of Eastwood, Henley, DS Paul Stanford, who was en route to the Old Bailey to give evidence in a serial rapist case, and now Salim Ramouter. Pellacia was in charge and these days very rarely left the office unless it was to answer the calls of his superiors, who were based at New Scotland Yard. The SCU was supported by a civilian admin team: Ezra, an ex-con at twenty-three years old and a computer genius who Pellacia had taken under his wing, and Joanna. No one knew how long Joanna had been knocking around the police stations of southeast London and neither did they know how old Joanna was, but the general consensus was that she definitely knew where all the bodies were buried and how many skeletons the Met had in their cupboards.

"We're overstretched as it is," said Eastwood. "I've worked eleven days straight with not one rest day. We've lost Stanford for the week."

"You're pointing out the obvious, Eastie."

"And the last time I checked we were running six active investigations…"

"Seven." Joanna walked through the door carrying a large cardboard box filled with various breakfast orders from the café across the road. She put the box down onto Eastwood's desk. "It's seven if you include the Thames Valley job that we're"—

she raised her hands and made the quotation signs in the air—"consulting on."

Henley watched Pellacia bite his tongue as Eastwood rolled her eyes.

"Look, you may not like it but that's what's happening. None of the other murder teams have the capacity to deal with it. The investigation is staying here. Is that clear?" said Pellacia.

"Crystal." Eastwood shook her head.

Pellacia turned his gaze to Henley, daring her to challenge the decision that he'd just made. "As Stanford is stuck in court, I've decided that Ramouter is staying on this body-part case with Henley."

"You're splitting up the twins?" Joanna exclaimed in mock shock.

"I didn't think that Stanford would take offense at no longer being Ramouter's mentor and temporarily separated from Henley."

"That's what you think." Joanna took a sausage sandwich from the box. "Ramouter, just to give you the heads-up, those two are as thick as thieves. Stanford is Henley's brother from another—"

"We get it, Joanna," said Pellacia. "Right, let's move on."

Henley mentally went through her own checklist. Muscle memory had taken over as she attended the crime scene: observe the surroundings, note the familiar and unfamiliar. Treat everything as evidence. Prepare a narrative. Secure and protect. To the outside world, she was calm and composed. Inside, her heart was about to burst out of her chest, and the knots in her stomach twisted and tightened.

Henley's phone began to vibrate on her desk. She felt sick as she read the text from her brother, Simon.

Just been around to Dad's. Wouldn't let me in. Bell you when I've finished work. x

"Now, about this river case," said Pellacia. "Potentially two victims?"

"It's not potentially two. There *are* two victims," said Henley. She began typing a reply to her brother. "The torso, legs and one arm belong to a white male. The second arm belongs to, although the sex hasn't been confirmed, a black female."

Henley's mobile phone vibrated across her desk for a second time. She picked it up.

"And no other parts have been found?"

"CSI recovered a head belonging to a white male in the skip outside 15 Nelson Mews," said Henley. "That was a text from Linh, by the way. The…parts have arrived at the mortuary."

"Two bloody victims," said Pellacia. "You never know though. This could still be a nice, straightforward investigation."

Henley didn't reply as she picked up her bag, because every nerve in her body told her Pellacia believed that even less than she did.

4

The building that housed the dead was walking distance from the police station, just off the high street where the cafés, pubs and estate agents gave way to more sparkling new hotels, unaffordable apartment buildings and a twenty-four-hour gym. It blended in anonymously among the Georgian houses and the council estate that shared the quiet road. Henley didn't feel out of place now that she had her uniform on, a sharp midnight blue suit. It screamed authority even though she had kept on the black Adidas Gazelles.

"Greenwich Public Mortuary," Ramouter read the sign on the wall as he finished the rest of his coffee. "They make it sound like a library. Like you can just walk in, show your card, pull up a seat and watch an autopsy."

"How long have you got left?" Henley asked.

"For what?" Ramouter waited for Henley to release the child safety lock.

"Until you're no longer a trainee?"

"What you're really asking is, how long are you stuck with me for?" The grin on Ramouter's smooth brown face quickly disappeared as he saw that Henley was not smiling back. "I've got four months left." He rubbed at his beard. "But I did spend six months working in the Homicide and Major Crime team. It was good solid work, but I wanted something more challenging and West Yorkshire Police have nothing like the SCU."

Henley felt a flush of empathy—it wasn't his fault that he had been dumped with her—but the warmth was brief.

"Well, things work a bit differently at the SCU. It's very rare that we hit the ground running like this. The cases are usually passed on to us once the potential emergence of a serial killer or rapist has been identified. The preliminary work that we're doing now has usually been done before we get going."

"But that's not all that the unit does," said Ramouter, following Henley toward the detached building in the middle of the grounds. "There was that serial kidnapping and human trafficking case a few years back and also the Jigsaw Killer case."

Henley winced as a muscle pulled in her neck. *The Jigsaw Killer.* The case that had changed everything. There had been praise from her colleagues, a commendation from the commissioner, a promotion to detective inspector. But the case had stolen a piece of her.

"That must have been amazing to work on," continued Ramouter. "It's what made me want to join the unit. The reason… Well, one of the reasons why I came down to London."

Henley turned and looked at Ramouter. Even though she knew that he was nervous, there was no mistaking that familiar look of excitement in his eyes.

"Don't let what you saw in the media fool you. The SCU is understaffed and underfunded. I'm surprised that your transfer was even authorized. Look, in your average Murder Squad it wouldn't be unusual to have up to a hundred people working on an investigation from the DSI down to your civilians, but at the SCU it's just us and we spend a lot of time pulling in favors. There's no glamour here and any praise is short-lived."

Henley turned her back, entered the passcode she wasn't meant to have and pushed open the door.

Head forensic pathologist Dr. Linh Choi was sitting at her desk with her back to the door, hunched over her lunch. Her long black hair was piled on top of her head, secured loosely with a ballpoint pen. She bobbed her head up and down in time to the heavy drum and bass that was escaping from the Bose wireless speakers on her desk. Henley had met Linh over fifteen years ago, when they were both starting out in their careers and feeling woefully out of their depth. Their friendship had flourished over time. Henley tapped Linh on the shoulder.

"Jesus Christ!" Linh jumped in her seat. The hot wing in her hand fell back into the box. "You nearly gave me a bloody heart attack."

"Reliving your raving days, are you?" Henley said with a smile.

"Don't you mean 'our' raving days. You love this as much as I do. I've got a wicked mix that I found at home. I'll have to send it to you." Linh muted the volume on her laptop. "You didn't tell me that you were back. Had to hear it from Anthony," she said.

"I'll talk to you about that later," Henley replied.

"And you've got a new partner? What did Stanford have to say about that?"

"This is TDC Salim Ramouter, and he's not my partner." Henley moved aside to allow Ramouter to step forward. "I'm his mentor. He's just transferred from West Yorkshire Police."

"Oh, I see. Well, you couldn't have asked for a better person to train you than DI Henley," said Linh, getting up from the chair. She cleaned her hand with an antibacterial wipe before extending it toward Ramouter. "Nice to meet you. Dr. Linh Choi."

She'd had the benefit of a private school scholarship and Cambridge University education, but you'd never have guessed from her thick south London accent. She pulled her glasses down from the top of her head.

"I've just completed a preliminary examination on your male victim, but let me tell you about the arm first. There wasn't much to go over, considering that we're missing bits. A head, legs, torso, another arm would be nice."

"What can you tell us?" asked Henley.

Linh shrugged. "Black female. Probably in her twenties but that's all that I can tell you until you find the rest of her."

Henley and Ramouter followed Linh out of her office, toward an examination room that resembled a hospital operating room. There was a chill in the air. Against the wall a row of metal cabinets provided temporary storage for the dead, while opposite were three deep sinks with a fridge in the corner. In the middle of the room stood four metal examination tables. Linh's assistant, Theresa, was working on a body on the far table while listening to music on her Beats headphones. The scents of industrial antiseptic and soured bodily fluids tickled Henley's nose.

Theresa inserted an expander into the body's chest.

"That used to be a twenty-three-year-old bodybuilder," Linh said, shaking her head. "Heart attack. Collapsed in the gym. I don't need a toxicology screening to tell me that he's going to be pumped full of steroids."

The sound of someone stepping on broken glass filled Henley's ears as Theresa cracked the chest open. Ramouter took a step back.

"The loo is the second door on your left," Linh said, amusement tickling her voice as Ramouter turned and ran.

"Sorry," said Ramouter when he returned a few minutes later with the look of shame in his eye.

"That's all right. You're not the first and you won't be the last," said Linh. "Right, are you ready?"

Henley nodded her assent and Linh pulled back the protective plastic sheet. The body parts that had been found along the riverbank and the driveway of 15 Nelson Mews were now arranged on the examination table, like a bloodied jigsaw that had yet to be fully put together. Henley felt light-headed. She took a step back and tried to anchor herself.

"Are you able to give us a time of death?" Henley asked, trying to hide the nervous quaver in her voice.

"Rough estimate," said Linh, "I would say between twenty-four to thirty-six hours for your man."

Henley took a closer look at the tattoo on the torso.

"It's a scene from *Full Metal Alchemist*," Linh said. She sounded quite pleased. "That's a Manga anime film, if you didn't know. Way before your time," she continued for the benefit of Ramouter. "He's got Ken from *Fist of the North Star* tattooed on his back."

"What can you tell me about the dismemberments? Before or after death?" Henley asked as she walked slowly around the body parts, taking every detail in, ignoring the mobile phone that was vibrating in her pocket.

"Both." Linh moved toward the top of the table. "Right arm and the left leg were removed first. If you take a look here"—she pointed to where the left leg had been cut—"the blood had already started to coagulate. Death would have occurred within four minutes."

Linh turned the lower end of the torso toward Henley, pointing out the bone, flesh and bowels. "There is hardly any coagulation at all here. So, four hours after death, your killer starts to remove the limbs. There's an interesting puncture wound in the chest, just above the heart. That was done before death. I'll know more once I start the autopsy after lunch. I will tell you one thing though. They made a right shit job of cutting this body up. Look here." Linh pointed a gloved finger to two long, jagged cuts on the right shoulder. "There were at least two attempts made before the arm was finally taken off. It's as if who-ever it was had never used a Black and Decker jigsaw before."

"Was it a Black and Decker jigsaw?" Ramouter asked. He was standing almost three feet away with his back to the sinks.

"I wouldn't have a bloody clue. You need a DIY expert for that." Linh's eyes crinkled with laughter as she straightened the right leg. "But more importantly, take a look at this."

Linh picked up the head and turned it toward Henley. She then prized the jaw open with her fingers. "Ramouter, grab the flashlight on the side," she said. "I haven't got enough hands."

Ramouter picked up the small silver penlight and walked over to the table.

"Come on. Don't be shy. Shine it here."

Ramouter did as he was told and shone the light into the opened mouth.

"Er… Where's his tongue?" Ramouter asked.

Henley forced herself to take the penlight from Ramouter and shone the light toward the back of the throat. The mouth was caked in dried blood and she could see the remnants of exposed striated muscle that formed the base of the tongue.

"How?" Henley asked.

"It was cut off," Linh replied. "A very clean dissection which could only be achieved by something like a very sharp fillet knife or a scalpel."

"But how easy is it to cut out someone's tongue?" Henley wriggled her own tongue around her mouth, feeling the small tendons at the base stretch and pull.

"While they're alive? Bloody difficult. Which is why it would have made sense if the tongue was cut off postmortem, but it wasn't."

"Hold on, he was still alive when his tongue was cut out?"

Linh nodded. "To grab hold of the tongue while the person is alive would be difficult and the cut is so clinical. My guess is your victim was unconscious. Also, there's another thing. Tell me if you notice anything about the legs."

Henley crouched down. The calf of the right leg, covered with small grains of sand, fragments of seaweed and dried vomit, was muscular with fine, light brown hair. The left leg was the same but, on the ankle, a strip of skin, about two inches wide, was paler than the rest.

"Our victim was wearing a tag?" Henley said.

"I think so," replied Linh. "If you look here." Linh turned the leg to examine the pale patch, which was no bigger than a matchbox. "Definitely, I would say that he was wearing a tag. I'm sure that if I got the measurements of a generic tag from one of the monitoring companies, it would fit."

"So, our victim was on court bail with a curfew?" asked Ramouter. "That should give us something to go on. There must be a way of finding out if anyone has breached their bail in the last few days."

"Do you have any idea how many people are granted bail and placed on tag?" said Henley.

"Good luck with that," replied Linh. "I've taken blood, urine samples, the usual, and sent them off this morning. Hopefully, I'll get something back by the end of the week. So, do we have a name? It feels a bit disrespectful to keep calling him…well, one of them, Manga Man, now that most of him is laid out on the table like this."

Henley pulled her phone out of her pocket, which had been buzzing with alerts, and read the message on the screen. It was from Anthony Thomas confirming that he had run the severed arm's fingerprints through Livescan, the police database. ·

"Actually, we do," said Henley. "Meet Daniel Kennedy."

5

It was almost 8 p.m. by the time Ramouter had entered his flat, taken off his shoes, which still had traces of dried mud on them, and placed them on the doormat. It had been four days since he moved in. The scent of the flat wasn't his. It still smelled of artificial air freshener and bleach. A lingering stack of unopened boxes occupied the open-plan living room and kitchen. He turned on the radio for company and took out a ready meal from the fridge, pulled off the cardboard sleeve and stabbed the taut plastic with a fork.

A few minutes later, Ramouter pushed aside the remains of the bland spaghetti carbonara and picked up his iPhone.

"Oh, we were expecting you to call earlier. We're just about to eat," said Pamela, stepping away from the camera. As always, her face was perfectly made up and not one muscle moved on her face. She was dressed in expensive yoga clothes, even though Ramouter knew for a fact that Pamela had no idea what downward-facing dog meant and probably thought Savasana was a type of tea.

"Sorry, I didn't realize how long it would take me to get back from the station. The traffic on the South Circular—"

"Well, perhaps you could leave on time tomorrow. Routine is important."

Ramouter bit his tongue to stop himself from saying, *Murder isn't a nine-to-five job.*

"Where's Michelle? I tried to FaceTime, but she didn't pick up."

"She's probably forgotten to charge her phone again but she's upstairs. They both are. She was feeling tired. I'm going to leave in a bit to pick the boys up from football practice. I'll bring my iPad up to her."

Pamela found Michelle sitting on the edge of the bed. Her bedroom mirrored his living room with suitcases and boxes taking up much of the space. He chuckled to himself.

"Michelle. Sweetheart," said Ramouter. "You OK, love? Where's Ethan? How was his first day at school? I miss you."

"He's already in bed," Michelle replied, steadying the iPad on the bedside table. "His first day at school completely knocked him out. I took loads of photographs for you."

"I know. Remember, you sent me the photos this morning?" Ramouter's heart sank as confusion spread across Michelle's face. Early onset dementia at the age of thirty-six. A rare genetic form of Alzheimer's, the specialist had said. Her father had died at fifty-eight, but the rest of the family had thought that maybe it would skip a couple of generations. He had received his transfer confirmation to join the SCU two weeks before Michelle's diagnosis. They had found the flat in Forest Hill, a school for Ethan and a job interview for Michelle lined up, but the diagnosis had changed everything. Michelle's older sister, Pamela, had argued that her sister needed stability, and a move to an unknown city away from her family and friends would be detrimental. Ramouter couldn't argue with that. He still had the email declining the transfer to the SCU saved in his draft folder. He had been ready to send it, but Michelle had told him no.

That it was a once-in-a-lifetime opportunity. That she didn't want him to regret it. To resent her.

"How was your day?" Ramouter asked.

"My day was OK. Pamela took me to lunch to meet some of her friends. You would hate them. How was your day?"

"It was good. They're a good team and I've been paired up with Anjelica Henley on a case. Do you remember her, the one I told you about?"

"The inspector?"

"Yes, that's right. The inspector," Ramouter replied, his voice brightening.

"What is she like?"

"She's, er... Tough. Smart. Don't think that she likes being stuck with me much, but it's early days."

"Hmm. Ethan wanted to stay up to tell you about school—"

Ramouter looked at Michelle through his screen and felt overwhelmed with sadness. She was distracted again. He could see it in her eyes. Staring back at him as she tried to hold on to her memories. He couldn't look back at her. He turned the phone screen down onto the counter. He should have ignored Michelle when she told him that it was OK for him to go to London. He should have stood by his wife like a man, but instead he ran at the first opportunity. He wore the guilt in his shoulders, as familiar as his work suit. He was angry with Michelle and her illness. And the guilt and embarrassment that he felt from that anger was suffocating.

"Sorry," Ramouter said as he picked up the phone. "The reception is a bit dodgy in this flat."

"You need to stop," Michelle said.

It was these moments of lucidity that made Ramouter feel worse. His eyes filled with tears as Michelle stared back at him with intense clarity. She knew him and how to manage him.

"We both agreed," she said.

"Aye. I'm just missing you and Ethan. That's all," Ramouter replied as he wiped away the tears.

"It's going to be OK. We're OK," Michelle said firmly.

"I know. I'll have a word with myself."

"Good. Now, let me tell you about lunch with Pamela's lunatic friends. I'm actually looking forward to the day when I don't remember them."

Ramouter laughed as he watched Michelle brighten up. The guilt was still there, but for the next hour, as he spoke to Michelle, the weight was not so heavy.

6

Henley knew that the collection time for the nonrecyclable rubbish was around 11 a.m. She put down the shopping bags and checked her watch: 8:26 p.m. The blue wheelie bin was blocking the front gate. Her dad probably hadn't left the house all day.

Henley dragged the wheelie bin to the side and opened the gate. The thorns on the overgrown rosebush caught on her jacket as she walked up the pathway. Weeds had forced themselves through the cracks in the paving stones.

"What the hell?" Henley said as the key to the front door refused to turn anticlockwise. It was the same key that had been attached to the same blue Tesco Clubcard fob for the past five years. She pushed the key in again. It wouldn't turn.

"Dad, for crying out loud."

Henley crouched down and shouted through the letterbox.

"Dad. It's me. Anjelica. Open the door."

She sat back on her heels, keeping the letterbox prized open with her fingers.

"Dad. Come on. Just… Please. I want to see if you're OK."

"I'm fine. Go away."

"Not until you open the door. I've bought you some shopping."

"Leave it at the door."

"Dad. Please. Let me see you. I promise that I won't come in."

Henley peered through the letterbox and saw his legs approaching in their faded gray tracksuit pants. The letterbox slammed shut as the front door opened.

"You need a haircut, Dad." It was the only thing that Henley could say as her stomach was twisted in knots. She hadn't seen her dad, Elijah, in almost three weeks and his appearance was shocking. He'd lost weight. The skin around his neck was folding into itself like a rumpled handkerchief. Henley felt the shock give way to the type of fear that came when you recognized your parents were tapping on the door of mortality.

Elijah patted his hair, which was now more white than gray. The number two fade devolved into a short unkempt Afro.

"Simon came around this morning." Henley placed her hand on top of her dad's hand. He pulled his hand away. "Why didn't you want to see him?" she asked softly.

"I don't want to see any of you."

"Dad. You have to let us help you."

"I don't need your help. I'm fine."

"Why did you change the lock?"

"To stop you and your brother coming here whenever you felt like it. I'm not a child."

"No one said that you were. We're just worried about you."

"Well, I'm fine. You've seen me. Now you can go."

"Dad… Don't be… Can you at least let me in for a minute?"

"I said no!"

"Fine. Fine." Henley grabbed the edge of the door. "I won't come in. Here, take this."

She picked up the shopping bags and pushed them through the gap in the door. "I haven't got a clue what you've got in your fridge. You could be living on crackers and sardines for all I know," she said angrily. "I've got you the basics—eggs, bread, ham, chicken and some party ring biscuits. I know that you like—"

Elijah pulled the bags toward him.

"Fuck," Henley said as he slammed the door shut in her face.

"Fourteen hours," Rob said without looking up from his laptop. He was sitting at the kitchen table, his temporary office, while the builders finished converting the shed in the back. He was a financial journalist who had taken the option to work remotely instead of depositing a redundancy check into his bank account. Once a week he left the house and ventured to Old Street where he graced the studios of a business channel to discuss breaking financial news. The arrangement suited Rob and Henley but he still wanted her home. Luna—part Alsatian, part Labrador, part something else—was asleep under the table. The French doors were open but the heat from the day still hung heavily in the air, mixed with the perfume of jasmine and honeysuckle that came from the garden. The seductive scents of a late summer's night couldn't cover up the strong odor of decay that had been with Henley since she'd seen the dismembered torso on the Watergate Steps.

"You left the house just after seven and you're walking in at twenty-one minutes past nine."

"Rob, I've had a really long day—"

"You had a long day? I had to pick up Emma from nursery because she was sick."

"And I texted you to see how she was."

"She didn't need a text. She needed her mum."

"Let's not do this," said Henley as she put her bag on the kitchen counter and walked toward the fridge. Rob being Rob, he wasn't selfish enough to cook for one. She pulled out the Pyrex dish covered with plastic film. Honey and garlic grilled chicken with vegetable fried rice and broccoli. She put the dish back and closed the fridge door. She needed to shower first to remove the thin film of death coating her body and the scent of failure that trailed her since she had left her dad's house. She wondered if Rob could tell that she was back working an investigation.

"I went to see Dad," she said.

"Oh." Rob's features softened a bit. "How is he?"

"Not good. He refused to let me in."

"This isn't good for him. What are you going to do?"

"I don't know." Henley opened the fridge door again and pulled out a bottle of wine. "I'll have to talk to Si, but... I don't know."

"Look, I know that things aren't great with your dad, but you could have let me know that you were going to be late. An apology would be nice."

"An apology for what?" Henley said, picking up a wineglass from the cupboard. "For seeing my dad?"

"No, of course not. I only meant—"

"Do you want me to apologize for going to work? I *have* to work, Rob. One of us needs to hold a stable job." Henley regretted the words as soon as they left her mouth.

"And what? I'm just sitting here playing the house husband, looking after our child and making jam while you go to work."

"You know exactly what I meant. I know what you do and I... I appreciate how hard you work for us, but we keep going around in circles with this."

"Appreciate?" Rob looked up at Henley for the first time since she entered the kitchen. He took off his glasses, and rubbed the small grooves on his nose where the frames had been pinching. "I'm not one of your colleagues. I'm your husband. I don't want you to *appreciate* me. I want you to understand what I'm saying to you, what I have been saying to you."

"You want me to stop working. To give up my job—"

"You know that's not what I'm saying. I don't want you to

stop working. All I want is for you to find another job. It's a miracle that Emma even knows what you look like."

"Don't be so bloody ridiculous. You're acting like I've abandoned her. I go to work to try and do my bit to make the world safer for her."

"From behind a desk? How is that helping her? You're on restricted duties. You're not out there catching rapists and murderers with your bare hands. I sometimes wonder what the real reason is why you won't leave."

The legs of Rob's chair screeched across the tiles as he stood up. Henley waited for the familiar accusation of the betrayal to be thrown in her face.

"I don't want to argue with you, Rob. Not about this. Not again. I know that we need to talk."

"That's the thing. You always know, but have you ever taken the time to sit down and talk to me? You're putting our lives on standstill because of what? You told me last Christmas that things were going to change but they haven't. We're still here. In the same place."

Rob grabbed his lighter and rolling papers off the table. "I'm going to walk Luna. I'll be back in half an hour."

The front door slammed and Henley let out a pent-up sigh. She should tell him now. Tell him that she was back out there. No longer restricted to the desk, that Pellacia had put her back on the streets. That their lives were going to be turned upside down again. Instead, she went upstairs to her daughter's bedroom. Emma was starfished across her bed. Henley was tempted to wake her just to hear her say "Mummy." Instead, she kissed the top of her head. She smelled of cocoa butter and baby powder. Emma was the one thing Henley could see the good in.

Henley sat on the edge of the bed and fell back, letting the towel fall loose around her. She'd showered but she didn't feel clean. The investigation had already crawled into her pores. She closed her eyes and ran her fingers across her body until she came to the familiar ridge of thickened, rippled skin. Two inches of scar tissue on the right. The second scar, three inches above, was slightly flatter. The knife had narrowly missed her liver, and if it had been any lower she would have lost the baby that she didn't know she was carrying. Two and a half years later she could still feel the hot steel piercing her skin. Henley squeezed her eyes tighter. She could see Daniel Kennedy's dismembered body in front of her. She took a deep breath. She had kicked up a fuss about being made the senior investigating officer on a murder investigation, but she couldn't ignore the electric thrill that had run through her. Death was her adrenaline and it scared her.

Walking along that riverbank, examining the corpse, she felt a renewed sense of purpose, but the tendons in her hand tightened and her fingers started to tremble; her body was telling her that something wasn't right. She shook her head to quiet her inner voice. The voice was slightly louder than a whisper, but it was insistent: *A storm is coming, and you're not ready.*

7

The rules of the High Security Unit at Belmarsh prison didn't apply to him. The doors to the prison cells accommodating the Category A prisoners, deemed too dangerous to associate with the rest of the prison population, were not opened until 8 a.m. Peter Olivier, prisoner number A0743TP, had been out of his cell since 6:30 a.m. He had brushed his teeth and taken a shower alone, before changing into a brand-new navy Nike tracksuit and a black pair of Air Force 1 trainers. He had worn the regulation prison-issued maroon tracksuit only once in the two and a half years he had been a prisoner. The first care package containing clothes, toiletries and books had arrived forty-eight hours after he had been escorted in as a remand prisoner.

He could have watched the breakfast news on the small television in the corner of his room, but he preferred not to have his morning routine disturbed by the thirty-eight-year-old drug trafficker in the cell next door who couldn't handle prison life and screamed and banged his head against the wall every morning. Olivier had left his cell and was sitting alone in the recreation room opposite the forty-six-inch television screen.

"It was coffee you were after?"

A prison officer was holding a steaming mug. Olivier smiled, his pale skin crinkling around piercing blue eyes. This officer was new. Olivier could smell the cotton fresh spray starch emanating from his shirt.

"Coffee is absolutely perfect. Thank you very much, sorry— I didn't catch your name."

"It's Paul."

"Ah, that's it. Paul. Just wait there, will you?"

The officer stood still as Olivier leaned back, blew the steam off the cup and took a sip.

"Hmm, it's a little bit heavy with the hazelnut syrup, but it will do. You couldn't do me a favor and pass the control? It's far too early in the morning for that Piers twat."

Olivier grinned as the officer handed him the remote control.

"Now, what is going on here?" Olivier said to himself as he switched the channel to BBC One where the local news had begun. The reporter was standing on Greenwich Pier.

"Investigating officers have now confirmed that the body of a young man found on the riverbank yesterday morning just a few meters behind me has been formally identified as Daniel Kennedy. It has been confirmed by the senior investigating officer that this is a murder investigation; however, she did not confirm local rumors that the body of Daniel Kennedy had been found dismembered."

"That's an awful way to go," said the prison officer, who hadn't moved. "How could someone cut him—" Paul stopped as Olivier turned slowly to face him and smiled.

"You are a very funny man, Paul. I doubt that it's a rumor though." Olivier approached the TV as a photograph of Daniel Kennedy appeared. He cocked his head to the side and tapped the screen three times.

"Why do you look familiar, son?" he asked.

"A press conference with investigating officers has been scheduled for this afternoon. In the meantime, Detective Inspector Anjelica Henley

has appealed for any witnesses to contact the Serial Crime Unit. The contact details should be appearing on the screen."

"Paul, did I hear that correctly? Did that reporter say *'Henley'*?"

"Henley, Henman. I'm not too sure."

"I'm pretty sure that she said *Henley*." Olivier picked up the control and turned off the TV. "And my girl is now an inspector."

8

Daniel Kennedy. Thirty-six years old. In a relationship. Lived in London. From London. The profile photograph on his Facebook page showed a smiling man standing on top of a quad bike with all his limbs intact. His criminal record from the Police National Computer showed a man with two aliases and four convictions: possession of Class A & B drugs, robbery when he was sixteen and, most recently, GBH.

"It makes you wonder, doesn't it?" Ramouter flicked over the pages of the report. He had toned down the back-to-school look of yesterday. Polished shoes swapped for black trainers. Suit jacket, but no tie.

"What makes you wonder?" Henley swerved to avoid a cyclist who appeared out of nowhere.

"Who Kennedy must have pissed off to end up in pieces on the bank of the Thames. He got an eighteen-month sentence for GBH. Came out of prison in 2018, completed his license period three months ago and then found himself on bail for an affray and ABH."

Henley had asked herself the same thing when she had lain

awake in bed, Rob snoring next to her with the sweet, intoxicating scent of cannabis still on his breath.

She pulled the car into the driveway of a three-floor Victorian house. The grass and bushes were overgrown, and the row of green wheelie bins were overflowing. Two residents sat on the low wall, smoking their cigarettes and eyeing up Henley as she parked between a white transit van and red Mini.

"It doesn't look like a bail hostel," Ramouter said, checking that his warrant card was visible around his neck.

"What were you expecting?" Henley cut the engine and took another look at the two men on the wall before opening the car door.

Ramouter shrugged. "I don't know. It's not the tidiest but I thought it would be…grittier."

"Disappointed that the residents aren't shooting up in the front garden?"

"No…but…"

Henley leaned over the roof of her car. "You have been to a bail hostel before?"

"Actually, no." Ramouter had the decency to look a bit embarrassed. "First time for everything, eh?"

"Hmm. Don't embarrass me," Henley warned, walking toward the reinforced front door.

"Sentinel have been here twice looking for him." Beryl took a long drag from her e-cigarette, leaving behind her neon pink lipstick on the vape as Henley and Ramouter signed their names in the visitors' book. "To be honest, I was shocked to see them at all. You can just about rely on them to come here and put the tag on in the first place. So, what's he done? I never did like him. Not that I really like any of them."

"When was the last time that you saw Mr. Kennedy?" Henley asked, ignoring Beryl's question.

Beryl closed the book and placed it under the counter. She

disappeared and returned with a bunch of keys in her hand. "Let's see. I don't work weekends and Mondays. I was off sick on Friday, so the last time I was here was Thursday and I only do the day shift, 8 a.m. to 5 p.m. and I don't recall seeing him then. I think the last time I saw Kennedy was maybe Tuesday."

"How long was he here before Sentinel came and fitted the tag?"

"He was here for at least two weeks before they came. Bloody stairs, he was on the third floor." Beryl tutted. She walked up the stairs with Henley and Ramouter close behind.

"Was he keeping to his curfew before they came?"

"Actually, he was. Pretty much kept his head down. He was sharing for the first week, but his roommate had a fight with the crackhead in room nine and got remanded. So, he had his own room." Beryl selected a key from the bunch and opened the door.

"Before you go," Henley asked, "did Daniel have any visitors?"

"No visitors are allowed but that's not to say that he didn't have any. We've got CCTV. The recordings get deleted every thirty days, but you can check that if you like."

Ramouter put a hand to his nose as he stepped inside. The room smelled of rotting food and stale clothes. There were two single beds on opposite sides of the room with a small wardrobe next to each. Henley opened the window as wide as it could go. The table was littered with empty takeaway boxes, beer cans and half a bottle of cheap whiskey. A bottle of soured milk was on the windowsill. Tiny black flies buzzed around an orange net bag of moldering clementines.

Henley donned the pair of latex gloves she kept in her pocket. She bent down and picked up a carrier bag. It was filled with junk mail, a court form confirming his bail conditions, his next appointment with his GP and letters from his solicitors.

"This is disgusting," Ramouter said as he walked around the

room. "How can anyone live like this? Whatever happened, it didn't happen here, but it smells like he hasn't been here for at least a week."

"I'll need you to speak to the other residents," said Henley. "Explain to them that we're not asking them to grass; all we want to know is when they last saw him and if they spoke to him. Then we can take a look at the CCTV. The footage from outside the house may be more useful."

"No problem. So, we're done here."

"It looks like—" Henley paused as something caught her eye near the foot of the bed. She pushed aside a pair of boxer shorts and picked up an iPhone.

"That looks new," said Ramouter. "Why would he leave a brand-new phone behind?"

"Have you got any evidence bags?"

Ramouter checked his pocket and shook his head. "Nowt. Sorry. I must have left them in the car."

Henley peeled off the glove from her left hand, wrapped it around the iPhone and handed it to Ramouter before reaching again under the bed. Her fingers touched something hard and cracked. She knew without seeing it what it was. She stood up and showed Ramouter a small, circular box attached to a strap. There was a visible crack on the black plastic.

"He cut off his tag?" Ramouter said as Henley turned it over in her gloved hand.

"Looks like he stepped on it too. He leaves his phone and re-moves his tag. What the hell was he up to?"

Ramouter took the broken tag from Henley as her own phone began to ring. Stanford's mobile number flashed on the screen.

"You need to get down to Ladywell Fields," Stanford said without giving Henley a chance to say hello.

"What for?"

"I think we've found our girl."

9

"One of the ladies from the boot camp found them. She's over there."

Stanford pointed to a black woman who was talking to a police officer. Her shoulders were visibly shaking. A taller white woman standing next to her put her arms around her.

"Needless to say, she's a mess." Stanford, who had the stature of a rugby player, folded his broad arms. "Sick bastard. Now that we've got two of them… I was thinking about the last time we had a case like this."

"I can't lie and say that it hasn't crossed my mind, but chopping up bodies and dumping them is not that unusual so let's not go there just yet," Henley replied as she looked around.

It had been years since she'd been to Ladywell Fields. The boot camp had taken place next to a tennis court, within view of Lewisham Hospital. The police had cordoned off the area, the grass parched from the summer heat. "So, what happened?"

"Aisha runs a women-only boot camp session here every Wednesday at 11:30 a.m."

Stanford, Ramouter and Henley began to walk toward the bushes. "Over the past couple of weeks there have been reports of a flasher," continued Stanford. "Stelian Vacarescu, forty-eight years old. Aisha had split the women into small groups, was walking around, and who does she see in the bushes?"

Henley ducked under the tape. "Surprise me," she said.

"Vacarescu, with his dick out. She runs toward him and tells him to fuck off and that she was calling the police. He zips up and starts to run, but he trips and takes a fall. Wonder Woman Aisha thinks her luck is in and decides to make a citizen's arrest. She reaches Vacarescu, looks down and sees what he's tripped over."

The caramel-colored leg was slim and streaked with dried blood. Three toenails, polished bright blue, had pushed through the black netting of a pair of tights, which had gathered at the foot.

"Shit," said Ramouter.

"She thought it was the leg of a mannequin at first until she noticed the dried blood and Vacarescu started screaming like a man possessed."

Three feet from the leg, an arm and a head had been dumped against a tree stump. The head was covered with long black and purple braids. There was a bald spot, the size of a two-pound coin, on the right side. Her forehead was crisscrossed with grazes and bruising pocked her right cheekbone. Traces of red lipstick cracked across her lips. Two blackened holes where her eyes used to be. Ramouter put a hand to his mouth and looked away as a woodlouse crawled into the left eye socket.

"Where's Linh?" Henley asked Stanford. "And why aren't you at court?"

"Sick juror, and Linh is on her way." Stanford turned his back on the body. Henley knew how he was feeling. They thought they had seen it all, until life presented them with a fresh kind of hell.

"How are you doing?" Stanford asked Henley.

"I'm fine," Henley replied. "Nothing for you to worry about."

Henley had prepared herself for the moment that they would find the rest of the girl. There was no anxiety, no tremors, but there was an overwhelming torrent of anger at the thought that someone could dump this girl like rubbish.

"We had a case up in Bradford last year," said Ramouter, his expression taut as he tried to regain control. "A PCSO found a woman, nearly half dead, at the back of a corner shop. Gouged her own eyes out. She was a drug addict. High on crystal meth. But look at our girl… It doesn't look like she gouged her eyes out, but why would someone take them out?"

"Where's Vacarescu now?" Henley asked.

"Sitting with a couple of uniforms on a bench. Shock got the better of him," Stanford replied as he pulled a crumpled tissue out of his pocket and blew his nose.

"Ramouter, go and talk to him. If he's a regular around here, then he must have noticed something that was off. Remember, it doesn't matter how big or irrelevant it may seem, make sure that he tells us everything."

"And tell him to keep his dick in his pants," said Stanford. The smile on his face quickly disappeared when he turned around and looked down at the woman's body. "Poor thing."

"How long until Forensics get here? We need to get a tent put up ASAP. Too many amateur photographers around here as it is." Henley turned to face the small crowd that had increased in size since she arrived. Teenage boys, their bikes discarded on the grass, stood holding their phones in the air. "CCTV?"

"Would you believe it? There're loads all over the place. Hopefully, we'll get something."

"God willing." Henley put her hands on top of her head and took a breath. "Who the hell would do something like this?"

Stanford shrugged. "Jealous lover, perhaps?"

"Maybe. We need to get an ID on her. We'll have to go through Missing Persons if she's not on the DNA database."

"OK. What do you want from me next, boss?"

Henley looked up to the sky. The sun was already at its zenith and the heat wave had resumed, bringing with it the humidity and the stench of the city. "I need you and Eastwood to pay a visit to Sentinel. Kennedy was on a tag, which he removed. The hostel has CCTV and we've got his phone. It's dead. We need to get the tech guys to take a look at the phone and the broken tag, but I want to see what Ezra can do it with it first."

"I've got you."

Stanford nodded and gave a Boy Scout salute as Henley beckoned Ramouter over. A police BMW X5, blue lights flashing but no sirens, closely followed by a transit van and a silver Hyundai, was heading in their direction.

"How was our flasher?" Henley asked Ramouter as he put his notebook in his pocket.

"Useless. My budgie speaks better English than he does."

"You have a budgie?"

"My son's. He's four." Ramouter gave Henley a look as though this was information she should know.

"Vacarescu? Romanian?"

Ramouter nodded. Henley pulled out her car keys, handed them to him and then took out her phone. The transit van, police car and the Hyundai came to a stop next to Henley's car. "The most that I could get out of him was his name, that he lived in Sydenham and that he was sorry. I had to use Google Translate just to get that. Then he kept saying, 'The girl, the girl.' Everything else after that was in Romanian and I can't type that fast."

"Fine. Take Vacarescu down to Lewisham," she said, scrolling through her contacts, and pressed call. "If I can get hold of Bianca, that's the interpreter, I'll ask her to meet you down there. If we wait for the Witness Care Unit to sort one out, you'll be there all day."

Bianca picked up the phone and told Henley that she was just finishing a job at Thames Magistrates' Court and that she should be there in about an hour.

"Right, it's sorted. I've sent her your number. She's going to call you once she's at the station. The last thing I want is for her to be kept waiting at the front desk for ages."

Ramouter's phone began to ring and he walked back toward Vacarescu. Henley turned and looked back at the area where the body parts had been dumped. Ladywell Fields was open twenty-four hours with various entry points. Just like the first victim, whoever it was knew the area. The location wasn't somewhere you came to by chance. At some point the woman, whoever she was, was bound to be found. Two bodies in two days. Both cut into pieces and displayed. Male and female. Black and white.

"Well, I would say that it's nice to get out of the office now and again."

Linh's voice pulled Henley out of her thoughts. "I was told that we've got another one."

"Not that I'm one for assumptions, but I think that it's the rest of what we found at the river yesterday. Like you said, she looks…looked between twenty and thirty years old."

"OK. Well, let me have a look at her. I don't know how long she's been out here, but this heat will accelerate decomposition quicker than a stripper picking up fifty-quid notes."

"You know that you're not funny, right?"

Linh grinned and adjusted the bag strap on her left shoulder. "Doing this job, can you blame me? Are you staying?"

"For a bit. I'm going to have a word with Aisha, the woman who found her, and then get one of the uniforms to drop me back to Greenwich."

"I doubt I'll be long. The sooner they get her back to my place, the better. If you hang on, after I'm done, I'll give you a lift back and maybe we can finally sort out a date for a girls' night out. It's been too long, Anjelica. I'm starting to feel neglected."

Twenty minutes later, Linh was tapping Henley on her shoulder. She had just given the go-ahead for Aisha to be taken home.

"I need a word," Linh said. The grin on her face had been

stripped away. Her forehead was creased with concern as she rubbed at the bags under her eyes. She held Henley's arm and led her toward the tennis court away from the forensics team gathering evidence in the bushes, away from the small crowd of thirty that had increased to fifty in the last hour.

"First, the eyes. Foxes, stray cats, I'm not sure which, have already been at her, but the eyes…they look like they've been cut out. I need to get her back to the mortuary to get an idea of time of death."

"How long do you reckon she's been out here?"

"Hard to tell. If I had to take a rough guess, she's been dead a few days at least, but how long she's actually been out here, waiting to be found? No idea, but that's not what I wanted to talk to you about. She has a mark," Linh said, her voice hushed.

"What?" Henley's mind started to race, stalling on one explanation. Bile had already risen from her stomach and was tickling the back of her throat.

"A symbol cut into the skin, Anjelica. She has one on her forearm. Not an old cut but new. The blood looks like it's coagulated. My guess is that it was done postmortem."

"Is it a…" Henley didn't need to finish the sentence. Linh knew. Nevertheless, she finished the question. "A double cross with a crescent on top?"

"Yes, about two inches in length."

"What about Kennedy?"

"There's evidence of what looks like self-harming, old scars on his arms and his torso, but what we've got of him is covered in tattoos. Detailed, intricate tattoos. If I'm honest—" Linh shook her head. "No, no way. I doubt that I would have missed something like that."

"Maybe you didn't miss anything. Maybe there isn't anything there." Henley put her forehead against the fence, hoping that she was talking rubbish.

"Fuck, I'm going to have to pull him back out of the freezer.

Just for my own peace of mind. I'm going to call Theresa. Tell her to get him ready and to take photos of every single inch of him."

"I'm coming with you. If he has the mark, I want to be there when you find it."

"If we find it. Then there's her."

Henley and Linh both looked in the direction of where the forensics team were gathered in the bushes.

"Who is she?" asked Henley as the image of the woman's head flashed in her mind.

10

"You took your time," said Henley as Ramouter walked into the SCU. It was almost 4 p.m. He looked frazzled. He had rolled up his shirtsleeves and his forehead glistened with sweat.

"Sorry. Had to get something to eat before I dropped." Ramouter held up a wet takeout bag with a chicken burger and chips. "So, first thing first. Vacarescu likes to talk. A lot. I then went to see the local council offices—they're only down the road from Ladywell Fields—and I spoke to the person responsible for park maintenance. Sorry, I should have told you."

"No, that's fine," Henley replied. "I'm the last person who will ever have a go at you for actually using your initiative. So, what did Vacarescu say?"

"Well, he was adamant that he wasn't going to talk until I promised him that he wouldn't be charged with exposure. I may have agreed to that, but technically no one had bothered to actually arrest him for flashing, and Aisha hasn't reported it."

"Once she saw the body that would have been the last thing on her mind."

"Aye." Ramouter scooped a couple of chips into his mouth. "So Vacarescu said that he got to the park about 10:30 a.m. He went to the café, had a cup of tea, read his book and afterward went for a walk. He then said that he was desperate for a piss and went into the bushes."

"He couldn't use the toilets in the café?"

Ramouter shrugged. "Apparently, he needs to go a lot because he caught an STD from his ex-girlfriend."

Henley pulled a face as Eastwood, who had just walked into the office, and started to laugh.

Ramouter wiped his hands with a napkin. "Anyway, he said that he was just taking a piss, not wanking, so he didn't see anything in the bushes until Aisha started screaming at him. He also said that he was there yesterday around the same time."

Henley nodded as she opened the photographs of the crime scene onto her computer screen.

"The body was found slightly further back and to the right." Henley pointed to the bushes on the left of the park. "Impossible to be seen from where the boot camp was but visible from where Vacarescu would have been standing. So, what did the council say?"

"Well, they've had issues with fires in the parks because of the really hot weather. Dry grass and idiots throwing cigarettes into the bushes and not disposing of those cheap barbecues properly is not a good combination. They said that the fire brigade was called out yesterday afternoon at 5:48 p.m. because there was a fire in the bushes next to the tennis court."

Henley clicked onto the next photograph and zoomed in on the scorch marks that were visible a few feet from the girl's head. "Did our killer want the body to be found or was he just looking for a way to dispose of her?" she asked.

"Why bother dumping her in the park or Kennedy along the river?" Ramouter asked. "He's already cut the bodies up so why not put the pieces in bin bags and dump them in the nearest wheelie bin? Rubbish men would have picked it up and we probably would have been none the wiser."

Henley thought back to the marks that Linh had seen on the girl's forearm. The marks were significant and not something that she could keep from Ramouter.

"There is something else," Henley said. "Our girl has two symbols cut into her skin. Peter Olivier cut those same symbols into all seven of his victims."

Ramouter's eyes widened and brightened with recognition. "The Jigsaw Killer?" he said through a mouthful of bread and chicken.

Henley shuddered. She hated the moniker that the press had given Olivier. It had unsettled her to see the trivialization of a serial killer.

"Whoever killed our mystery girl has branded her the same way that Olivier did," Henley explained. "A crescent and a double cross."

"But Olivier is in prison, right?"

Henley repeated the words that the sentencing judge had spoken to reassure herself. "He's serving seven life sentences. Whole life tariff. No chance of parole. He will die in prison."

Henley looked down at the crime scene photos. Scattered dismembered limbs across southeast London. Her home. One of the victims had a name, but this young black woman who had once been full of life was still nameless and had been murdered, butchered and then discarded like a broken doll.

"Who are you?" Henley said out loud. The photograph of the woman revealed empty eye sockets, the absence of the milky film of death that usually covered the eyes of a corpse. Henley shivered involuntarily. It wasn't lost on her that a few years ago she could have been the woman in that photograph, butchered and left for dead in a park.

"Still ain't got a name yet?"

Henley looked up to see Stanford standing in front of her

desk. She had been so lost in her thoughts that she hadn't even realized he had walked into the office.

"We've run her prints and DNA through the database, but we haven't got anything back. What did Sentinel say?" asked Henley.

"That it would take a few days to get a full report." Stanford pulled off the red tie he wore every time he had to appear in court and threw the jacket that only came out for weddings, funerals and the occasional disciplinary hearing onto his desk.

"You didn't have to come back here. You could have gone home. I would have done."

"And have to put up with Gene shoving another tile sample in my face. No thanks."

Henley laughed as she imagined Paul's partner trying to convince him to join him in another house renovation project.

"So, what you're saying is that you thought you'd check up on me," said Henley.

"Never. He said to invite you around for Sunday lunch. You don't have to bring Misery Guts with you, just you and the munchkin."

"You really want to spend Sunday with a toddler?"

"No, I plan on getting drunk in the kitchen with you."

Stanford picked up the bottle of water that had been sitting on his desk for more than a week and unscrewed the top. "So, I heard from Eastie that we're keeping this one and that you're running it?"

"I wasn't given much of a choice." Henley began to straighten up her already clean desk. She rearranged the pens in the mug and made sure that her files were together six inches from the edge of her desk, listening to Stanford rattling on about the trial and complaining about the latest Met Police protocol announcement.

"So, where is he, then?" asked Stanford. "Your trainee. Thought he would have been with you. Clipping at your heels."

"He's supposed to be your trainee."

"No thanks. He seems a bit wet if you ask me."

"You were like that once," Henley replied with a smirk.

Stanford pulled a face. "Never."

"As much I love our chats, Ramouter's waiting for me downstairs. We're heading to Camden to speak to Daniel Kennedy's brother."

Stanford raised a thick eyebrow. "North of the river? Rather you than me. So, how far have we got with this case?"

"Linh found a mark on the girl's body."

"A mark?"

"A double cross with a crescent on top."

The humor drained from Stanford's face. "And the other one. The body found on the river?" he asked.

"She's checking now. I'm just waiting for her to come back to me."

"Well, it can't be…"

"We've been here before, Paul." Henley picked up the iPad. On-screen, the double cross and crescent cut into her skin.

"Olivier was out and rampaging all over the place back then, but this is different. Olivier is sitting in a prison cell. This could be down to anyone."

"After everything that Olivier did, are you seriously saying that we should dismiss the possibility that this has something to do with him?" Henley said anxiously.

"Sit down, Anj." Stanford pulled a chair across and sat down himself.

"I know what you're going to say, Paul, and there's no need."

"There's every need."

Henley sighed and sat on her desk as a compromise.

"You don't have to do this," Stanford said. "You don't have to put yourself in a place which is going to drag up painful memories."

"And what do you think talking about it now is going to do?" Henley snapped.

Stanford leaned back and folded his arms.

"Don't do that. I'm your mate and I know what it's like."

"I know that you're concerned but there's no need."

"You could give the case to Eastie. She proved herself more than once while you were on restrictive duties. You know that Eastie can handle it."

"And I can't?"

Stanford's tipped his head back and spoke his words to the ceiling. "That's not what I'm saying."

"And how would it look if I just handed the case over to Eastwood? People would gossip, Paul. There're enough rumors floating around me as it is. I'll lose respect."

"You won't lose—" Stanford stopped as Henley turned her back and headed toward the door. "Anjelica," he pleaded.

"I know that you care, but don't ever ask me to drop a case again."

"Bollocks," Stanford said as Henley slammed the door behind her.

11

"I still can't believe it," Jacob Kennedy said as he sat on the sofa. Three cups of coffee rested on the table. Henley hadn't wanted any, but she could see that Jacob had needed something to do. They only had one photo of Daniel, taken six months earlier in custody, but she could see the similarities. The same thick curly brown hair and sharp hazel eyes. "I'm supposed to be working from home this week but that's all gone to pot. I can't really concentrate on anything."

"What do you do?" Ramouter asked.

"Financial consultant. I advise people who are setting up new businesses, help them find investors, that sort of thing. Dan… my brother works with me. Design and construction. He is… sorry…oh God…*was* really good… Don't get me wrong. I know that he wasn't an angel. He had a rough few years. He had to go inside for a bit, but you probably already know that…"

His voice trailed off as he looked toward the mantelpiece where there was a collection of photographs.

"When was the last time you spoke to him or saw him?" asked Henley.

"Dan? I think that it was the bank holiday weekend. It was the missus's birthday, so we had a barbecue."

"And how was he?"

"He was fine. I mean, he was pissed off about his curfew, so he couldn't stay late, but other than that he was fine."

"And had you spoken to him after your wife's birthday?"

"I must have done." Jacob squinted and rubbed his temples. "As I said, we were talking about him coming back to work. Oh, I did see him after my wife's party. We went to watch West Ham at home against Arsenal. That was about three weeks ago."

"You were close?" Ramouter asked.

"He was my little brother. Our dad died when we were kids and our mum couldn't really cope. Drank a lot. Drugs. So, it was just me and him looking out for each other."

Jacob rocked back and forth as his shoulders heaved and he began to cry. "Sorry, I'm sorry."

"It's OK," Henley said gently, and indicated for Ramouter to pass the tissues from the coffee table. "I really am sorry."

Jacob nodded his thanks as he took the tissues from Ramouter.

"Your brother was on court bail for affray and ABH?" asked Henley.

"The court said that his flat was too close to where the victim lived," Jacob said bitterly. "I wanted him to stay here with us. I could have kept an eye on him, but the wife said that it would be too disruptive for the kids, which is rubbish. The kids love their uncle Dan. Maybe... I dunno. None of this would have happened... It's my fault."

"Please. It's not your fault." Henley could feel her own bruised heart ache at the rawness of Jacob's grief. She put a hand on his shoulder, not sure how reassuring the gesture actually was. "What do you know about the charges your brother faced?"

"Dan was just defending himself. We were working on a project in Dalston and Dan suspected that one of the builders was stealing material. The thing is, Dan has...had a bit of a temper.

I doubt very much that he would have been polite about confronting him. Apparently, they got into an argument—"

"You were there?" Henley asked.

"No. This is what Dan told me. There was a fight. It spilled out onto the street and Dan hit him on the head. Dan was the one who was arrested and charged."

Ramouter flicked back through the pages of his notebook. "Tomas Nowak," he said. "That was the builder that Dan got into a fight with?"

Jacob's expression brightened slightly. "Yeah, that's him. Do you think he's got something to do with what happened to Dan?"

"We will be talking to him," said Henley. "Is there anything else that you can think off?"

Just then a woman's voice shouted out: "Jay. I'm back."

"My wife," said Jacob, almost apologetically.

Henley and Ramouter stood up as a well-dressed woman with long straight brown hair stood in the doorway.

The woman dropped the large yellow shopping bags at her feet. "Who are you?"

"I'm Detective Inspector Anjelica Henley and this is Trainee Detective Constable Salim Ramouter," answered Henley.

"You're here about Daniel?" the woman asked unsympathetically. "Whatever he was into has nothing to do with us."

"Zara! He wasn't *into* anything," said Jacob, jumping to his feet.

"I was only saying—"

"Well, don't."

"Didn't they get on?" Henley asked as Zara turned around and left, her heels clacking against the wooden floorboards. Jacob shuddered as a door slammed shut.

"She's just upset," he said. "We all are."

"There was one other thing," Henley admitted. "Daniel went into prison for a GBH."

Jacob huffed and wiped his face with the back of his hand. "He was trying to defend Zara, if you can believe it. We were at a party and this idiot wouldn't leave Zara alone. Dan told him to get lost and then it all kicked off. There was a fight and the guy fell against a table and cracked his eye socket. Dan said he was acting in self-defense, but the jury didn't believe him."

"Did you believe him?"

Jacob shot Henley an indignant look. "Of course," he said. "My little brother had a bad temper and he was an idiot at times, but he never went out looking for trouble. I didn't bring him up like that."

12

"Did you feel that?"

The man looked down. He tried to open his mouth as he watched fingers curl around a silver-handled knife. He tried to move his tongue. To form words as the six-inch blade pierced his flesh. Blood, dark in the dimmed light, ran across his thigh, but there was no pain. The fingers uncurled and the knife stayed rigid in place.

"That was a stupid question. You can't feel a thing. It probably seems like one of those dreams. You know the one, don't you?"

The man tried to move his head. To follow the voice that was circling the room. "You think that you're awake, but you can't move. Not one single muscle. Not even your little finger, but you're scared, aren't you? That's something you *can* feel. All-consuming, suffocating fear."

The man tried to move his hand. He wanted to pull out the knife, but nothing happened. All he could do was stare straight ahead at his bare legs stretched out in front of him. His ankles were bound with clear plastic ties that were cutting into his skin. His feet had turned white with patches of purple and blue. He wasn't sure where he was or how he'd got to this place. He couldn't tell if it was night or early morning. He wanted to shake his head. To try and dislodge a memory. To sharpen the image of opening the door to someone who he thought he knew.

"I can't make false promises and tell you that this is going to be quick, because it won't be. It's going to be slow."

He couldn't feel anything, but he could hear everything. Cats fighting outside. Rain falling like heavy nails against the roof. And the person that he couldn't see, moving around the room. He heard the sound of a zip being pulled back. Metal caught against metal. Then something was pulled out of a bag.

His heart jumped, but his body didn't, as something heavy bounced along the concrete floor. He could smell rusted metal, damp dirt, the earthy scent of rain and spilled blood. The odor of stale sweat swam up his nose. A nauseating combination of soured fruit and rancid fish.

A voice buzzed in his ear like a mosquito.

"If it makes you feel better, you won't feel a thing, but I think that watching what I'm going to do to you—that has to be a mind-fuck."

He blinked. That was all he could do. Then the buzzing stopped. He smelled fresh blood and then he couldn't hear anymore.

13

Her name was Uzomamaka Darego, but she liked to be called Zoe. She was twenty-six years old. A description of the girl in the park and an artist's sketch of her face circulated in the local press. No one needed to see a photograph of a dead girl with missing eyes. Her uncle had formally identified her while Henley had been dropping Emma off at the nursery. Linh had done a good job of making it look as though Zoe were whole, her eyelids lowered as though she was sleeping. Henley placed Blu Tack onto the A4-sized photograph and placed it on the whiteboard next to the photograph of Daniel Kennedy. It was a recent photograph, taken three weeks ago on a girls' night out. Zoe's eyes were large, light brown and bright.

"She was working as a nurse at Lewisham Hospital, and as we know, Lewisham Hospital backs onto Ladywell Fields." Henley turned her back on the whiteboard and faced the office. Stanford, Eastwood and Ramouter had all arrived at the SCU early. It was almost nine and, unusually, there was no sign of Pellacia.

"Pretty girl," Eastwood said, peeling back the plastic cover of her coffee cup. "What are we thinking? Maybe she was killed on the hospital grounds and dumped nearby?"

"It's a possibility, but remember her right arm was found the day before in Greenwich. There's 2.4 miles between the two locations. Her grandparents reported her missing on Sunday evening at Forest Gate police station, but her details weren't sent to the Missing Persons Unit until the next day. Her information wasn't circulated among the station, social media or the press. The last time that I checked our internal database there were 10,980 black females missing but the public website that Ramouter checked only shows details for fourteen."

"Fourteen!" Stanford said incredulously. "How could it only be showing fourteen?"

"The website only shows unidentified missing people, but let's not get distracted with how rubbish the system is. Right now, we've got names for our two victims. Linh is carrying out a postmortem this morning. Daniel Kennedy's postmortem has been completed but we're still missing his left arm." Henley flipped open her notebook. "Stanford, I know that you're due back at court this afternoon but I want you and Eastie to go to Lewisham Hospital. Speak to her colleagues and also check with hospital security. They must have CCTV of Zoe Darego leaving the hospital. Uniform have completed house-to-house on Watergate Street. No one saw anything that could be described as suspicious behavior and there are no CCTV cameras on that street. So, in terms of eyewitnesses we've come up short."

"Right, boss." Stanford screwed up the paper bag that had contained his bacon sandwich and threw it into the bin.

"What about Greenwich Pier?" asked Pellacia.

Henley hadn't heard him come in and wondered how long he had been standing there watching her. The look in his eye signaled more than professional interest. Henley looked away.

"I've asked Joanna to chase Greenwich Council and also the service management company for the flats along the river," she replied.

"Good. She'll definitely put the fear of God into them."

"Oi," said Joanna from her desk at the back of the room. "I'm right here, you know. Manners will take you far."

"My apologies, Jo," said Pellacia as he bowed mockingly. "Can you pull up the CRIS reports for the Daniel Kennedy GBH case and his current ABH case?"

"Already on it. Ramouter emailed me last night."

"In that case, I'll leave you all to it. I'm going to give the guv'nor at Lewisham a call. See if they're prepared to spare us any bodies from the Community Safety Unit to help us with the CCTV."

Henley nodded her thanks and caught Pellacia's gaze a second longer than she should have.

"And what will you be up to?" Pellacia asked Henley.

"Ramouter and I are going to pay a visit to Zoe Darego's grandparents."

"We tried to report her missing on Friday night, but they said that we had to wait forty-eight hours. Why forty-eight hours? I told the woman at the counter that there was something wrong, but no one cares about a black girl going missing."

Henley saw Ramouter flinch, but she didn't. It wasn't the first time that she had heard those words: "No one cares about a black girl." She had echoed those words herself throughout her life and career, knowing that the usual stereotypes and negative images of black people meant that the media didn't care and were biased toward reporting the disappearance of a blonde, blue-eyed white girl instead of a black woman.

Khalifa looked up at Henley with angry red eyes. Looking at her as if she was responsible, as though she could have done more. Khalifa's wife, Ndidi, sat next to him and reached for his hand. She hadn't said a word since she opened the door to Henley and Ramouter. Just silent acceptance when they showed her their warrant cards.

They weren't the only ones in the house. A man who looked

to be in his mid-fifties sat on a high-backed chair in the corner of the room. Khalifa had introduced him as their pastor and he eyed Henley cautiously. She knew that internally he was asking why a black woman had chosen to work for "them"? The rest of the family—an aunt, an uncle, a family friend and a boy and a girl who were no more than fifteen and sixteen—had been sequestered into the back room. Through the closed door, Henley could faintly hear someone crying.

"No one cares," Khalifa said again. "And they did nothing." He pulled his calloused hand away from his wife and she clutched the gold crucifix around her neck. They were probably in their early seventies. The room they were sitting in was clearly the "good room." The hoover had left faint lines in the oatmeal-colored carpet. The couch cushions were still firm, hardly sat on. The room smelled of pine furniture polish and sandalwood air freshener. Against the far wall was a fake mahogany sideboard covered with framed photographs. A photograph of their granddaughter showed her in a graduation gown and holding a scroll, a mortarboard balancing precariously on top of her long braids. Her smile was large and bright. Henley could see the mixture of excitement and anticipation in her eyes.

"Uzomamaka," Henley said gently.

"Zoe." Ndidi spoke for the first time. Her voice, filled with pain, carried a hint of a Nigerian accent that had anglicized over time. Henley couldn't help but feel sorry for her.

"Uzomamaka," Khalifa said stubbornly. "Our granddaughter. She always came home. Always. She was a good girl. Not running around the streets. She was training to become a midwife. She could have been a doctor, but she said no." His wife nodded in agreement.

"When was the last time that you saw Zoe?" asked Henley.

Ndidi reached for a black leather bag and pulled out a slim red diary. "I always put Zoe's shift times in my diary. On Friday, her shift was 6 a.m. to 6 p.m. but sometimes she finished later. They're short-staffed."

"How long had she been working at Lewisham?"

"Almost two years now. She started at Park Royal Hospital but that was too far. It used to take her almost two and a half hours to get home. It takes her about an hour to get home from Lewisham. She didn't have a car. If she had a late shift, Khalifa would sometimes pick her up."

"But she didn't come home?"

Khalifa shook his head. "Sometimes the traffic makes her late. I called her phone, but it went straight to voice mail. My son texted her, but nothing. At eleven o'clock we went to the hospital, but no one had seen her. I went to the police station. They refused to report her missing. They said that maybe she was with her boyfriend."

"Her boyfriend? Do you know his name?"

"Daniel. I can't remember his last name."

"Was it Daniel Kennedy?" asked Ramouter.

"I don't know." Ndidi looked confused. "Maybe. I'm not sure."

"He was a bad influence," Khalifa shouted. "Uzomamaka was a good girl. She went to work, and she went to church. She was a good…" His shoulders collapsed, and he let out a guttural wail.

The pastor, who had been sitting silently, got up and gently lifted up Khalifa by the arm. "Maybe some air will be good for him," he said. Henley nodded her agreement.

"She loved him, and he loved her very much," Ndidi said as soon as the door was closed. "Daniel wouldn't have been my choice but… What can you do?"

"How would you describe their relationship?" asked Henley.

"They seemed happy."

"Happy?" Ramouter seemed surprised. He bent his head as Henley shot him a disapproving look.

"Yes. Happy. I mean, she didn't talk about him all of the time. Zoe wasn't like that. She was discreet."

"You weren't aware of any problems?" asked Henley.

"No. I don't know how things were in the beginning. She didn't tell us straightaway that she was seeing Daniel."

"When did she tell you?"

"About a year later."

"How long have...had they been together?"

"I'm not too sure. A couple of years."

"They didn't live together?" Henley asked.

"No." Ndidi's eyes were filled with water but the tears did not fall. "They were planning to. They had found a flat near Zoe's work, but after all of the trouble they couldn't move there because of his bail conditions, so they had to wait. Have you spoken to him yet?"

Henley shot a glance at Ramouter. "I'm afraid that Daniel Kennedy is dead," she said.

Ndidi's hands flew to her mouth. Her eyes widened with shock. "I don't understand."

"His body was found on Monday morning in Deptford."

Ndidi began to cry. "Who would do such a thing?" She reached into her cardigan pocket and pulled out a tissue. "Why would they...why?"

"I wish that I could tell you, but I honestly don't know," Henley said. "That's why we have to investigate. Did Zoe mention anything to you? Anything that would have made you concerned about her safety?"

Ndidi began to cry again and Henley let her.

"If there was anything," Ndidi said after a minute had passed, "I would have told you. She was a good girl, but who knows? She kept Daniel a secret for so long. Who knew what else she was keeping from us?"

"What about her work? Any problems?"

Ndidi shook her head. "She loved her job. She loved to help

people. She wanted to bring life into the world. How could anyone want to kill her for doing that?"

Henley's throat tightened. "We will find who took Zoe away from you," she managed to say.

Ndidi got up and walked to the mantelpiece. She picked up a photograph of a smiling baby. "When can we bring her home?" she asked, gently stroking the glass.

Henley hated this question the most. There was never a satisfactory answer, because the truth was that she didn't know.

"The police didn't care when we said that she was missing," said Ndidi. "You need to promise me that you will not let Zoe be forgotten."

Henley could hear her old boss's words echoing in her head. Rhimes had repeatedly told her, *"Don't make promises to the family that you can't keep. This ain't about you."*

"I promise," said Henley.

14

Henley put down the phone with a heavy heart.

"What's wrong?" Stanford placed a cup of tea on Henley's desk.

Pellacia looked up from his seat by the window where he'd been reviewing the Ladywell Fields crime scene photographs. He was one of the few officers who, after years on the force, remained uncomfortable with images of death.

"That was Linh," said Henley. "She's completed the autopsy of Zoe. She was six weeks pregnant."

"Damn. Poor girl."

"You've been to the hospital and spoken to friends. Any possibility that Daniel Kennedy wasn't the father?"

"Feel like I'm on an episode of *Jeremy Kyle*. Give me a sec," said Stanford.

"Chance would be a fine thing," said Eastwood, throwing her empty crisp packet in the bin and reaching for the KitKat on her desk. Eastwood loved her junk food.

The stillness as the team waited for Stanford to answer was broken by Ramouter entering the room.

"Sorry I'm late," Ramouter said.

"Short answer to that is no," said Stanford. "According to her best friend, Rachel Bishop, who has been working on the same ward as Zoe for the past eight months, Zoe was head over heels in love with Kennedy. Rachel said that Kennedy was a bit overprotective but was adamant that he would never hurt Zoe."

"OK, so why keep the relationship a secret if Daniel was such a good boyfriend?" asked Ramouter.

"The family are strict Seventh Day Adventists and completely against interfaith relationships," explained Stanford. "Kennedy is Catholic so that was a no-no. Rachel says that Zoe's grandmother was fine with it, but her granddad and uncle didn't like it one little bit. They threatened to disown her and actually kicked her out before they finally came to their senses."

"Her nan didn't mention any of this," Ramouter said.

"They described her as a good girl. They wouldn't want to taint her image. Where are Zoe's parents?" Henley said, and then mentally kicked herself for not thinking to ask Ndidi when they were at the house. She had allowed Ndidi's grief to distract her.

"No one knows where or who her father is." Stanford flipped over a page in his notebook. "Rachel said that Zoe's mum had her at eighteen, handed her over to the grandparents and disappeared to Canada."

"Kindred spirits," said Henley. "Kennedy's dad died young. No mum. So back to Friday night."

"Her shift finished at 6 p.m. but she didn't sign out until 10:08 p.m. As we know, the NHS is short-staffed. Security cameras show her leaving the High Dependency Unit at 10:17 p.m. and she leaves the building at 10:32 p.m."

"Her grandfather said that he went to the hospital at eleven," said Ramouter. "Why would he leave it so long if he knew that she was finishing at 6 p.m.?"

"Boy Wonder has a point." Stanford closed his notebook and threw it onto his desk. "You're going to ask me to have a word with her grandfather, aren't you?"

Henley smiled. "And the uncle. Bring them in if you have to. Voluntary interview. See if you can pin them down on exactly what they were doing from 6 p.m."

"Will do. But there's one other thing. Rachel said that two weeks before she went missing, Zoe had arrived at work very upset. Crying, shaking, the works."

"What happened?" Ramouter asked.

"According to Rachel, Zoe told her that a man had grabbed her and called her a bitch. He told her that she had ruined his life. A couple of days later the same man was seen outside the hospital."

"Did she report it?" asked Henley.

"Rachel isn't sure if Zoe called the police, but she did report it to hospital security."

Henley's confidence grew. They were getting somewhere. Promises wouldn't be broken.

"But what about the symbols on her body? We're not just ignoring that this may be connected to Olivier in some way?" asked Eastwood.

"If we were only dealing with chopped-up bodies, I would have said no, but with the branding…" Henley's voice trailed off.

"I don't like where this is going," said Pellacia.

"We have to look at the possibility of our victims having links to Olivier or to his seven victims."

"What could the link be? Olivier already got his revenge when he went on his murder spree," said Eastwood.

"Why did he want revenge?" asked Ramouter.

"Olivier joined the army when he was nineteen," Eastwood explained. "He was a walking cliché." She ticked each item off her fingers. "Parents couldn't handle him. Expelled from school. Moved from foster home to foster home. Put into care and then kicked out at eighteen with a check for two grand and no clue what to do with his life. So, Olivier joins the army. Six months later he is raped. The army doctor said that it was one of the worst cases she had seen."

Henley leaned forward on her desk, grateful that Eastwood was telling the story.

"What did she mean by 'worst case'?" Ramouter asked.

"He was gang-raped. They used a broom handle and a broken glass bottle as well as their dicks. Olivier was in the hospital for six weeks."

"Shit."

"He reported it. Named his six attackers. Adrian Flynn, Toby Kendrick, Jeremy Hicks, Gary Forde, Richard Lewis and Alastair Nash. All members of his squad. There was a court-martial which lasted twelve days. All six of them were cleared. Fast-forward eighteen years and Sergeant Adrian Flynn is accused of rape by a civilian. Again, he's acquitted, and three months later Olivier hacks him into pieces and scatters him along the A2 between the Sun in the Sands roundabout and the Kidbrooke turn-off. Two weeks after that, Tony Kendrick is found in pieces under a railway arch in Lewisham—"

"Well, this is bloody depressing," said Stanford. "Is it too early for the pub?"

"I might join you," said Pellacia. The air was warm, but heavy. There was a stillness in the room as though they were sitting in the eye of a storm.

"Olivier killed every single one of his attackers," Eastwood continued. "And he would have killed the prosecutor and the judge who presided over the court-martial if Henley hadn't stopped him."

"You said that he killed *all* of his attackers, but there were seven victims. Who was number seven?" asked Ramouter.

"We have absolutely no idea. Olivier refused to tell us."

Henley blinked away the memories and turned her attention back to the room. "The branding on the body means that it's more than just a coincidence, but it also means that we're not dealing with our usual killer. We're looking for a copycat."

"I don't understand," said Ramouter as he leaned forward onto the desk. "Why would a copycat start now? Olivier has been in prison for two and a half years."

"They're not the first," Henley said, staring straight at Ramouter. "Whoever we're dealing with is calculating, and they want to keep us on our toes. Why else would they dump the bodies where they did and within one day of each other? And there's something else."

Henley looked at the ones who knew. Pellacia, Eastwood and Stanford. They all looked everywhere but at her. Trying to escape that feeling of old ghosts coming back to haunt them.

"No one knew about this." Henley opened up the image of the symbols that had been cut into Zoe's skin. "These symbols were part of Olivier's MO. His tag. His brand."

"I didn't know about that," said Ramouter. "The symbols. That wasn't in anything I read."

"That's the point, Junior," Eastwood said. "It was never disclosed."

"This was information that we kept away from the press during the investigation and the trial," continued Henley. "We'd already had two copycat killings before we went to trial, so the judge issued reporting restrictions. The newspapers went to the High Court to appeal the order but the judges hearing the appeal agreed that publication of the symbols would be prejudicial—"

"How many people knew about the branding?" asked Ramouter.

"Everyone on our team at the time. Linh, Theresa and Anthony's CSI team."

"Last time I checked," said Pellacia, "Olivier was sitting in the segregated unit at Belmarsh. He spends nineteen hours a day in a cell. With the exception of the prison officers and whatever unlucky lawyer he's convinced to try and appeal his conviction, he communicates with no one."

"The bodies that have been found suggest otherwise," said Henley. "It's one of three things. We've either got a copycat who's a psychic, or it's someone who was involved in the original investigation and the trial, or Olivier has been talking to someone."

"Are you sure that we can't go to the pub?" Stanford asked again.

"Seriously?" Henley snapped.

"Sorry, boss." Stanford sat up straighter in his chair. "OK, who could Olivier be talking to?"

"Someone with a direct line to him," suggested Ramouter. "Maybe someone he's writing to? But what would be the point?"

"Olivier is a narcissistic, egotistical psychopath," said Henley. "Maybe he wants to gloat."

"But what if it's not him and he's really just sitting in Belmarsh minding his own business and doing Sudoku," said Eastwood. "It could be a leak?"

Henley shook her head. "Doesn't make any sense. Why would anyone leak that information now?"

"I'm not talking about now. I'm talking about back when Rhimes was in charge."

"Don't even go there, Eastwood," said Pellacia. His voice was hard and filled with warning.

Eastwood held her hands up. "It's not like I'm speaking ill of the dead. I'm only saying what most of us may be thinking. Look, it's just us here and we all know that Rhimes wasn't an angel."

"He was a lot of things, Eastie, but he would never have leaked sensitive information like that," said Henley. She felt more protective of him in death than she had when he was alive.

"You can say that, even with all the rumors that were running around? Why else would he top himself?"

"OK," said Stanford in an effort to take the heat off East-wood. "It wouldn't have been us. What about the CPS? They're not exactly reliable. I wouldn't be surprised if some nitwit temp had dug up the file and left it on the Northern line. Wouldn't be the first time."

"Look," said Pellacia. "What's not to say that the murderer is some jealous ex-lover? Darego wasn't exactly honest about her relationship with Kennedy."

"Don't be ridiculous," Henley muttered under her breath.

"Or maybe Kennedy annoyed the wrong person," Pellacia continued. "He's got previous for drugs."

"A drug debt?" said Ramouter. "His last conviction was when he was twenty-two years old. That's fourteen years ago. A bit late for someone to realize that Kennedy may have sold them an eighth of weed instead of an ounce."

"I'm just playing devil's advocate," continued Pellacia. "From what we know of Daniel Kennedy so far, the only person singing his praises is his brother."

"Sorry, guv." Ramouter raised his shoulders. "The timing doesn't sit right with me, for this to be drug-related."

"I agree with Ramouter," said Henley. "And I don't think it's a leak either." She understood that Pellacia wanted to cover all angles, but she couldn't ignore the feeling that this would only lead them on a wild-goose chase.

"Most people who leak information are either doing it out of some misguided notion that they're doing good or it's all about getting paid. This guy, if it is a guy, he's more interested in getting noticed. Standing out from the crowd," said Ramouter. "And branding the body with... What is it? A crescent and a double cross?"

Pellacia nodded.

"That's definitely going to make him stand out."

15

"He's bit of a bright spark, isn't he?" said Pellacia, closing his office door.

"He's asking the right questions," Henley answered. "But it's still early days."

"It's been two days. Well, actually"—Pellacia checked his watch—"two days, eight hours and forty-two minutes since you've been on this case as an SIO."

She sat down. "Have you called me in here for a checkup?"

"Don't say it like that. One, I'm doing my job, and two, don't you think that I would rather be out there than in here? I did hear what you said. Calling me ridiculous."

Henley tried to ignore the hurt in Pellacia's tone. She didn't answer. Her mind flashed back to those late-night conversations in bed, where Pellacia had talked about his career ambitions. Now he had the face of a man who had reached for the largest orange in the tree, only to realize the fruit was bitter.

"What is it about her?" Pellacia asked.

"About who?"

"The girl. Uzomamaka Darego. Zoe."

Henley thought about lying to him. To fob him off with the

usual line of just wanting to do a good job, but Pellacia knew
her too well.

"Zoe reminds me of her," Henley admitted. "Melissa Gy-
imah. I've told you about her."

"The girl who went missing from your school?"

"She didn't just go to my school. I grew up with her. She lived
in the flats across the road from my house. The police didn't
bother and the press didn't bat an eyelid until a fifteen-year-old
white girl went missing. Her face was everywhere. All over the
papers, all over the news, but Melissa…we had to do it all ourselves. We were the ones who looked for her and put posters up,
and nine months later I found her."

"In the river," Pellacia said softly. He knew the story.

"Zoe reminds me of her, that's all. Someone dumped her like
rubbish. Melissa's killer was never caught. I don't want that for
Zoe's family or for Kennedy's."

"It won't happen." Pellacia stepped forward as if he wanted
to hug Henley but put his hands in his pockets instead. "How
have you been otherwise?"

Henley watched Pellacia carefully, trying to work out if he
was asking about her professionally or personally. They had
blurred the lines so long ago that she could never really tell.

"Work," she said slowly and precisely. "It's fine. What more
can I say about working a double murder investigation? The
victims' families, both of them, seem genuine, but you know
what families are like—lots of buried secrets."

"And nothing stays buried forever. Secrets have a way of
coming out."

"Like the branding. The symbols." Henley picked up a packet
of yellow Post-it Notes from the desk, turning it over in her
hands. "We kept that a secret and now…someone knows."

"Benefit of the doubt… It could be a coincidence."

Henley smiled tightly. "We both know that it's not. Someone

has talked. We just need to work out who, which means that I need to see Olivier."

"Excuse me. Why? You know what, don't answer that. For fuck's sake. There must be another way."

"There isn't. I won't lie, I'd rather *not* be seeing him, but I don't think that I've got much of a choice. Someone is using his MO right down to carving his symbols into the bodies."

Pellacia turned his back and picked up the phone.

"Stephen, don't turn your back on me. What are you doing?"

"What you've asked me to. I'm calling the prison liaison officer, whoever the fuck that is."

"This can't wait."

"I know. If I can't get you in there tonight, then one way or another, you're seeing him tomorrow morning."

Henley ran hard. She could see him just in front of her, sprinting across the heath. She could hear Pellacia's voice shouting out, "Stop! Police!" Sharp jolts of pain shot down her shins, but she ran faster, ignoring the metal rings of the handcuffs banging against her ribs. She lost him for just a second as her breathing grew more rapid. The exhaust fumes pushed down her throat, when suddenly he stopped, turned toward her and ran—

"No, no, no, no," Henley murmured before she jolted awake. The back of her pajama top was soaked and clung to the cotton sheet under her. Sweat rivered between her breasts. She tried to kick off the bedsheets entangled in her legs. As her eyes adjusted to the darkness, she could see Rob lying on his back, mouth slightly open, snoring and oblivious to her anxiety. The green digits on the clock on the bedside table flashed to 3:48 a.m.

Henley pulled off her pajama top and got out of bed. She thought it had stopped. The nightmares and the panic attacks that had consumed her for months. Her eyes burned with tears as fear gripped her in the bathroom. She pulled off her shorts and turned on the shower.

"No…" Henley said as she felt the warm stream of urine leave her and run down the inside of her leg. Henley flushed with shame, reached for a towel, soaked it under the running water and wiped up her piss from the floor. The slow breaking down of her body, telling her that she couldn't do the job. She threw the damp towel into the laundry basket and stepped into the shower. She rested her head against the tiled wall and breathed in the steam.

"I won't let it happen," she said, water running down her back. "I won't let you break me."

16

"Oh God, this place is still depressing," said Henley as she and Ramouter walked through the rust-colored doors to HMP Belmarsh. The reception area was devoid of any sort of personality. The walls were painted the same neglectful gray as the security exterior. Henley resisted the urge to wave at one of the small black domes covering the security cameras in each corner of the ceiling. The security guard, stationed behind reinforced glass, looked up from her copy of the *Daily Mail*. Her gaze flicked from Henley to Ramouter and she let out a huff.

Ramouter stole a look at Henley that didn't need explanation. They shared an inherent understanding that came from a lifetime of assumptions based on the color of their skin. Henley felt her face prickling with heat as she sensed the subtle racism. The unspoken words of *What are you doing here?*

Henley tapped the glass harshly when she realized that the woman behind the glass was smirking. She dropped the warrant cards and folded piece of A4 paper into the metal tray and waited.

"Detective Inspector?" the woman said.

Henley waited for her to attach the word *Really?* to the disbelief that was evident in her voice. It never came. She walked to the back of the office, picked up the phone and said, "Yeah. Two of them… OK… OK… Yeah, I know. Ta."

Henley sighed with annoyance and worked out the crick that had been growing in her neck. The woman handed back the warrant cards and the security door opened. Henley and Ramouter were body searched, and Henley's hair clip got thrown into the waste bin. They waited for the faceless officers in the control room to check their fingerprints against their ID cards.

"That was a bit intense." Ramouter put his jacket back on and the security doors in front of him opened. An officer led them past a small garden that was being tended to by three prisoners all dressed in burgundy tracksuits. The almost fluorescent bed of dahlias looked out of place against the otherwise drab background. The prisoners had stopped working and were staring at Henley. She ignored a wolf whistle as they walked past the main prison building and headed toward the High Security Unit.

Fifteen security doors later and Henley and Ramouter were in the prison within the prison.

"Wait here," said the officer. In the distance Henley could hear the murmur of a television and doors slamming shut.

A second officer, flanked by a smaller man, entered the corridor with a black Labrador.

"Good morning. I'm Terry Wallace, the acting governor. You must be Inspector Henley?" He extended his hand to Ramouter.

"Er… No," said Ramouter as he took a step back.

"Oh…my apologies." The governor turned toward Henley. His forced smile disappeared when Henley ignored his hand. He pulled at the lapels of his beige jacket, which was far too big for him, and then clasped his small hands in front of him.

"We informed Mr. Olivier of your visit."

Henley raised an eyebrow.

"It's my policy to remind the prisoners that even though they are considered to be high risk, it is not my intention to dehumanize them. Not everyone in the HSU is a killer."

"No, just your average rapist, gangland boss or terrorist leader," said Henley. She stood a little bit straighter, trying not to betray her nerves. She had barely slept and hadn't been able to eat breakfast. The corridor was narrow with no natural light. The body heat from four people and a dog made the dead air rise. It was claustrophobic.

"We have a room that we use for legal visits available for you. Even though he expressed surprise, he appeared quite eager to see you."

"Eager?"

"You can hardly blame him. The only people he sees are the nine other men in the unit and the guards."

The governor pulled up the sleeve of his jacket and looked at his watch.

"How long do you anticipate this…meeting will be? It's important that there is as little disruption to Mr. Olivier's routine as possible."

"It takes as long as it takes."

The acting governor sniffed and wiped away a trickle of sweat from his temple. "Ah, this is Officer Bajarami."

A female officer walked through the door. She was shorter than Henley, but not by much. Her auburn hair was tied back into a bun. She looked to be in her mid-thirties. There was nothing distinguishing about her and the uniform was unflattering. She was the sort of woman who would be lost in a crowd if it wasn't for the purple remains of a bruise under her left eye. Bajarami was wearing a short-sleeved shirt and Henley's eyes moved down to the visible scratches on her right arm, which added color to a tattoo of shooting stars.

"You should see the other guy," the governor said with a weak laugh. "Anyway, places for me to be. Inspector Henley, Detective Ramouter." He nodded, before walking out of the door that Bajarami was holding for him. She locked the door behind him.

"It was a prisoner on the remand wing. He got refused bail

and he kicked off," said Bajarami. She opened another door and waited for Henley and Ramouter to walk through before locking it behind her. "To be fair on him, the judge was a bit harsh. He's only twenty-two and he's never been inside before."

"And then he finds out that he's coming here?" said Ramouter as they walked up a set of stairs.

"Exactly," replied Bajarami. She opened the door to a room unlike the others. It was small and bright and with a large window, a table and chairs. Everything was bolted securely to the floor. A red light above a security camera flashed intermittently in the far corner and a long black rubber strip, just an arm's length away from the table, ran along the wall. Henley wondered how many lawyers, doctors or police officers had had to press the alarm over the years.

The last time Henley had seen Olivier he'd been standing in the dock at the Old Bailey as the forewoman stood up, visibly shaking as the clerk asked her if the jury had reached a unanimous verdict. Her voice cracked when she replied, "No." It had cracked again when she had replied, "Yes," to the next question: "Have the jury reached a verdict where at least ten of you have agreed?" Her voice had grown quieter as she said that Olivier was guilty of murder seven times.

He had stood motionless as the verdicts were read out. His face unmoving, in the same navy Hugo Boss suit he'd worn for every day of his trial. From the sharpness of his suit to the shine on his shoes, he didn't look like a killer. He looked smooth, like he was ready to advise you on how to make the best return on your investments. The only crack in his demeanor came when the forewoman had confirmed the majority verdict of 10-2. Two people on that jury had thought that he was innocent.

Henley watched Olivier through the shatterproof window. He spoke to one officer while another officer inserted a key into the handcuffs around Olivier's wrists. Olivier said something, and the short Asian officer shook his head and laughed. Olivier placed his hand on the second officer's arm, and Henley flinched. The cuffs were removed and Olivier walked into the room. Henley's breath caught in her throat.

"It's been a long time," said Olivier, his voice hoarse. "You're looking well. You will have to excuse the voice. Haven't been feeling too well. Those cells get a bit drafty at night." Olivier extended his hand. Henley ignored it. "I saw you on the news yesterday morning. It's inspector now, isn't it?"

Olivier's dark blue gaze shifted down to her stomach, looking for the scars that he had left behind. His smile grew wider, revealing perfectly aligned but nicotine-stained teeth. The charm was still there, but there was something else too. He was not the same man who had walked into Belmarsh two and a half years ago, but he was not entirely broken either.

"Sit down," Henley said firmly, pointing at the chair opposite Ramouter. Bajarami, who had been standing expressionless by the door, left the room.

"There's no need to be so unfriendly, Inspector. Enough time has passed. The path to redemption is forgiveness, so we can be civil to each other."

"I said sit down. And I'm in no mood for games."

"I don't get any visitors. I get my fair share of fan mail but they're hardly going to let them come here and see me. I see the doctor now and again but it's not the same as having someone who wants to see you. So, I'm flattered you're here, Inspector. It's a shame you felt the need to bring a friend, but luckily for you I'm not a jealous man."

Olivier looked Ramouter up and down.

"Well, you're certainly better-looking than that other one the inspector used to hang around with. This place makes you forget your manners. We didn't introduce ourselves. What's your name? You look new. Fresh."

"Ramouter. TDC Ramouter."

"Is there a first name?"

"Salim. Salim Ramouter."

"Pleasure to meet you, Salim Ramouter. Are you the inspector's new partner?"

"Yes, I am."

Henley silently cursed and gave Ramouter a look. The last thing that she wanted was for Olivier to think that he had made a connection with Ramouter.

"I think that the inspector just wants you to sit back and observe," Olivier said matter-of-factly. He folded his blue-veined arms across his chest. "She's always had an obsession with me. I remember the first time that I saw her, standing outside Scotland Yard, calling me out—"

"We're here to ask you some questions," Henley interrupted, careful not to call him by his name, first or last.

"She called me a monster," Olivier said. "And then was surprised when I stabbed her. I was only defending myself."

Henley made a fist with her right hand again and squeezed so tightly that the pain came once more. "We're here to ask you a few questions," she repeated.

"Go on."

"On Monday morning, body parts were found on the banks of the River Thames in Deptford and Greenwich. A man and a woman."

Olivier didn't respond. His face was fixed like granite.

"Yesterday morning, the rest of the woman's body was found in Ladywell Fields. Both bodies were dismembered. Legs. Arms. Head cut off and dumped."

"So the rumors are true," said Olivier, "but they haven't confirmed that in the news? There was no mention of there being two victims."

"The public doesn't need to know that just yet."

"Trying to control the flow of information. Sensible, but always fraught with difficulty in these days of social media. What does the public know?"

Henley paused. Olivier was trying to take control of the interview. To show Ramouter and herself where the true balance of power lay. Reluctantly, she answered Olivier's question.

"The man has been identified as Daniel Kennedy."

"Daniel Kennedy." Olivier said the name slowly. "You say his name as though he's someone I should know. Did he serve at Her Majesty's pleasure?"

"For a while," answered Ramouter. "About two years ago. He spent six months at Belmarsh before he was transferred to High Down."

"Salim, I'm serving a very long sentence in the High Secure Unit. I'm Category A. I don't get to mingle with the general population. They think I'm a monster."

You are a monster, Henley said to herself. The longer that she sat across from him, the more agitated she became. She realized how closely she was watching his movements, hypervigilant to the fact that at any moment Olivier could try to kill her.

"The name doesn't mean anything to you?" she asked.

Olivier didn't answer. Instead, he stood up, walked to the door and tapped on the small window. The prison officer appeared and opened the door. "You couldn't get me some water? I'm a bit parched in here. All of that body heat."

The prison officer nodded. Ramouter mouthed to Henley, *What about Zoe?*

Not yet? Henley mouthed back. Olivier may be spending his days in prison but he was clearly in command. No one seemed to recognize the danger in him, except Henley.

Olivier returned to his seat, and watched Henley for a beat too long. "I don't know any Daniel Kennedy," he said eventually. "What else is there?"

"One of the victims was found with a crescent and double cross cut into their skin."

Henley purposefully didn't tell him which victim had been stamped with his symbols. She watched Olivier for a reaction, but there was nothing. The prison officer returned with a cup of water.

"I sincerely hope that you don't think this has anything to do with me," Olivier said.

"They're the same symbols that you cut into your victims' skin, all seven of them."

Olivier turned his gaze to Ramouter as he raised the cup to his lips and drank.

Henley continued. "There aren't many people who knew about those symbols. Your—"

Olivier held up his left index finger as he continued to drink, forcing Henley to pause.

"They're your marks. Your brands." Henley's voice rose with frustration. The concrete walls of the small room amplified her every word. Olivier placed his empty cup onto the table. The corners of his mouth twitched.

"The two victims mean nothing to you but your style of killing is all over them. It all points—"

"Surely a coincidence?" Olivier asked with almost genuine curiosity.

"Unlikely. I need to know if you've spoken to anyone about what you did to your victims."

Olivier didn't answer.

"Any other prisoners, jailers, social visits?" asked Ramouter.

Olivier laughed. A deep throaty laugh. "Social visits? Really? They don't let anyone see me, except my legal team."

"Legal team?" Henley asked cautiously.

"Of course. I've still got one. We've been discussing the merits of an appeal. Being called the Jigsaw Killer is not very flattering, Inspector."

"You killed seven people?" Ramouter said incredulously. "And you think that you've got grounds to appeal?"

Olivier laughed again. He turned to Henley and winked.

"Can you think of any reason why these victims would have been branded with your symbols?" Henley asked firmly, trying to get them back on track.

There was no reply.

"Is there someone out there trying to send you a message?" Olivier folded his arms and leaned back.

"Is someone trying to get your attention?" Henley continued. A cracking sound. Olivier swiveled his head.

"*If* you are working with anyone. *If* these murders have absolutely anything to do with you, I'm telling you right now—"

"This must be killing you," Olivier said slowly.

The muscles in Henley's back seized as Olivier kept his eyes firmly focused on her.

"Here you are. Sitting here with me. Asking me for help."

"Don't flatter yourself," said Henley. "This is not a request for help."

"What is it, then? You came here to ask me what I know. You're struggling."

Henley sat back. "I'm struggling? Not likely. You know what I think? I think this is burning you up inside. You're stuck in here, no chance of parole. They'll wheel you out of here in a wooden box, cremate you and dump your ashes in the nearest bin."

"Careful, Inspector."

"You're stuck in here while someone is out there, chopping up bodies, using your sign, and you can't do a thing about it."

"Careful," Olivier repeated, his voice dropping, low and dangerous.

"You're not in control here," Henley said firmly.

Olivier smiled, but said nothing more. Ramouter tried to suppress a cough in the silence. Henley's watch was locked away in the glove box. There were no clocks in the room. A minute felt like an hour.

"We're done," she said to Ramouter.

Henley braced herself as Ramouter stood up and made his way quickly to the door. She heard the rustle of Olivier's clothing as he turned his body to watch her leave the room. Henley didn't look back. She couldn't let Olivier see the frustration in her face, nor could he see that she was fighting to stay in control.

17

Dr. Mark Ryan looked like a forensic psychologist. Confident. Trustworthy. His office, in the old biscuit factory in Bermondsey, was homey. Warm. Comfortable. Safe. You couldn't tell that this was a space filled with stories of trauma, betrayal, limiting beliefs, anxiety and sometimes just deafening silence, but Henley was not relaxed.

"You look as though you're pissed off with me, Anjelica?" Mark asked as he sat down in the leather armchair across from her.

"You know full well that I'm pissed off with you," said Henley. She picked up the cup of tea that Mark had put on the coffee table.

"I don't know why. I've been telling you for the past three months that you weren't ready to go back. You just weren't listening. I'm pretty sure that your own therapist would have told you the same thing."

"I've stopped seeing him," she said.

"What do you mean you've stopped seeing him? Since when?"

"About seven weeks."

"For God's sake. Why?"

"You know why. Dr. Afzal is too judgmental."

"You're projecting."

"Whatever. I would have preferred you."

"And I've told you before that there's a fundamental rule in therapy that there have to be appropriate boundaries between the therapist and the patient. You and I getting pissed in the Market Tavern would definitely cross that line."

Henley smiled at the memory of the mini pub crawl that she and Mark had gone on after Abigail Burnley had been convicted of fifteen murders.

"So, as a friend—not a therapist, because that's unethical," said Mark, "how have you found it being back?"

Henley leaned into the sofa and searched for the right words. She couldn't tell him about the panic attack last night. She had already pushed that to the back of her mind.

"Comfortable. It feels comfortable. And that's wrong, isn't it?" Henley continued, looking out of the window behind Mark's head. They were on the fourth floor with a view of the city skyline. "I shouldn't be feeling comfortable among all of that."

"If I was your therapist, which I'm not, I would say that it's not for me to say whether being comfortable is wrong or right. If that's how you feel, then that's how you feel."

"Safe."

"What?" Mark raised his head.

"Being out there, back on the street, feels safe. Which is odd because the streets are anything but safe, whereas being stuck in that office..." Henley paused, but Mark's expression was encouraging, devoid of judgment, and she continued. "It felt as though I was being punished for something that wasn't my fault. *He* punished me for a mistake that *he* made."

"He? You mean Pellacia?"

"No." Henley put the tea down. Mark had forgotten to add sugar. "No. I mean *him*. Rhimes."

"You hardly talk about him, which, considering how close you were, is odd."

"There's nothing to talk about. He's dead. We have to get on with it."

Mark opened his mouth to say something, but then thought better of it.

"He took the easy way out. Left us all in an absolute mess. I expected more from him."

Henley wasn't sure where all of this was coming from. She had resented therapy since she'd been ordered into weekly sessions with Dr. Afzal. For the first six months, once she was able to leave the house, she sat rigid, hardly speaking. She didn't like being forced to do anything and she especially didn't like being forced to talk about something that had been done to her.

"You're still angry with him? With Rhimes?" Mark asked. "It's not uncommon to feel that way when someone close to you commits suicide."

"I'm not angry. It's a waste of energy and my time."

Henley wondered if Mark knew that she was lying. She *was* still angry with Rhimes. Every memory carried a jolt of pain. Her heart broke every time she thought about what Rhimes had done.

"Have you told Rob that you're back on the street?" Mark asked.

"Back on the street?" Henley couldn't help herself from laughing. "You make it sound like I'm a sex worker."

"I'm sorry. It's been a long day, but you know what I mean."

"Yeah, I told him last night. He wasn't exactly jumping up and down and wishing me well." Henley could feel the knots of tension in her shoulders as she thought back to Rob's reaction. He'd accused Henley of lying to him, of putting her career before their marriage. Rob was still giving Henley the silent treatment when she'd left for work that morning.

"You can't really blame him," said Mark.

"I know that I can't, but listen, I didn't come here to talk about me. It's about this case." Henley told Mark about the investigation so far.

"I haven't heard anything in the news about this," said Mark.

"We're not releasing a press statement just yet. Bodies get pulled out of the Thames every day. That's hardly news, but two dismembered bodies being found within a day of each other. Now that's news, and the last thing that we need is speculation."

"So, do you have any leads? Any suspects?"

"We've got a couple of theories that we're following. Revenge, possible ex-boyfriend or girlfriend—"

"Even though dismemberment is about power and it's a display of extreme hatred toward the victim, it's not something that women typically do. Dismemberment is a psychological form of closure and gratification and it takes determination. Women, no offense to you, Anjelica, are more...emotional."

"No offense taken. So, what about revenge?"

"Your murderer would be more focused if it was revenge. They would either kill the new girlfriend or boyfriend, but to kill both and then dismember... In my opinion, no."

"What about a copycat?" Henley pulled up the photos on her phone, the symbols cut into Zoe's skin.

"Hold on a sec." Mark took off his glasses and cleaned the lenses with the end of his tie. "Is that a crescent and a double cross?"

Henley nodded.

"The last time that I saw anything like this was back when Peter Olivier was on the loose. Was this carved on both bodies?"

"Only on Zoe's. Which meant that I had to see Peter Olivier this morning."

"Excuse me. You did *what*?"

"You heard what I said, Mark."

"And you didn't call me first. I could have talked you through it. Prepared you."

"You're not my therapist, remember."

"But still… How was it? How was he?"

"Frustrating. Unhelpful. I don't want to talk about it," said Henley dismissively. "I need something from you. Would you be able to prepare a profile for me?"

"Of course I can, but I'll need the investigation report… Well, as much as you're prepared to give me and all the information you have about the two victims."

"I've already got it for you." Henley handed over a memory stick.

"Great. Give me a couple of days to put something together."

A wave of nausea overtook Henley as she stood up. She placed a hand on the back of the chair to steady herself.

"Hey, are you OK?"

"I just got up too quickly. I'm fine."

"No. You're not. Seeing Olivier would have triggered something in you. Anjelica, at some point you're going to have to talk about what happened to you and not from the viewpoint as a detective but as a victim. A survivor of a horrific ordeal."

"Don't call me that. Don't call me a survivor. It makes me sound… Weak."

"How is being called a survivor a sign of weakness?"

"I don't want labels."

"PTSD doesn't just go away. I know what you're like, Anjelica. You're very good at compartmentalizing."

"It's what makes me good at my job."

"Your job is one thing but compartmentalizing your actual life. That's different."

"It works for me."

"At some point, you're going to overfill those compartments. You've been through a lot. You're still processing things. It's only been seven months since your mum died. I'm not even sure if you've properly grieved yet."

"It's too late to grieve and you're not supposed to be giving me therapy." Henley tried to smile but failed. She checked her watch. It was twenty past eight. She had already missed Emma's bedtime and Rob would likely greet her with stony silence once she got home, not that she could blame him.

Mark walked over to his desk and opened a drawer. "If you're not going to talk to Dr. Afzal, at least let me recommend someone to you."

Henley took the business card from Mark's hand. "Dr. Isabelle Collins?"

"She's very good. Call her if you ever change your mind about going back to therapy."

"I'm not promising anything." Henley's phone began to vibrate in her pocket. She read the message from Ezra: Can U come back to SCU? V. imp info on Ladywell.

Henley wanted to reply *No*. She needed to be home and spend time with her own child, to watch Emma sleep, kiss her forehead. Be a mother.

"Mark, something has come up. I've got to get back to the station," said Henley grudgingly. "Thank you for everything."

"Not a problem. Just remember, if this is a copycat and he's following Olivier's MO, there will be more bodies and probably a lot sooner than you think."

18

"He's a thieving little con artist."

Those were the words Rhimes had used when Pellacia had told him of his bright idea to give Ezra Williams a job at the SCU, two weeks after Ezra had been released from Coldingly prison.

Ezra had replied, "It takes one to know one," as he peeled back the plastic film from the container of sweet curry sauce.

Rhimes had muttered something unintelligible as he bit into his Quarter Pounder and Ezra had said, "This is a breach of my human rights, bruv."

Ezra had reluctantly turned up at the SCU with his laptop in his bag, an electronic tag on his ankle and, to Rhimes's unspoken delight, two bacon and Egg McMuffin breakfasts. He had spent two days sitting with a laptop in the corner of the incident room before demanding that he was moved to a room where he didn't have to look at photos of dead bodies all day.

Ramouter walked into Ezra's office.

"Give me one sec," Ezra said as he tapped away at his keyboard. "Right, I'm done." He spun around dramatically on a large leather chair that wouldn't look out of place on the *Mastermind* set. "So, the phone?"

"Yeah, Kennedy's phone and his tag. Henley said that you were done with it."

"They will never know that I've even been in it," Ezra said proudly as he stood up, stretched and walked over to the filing cabinet in the corner of the room. He opened a drawer and pulled out two sealed evidence bags.

"So, did you find anything?" Ramouter asked, taking the phones from Ezra's hand.

Ezra folded his arms and cocked his head. "Are you seriously asking me if I found something?"

"Well, I don't know how good you are, so I have to ask."

"No, you don't. I know that you've Googled me. Probably tried to get into the system and dig up the case files about me. You probably did it at the same time as you were trying to retrieve the Olivier case files from Archives."

"How do you—"

"Think of me as SCU's gatekeeper."

"So, how can I get access to the case files?"

"Mate, you need to learn a bit of patience. Have you tried meditation?"

"What?"

"A little bit of mindfulness will help you before you blow a fuse. I've already sorted out your access to the files. It connects to a secure server. Don't like all this cloud business."

"You've got the actual files here?"

Ezra nodded. "In the basement. Anyway, Kennedy's mobile phone. Brand-new. Only three months old. The SIM in it is new too. Pay-as-you-go. Only a few numbers saved. His brother, probation officer and someone called Rinse. Sounds like a dealer, if you ask me."

"What about text messages? WhatsApp? Messenger?"

"Nothing. The phone was wiped clean. Text messages empty.

WhatsApp chat cleared but that's nothing. People are idiots. They think that just because you hit delete you're in the clear."

"So, you found stuff?"

Ezra walked over to a small fridge and took out a bottle of luminescent green juice. "The WhatsApp account number wasn't linked to that phone, or to be more accurate the SIM that you've got in your hand."

"What was it linked to?"

"Bruv, another SIM, phone number and handset obviously."

Ramouter was struggling to connect the dots. He was tired. He pulled up a chair and sat down.

"Do you want some green juice?" Ezra extended the bottle. "Spinach, kale, apple, a bit of lime and ginger. Perk you right up."

"Nah, I'm good. So, there's another phone?"

"OK. Don't get offended, but I'm going to talk to you as if you're my granddad who spends eighty percent of our Skype conversations showing me the bloody ceiling."

Ramouter laughed.

"When you register for WhatsApp you have to enter a phone number. You're then sent a verification code by text. You enter that and then you're up and running. Got it?"

"Aye, got it."

"Right, so imagine that you need a new phone. You get the new phone and a new SIM, but for some dodgy reason you still want people to contact you on WhatsApp, but you don't want them to have your new number."

Ramouter nodded. So far it was all making sense.

"So, you download WhatsApp and they ask if you want to use an existing account. Got that?"

"Yes. Do you have details for the old number?"

"Of course. I retrieved the number and then I did my thing."

"What thing?"

"That is something that you don't need to know the details

about. All I can tell you is that I found the phone provider and that phone was full and still active up until Tuesday morning."

"Tuesday? But Kennedy's body was found on Monday morning."

"Curiouser and curiouser. Well, it's one of two things. Someone nicked it and was still using it until it ran out of credit. Or whoever took him still has it."

"Shit. What about the tag?" asked Ramouter.

"Now, the tag was even more interesting. He was given one of those fancy tags with GPS. Not the crappy, useless one that I had. Bad for him. Good for us. It tracks everything and he was always out. Solicitors in London Bridge, Camden, Upton Park? Couldn't pay me enough to watch West Ham but anyway." Ezra paused and squinted his eyes. "Oh yeah, Blackfriars Crown Court, Lewisham Hospital and the local library. He was a busy man, but once the curfew kicked in, he stayed put. But that's not to say that he was such a good boy *before* the tag was fitted."

"When did they fit it?"

"The tag was activated on August 29."

"Kennedy was granted bail on the twenty-sixth. When did the signal go dead?"

"September 6 at 11:47 p.m., but he wasn't at the hostel when it went dead."

Ezra's eyes flicked away from Ramouter's to where Henley was standing in the doorway, holding a coffee cup with her name spelled incorrectly on the side.

"All right, boss. Sorry to drag you back up here."

"Hey, Ezra. That's all right. What do you mean he wasn't at the hostel?" asked Henley.

"Like I said," Ezra continued. One of the mobile phones on the desk started to ring. "Kennedy wasn't at the hostel when his tag went dead. He was in Ladywell Fields."

19

Henley couldn't pull herself away from the photographs of Daniel Kennedy and Zoe Darego. Fated lovers. The pull to find their killer had grown stronger but it was the connection that she felt with Zoe that was driving her. Like Melissa, her story had been cut short. She had been a daughter, someone's friend. A sister. From her nail polish and lipstick, the black and purple braids that looked to Henley freshly done, this was a woman who had cared about her appearance. But her fingernails, ragged and split, told a different story. Signs that she had tried to escape from somewhere. She had scratched and had clawed to get out, to get away, but away from where?

"What do we know?" Henley asked Ramouter.

They were sitting in a room two doors down from what Ezra called his laboratory. The room was quiet and cool but Ramouter was starting to look flustered. Henley knew that he wanted to question her about what Olivier had said to him earlier. She lifted up her shirt, just above the belly button.

"Olivier stabbed me when I tried to arrest him." She pointed to the scars on her stomach. "I spent a week in the hospital, and he was charged with my attempted murder. Any questions?"

"No. None at all."

There were a few seconds of awkward silence as Henley tucked her shirt back in.

"What do we know?" she asked again. Ramouter consulted his notes.

"Daniel Kennedy and Zoe Darego had been in a relationship for about two years, but they didn't live together. Zoe worked at Lewisham Hospital."

"And Kennedy was in the park when his tag went dead, and Zoe was found in the park," said Henley.

"There's a gap of four days between Kennedy disappearing and his body being found, but the rest of Zoe was found after five days. Dr. Choi says that her arm was cut off first and the rest of her was cut up one or two days later. So, what did our killer do? Keep Zoe around for a few days to watch her suffer before he finished her off? It's sick."

Ramouter leaned back in his chair.

"We know that Kennedy was fully compliant with his bail conditions," said Henley. "He's a creature of habit, but something, not necessarily someone, forces him to remove his tag. Now, what would make you do something that you didn't want to do?"

"My sister-in-law."

Henley couldn't help herself. She almost smiled. "Someone other than your sister-in-law. Lesson number one, don't jump ahead. Always listen to the question. The question is not *who* but *what*? What would make you do something that you didn't want to?"

"A threat. If someone was threatening me or someone close to me—but there is something else that's bugging me. Kennedy's tag. Why would he take the time to cut off his tag and break it if he believed that Zoe was in danger? If that was me, I wouldn't bother. I would take my chances with the judge when they arrested me for breach of bail and the tag. The tag went dead in Ladywell Fields but we found it broken and under his bed. How did it get there?"

"That's good but we're still missing answers to the where, who and why? *Where* were they killed, *who* killed them and *why*?"

"The connection between Zoe and Kennedy isn't enough, is it?" said Ramouter.

"No, it isn't." Henley closed her notebook. "So, what are our next steps? What other evidence have we got?"

"CCTV from the area where Zoe was found and also CCTV from Greenwich Council but no actual footage of the river-bank."

"What don't we have?"

"Eyewitnesses and an actual complete body for Daniel Kennedy. We're missing his right arm," Ramouter said with a grimace.

Henley looked at her watch. "It's late. You should go home. I'll be here first thing. Ezra told me that you were trying to access the original case files."

"I wasn't snooping or anything like that," Ramouter said quickly. "I just thought it wouldn't hurt to take a look."

"To see if we missed something?"

Henley put her hand to her chest, as though she was offended. "What? No. Of course not... I just..."

"Calm down. I'm only joking. You're a fresh pair of eyes. See if there's anything about the original investigation that jumps out at you."

As Henley watched Ramouter pack up, she couldn't get rid of the one thought that was running through her mind. What if Ramouter discovered that she *had* missed something?

Ramouter sat on his living-room floor wearing a pair of shorts and his ancient number 8 West Bromwich Albion football shirt. He had opened all the windows but the overpriced fan was doing nothing but pushing around hot air. He picked up the last spring roll and dipped it in sriracha chili sauce. He was ashamed of his current diet. The contents of his fridge hadn't expanded beyond the two pints of milk, half a loaf of bread, eggs and sausage rolls that he'd bought on Sunday night.

He had printed out the investigation file from the memory stick. The papers were fanned across the floor, held down by the remote control, mobile phone and a 12 kg kettlebell. He picked up Olivier's arrest photo. He had smiled for the camera, his face all sharp angles, but there was a handsome ruggedness to him, a magnetism. Ramouter could feel himself being drawn in when he met him. In the photo he had a cut lip and dried blood on his nose. His left eye was swollen and bloodshot. According to the report, Olivier had been apprehended by Pellacia and resisted arrest. From the look of Olivier, Ramouter was pretty confident that Pellacia had done more than Taser him after he'd stabbed Henley.

Over the course of eight weeks Olivier had murdered seven people and dumped their bodies in various locations across southeast London. Ramouter picked up another photograph, smudging sauce on the bottom of the page. The last victim. Unidentified and to date they had never recovered his head. Ramouter's laptop pinged with the arrival of an email. The email was from the visitors' department at Belmarsh prison. Olivier had no family or friends to speak of but in the past three months forty-three people had applied to visit him. Olivier had only agreed to see one person.

"Who the fuck is Chance Blaine?" Ramouter asked the empty room.

20

Henley and Ramouter had been in the SCU for less than an hour on Thursday morning when Joanna received a call from an officer at Deptford police station. A body had been found, in pieces, in the churchyard of St. Nicholas church. The actual church was partially obscured by a wall that separated it from the surrounding council estate and a gated private development.

"Not very welcoming, is it? For a church, it's kind of grim," said Ramouter as he stopped at the open gates. On either side of the gates, a skull and crossbones sat on top of the posts. The empty black eye bored into them as if daring them to enter. In Henley's mind's eye, the skulls were replaced with Zoe's head. She shuddered.

"When we were younger, they used to say that this was a pirate's church." Henley almost smiled at the memory. "They told us that the skull and crossbones on the gates were the inspiration for the Jolly Roger."

"Seriously?" Ramouter looked up before following Henley along the concrete path that headed toward the church building.

"Yep, but really it was meant to remind parishioners of their own mortality and the fact that there's an afterlife."

"You grew up around here? I remember that senior CSI guy, Anthony, said that you knew the river well."

"I did," said Henley. "On the other side of the park."

"Local girl made good."

"Depends on who you're talking to. Right, let's get—"

The sound of Ramouter's mobile phone cut Henley off. She held her tongue as Ramouter looked at her apologetically before turning his back to answer the phone, then walked away. A few minutes later, Ramouter walked sheepishly around a white transit van and a police officer rolling out the blue-and-white police tape.

"Finished, have you?" Henley asked sarcastically when Ramouter came back.

"Sorry about that. It was... Never mind. Sorry."

Henley thought about asking him more about the phone call but changed her mind. The last thing she needed was to start getting close to him.

"Come on," said Henley, checking her pockets for gloves. She stepped off the path and walked through the overgrown grass, gravestones and tombs where the names of the dead had long been eroded. All of the activity was at the back of the church where the medieval tower stood. Anthony and his team of forensic investigators were already at work, while a young man, with the familiar black-and-white dog collar, his shirtsleeves rolled up, stood talking to a couple of uniformed officers.

"There are three entrances to the churchyard." Henley waved over a policewoman who was standing next to a petite white woman holding tightly to a dog leash. The Staffordshire bull terrier lay quietly on the ground. "We'll have to speak to the reverend. The woman who was standing with you. I take it that's the witness, Janine Mullins?" Henley asked the policewoman, who looked down at Henley's warrant card.

"Yes, ma'am. I've got her statement here." The officer reached into her back pocket and took out her notebook and handed it to Henley. "You will have to excuse my handwriting."

"That's OK." Henley flicked through the pages before handing the blue book over to Ramouter.

Ramouter handed the book back with a grimace. "She saw the foxes eating an arm."

The foxes had discarded the arm a few feet away from the memorial plaque for Christopher Marlowe. The rest of the body was a jumbled mess at the bottom of the stairs that led down to the door of the tower.

"Jesus Christ," said Henley, making her descent. She stopped three steps from the bottom and gagged. Among the broken beer bottles, weathered crisp packets and greasy chicken boxes lay a man, broken, cut in pieces and decomposing.

"How long do you reckon he's been down there?" Ramouter peered into what looked like a shadowy exposed grave.

The flesh on the back of the man's neck, where the head had been detached, was crawling with bloated white maggots. The limbs were wrapped in a clear plastic sheet that was shredded in the parts where the foxes had been clawing at it. The once white skin on the torso had taken on a mottled green tone and was taut like an overcooked sausage. Henley backed up the stairs.

"If the foxes have only just found him, then someone must have put him here in the early hours of this morning, but how long he's been dead for?" Henley said. "No idea. Where's the reverend?"

"He went back into the church," said Ramouter. "What I don't understand is why *here*?"

"I don't know," Henley admitted. "But it's someone who knows the area. It's no coincidence that Kennedy and Zoe were found just up the road and—"

"Do you think that it's another one of his?" Ramouter asked.

Henley nodded. She didn't need to see the symbols cut into

this man's skin to know that this was the copycat's third victim and that they were now looking for a serial killer.

"This isn't normal, is it? Three bodies in four days."

"No, it's not." The shrill ringtone from Henley's phone interrupted them. NO CALLER ID flashed across the screen.

"Hello... Yes. This is DI Henley... Right. Where did you pick it up?... How long ago?... Was it found in the water or on the riverbank?... OK... Let me know as soon as it does. Thanks."

"Who was that?" asked Ramouter.

"Sergeant Caballero from the River Police. They found an arm in the water near the Woolwich Ferry."

"It could belong to Kennedy."

"Maybe, but this river has a habit of spewing up all sorts. Could belong to anyone. They're waiting for CSI and then they'll send it on to Greenwich mortuary. Come on, let's go talk to Janine Mullins."

21

The teacup rattled on the saucer that Janine Mullins was holding in her hands. Henley was giving it two minutes before the cream china cup with a scattering of delicate pink roses around it ended up in pieces on the floor in the reverend's office. It took less than one.

"I'm sorry, Father. I'm so sorry." Janine stared at the broken pieces on the floor.

"Don't worry about it, Mrs. Mullins. I'll go and get a dustpan and brush. Perhaps I can find you something a little bit stronger in the kitchen." Reverend Undrill gently touched her arm as he walked out.

Janine rubbed at the creased, blue-veined skin on her hands and twisted the gold band on her ring finger.

"We walk in the churchyard all the time but I've never been in the actual church," she said as her dog lapped up the brown liquid running along the tiles. "Then again, I'm Catholic and this is Church of England. Brian's mum would have a fit."

The reverend came back in and quickly swept up the broken cup and saucer and wiped up the spilled tea.

"Do you go to church?" Henley asked.

Janine nodded. "Our Lady. Up the high street. Do you know it?"

"I was christened there. Had my first holy communion and my confirmation there."

"Really?"

"It's a small world."

The door opened and Ramouter entered holding a fresh cup of tea. "The caretaker is here so I'm going to have a word with him. Linh has just pulled up too."

"He seems nice," Janine said. "They make them so young these days. Even you look too young to be an inspector."

"Don't let the face fool you. There are some days where I feel ancient," said Henley.

"I've never seen a dead body before." Janine clutched her tea tightly. "Never. Not even my dad's when he passed."

"It's OK." Henley placed her hand gently on Janine's wrist. "Just tell me what you saw."

"It's like I told that other officer out there. There were a couple of vans having a standoff around the corner. They're always cutting around the back to avoid the traffic. There was a couple jogging, but they jogged past the church; they didn't come in. I came in, sat on the bench, and I hadn't even taken a sip of my tea when I started to hear rustling behind me and then I noticed the smell. I turned around and that's when I saw the... The—"

Janine convulsed with sobs.

A small crowd of parents, dropping their children off at the nursery across the road, had gathered on the corner by the crime scene. Their gossip simmered to a hum when the transit van bearing the words PRIVATE AMBULANCE passed through the church entrance.

The air was heavy with the scent of death. It was almost suffocating. Henley grew irritable and restless.

"I took a look around and had a good chat with Reverend Undrill," Ramouter said as they headed to Henley's car. "They usually close the doors to the church at 8 p.m., but the hall next door doesn't close until ten. It depends on whether they have events or meetings. The reverend doesn't live on the premises. Apparently, there isn't enough money to fund a residence."

"Get to the point," Henley said impatiently.

"OK. There's a caretaker that closes all three gates at 10:30 p.m. and they're not opened again until 6 a.m. There's only two sets of keys. The caretaker has one set and the reverend has the other. So, last night the caretaker does the same thing that he does every night. Checks the churchyard, throws out any drunks and locks up. When he went to open the gates this morning, he discovers that the back gate next to the flats has been forced open."

"CCTV?"

Ramouter shook his head. "All of the cameras were damaged a couple of days ago. The caretaker thought it was kids, but I'm not so sure."

"But Janine found the body. How come the caretaker didn't see anything?" Henley spotted Linh talking to Anthony while another forensic investigator took photographs.

"He says he didn't see it, and to be fair, sunrise wasn't until 6:32 a.m. so it would still have been dark."

Henley sucked her teeth in frustration as they walked toward Linh. "Do you realize that in four days we've had three dead bodies that have been dumped in public places, but we haven't got one independent witness."

"Whoever it is, they're clever," Ramouter said as he pulled a packet of Polo mints from his pocket. "Literally knows how to move like a ghost."

"I will never, ever get used to maggots. They make my skin crawl." Linh turned her arms over to check that she was insect-free. "I've been up since 3 a.m. Fifteen-year-old boy hanged himself in his bedroom in Kidbrooke. He's the third one this week and then when I'm two minutes away from my house I get a call to go to Nunhead and do you know what I find?"

"Go on, tell me."

"A skeleton. A bona fide skeleton. Not a strip of flesh on it. Just sitting in an armchair. Fucking mad. Anyway, back to your guy down there. White male. Mid-thirties to early forties. Like your other two bodies, he's been dismembered. All six pieces are there. Ligature marks on the wrists and ankles. Stab wound to his right thigh."

"How long do you reckon that he's been dead for?" asked Ramouter.

"Well, as you could clearly see, the body is covered with mag-gots. The blowflies, especially in this weather, will arrive within twenty-four hours of death." Linh pulled a face. "I'm not an ex-pert, but I do know that flies can lay up to 150 eggs in a batch. Another day for the larvae to hatch, three to five days before they pupate into flies... If I had to hazard a guess, I would say that this guy has been dead at least four days. I'm going to have to send some of those nasty little maggots to an entomologist, but there's another thing." Linh stepped closer to Henley and Ramouter. "Left thigh. Three inches above his knee. It looks like a double cross has been cut into his leg."

"Are you sure?" Henley asked.

"I need to get him on the table before I can be one hundred percent sure, but there is something else. His ears have been cut off."

"Excuse me—his what?"

"Ears. Both of them. Cut off. I know. I haven't seen anything like it before. I'm going to go. I'll give you a bell later."

"Let's make a move," Henley said to Ramouter.

"I think that you may want to take a look at this first." Ra-mouter handed Henley his phone, which was opened on the front page of the *Evening Standard*.

LADYWELL FIELDS: POLICE LAUNCH SERIAL KILLER INVESTIGATION AFTER SECOND BODY FOUND IN SOUTHEAST LONDON

—Callum O'Brien

Murder detectives from the Serial Crime Unit are investigating after a woman's body was discovered in a park in southeast London. Police were called to Ladywell Fields shortly before 10 a.m. on Tuesday after members of the public made the gruesome discovery. Three days ago, the remains of Daniel Kennedy, 36, from Camden, northwest London, were found on the riverbank in Deptford, southeast London.

Scotland Yard refused to confirm if the woman's body, found in bushes, had been dismembered, but did confirm that her next of kin had been informed. A Met Police spokesman said: "Inquiries are ongoing and we are investigating whether the person responsible for the murder of Daniel Kennedy is also responsible for the tragic death of this young woman."

"Shit, shit, shit!" Henley handed Ramouter his phone as her own began to ring. "It's Pellacia."

"Have you seen it?" Pellacia asked.

"I'm looking at it now. I thought that we were going to wait a bit before we started talking to the press about any possible links? Who's the spokesman?"

"Someone from the commissioner's office."

"I'm not happy about this."

"I'm not exactly jumping up and down about it either."

"This is a load of—"

"Anj, the chief superintendent wants to see us now."

"What do you mean *now*? I'm in the middle of a—"

"I know what you're in the middle of, but I need you to be at the Yard this afternoon at 12 p.m. Anjelica, did you hear me?"

"I heard you. I'll see you at 12 p.m."

22

Standstill traffic on the Old Kent Road meant that it had taken forty minutes longer to get to the Victoria Embankment. Henley had almost been tempted to turn on the sirens.

The tourists were out in force. Henley wondered how many of them would get their phones and wallets nicked as they stood in front of the "magicians" and three-card hustlers on the bridge. The air was thick with exhaust as the traffic continued to build up.

She carried out a quick rescue job with her compact powder and nude lipstick. There wasn't much that she could do about her hair.

Henley made sure that her police credentials were prominently displayed around her neck. She had lost count of how many times she walked through the doors of New Scotland Yard, only to be stopped by some overzealous officer.

She checked the rearview mirror and spotted Pellacia, hands deep in his pockets, making his way toward her. As Henley left the cool refuge of the air-conditioned car, she could feel the heavy air cling to her skin like an oil slick. She thought back to the last time she'd visited the Yard. Three weeks after she had been discharged from the hospital, her stitches still tight and the wounds seeping, she had been forced to explain her actions and how she had allowed Olivier to stab her. All eyes were on her that day. Blaming her, her sex and race, for the mistake she'd apparently made.

"This weather is shit," Pellacia said as he pulled at the collar of his shirt. "I feel like I'm sitting in an oven."

"Your tie isn't straight." Henley resisted the temptation to fix it. She watched him adjust it.

"Better?"

"Much."

They stood at the top of the stairs watching officers walk in and out of the building. The last place that either of them wanted to be was sitting in front of their boss, Chief Superintendent James Larsen, while he played the blame game. Pellacia pulled out a packet of cigarettes.

"Don't you think that you're smoking too much?" Henley asked.

"I didn't think that you cared."

Henley stopped herself from saying, *Of course I do.*

"We wouldn't even be here if it wasn't for Callum O'Brien," Pellacia replied as he lit his cigarette. "The man is a fucking snake. Rhimes would still be here if it wasn't for O'Brien poking around the SCU and accusing him of corruption. I don't trust him and I don't trust Larsen."

Larsen and Rhimes always had a contentious relationship and, as a result, Larsen was openly hostile toward the SCU. Henley shared the team's belief that Larsen was responsible for the corruption allegations against Rhimes that had been fed to Callum O'Brien and that Larsen was the reason why Rhimes was six feet underground.

From his slick gray hair to his polished cuff links, Larsen looked the part. But Henley and Pellacia knew he was full of shit. They sat there, listening to him threaten to slash the SCU's budget and transfer their investigation to the National Crime Agency.

"I thought that the reason you demanded to see us was because of the article in the *Standard*," Pellacia said when Larsen finally shut up.

"I'll come to that. My main concern is that in less than a week three people have been brutally murdered and their remains have been scattered all over southeast London."

"With all due respect," Pellacia snarled, "you can't apply a textbook approach to the investigation of a serial crime. By their very nature—"

"DSI Pellacia, the last thing that I need is an amateur psychology lecture from you."

"Sir," Henley said as she subtly placed a hand on Pellacia's leg. She felt his body rise with tension and then subside. "We're dedicated to completing this investigation and finding this murderer. We're not sitting idly by and waiting for the bodies to fall."

"Unfortunately, Inspector Henley, dedication isn't enough," said Larsen. "The pressing issue for me is whether or not I can continue to justify the existence of the SCU and the leaking of information to the press…well, it's a struggle."

Pellacia's voice sounded unusual and terse as he interrupted. "There is no leak."

"The SCU is a very tight unit and we've always done our job," said Henley. "It's a very risky strategy and it's one that will come at a cost if you take us off this investigation."

"Not necessarily," Larsen replied. "The SCU is not indispensable. You need to be aware that I'm keeping a very close eye on the unit, and if the current investigation seems too much for the SCU to handle, then the NCA have the capacity to deal with it."

The pub was a good fifteen-minute walk away from New Scotland Yard and not one of the drinking haunts of their fellow officers.

"The man is an absolute tool." Pellacia drummed his debit card against the edge of the bar while the young barman poured his pint. "Are you sure that you don't want a double?"

"Go on, then." Henley knew better than to challenge Pellacia with something as innocent as alcohol measures when he was in this sort of mood and she couldn't pretend that she didn't need it. "I'll get a table."

"He hasn't got a clue how an actual police investigation works." Pellacia handed Henley her drink and they walked toward a small table in the back of the pub. They sat down and said nothing for a short while as they drank.

"How are you coping?" Pellacia asked.

"Coping?"

"Sorry. Wrong choice of words. I just wanted to… I'm always going to worry about you."

"You don't need to worry about me." She hated the feeling that she was being micromanaged, but she couldn't admit the truth. That the past forty-eight hours had drained her. That she hadn't been sleeping. "There's no coping. I'm doing my job."

"I know that you are. I wasn't patronizing you. We haven't spoken properly about you seeing Olivier."

"And there isn't any need to. It was work. We're going to have to issue a statement." Henley didn't want to spend any time talking about herself. "Our own statement."

"The sooner, the better. I don't want the NCA getting their hands on this investigation. I'll go back to the Yard and speak to the press office."

"Are you going to mention the body in the churchyard?"

"I think that it would be a mistake not to mention him."

"It would also be a mistake to link him to Kennedy and Zoe right now, but with that article—" Henley put down her drink. "What? Why are you looking at me like that?"

"You keep calling her by her first name?"

"Who do I keep calling—"

"Zoe."

"And?"

"You don't do that with Kennedy, but with her. It's always her first name. As if you're attached to her. I understand why, but it's not helpful."

"You're reading too much into it."

"I think that you forget that I know you. You can get so obsessed with a case that it becomes an extension of you."

"You need to stop talking to Mark."

"I just worry about you."

"You don't need to worry about me."

"I'll always worry about you." Pellacia clasped Henley's hand.

"Don't." Henley pulled her hand quickly, knocking over her glass. She mopped up the vodka and tonic with a napkin.

"I'll get you another."

"No, don't bother. I'm going to go."

"Anj—"

"Stephen, please. I can't do this. I know what you want. I'm not an idiot and I can't do this."

"You act as if there isn't anything between us."

"Past tense. Was. There was something between us. For crying out loud. I got married, I had a baby. I had to have a life outside of this job."

"And even after all of that, you came back to me. Don't—"

"Stephen, that was a mistake. My mum had just died. You knew that I wasn't myself. Christ, everyone knew that I wasn't—"

"Are you saying that I took advantage of you?"

Henley was grateful for her mobile phone choosing that moment to ring.

"Linh."

"Your man in the churchyard." Linh's voice was echoing as though she was standing in a tunnel.

"What about him?"

"The advanced stage of decomposition made it a bit difficult, but I found it. A double cross and a crescent on the left thigh."

Henley exhaled.

"But that's not all. The arm that the River Police fished out of the Thames this morning? I can't confirm ID because the fish and whatever else is in the river has eaten away at the fingertips, but I've managed to retrieve ridge detail from the underside. I've also taken Kennedy out of the freezer and I would say that the arm is a fit."

"Did you find anything else?"

Linh sighed. "Crook of the elbow. A double cross and a crescent."

23

Ramouter scanned the empty office. It was the first time that he had been alone in the SCU since he'd joined the team almost a week ago. He hadn't had a chance to breathe.

Ramouter typed the name on Olivier's visitors' register into Google. *Chance Blaine.* Helpfully, the prison had provided a copy of the passport that Blaine had used as ID.

"That's odd," Ramouter said out loud. Blaine's passport confirmed that he was twenty-nine years old. A sparkling millennial with no social media presence whatsoever. He didn't even appear on the electoral register. Ramouter searched Blaine's information in the Police National Computer. He had previous convictions for possession of cannabis, drunk and disorderly earlier in the year and perverting the course of justice in January 2015. He lived on Ha-Ha Road in Woolwich. A mere two miles from Belmarsh prison and four miles from where Daniel Kennedy's body parts were found on the river. Alarm bells rang in Ramouter's head when he saw that Blaine had an alias. Joseph McGrath.

This was a man with something to hide.

As Ramouter repeated his searches, this time for Joseph Mc-Grath, he didn't notice Eastwood and Ezra walk into the room.

"Oi. Ramouter," Ezra said, slamming his hands on Ramouter's shoulders and causing him to jump. "While the bosses are away, getting a bollocking, we've decided to go to the pub. And you're buying."

"Fuck me," Ramouter said, too distracted by what was on his screen to fully register Ezra's words. Ramouter quickly copied and pasted the link to the article and emailed it to Henley.

NQ SOLICITOR JAILED FOR PERVERTING COURSE OF JUSTICE

—Farha Winter, June 12, 2018

A newly qualified solicitor of north London firm Osbourne Barrett Solicitors, who was part of the legal team representing the convicted serial killer Peter Olivier, was today sentenced to fourteen months in prison.

Joseph McGrath, 24, from Dalston, London, was found guilty of perverting the course of justice on May 22, 2018. The verdict followed a three-day trial at Southwark Crown Court.

In September 2017, McGrath had contacted members of the jury on the Peter Olivier murder trial and offered them money in return for a not guilty verdict. CCTV footage showed McGrath following a jury member onto a bus as she made her way home. McGrath maintained his innocence and gave evidence that it was a case of mistaken identity.

In her sentencing remarks, Her Honor Judge Henry said the matter "struck at the very root of our system of justice." She added that as a qualified solicitor—albeit an inexperienced one—McGrath must have known that seeking to

influence members of a jury was thoroughly inappropri-
ate and showed a blatant disregard for our judicial system.
"A solicitor must uphold the rule of law and administra-
tion of justice. Sadly, in this case, Mr. McGrath, you have
failed in those duties and the sentence must be one of immediate custody."

Joseph McGrath has been struck off the roll of solicitors
over his conviction and ordered to pay £19,786 in costs.

24

"So, Ramouter, how are you finding it so far?" Stanford asked.

Ramouter took a sip of his beer, giving himself a few seconds to think of a satisfactory answer for Stanford, who was staring at him intently. He had sensed that Stanford resented the fact that Henley had been taken away from him. "I'm learning a lot. I wasn't expecting to be on such a big case so quickly. It's a good thing for me that you're away on this trial."

Stanford didn't laugh.

"Anyway," Ramouter continued. "I'm sure that I'll be sent back to CID once this case is over or I've finished training. Whichever comes first, I suppose. So, how long have you been working with Henley?"

"Almost ten years."

"But the SCU has only been running for six."

"We were together at the Murder Squad at Lewisham with Pellacia. Our old guv'nor asked us to join the unit, so we did."

"That was DCSI Rhimes, wasn't it? The one who died. I heard that he——"

"You heard what?"

Ramouter shifted uncomfortably in his seat as Ezra Williams,

Roxanne Eastwood and Stanford stared at him. Almost daring him to continue.

"I mean, there's other stuff… Like I heard that he was under investigation when—"

"You should leave it," Eastwood said with a clear warning in her eyes.

"I was just—"

"Leave it," Stanford said firmly. "It's bad enough that Rhimes gassed himself to death in his garage. I suggest that you leave those rumors well enough alone."

Ezra stormed off.

"Ezra and Rhimes were close," Eastwood explained. "He took Rhimes's death badly."

A few minutes later Ezra returned to the table. Ramouter sat and drank his pint in silence for the next twenty minutes, listening to the others talk about officers he had never heard of and the latest rumors about the next set of budget cuts.

"I heard that they've finally sold our building?" said Eastwood, pushing aside her empty glass.

"They've been saying that for the past three years and we're still there. I keep telling you, they don't care about us. My round, I think," said Stanford as he handed his debit card to Eastwood. "Would you like to do the honors?"

Eastwood took the card and headed off to the bar. "You are such a lazy git."

"There's something else I wanted to ask about," Ramouter said.

"What did you want to ask?" Stanford interrupted.

"Olivier."

Stanford raised an eyebrow and Ezra leaned back in his chair. "What exactly do you want to know?"

Ramouter heard the warning in Stanford's voice but proceeded anyway.

"I was wondering what happened afterward. I mean, I've

been going through the case files. Henley told me that Olivier was convicted of attempting to kill her, but then she was off work for ages—"

"She had a baby," said Ezra.

"I know that, but even after that, it's like she just disappeared. Was she seconded somewhere? It seems a bit odd that after such a big case she would—"

"That trainee detective mind of yours seems to be running overtime," Stanford said.

Eastwood returned to their table, precariously carrying three pints and a gin and tonic in her hands.

"What did I miss?" she said.

"Young Sherlock wants to know what happened to Henley after we caught Olivier."

"Not Olivier exactly," said Ramouter. "I only wanted to know what Henley was doing afterward. I would ask her myself but—"

"There is nothing to ask her," Eastwood said as Stanford shot her a look. The atmosphere had grown leaden and it had nothing to do with the football result. "If there's anything that you want to know about Olivier's case, and only the case, then you can ask me."

Ramouter knew that wasn't an invitation. He knew when he was being warned off.

"Your only concern, son, is what you're working on now," said Stanford. "Now drink your pint."

Ramouter did what he was told. If anything, the way that Eastwood, Ezra and Stanford had gathered the wagons around Henley had made him even more curious. He was pretty sure that if he was to ask them again about Rhimes that they would be more willing to answer his questions instead of talking about Henley.

"Her ears must have been burning," said Stanford as his phone began to vibrate across the table. "All right, boss… Yeah, we're at the Tavern… Are you… Oh, I see. OK. I'll pass it on."

"Something happened?" asked Eastwood.

"Yeah, it has." Stanford put his phone inside his jacket pocket. "The boss wants us back at the SCU, now."

25

Henley flicked through the photographs from the smartboard on her laptop. Displaced limbs pressed against aged stone, cheap plastic and faded crisp bags. Dark blond hair matted with dried blood lay flat against a white scalp. A wedding band. Someone's husband, maybe someone's father. Henley placed her own hands on the desk, waiting for the tremor. It didn't come, but her stomach was fluttering. She zoomed in on a photo of the head. The area where the ears had been cut off was speckled with the husks of maggots that had turned into flies.

"As you can see," said Henley, "our killer has cut off Churchyard's ears."

"His ears?" Eastwood walked up to the smartboard and traced the section where the ears should have been. "Was that it? Just his ears?"

"Yep. Nothing else is missing. Our killer has also taken Kennedy's tongue and Zoe's eyes, but all three have been dismembered and all three have had a double cross and crescent cut into their skin."

"Why would someone go to all the effort of cutting up a body and dumping it, but keep such random body parts?" Eastwood returned to her seat.

"A trophy. It's not unheard of. Remember that Marques case seven years ago? He would pick up men outside gay nightclubs, take them home, kill them and remove their penises."

Pellacia grimaced at the memory. "He kept them in a container in his bedside table, but cutting off someone's dick is very different than removing someone's eyes, ears and tongue. What are you going to do with all of that? Keep them in the freezer next to the frozen peas?"

Henley didn't laugh.

"Olivier didn't keep trophies," said Ramouter.

"It was never about trophies with Olivier." Henley closed down the photographs. "He wasn't interested in collecting mementos. He wanted to show us what he could do. But the double cross and crescent were personal to him. Our symbolism expert suggested that the crescent represented disillusionment and the double cross was betrayal."

"Olivier was just fucked up if you ask me," Stanford muttered.

"Thank you for that, Stanford. Right now, we have to establish how our killer found out about the symbols. I'm not prepared to accept that it's a coincidence."

"I agree with you," said Pellacia. "But why remove Churchyard's ears, Kennedy's tongue and Darego's eyes?"

"Three wise monkeys." Ramouter's voice sang out from where he was standing in the kitchen, pouring himself a glass of water.

"What are you banging on about, trainee?" asked Stanford.

"Three wise monkeys. It's a proverb. See no evil. Hear no evil. Speak no evil. You must know? One monkey is covering its ears, the other its mouth, the—"

"Yeah, yeah, I get it."

Henley tried to organize her thoughts as she processed what Ramouter had just said. "Our killer has a vendetta," she said.

"Each of our victims have been targeted for some reason. What did Zoe see, what did Kennedy say and what did Churchyard hear?"

No one responded. The sound of early evening traffic, making its way through Greenwich, crept through the window. The sky was almost purple, as though it were holding back a storm.

"Three monkeys. Three victims. That should be it, right?" asked Ramouter.

Henley could sense the lack of conviction in Ramouter's question. "There has to be a psychological motive," she said. "There's a reason why they were killed. We need to establish the reason."

Pellacia's phone started ringing and he went to his office to answer it. Henley waited for him to return before she continued.

"There is another thing," Henley said. "Ramouter, go ahead."

"Right." Ramouter cleared his throat. "It's something that Olivier said to us when we saw him the other day. He claimed he didn't get any visitors, just fan mail. But then he told us that he has had a few legal visits."

"So?" said Pellacia.

"So, while you were out, I asked the prison governor for a list. Olivier was lying about the legal visits but he did see someone on a social visit."

Ramouter explained his investigation into Chance Blaine.

"Why on earth would a struck-off solicitor be visiting Olivier?" asked Eastwood.

"I have no idea, but there's something dodgy going on. Firstly, Olivier lied about it, and secondly, the prison confirmed that Blaine had initially tried to book a visit after his own release from prison, in his original name, but he was on the prison's blacklist. Four months later, he's changed his name and has a new passport," said Ramouter.

"And he's booking visits and seeing Olivier," Henley concluded.

"Olivier isn't an idiot," said Eastwood. "He would have

known that you would check the visits register and find out about Blaine."

"And that's why we're going back to see Olivier tomorrow," Henley said. "We've got three bodies lying in bits in a freezer down the road. I can't have Olivier thinking that he can pull the strings in our investigation."

"This Blaine/McGrath geezer," said Stanford. "As part of his legal team, he would have known about the symbols that Olivier used. In fact, he would know everything."

"Exactly," Henley replied. She picked up a black marker and walked over to the whiteboard. She wrote the name *Chance Blaine* in the empty suspect box.

26

Luna began barking and jumping before Henley had even stepped a foot into the house. It was after 7 p.m. when she'd finally left the SCU.

"OK, OK. I know that I'm late," Henley said when Rob entered the hallway.

"Don't worry about it. It's fine. I understand that this case is important to you."

"I'm sorry. I thought that I would have been out by five, but... It's been a hard day."

Henley held on to Luna, a barrier between her and Rob.

"I thought that you weren't talking to me," Henley said.

"I'm sorry about that. I've barely seen you for most of the week, and when you told me that you were working a case again, I should have done better. I was being immature and an idiot."

"You're not an idiot."

"You didn't deny that I was immature though?"

"How's Emma?" Henley finally let go of Luna and kicked off her trainers. "Is she OK?"

"She was a bit moody. Fighting sleep, asking for you."

"Don't make me feel bad for not being here. Don't you think

that I feel like shit every time I leave her? I just need a bit of support from you. This isn't easy for me. I'm trying to get it right but it's hard." Henley's shoulders sagged.

"Hey, I'm sorry. I didn't mean for it to sound like that." Rob's face softened. "Come here." He pulled Henley toward him and held her. She breathed in the scent of him and buried her head into his neck.

"I can't ever pretend to know what you're going through," Rob said. "Do you know how bad I felt knowing that I didn't do my job as a husband?"

"Sweetheart, I know that you want to protect me and I know that you sometimes think that I care more about the dead than you—"

"Don't even go there, Anj. I've never thought that. I would just like you to have a job where I didn't worry that you may not come home one day."

"I've got something to tell you," Henley said, pulling herself away from him.

"What's happened?" Rob asked quietly.

"Nothing has happened. It's just that… Tomorrow morning… This case. I have to see Olivier." She held back on saying the word *again*. She felt guilty but she needed Rob to be sympathetic.

Rob didn't say anything. The only sound came from the television. Henley sat down on the stairs and waited.

"Breathe," Rob said as he sat next to Henley on the bed and gently massaged her shoulders. "You need to relax. You need to breathe."

"I can't," Henley gasped. Her pulse quickened.

"Come on. I'll do it with you. In for three, hold and out for three."

Henley leaned into her husband as her breathing became softer, the ringing in her ears stopped and her pulse slowed down.

"I don't want you to see Olivier," Rob said as Henley lay down next to him. "I don't want him to hurt you again."

"He can't hurt me."

"No one will judge you for walking away."

You're wrong, Henley said to herself. She moved her head onto Rob's chest and listened to the calming rhythm of his heartbeat.

"I can't walk away," Henley whispered, the words lost in the soft cotton of Rob's shirt.

27

Chance Blaine looked miserable as he stood inside the estate agents on Sydenham Road, changing the available property posters. Despite his downtrodden face, he was dressed well in a charcoal gray suit and a light blue shirt. He noticed two people watching him through the window and opened the door.

"Can I help you?"

"Good morning, I'm DI Henley and this is TDC Ramouter. We need to have a chat with you."

Henley held out her warrant card, but Blaine didn't take it. In fact, he didn't look that surprised to see a couple of police officers turning up at his place of work.

"Is this about the fraud we reported? It's taken you long enough," he said as he remained standing in the doorway.

"Mr. Blaine, this isn't about a fraud and I would prefer to discuss this inside. We did go to your flat first but it seems that you're a bit of an early riser."

"You've been to my… What is this about?" Blaine's voice rose slightly.

"Peter Olivier."

Henley and Ramouter entered the office, ignoring the stares

from the other two estate agents at their desks. From the look of the place, Henley was convinced that the agency wasn't totally legit.

"Do you want a cup of tea or something?" Blaine asked, pushing open a door to a small cramped office at the back. There were half-empty cups of day-old tea on the desk, resting on top of old copies of the local paper.

"No, thank you." Henley took a look at the old chair in front of her and chose to remain standing. "A bit of a change for you, isn't it? From criminal defense solicitor to estate agent."

"Didn't have much of a choice," Blaine said bitterly. "It's not easy getting a job after you've been in prison."

"I can imagine. Look, Mr. Blaine, we're conducting a murder investigation, and there are certain features of our new case that are similar to the murders that Peter Olivier committed."

"What's that got to do with me?"

"We know that you've been visiting Peter Olivier in prison."

"Last time I checked, that wasn't illegal."

"No, it's not, but we've also been to see Olivier," said Ramouter, sitting down on one of the chairs. "And he denied that he's had any social visits. Didn't mention you at all."

Henley caught it. The flash of hurt across Blaine's face.

"That's understandable. Peter is a very private person."

"Well, private or not, there are some questions that we need to ask you."

Henley stepped back and let Ramouter continue. She had to admit that she was impressed with his authority.

"As my boss said, we're investigating a series of murders. Three people have been found dismembered and all three had these symbols carved onto their bodies." Ramouter reached for the pen on the table and drew the crescent and double cross on the back of a property leaflet. "Now, I'm sure that you recognize it. That was disclosed to you when you were part of Olivier's legal team and called yourself Joseph McGrath."

"I can't discuss anything with you about the case," Blaine said smugly. "Legal professional privilege. Anything that I discussed with Olivier is still confidential."

Henley shook her head in disbelief.

"Mr. Blaine, I wouldn't expect you to breach the conduct rules for a second time, but your social visits aren't covered by any sort of privilege and you've been seeing him every month since you changed your name. Why have you been seeing him?"

"We became friends," Blaine said. "He felt bad about what happened to me. He said that he felt responsible."

"Did he tell you to pervert the course of justice? To bribe jurors?" asked Henley.

"Of course not. It was a stupid decision that I made. He doesn't have anyone and we always got on when I was representing him."

"Even though you were struck off? And went to prison?" Ramouter didn't bother to mask the disbelief in his voice.

"I've tried to move on since then," Blaine replied.

"Mr. Blaine, you knew about the symbols," Henley said impatiently. "Have you in the past few months disclosed that information to anyone? If you have, even in passing, then it's important that you tell us."

"No, why should I?" Blaine said. He looked convincingly baffled. "Look, if I'm honest, I try not to think about what happened in that case. It ruined my life."

"It ruined your life but you still keep in touch with Olivier?"

"As a friend," Blaine said firmly. "He still needs friends."

"You want to be friends with a serial killer?" Henley waited for Blaine to answer as she reconciled herself with the absurdity of his admission. He had the good sense not to try and explain himself.

"We've identified two of the people who have been murdered," said Henley. "Daniel Kennedy and Uzomamaka Darego. Do those names mean anything to you?"

"Never heard of them," he said quickly. "Is there anything else? I've got viewings starting at ten."

"Not just yet, but we're going to need to confirm your whereabouts over the past week."

"Why? Am I a suspect? That's ridiculous. I'm a bloody estate agent. I'm in debt up to my eyeballs. I've already been to prison once and I've got no intention of going again."

"In that case, you'll have no problem with providing us with the information. You may not be a criminal solicitor anymore, but you know exactly how this works," Henley said. She threw her business card onto his desk.

Blaine grabbed his jacket, which was hanging from a nail on the wall. "I'll email you my work diary. Not that it's very exciting. I'm working twelve hours a day, six days a week. A couple of nights a week I go to the gym and the rest of the time I'm with my girlfriend, Lorelei."

"We'll need her details too."

"Fine."

Blaine felt sick as he waited for Henley and Ramouter to drive off. As they pulled away, he committed the car's license plate to memory. Back in the office he ignored his colleagues' questions, closed his office door and pulled out a SIM card taped to the back of a loyalty card in his wallet. He swapped it with the SIM card in his phone, waited for the phone to connect to the network and then he sent a single text.

You were right. They found me at work. Just left. Asked me about ‡℃. Don't worry. Said nothing. xx

28

"So, are we going to tell Olivier that we've just paid his mate a visit?" asked Ramouter as they entered the legal visits room in Belmarsh prison.

"No, not yet. To be fair, Olivier's not stupid. He's probably worked out that we would have been to see Blaine and that we know he lied."

"I don't understand why he would do that. What's he going to gain from it?"

"Who knows? He probably needs a way to amuse himself."

Henley held her finger to her lips as she heard Olivier's raspy voice down the hall as he talked to the prison officer.

"Inspector Henley and TDC Ramouter. We meet again," said Olivier. He stopped at the door and waited for the officer to remove his cuffs. "Thank you very much, Paul."

"I'll only be down the corridor," Paul said to Olivier. Henley was slightly amazed; was the prison officer warning her that he had Olivier's back?

"So, what's happened? Has another one turned up? In pieces, covered in X's and O's?" Olivier took a seat. "I prefer this room. It's a lot brighter and you can see people." He nodded at the female solicitor passing by the window. The woman paused, smiled hesitantly before walking off.

"TDC Ramouter." Olivier held out his hand.

"Yes?" Ramouter shook his hand hesitantly.

"I've been thinking about you. I was thinking about the letter T."

"What about it?"

"It's a new one, isn't it? I was trying to work out what the T stood for and then it hit me. T for Trainee. So, you're Inspector Henley's trainee. Someone to look after. To groom. It made me wonder what happened to—"

"Olivier!" Henley said forcefully.

"Pellacia," Olivier said. "The one who used to groom *you*. He told you to stop, but you didn't. Pellacia."

He said the name with such force that Ramouter had to wipe away the traces of spittle that had landed on his face.

"Pellacia. It's Italian, isn't it?" said Olivier. "He was and probably still is a cunt."

Henley willed herself to remain calm. Olivier wasn't prepared to be compliant. He wanted to play. She wasn't going to let him.

"A third body was found yesterday morning in a churchyard in Deptford," said Henley.

Olivier raised an eyebrow. "That's it? You're not going to jump to your boyfriend's defense?"

"Shut up and listen."

Olivier smiled, his expression unreadable.

"It's been confirmed that all three had a double cross and a crescent cut into them," Henley continued. "That's your MO. That's what you like to do. Carve symbols into their skin. To claim ownership."

"I didn't do anything," Olivier said, leaning across the table.

"What do you mean you didn't do anything?" Ramouter asked.

"What do I mean? Ten misinformed idiots believed that I

killed seven people but I didn't. I put my hand on the Bible and I swore to my god that I didn't do anything."

"You were found guilty."

"*Found* being the operative word," Olivier replied. He waved his hand in front of Ramouter's face. "What exactly do you know, trainee? You come in here in your nice suit and hipster beard, acting like you know things about me. You know nothing." Olivier fixed his gaze onto Henley. "Why don't you tell him, Inspector? Tell your trainee that I was found guilty. I didn't plead guilty. I didn't admit to anything because I didn't do anything." Olivier sat back. "It was a miscarriage of justice."

"You know that the information about the branding was never released, and now I've got someone on the streets doing a very poor imitation of your work. It's a hatchet job."

"Poor choice of words." Olivier smirked.

"Tool of your trade."

"Alleged work. As I said—"

"I heard what you said," Henley snapped.

"Be nice. I could have refused to come up here."

"Who did you tell?"

"I didn't do anything." Olivier sounded bored.

"Well, let's talk hypothetically, then," Henley said. "If you *had* killed seven people and chopped up their bodies, would you have told anyone, not including your crap legal team, about cutting the symbols in their flesh?"

The room went quiet. Henley held Olivier's gaze, daring him to blink first. In the distance, a door slammed shut, a set of keys jangled. Paul the prison officer walked past the window, paused briefly, nodded at Olivier and carried on walking.

"Hypothetically speaking. No one. They remanded me and kept me on the segregation unit until my trial in that kangaroo court. I didn't see anyone. I didn't talk to anyone. Don't get me wrong, I was asked about the bodies."

"By whom?"

"The others in here. Bloody nosy lot those prison officers are. Wanting to know how I did it, why I did it. Did I enjoy it? Hypothetically, of course."

"And did you enjoy it?"

Olivier laughed loudly. "Ramouter, did you hear her? Your boss thought that she was being clever."

"Did you tell them?" Henley asked again.

"Nothing to tell because I didn't do anything. I can imagine that it would be quite messy though." Olivier's voice was soft. "There would be a lot of blood. It would take a lot of work and patience to position the jigsaw just right. I would think that it's the bone that would be the problem. It's probably quite tough and if you haven't got the right blade—well, you could easily go through a couple of blades before you perfected the technique—but once you got through the marrow, it would be soft, almost jellylike."

The silence was heavy. "And the symbols?" Henley forced herself to ask.

"It would be my tag, my artist's signature. Why would I want anyone to use my tag? I made you a present."

Henley blinked, thrown by the sudden change of subject.

Olivier placed a hand under his bib. "I didn't want to squash it, so I kept it somewhere safe." He placed a small origami bird, made out of prison-issued writing paper, on the table. "I know what you're thinking," he said. "It's not a swan. It's an egret. Do you know about egrets, Trainee Ramouter?"

Ramouter didn't reply.

Olivier shook his head and tutted. "It's good manners to reply when someone asks you a question. Egrets are common around the Thames, especially on Deptford Creek when it's low tide. They like to travel in pairs. I made it for you."

Henley refused to look down at the origami egret on the table.

"You could at least look at it." Olivier's voice was harsh, suddenly irritated. "Oi, you. Trainee."

Olivier slammed his hand on the table with such force that Henley was surprised the Formica didn't crack. She could hear Ramouter's breathing, shallow but rapid. The sound was familiar to her—the sound of someone trying to control a panic attack.

"Why are you not paying attention, trainee? Someone cut your tongue out?"

"I'm… I'm not—" Ramouter stuttered.

"What was that? *I'm not.* You're not what? Not worthy of carrying that pathetic badge in your wallet?"

Olivier placed his elbow on the table and leaned his head against his hand, creating a barrier between Henley and Ramouter. She pulled back quickly as Olivier's arm brushed against her.

"What makes you think that you're up to this job? Maybe you should think about going back to where you came from." Olivier hissed at Ramouter. "Don't look at me like that. I'm not a racist. I just think that our little trainee would be better off playing cops and robbers back on the moors."

"Stop it," said Henley.

Olivier smiled with satisfaction as he turned his body toward Ramouter. "What are you? Thirty-three, thirty-four years old. Married." Olivier stretched his long fingers and tapped the solid gold band on Ramouter's finger. Ramouter recoiled and his hand disappeared under the table.

"I doubt that it can be a very happy marriage," said Olivier. "Not if you're spending all your time with the inspector. Did they warn you about her? She has quite a way with men."

"I told you to stop," Henley interjected.

"No," said Olivier. "I'm talking to the trainee. Has your wife met the inspector yet? I would imagine that she would feel a bit threatened. Insecure. Lonely. Or maybe you're the one who's lonely." Olivier's face fractured into a smile. "That's it, isn't it? You're here. Alone. With just me and the inspector for company."

Ramouter's eyes widened.

"Don't you think that he looks like him, Inspector?" Olivier asked as he turned toward Henley and held up eight fingers. "Jeremy Hicks. Same build. Same height. Same nervous eyes. Out of his depth."

Hicks was Olivier's fifth victim and had been found in eight pieces by a group of schoolchildren.

"They found him in Bermondsey," said Olivier. "He begged. Doesn't Ramouter look like someone who pathetically begs for you not to kill him?"

Ramouter got up from the table and moved toward the door.

"Going already? I'm not the same man who put a knife into your inspector's stomach." Olivier stood up and Ramouter pressed the red alarm button on the wall.

"Sit down!" Henley shouted.

"Look at him." Olivier slowly sat back down and placed both hands on the table as the alarm rang out. "I think that your trainee might need a fresh pair of pants."

Henley held up her hand as three prison officers appeared at the door. She indicated for Ramouter to leave. Now it was just her and Olivier. She tried to calm herself as the silence between them stretched on.

"What do you know about these murders?" she asked eventually.

"I don't think you should keep him. He won't last a month."

"Shut up."

"That's why I like you." Olivier smiled. It was almost affectionate. "You always had a lot of passion. Nice to know that you didn't lose it when all that blood was spilled."

Henley held her breath as the anger raged inside of her.

"You're shaking, Inspector."

Henley looked down at her right hand and saw that Olivier was right. She placed her hands under the table.

"You've been talking to someone about what you did. How

you killed those seven people, and now that person is mocking you."

Henley saw the change in Olivier's demeanor. The games had stopped.

"It must wind you up," said Henley as she pushed on slowly. She wanted it to sting—lemon juice on a paper cut.

"Careful, Inspector."

"It must be frustrating, to be stuck in here, unable to do anything about this person claiming to be better than you. I don't know, it must make you feel…impotent."

Olivier held her gaze. "I told you before, I didn't do it."

"You've told someone about carving those symbols into your victims' bodies. Maybe you've got Joseph McGrath, sorry, Chance Blaine, helping you out."

Olivier's gaze was steady, unflinching. "Get the evidence to prove it and come back to me. I'll be right here. Waiting for you."

Olivier walked around the empty exercise yard. Two prison officers watched from the back. He had demanded to be let out, even though he knew that access to the yard wasn't allowed until after lunch. They watched him circle the yard, knowing that it was better for him to be outside instead of taking his anger out again on one of the other prisoners. They had learned their lesson eight months ago, when he had broken the jaw of the inmate who hummed continuously while he ate his lunch.

Impotent. She had called him impotent. The growing fury accelerated his footsteps. He wanted to hurt someone. He needed to feel the raw pleasure of release as he inflicted pain on Henley. It wasn't flattering; it was insulting to have someone out there killing people in his name. He didn't want to be motivating or inspiring anyone. It was *his* notoriety. *His* infamy. He was the one to be feared, not a cheap mimic.

"Fucking bitch," he hissed. It had been grating on him since

Henley had told him about the first victim. One victim he could cope with, but now there were three. He could see Henley's face as she took pleasure in telling him about the copycat. She was mistaken if she thought that the copycat had more power than him. The fucker wasn't going to get away with it.

"Who are you?"

Olivier's voice penetrated the air, rising above the sound of the crows screeching as they sat on top of the prison wall.

29

As soon as the fresh air hit Ramouter's lungs, he threw up. Henley couldn't blame him. Forty minutes in an airless room with Olivier, she couldn't wait to get out. She wanted to throw herself into a hot bath filled with Dettol. Olivier's malicious toxicity had managed to work itself into her pores and fuse with the cells in her bloodstream. She handed Ramouter a packet of tissues. He had been doing fine until Olivier had turned off the charm and switched to venom. He had used Ramouter like a punching bag and she had let him.

"I'm sorry," Ramouter said as he wiped his mouth and then looked down at the ground in disgust. "I should have been prepared. I knew what was coming. I should have been better."

"It's not your fault. To call him the devil would be too kind," Henley replied as they walked toward the car park. "I know that you've thrown up your breakfast and it's not even ten-thirty yet, but I think that we could both do with a drink... Do you drink?"

Ramouter smiled weakly. "Yeah. But we're still on duty."

"I'm not going to tell anyone. Come on. I could murder one."

"Do you want anything to eat? Not that I can recommend anything." Henley stabbed at the wedge of lemon in the bottom of her glass. They were at a nearby bar, the Duke of Gloucester Carvery, which sat under the flight path of the planes escaping London from City Airport. Their booth had a fantastic view of the dual carriageway and the Tesco Express.

"No, I'm good," Ramouter replied as he swirled his tumbler.

"Never took you for a whiskey drinker."

"I'm not, but my dad always says that it's good for a dodgy tummy. Well, that was his excuse. Funny, I spent the first half of the morning looking at decomposing body parts—I'm not saying that it didn't bother me, because it did—but when he started on me—"

A group of cheering people barreled into the bar.

"Justice!" someone screamed as a woman in her mid-fifties began to cry.

"Someone's happy," said Ramouter.

"Jury must have come back with a verdict," Henley said, watching the man put his arms around the crying woman.

"How do you know?"

"Social visits don't start at the prison until 1:30 p.m. It's Thursday so chances are that the jury has been deliberating for a couple of days and they came back with verdicts this morning. You're not going to get that excited over a conviction, even if you're the victim's family, so odds are that our man in the smart shirt and Marks and Spencer's suit was found not guilty this morning. Also, he's local."

"You can tell?" Ramouter asked as he tried and failed to discreetly turn around.

"If you had traipsed halfway across London to have a trial at Woolwich Crown Court and had been found not guilty, would you want to hang around?"

"God, no. I would get out of here as quick as I could."

"As I said. Local."

Her right hand began to tremble as she raised her glass to her lips. She checked to see if Ramouter had noticed, but he was deep in his own thoughts. She took a quick drink and waited for the vodka and tonic to hit.

"Feeling better?" Henley asked.

"Yeah. Much. I made a mistake. I underestimated him. I thought after last time that he wasn't that bad. I shouldn't have shaken his hand."

"It wouldn't have mattered. He's good at reading people. It's a skill and he knows how to use it well."

Ramouter nodded but he wasn't satisfied with the answer.

"But you were number one," said Henley, trying to soften the impact of Olivier's attack on Ramouter. "Top of your class. Highest marks in the National Investigators exam."

A look of surprise mixed with embarrassment flashed across Ramouter's face. "May have been top of my class but they didn't teach me how to recognize a cold-blooded, psychopathic murderer. There wasn't a question on the exam papers about that."

The Duke of Gloucester Carvery had begun to fill with more defendants and relieved or distraught family members. It was nearly 11 a.m., another two hours before the lawyers turned up.

"He doesn't like the gaffer much, does he?" said Ramouter.

"He doesn't like anyone," Henley said. "Everything he does, everything he says, is meant to get a reaction. You said that you had read the transcripts, right?"

"Yeah."

"When Olivier was being interviewed, his answer to every question that Pellacia asked was 'cunt.' Can you explain why your thumbprint was found above the left tibia on victim number two? *Cunt.* Did you send Sergeant Adrian Flynn abusive texts? *Cunt.* For an entire hour. That was his response. Until he piped up and said that he wanted a solicitor because he was fed up of looking at Pellacia's cunt face."

"Charming."

"An absolute delight."

"I didn't understand why he did that. Ask for a solicitor, I mean."

"Control. It's all about control with Olivier. The way he taunted you. He wants to control the narrative. Even his denial is all about control and he hates that Pellacia took that control away from him."

"But you were the one who apprehended him before he..." Ramouter stopped. "I'm sorry."

Henley felt her stomach muscles contract. Her mind flashed back to that moment when she had first tried to place her handcuffs around Olivier's wrists. She had pushed his face into the mud of the heath and he had kicked out, breaking two of her ribs. She didn't see the knife in his hand until Olivier had pulled it out and raised his hand. Her own blood had dripped from the tip of the knife and onto her face. She'd screamed out for Pellacia when Olivier had stabbed her again. She'd wanted to fight back but Olivier had pinned her to the ground, whispering into her ear that he wanted her to feel every single part of him and that there was nowhere for her to go. Time slowed down. She thought that Pellacia had abandoned her and left her to die on the heath. She could remember the sharp stabbing pain in her chest every time she tried to breathe, holding a hand to her stomach. Trying to stop the flow of blood. She remembered the flashing blue lights illuminating Olivier's face when he pressed the knife to her neck. Henley had closed her eyes shut. She didn't want Olivier to be the last face that she saw when she died. Pellacia shouted out her name and she felt the pressure release from her chest as Pellacia propelled himself at Olivier. Henley had opened her eyes, rolled over to her side and saw Olivier on his back as Pellacia approached him. She had looked into Olivier's face. His bloodied mouth and broken front tooth. She'd screamed for help as Olivier scrambled up and punched Pellacia, twice, in his face. Olivier had then walked over to Henley, spat in her face and smiled. The last thing that Henley remembered was Olivier screaming out as the two electrified darts from Pellacia's Taser hit his chest.

"Olivier hates me too," she said.

"Why? After what he did to you."

Henley squeezed her eyes shut as the first signs of a migraine surfaced. "I made a promise at the TV conference to catch the monster responsible," she said. "I called him a pathetic monster and I promised to catch him. He didn't like the fact that I kept my word."

30

"You're back," said Pellacia as Henley entered his office. "How did it go with Chance Blaine?"

"He's smug, nervous and hiding something," answered Henley.

"And Olivier?"

"How do you think it went? He was as much use as a chocolate teapot. Too busy playing his stupid games. Today's gem was that it's a miscarriage of justice that he's sitting in Belmarsh doing life."

"That old chestnut."

"He took it out on Ramouter. He handled it…well enough." She felt the need to protect Ramouter.

"So, we're back to square one. Where's Ramouter now?"

"At his desk. Working."

"And what about you?"

"What about me?"

"You haven't seen Olivier for years and now you've seen him twice in a couple of days."

Henley's tremors had subsided, but her headache was still there, silently throbbing.

"I'm not going to lie and say that it was fun and games sitting with him," said Henley.

"That doesn't answer my question. How are you?"

"I'm not about to break down in the corner, if that's what you're asking."

"You're something else, you really are. Did he give you anything that could help?"

"Nope. Denied that he had spoken to anyone. Denied that he had killed anyone, but he did ask Ramouter if someone had cut his tongue out."

"His tongue? Do you think that—"

Henley shook her head. "He wouldn't have mentioned it if he knew about the tongue, eyes and ears being taken. Olivier is too smart to give us any reason to suspect his involvement."

The report from Sentinel, the company who provided the electronic tagging system and prison officers, pretty much confirmed what Ezra had said. Kennedy had kept to his curfew until September 6 at 11:47 p.m. when the signal had gone dead in Ladywell Fields.

On the whiteboard were photographs of Daniel Kennedy and Zoe Darego.

"They're not a bad-looking couple, really," said Ramouter as he sat down.

"Are those the itemized bills for both of Kennedy's phones?" asked Henley. She pushed the reports to the side and opened up a brown envelope. She pulled out three DVDs. They all contained CCTV footage. One from the bail hostel and the remaining two courtesy of Lewisham Council. She put the DVD from the bail hostel into the disk drive first.

"Yeah, they are. The mobile provider confirmed that Zoe's phone is a contract. They promised to get her records to me by the end of the day and, before you ask, I spoke to Ezra. He's a bit limited with what he can do until he gets her phone, but he might have better luck with her laptop."

The laptop had been found in Zoe's bedroom by her grandmother. It had a password, but that was child's play for Ezra.

"What was her number again?" Ramouter asked, reaching for a yellow highlighter.

"The last four digits are 7432." Henley pressed play. "Start from the last entry and work backward."

Henley enlarged the video so that it filled the screen. The cameras outside the hostel hadn't been working for six months so the only footage they had was taken from the hostel's reception area. Henley fast-forwarded to the morning that Kennedy broke his curfew.

"Her number doesn't appear on his pay-as-you-go phone," Ramouter mumbled as he reviewed the call records.

"There he is," Henley said. She paused the footage and scribbled down the time on her notepad. Kennedy came into view at 11:43 a.m. He stopped in the hallway and spent two minutes and eighteen seconds talking to another man. He was wearing a Superdry T-shirt and jeans. At 11:46 a.m., he pulled out his phone from his back pocket and looked at the screen. Henley zoomed in. It wasn't the silver iPhone that Henley had found under his bed.

"Aye. I've found her," Ramouter said. He was highlighting the pages vigorously. "It's his second phone number." There was no mistaking the excitement on his face. "Kennedy's body was found on Monday morning, right?"

Henley hit pause on the video. "Linh says that he'd probably been dead for about forty-eight hours before he was found. So, we're talking early hours of Saturday morning or late Friday night when he was killed," said Henley.

"Zoe calls his phone at 10:46 p.m. on Friday, twice. He doesn't pick up. Remember his curfew starts at 9 p.m. so he should be at the hostel. She calls a third time. At 10:47 p.m. This time he does pick up and they talk for forty-five seconds. At 10:57 p.m. she calls him again and they speak for eighteen seconds."

"Hold on," said Henley. She fast-forwarded the footage. Kennedy reentered the hostel at 8:02 p.m. "There, he's leaving." Henley paused the video at 11:02 p.m. He was wearing a bomber jacket and walked quickly out of the hostel.

"That's the last call that she makes. He doesn't call her back, but he does text her. 11:07 p.m. I'm coming. Stay where you are. I'm getting a cab. She replies back, OK. 11:19 p.m. She texts him again. How long are you going to be? He replies, About 15 mins. I'm coming, babe. He then texts her again at 11:19 p.m. Wait for me in the hospital. I'm coming. x. There are no other calls or texts from her or to her after that. Ezra's right. The phone is still active until Tuesday, but they all go to voice mail. Couple of 0345 and 0800 numbers, and 0161—that's Manchester. Could be call centers."

"Zoe calls him because she's in some kind of trouble. Something has scared her enough to make him break his bail conditions."

"But you found his tag under his bed?"

Henley speeded up the footage and waited. The clock in the corner of the screen went past midnight and then 1 a.m., 2 a.m., 3 a.m. The doors to the hostel opened again at 3:06 a.m. "That's not him," said Henley, pausing on the image of a man wearing a bomber jacket and T-shirt.

"What do you mean? It's the same clothing that he was wearing when he left."

Henley tutted and shook her head. "Do you see the green emergency sign on the wall? On the earlier footage, when we first see Kennedy, his head reaches the top of the sign. When he was last arrested the custody record stated that he was six foot three. This guy—"

"He's at least three inches shorter."

"Exactly. He keeps his head down and he's wearing a baseball cap. Kennedy wasn't wearing a hat when he left." She stood up and walked over to the window. The sky had darkened, and rain struck the dirty window. A distant rumble of thunder, the first sign that the heat wave was beginning to break.

"But why bother? Why would this person go through the hassle of putting Kennedy's tag back in his room? Why not chuck it in a bin somewhere?" asked Ramouter.

The sky flashed. Henley jumped. "I'm going down the road to see Linh. Chase up Forensics and see if we're any closer to getting Churchyard identified."

"This guy…" Ramouter tapped the screen with his pen. The image of a man wearing a baseball cap, frozen on the screen. "Do you think—"

"Go back over the CCTV. See if anything picks him up leaving the bail hostel. This could be our killer." Henley paused, looking again at the frozen image. "How tall would you say Chance Blaine is?"

"Not that much taller than me. About six feet, maybe five-eleven."

"We need to find out where Blaine was on Friday night. Has he emailed us his diary yet?"

"No, nothing yet."

"Chase him up. Tell him that he's got two options. Send us his information or we'll arrest him at his next viewing."

31

It came quickly. A wave of nausea, a pain under her right arm-
pit, then pins and needles in her hand. Henley's scalp prickled
with sweat.

Inhale for three. Exhale for three.

She tried the breathing techniques her therapist had taught
her, but her lungs were not cooperating. She hadn't anticipated
the panic would grip her like this. It had only been five days
since the first body appeared.

"Everything OK?" Linh asked. Henley didn't respond. "No.
You're not OK."

Henley took a deep breath and tried to get rid of the nausea
that was sweeping through her.

"Come on. Let's go outside."

They walked up the stairs and Linh pushed open the fire exit
door that led to what she mockingly called the roof garden. The
thunderstorm had been brief. The air was still muggy.

Linh pulled out a tissue from her pocket and wiped the seat
of one of the chairs.

"Thanks," said Henley as she sat down and opened the bottle of water.

"Feeling a bit better?" Linh pulled out a vaporizer from her other pocket. She took a deep drag and exhaled a large cloud of raspberry-flavored mist.

Henley leaned forward and put her hand under her chin. They were on the first floor, so the view was limited to the court car park next door.

"I can't believe that happened," Henley said. "It's been so long since I've had—" She stopped. She didn't want to qualify what had just happened to her in Linh's office by giving it a name. "It's fine."

"But it's not the first."

Henley didn't confirm the truth. Instead, she said, "It's fine. I'm fine. I've had a lot on and haven't been eating properly, that's all. I can't survive on cups of tea and fast food."

"Coffee and cigarettes for me. Well, it used to be. God, I miss cigarettes," Linh said. "I know that it hasn't been easy for you. You were off for so long."

"I wasn't *off*, Linh. I was still working cases. I just wasn't out here."

"Yeah, but it's a bit different working a paper case than an actual blood-and-guts case, isn't it? Anyone can—"

"What have you got for me?" Henley cut her off.

"God, you can be a moody cow sometimes." Linh took another drag of her vaporizer before opening the folder that had been balancing on her lap.

"I'm still waiting for the toxicology results for Churchyard. But the toxicology results for both Kennedy and Darego show the presence of propofol, a general anesthetic, and atracurium besilate."

"Atracu… What is that?" Henley asked. She sat up. That feeling in her chest, like a trapped bird in a cage, had subsided and the pins and needles in her right hand were now gone.

"Atracurium besilate," Linh said slowly as though she were teaching spelling to a five-year-old. Henley did not take offense. "It's a muscle relaxant that they use during surgery. It works by blocking the pathways in the central nervous system and causes paralysis. Depending on the dosage, the effects could last for a minimum of four minutes or as long as an hour. I've forwarded the autopsy report for both of them to your secured email, but the injection site was here." Linh turned her head and tapped below her left ear. "Straight in the jugular vein. From the amounts that were found in their blood, I would guess that paralysis would have lasted thirty to forty minutes."

"Would it knock them out or only cause paralysis?"

"Just paralysis. This isn't like giving someone a roofie, which is really a sedative and takes about twenty minutes to kick in. This will get to work within three to five minutes of hitting your bloodstream and once it does paralysis is induced. Blood pressure lowers and blood flow to the muscles decreases, but you're still conscious."

"Olivier didn't work like that."

"Not from what I remember. He cut their jugular and then cut them up. Your new guy appears to be injecting them with the AB *before* he cuts them up."

"What do you mean before he cuts them up? Is that how they all died?"

"With the exception of Churchyard, your victims don't have stab wounds. They either bled out once the femoral artery was cut or once they were decapitated. If you ask me, this new one is a bit of a sadist. Darego had more atracurium besilate in her system than Kennedy. I'm not telling you how to do your job, but I would say that—"

"Our killer kept Zoe alive for longer."

Henley walked over to the edge of the roof and looked down to the street. It was nearly rush hour. A police motorbike silently weaved between a queue of cars, its blue lights flashing. It suddenly dawned on her. The copycat was playing by his own rules, new rules. Not Olivier's.

"If blood flow is reduced, then they're not going to die straightaway," she said. "He wants them to see him cutting off their limbs. He wants them to watch. He wanted Zoe to suffer."

Henley picked at the prawn crackers as the credits rolled. Emma was asleep on her lap, yellow blanket clutched tightly in her small fist. She should have put Emma to bed but she needed to hold on to her, like a lifeboat.

"Bottle's empty." Rob eased himself up from the sofa. "I'll grab another."

Henley groaned as her mobile began to ring from the other side of the room. Rob handed it to her. It was Anthony.

"Anj, sorry to call you at home. But you know that I wouldn't bother you if it wasn't important."

"I know. What is it?"

Anthony sighed. He sounded tired. "We've identified Churchyard."

"You have?"

"Yeah. We had to use dental records, which is why it's taken so long."

"Who is he?"

"His name is Sean Thomas Delaney. Date of birth May 16, 1978. He was reported missing by his mum on Monday. I'll email over what we've got to you. I have to run. There's been another stabbing, down in Kennington this time. Another kid."

"How old?"

"Thirteen," Anthony said with reluctant acceptance.

Henley opened the report. There was a photo attached. She didn't notice that Rob had come back into the room.

"Who's that?" Rob asked.

"That is Sean Delaney."

"Hmm. Good-looking man." Rob refilled Henley's wineglass. "I take it that he's something to do with work."

"Yes. It's work."

"Come on. Leave it. Let me take Ems up to bed. We're supposed to be having a boring Friday night in, remember?"

"You're right." Henley put the phone down and watched Rob gently pick their daughter up. She reached for her glass of wine and tried to focus on the TV, but she couldn't follow what was happening. Something niggled away at her. The thought that Sean Delaney looked familiar. That she had met him before.

32

"You're joking, aren't you? It's Saturday."

Rob stood in the bathroom doorway as Henley knelt by the side of the bath, holding on to Emma, who was pretending to swim.

"It's only for a couple of hours," said Henley.

"You shouldn't be going in at all. We have plans."

"It's a children's party. Simon will understand."

"You're just looking for an excuse to get out of it."

"I'm not. It's my nephew's birthday. I promise that I will be back in time. I'm not going to miss it."

"That's not the point and you know it. You're letting this case take over. Exactly like the last one."

"I can't just leave my team to get on with it. I thought that you understood that."

"I do understand, but this is shit."

"Don't swear in front of Ems. Pass me her towel."

Rob moved sullenly from the doorway and handed Henley the pink towel from the rail.

"Is Stephen going to be there?"

Henley didn't answer as she lifted Emma out from the bath and wrapped the towel around her.

"Well, is he?"

"Stop trying to make this into something that it isn't," Henley replied. "Of course he's going to be there. It's work. Believe me, no one wants to be at the SCU on a Saturday."

Henley focused on drying Emma. She wasn't going to rise to it.

"Come on, baby," she said to Emma. "Let's get you dressed. Mummy has to go to work."

Rob sighed heavily as he realized that he was fighting a losing battle. "Just make sure that you're back by one," Rob said as Henley picked up Emma and walked down the hallway toward their bedroom.

"The desecration of the body is clearly overkill," said Dr. Mark Ryan.

"I thought that chopping up a body into pieces was overkill," said Stanford.

Despite the fact that no one in the SCU had been paid for overtime since April the team was all there. Mark looked directly at Stanford, who was sitting on his desk in the incident room, sharing a tube of salt-and-vinegar Pringles with Eastwood. There was no love between Mark and Stanford. Stanford was of the opinion that criminal profilers were overpaid for pointing out the obvious. Mark, who objected to the title *profiler* and maintained that he was a forensic psychologist, had made it clear that he thought Stanford was arrogant, untrustworthy and insecure.

"Stanford, behave." Henley poured a brown sugar packet into her tea and took a bite of her McDonald's hash browns. Her diet really had gone to shit.

"The dismembering of the body wasn't overkill," Mark said sternly. "This is all about cruelty. People like Olivier have suppressed their pain and rage for years. Their pain usually stems from a trauma in their past."

"But what triggered him? You don't suddenly wake up one morning feeling a bit mardy and decide to go on a killing spree, and why not stop at killing them?" asked Ramouter. He leaned forward, clearly intrigued. This was what Henley liked about Mark, what made him so good with juries when he was appearing as an expert witness.

"Because dismemberment is a release. The killing isn't enough. Olivier is a psychopath. For him, cutting up the bodies and displaying them in public was a reflection of his disrespect, grandiosity and narcissism. He took pride in his work, which is the only emotion that he would feel."

"You don't need a bloody degree to work that out," Stanford muttered under his breath.

Henley screwed up the greasy McDonald's bag and threw it at Stanford's head. "Stop," she said. Stanford mouthed, *Sorry*, and bent down to pick up the screwed-up bag.

"Our copycat, on the other hand, is different." Mark began to pace the room like a college lecturer. As much as he openly expressed his dislike for the Hollywood myth of the criminal profiler, he did enjoy the audience.

"For copycat killers, it's all about attention. This person probably has the same psychological issues as Olivier. A loner. Childhood trauma. Psychopathic traits, but the difference is that there is also an inferiority complex. Our copycat isn't interested in the cat-and-mouse game of you catching him. He wants recognition and even approval from Olivier."

Stanford snorted as Dr. Ryan stopped at his desk, looked straight at him and smirked.

"The copycat's ego will always come into play. They will try, in some small way, to make the crime their own."

"That would explain the use of the muscle relaxant and the missing parts," said Henley.

"Exactly. There are two types of serial killers. Those who are act-focused and those who are process-focused," said Dr. Ryan.

"What's the difference?" asked Henley.

"Olivier is act-focused. He kills quickly because it's all about expressing his rage, but your copycat is process-focused. Incapacitating them so that they can see their limbs being removed, watching them die and then further mutilating their bodies. He kills slowly because he gains enjoyment from the torture. Olivier's main motivation was revenge. Your copycat is killing because he likes it."

Dr. Ryan stopped walking and the room grew silent. Henley pushed aside her half-eaten bacon and Egg McMuffin. She had lost her appetite.

"I've given up Arsenal at home for this," said Stanford. "Tell us something that we don't know."

"Who should we be looking for?" Henley jumped in. "Is it just an obsessed fan or someone actually connected to Olivier?"

"If it was just an obsessed fan, I would have expected the selections of the victims to be random, but that's not the case here," said Mark. "There are four reasons why people kill. Love, lust, money or pure hate. I suspect that it's the latter for your copycat. Kennedy and Darego were in a relationship and I'd be very surprised if there wasn't some connection between them and Delaney. Your copycat hates your victims for something they did to him collectively."

"What do we know about Delaney?" asked Eastwood.

"Not much," said Ramouter. "Other than that he's forty-one years old, worked as a support worker for the Leopold Drug and Alcohol Centre in Catford. He's married to Jamie Hawkins-Delaney. I went around to see him first thing, but he was in no state to talk to me. I'm going to try again this evening."

"But our copycat knows about the symbols," said Eastwood. "I've been through the court transcripts for Olivier's trial. They confirmed that the only people present were the judge, jurors,

court clerk, usher, the prosecutor and his junior defense barrister and the two officers who sat in the dock with Olivier."

"And at no point was that information in the press?" asked
Mark.

"Never. We've spoken to the twelve jurors and they're all adamant that they didn't discuss the case with anyone."

"So, our copycat has to be someone who is connected to Olivier?" asked Henley.

"Friends. Family," suggested Ramouter.

Mark shook his head. "Olivier was a loner, but that's not to say
that people wouldn't want to be his friends. People write to prisoners all the time. He may be a psychopath but he's personable."

"It makes Blaine look like a stronger candidate," said Ramouter. "He was part of Olivier's legal team, he's still visiting
him and he has no alibi for Friday night. Even though when I
asked him he said that he was with his girlfriend."

"OK, if our copycat is connected to Olivier, why is he moving so quickly?" asked Eastwood.

It was the question that had been troubling Henley the most.

"He's killed three people in a week," Eastwood continued.
"Olivier killed seven people over eight weeks."

"I'll admit," said Mark, "it's a concern, but as I said, it's not
about you. Your copycat wants to impress. The one thing that
may work in your favor is that he's more likely to slip up. It's
probable that he's killed previously, that there were others before
Kennedy and Darego, but a lag between victims is not unusual.
I don't know if you remember the case of Futoshi Kobayashi
in Japan, about five years ago. He killed nine women in three
weeks. It's quite fascinating—"

"You *would* find it fascinating," Stanford mumbled under his
breath.

"Kobayashi," Mark continued, "preyed on suicidal women
online. Convinced them to come to his home and to take part
in a suicide pact. Obviously, that didn't happen."

"What did he do?" Ramouter asked.

"Funnily enough, he dismembered them too. He also went a little bit further than that. He completely dissected them, threw their organs and flesh into the communal rubbish bin and kept the bones in storage boxes."

Henley looked around the room. Everyone was frozen. Stanford's face was a mixture of disgust and disbelief.

"I wish I'd never asked," said Ramouter.

33

Henley had been lying in bed staring at the dead spider in the corner of the ceiling for almost an hour while the sounds of London stirred outside. The clock read 7:42 a.m. Rob's side of the bed was empty. He was pissed at her for arriving late to the party. He had gone out again, ten minutes after they'd arrived home. Henley had spent the rest of the evening with a bottle of red wine while Emma slept. Through the open window she heard a helicopter, a gate being slammed and a car engine starting. A million thoughts had been running through her head. The box of sleeping pills sat unopened on her nightstand. She hadn't seen the point of taking any once she had heard the birds singing at 4 a.m.

Henley sighed and finally got out of bed. As she checked on Emma, who was still asleep, her mind wandered to the victims' families, their grief. The only common denominator was that they had all been murdered and that their bodies had been dumped locally. Local to Henley.

She turned on the kettle and then went to the fridge. Maybe it was time that she did something nice for once. Acted more like a wife. She had tried on Friday night and she knew that she should carry on trying. She wasn't entirely convinced that making Rob a full English breakfast would put their relationship back on the road to redemption, but it was a start.

"Witnesses at the scene have said that the body found in the churchyard of St. Nicholas in Deptford had been dismembered. The identity of the man has not been disclosed but it is believed that the murder may have links to the murder of Uzomamaka Darego, a twenty-six-year-old nurse from Stratford whose body..."

"What the actual—" Henley exclaimed, turning up the volume on the radio. She listened to the newsreader, who continued to give information that hadn't been released to the press. The last time that anyone from the SCU had spoken to the press was when Pellacia released a statement confirming the identity of Daniel Kennedy.

There was a loud knock on the door and Henley jumped, spilling hot tea onto her bare legs. It was almost eight and Emma had shuffled down the stairs.

"Morning, sweetie." Henley picked up her daughter. "Ooh, you're getting heavy."

She peered through the front door's frosted-glass panel, but couldn't see anyone. She brought Emma into the front room, placed her on the sofa and turned on the television. Someone had definitely knocked. Henley went back and opened the door. No one was there, but she spotted a cardboard box on the doorstep, her name written neatly on the top in black ink. No address labels.

Henley walked up the gravel path and placed her hands on the black iron gate. No cars. No people. Not even a stray cat or a wayward squirrel.

"Luna, come here." Luna was sniffing the box and Henley dragged her back inside. She knelt down and lifted the box's flaps, pushing aside shredded newspaper.

Her body froze as her fingers became entangled in matted

hair. Her fingers were stained with blood. She raced up the stairs and grabbed her mobile phone, which was charging in the bedroom. She left two sticky red thumbprints on the screen as she called Pellacia. She rushed back down the stairs, where Emma was still watching TV, completely unaware.

"Come on. Pick up," said Henley. The phone went to voice mail. Henley pressed call for the second time, not waiting to leave a message.

She heard the screeching sound of the rusty gate being pushed open.

"Don't move," Henley shouted to Rob. His hair was damp with sweat. He had taken off his running vest and tied it around his waist.

"What?" Rob shouted as he removed his wireless headphones and placed them around his neck.

"Don't move. Just stay there."

"What do you mean, don't move?" Rob began to walk up the gravel path. "What's going on with you?"

"For fuck's sake," Henley said as her phone began to vibrate. She pressed accept, smearing blood across the screen. She didn't take her eyes off Rob.

"What's this?" Rob said. He stopped at the box and bent down.

"Don't touch it!" Henley shouted, taking an urgent step toward him.

"Anj," said Pellacia on the other end of the phone. "What's wrong?"

"Stephen, I need you to—" The sound of Emma shouting for her mummy distracted Henley and she turned her back for just a second, but it was enough time for Rob to pick up the box. There was a loud scream and a heavy thud. Gravel scattered across the drive as he staggered back, tripped and fell.

"Anjelica," Pellacia said.

"I need you to dispatch a unit and Forensics to my house."

"What the hell for?"

Henley instinctively reached out her hand to grab Emma, who had appeared at her feet. Emma took a step toward her, stopped and began to cry. Henley looked down and saw her bloodstained hand. "It's OK, baby. Mummy's OK," said Henley. She kneeled and carefully put her arm around Emma, making sure that she didn't stain her daughter.

"Are you still there?" said Pellacia.

"*Now*, Stephen. Send a unit *now*."

34

Anthony, who had driven at speed from Shepherd's Bush, crouched inside the small forensics tent pitched on Henley's lawn. From a distance, it looked like a gazebo for a garden party. Stanford had also arrived and Linh was on her way.

Stanford had taken charge of Emma and was currently sitting in the back garden trying to distract her and Luna from the onlookers by the gate.

"Tell me again what happened," said Pellacia. He was sitting on a chair opposite Henley while Rob stood by the kitchen sink, his arms folded across his chest, not moving. Just watching.

Henley shifted her chair back, away from Pellacia, closer to her husband.

"I was in here," she said. "Listening to the radio. Drinking my tea. I was about to make breakfast as I knew that Rob would be back from his run." She looked across to him. His face hadn't changed, no acknowledgment that she had been thinking about him. "The news came on, so it must have been coming up to eight. Then someone knocked. It was loud enough to make me jump. I got up and met Emma at the bottom of the stairs. I looked through the window, but I couldn't see anybody. I put

Emma in the living room, turned on the TV and then opened the door."

Henley felt flushed. She pulled off the headscarf that was still wrapped around her head.

"I shouldn't have opened it. I knew that something wasn't right. There was no address. Just my name. It didn't feel right."

"And you didn't see anyone?"

"She's told you twice that she didn't see anyone," said Rob from his position by the sink.

"What about you?" Pellacia challenged. "You were the first one out of the house this morning. Did you notice anything suspicious?"

"Are you saying that this is my fault?" Rob said aggressively.

"That's not what I'm saying," Pellacia replied through gritted teeth.

"I left at half seven. I would have noticed if someone was hovering outside my house."

"What about cars, mopeds?"

"Flying saucers?"

"Rob, stop it," said Henley. She went to him. "Stop being a dick," she whispered as she reached behind him, picked up a glass from the draining board and turned on the tap.

"There was nothing unusual," Rob huffed. "I saw Mr. Flores from number 8 walking his dog when I left."

Pellacia scribbled the information in his notebook.

"And number 5's son."

"Liam?" asked Henley, sitting back down.

"No, the younger one. Terrell. That's it. He was leaving to go to football. I ran past him as he came out of his house, but that was on my way back."

Pellacia nodded. Henley noticed that he didn't thank him.

"We're going to have to take your prints," Pellacia said.

"What the hell for?" Rob stepped toward Pellacia, who stood up. There wasn't enough time for Henley to act as a physical buffer between them. Rob was taller and broader than Pellacia, but he didn't tower over him.

"You handled evidence," said Pellacia with a barely susceptible smirk. "We need your prints in order to eliminate them from our inquiries."

"That's fine. I'll ask Anthony to do it." Henley placed a hand on Rob's arm.

Rob angrily pushed Henley's hand away. "Is there anything else?" But he didn't wait for an answer, brushing past Pellacia and stalking out of the kitchen.

"You didn't have to do that," said Henley as Rob turned the corner and disappeared up the stairs. "You're both as bad as each other."

"Your husband's an idiot," Pellacia replied. "You told him not to touch it and what does he go and do?"

"That's not the point. If that was any other witness you wouldn't have spoken to them like that," said Henley.

"Well, he's not just any witness. He's… Sorry, I'm sorry." Pellacia pulled Henley toward him. She breathed him in, feeling safe for a moment.

Someone coughed loudly. Twice. They both pulled away as Stanford appeared at the doorway, carrying Emma.

"Madam here has just pointed out that she hasn't had breakfast," said Stanford, giving Pellacia a look of warning. At this moment, the rules of seniority didn't apply.

"Oh my God," said Henley. The eggs, sausages and bacon still sat where she'd left them on the worktop.

"Don't worry about it," said Stanford. "I'll get her dressed and take her to McDonald's. She can have some pancakes with her uncle Paul. Would you like that, princess?"

"Yes," Emma said. Henley felt a tugging at her heart as Paul blew a raspberry at Emma and she began to laugh.

"Thank you," Henley said softly.

"She's grown a lot," Pellacia said, watching Stanford walk away with Emma.

"Don't," Henley said. She picked up the food from the counter and went to the fridge. "Don't talk about her."

The muscle in his jaw tensed again. "Did you recognize who it was?" asked Pellacia.

"Who?"

"The head in the box?"

"No, no. I didn't even look. I just felt the… No, I didn't look. I don't have a clue who it is, or why it's on my doorstep, and before you ask, I'm not going out there to take a fucking look!"

Pellacia put his hands on his hips and sighed heavily as Henley stood at the doorway.

"I'm going to arrange for a couple of the officers outside to start making door-to-door inquiries. Talk to that Mr. Flores and what was his name? Terry?"

"Terrell. He's a good kid and he's only twelve, so don't frighten him. And forget about CCTV. There's nothing on this road."

"That box was hand-delivered. Someone must have seen something."

"Hmm," was all Henley said.

"Are you OK?"

"Of course I'm not OK. The sooner these lot are done—"

"Thanks very much," said Anthony as he walked into the kitchen.

"I'm sorry. *Are* you nearly done?" asked Henley.

"Yeah. Should be another half hour or so, then we'll be out of your hair." Anthony peeled off his purple latex gloves. "Shit, wrong choice of words."

"Can you tell us anything about it?"

"Definitely human. Definitely male. Definitely dead."

"Anthony!"

"Sorry. I don't know what else to tell you. We've recovered prints from the box and the tape. Cross fingers, those prints don't just belong to you and Rob. The most interesting thing about the head is…" Anthony paused, as though he couldn't quite believe what he was going to say next. "It's defrosting."

"What?"

"Linh can't guess how long he's been dead for because someone's been keeping his head in the freezer."

35

Henley couldn't stop the shaking. She stood at the sink, splashed her face with cold water and brushed her teeth. The house felt different; it felt cursed. She had to sit down and make a plan, but she wasn't sure where to start or what she was planning for.

"Where's Emma's toy zebra?" Rob asked.

"It should be on her bed. Why?"

"I'm packing our stuff." He flung open the wardrobe and started pulling clothes off the hangers.

"Hold on. You're just going to leave without talking to me first?"

"Have you finally lost it, Anj?" Rob shouted.

"Lower your voice. You're going to wake Emma up."

"Right now, I don't give a shit. Some lunatic dumped a head at our front door. A head, Anjelica. I asked you to give up this crazy job—"

"You haven't asked. You've demanded."

"With good bloody reason. I'm not staying, and our daughter isn't staying here either. It's up to you if you want to come or not."

"Not like this. Not without discussing it first."

"You didn't discuss it with me when you went back to him."

"I went back to the job, not to a fucking *man*," Henley shouted back with fury, forgetting her own warning about waking up Emma. She sat on the bed, overcome by a throbbing pain in her temple.

"Where are you going?" she finally asked.

"I haven't decided yet. Maybe to my brother's or my parents', but this is the last straw, Anjelica. I tried. I really did try to see this from your point of view, but it's gone too far now. You need to make your mind up."

"You're giving me an ultimatum?"

"Call it what you like, but you need to decide what's more important—your career or your family."

"I married a Neanderthal. You knew what you were signing up for when you married me."

"You've got a week."

"How gracious of you."

"You're lucky that I'm giving you that. Be clear about one thing. Emma and I are not staying here tonight. Who knows what will turn up on the doorstep tomorrow morning?"

36

"Are you ready for this, Henley?"

"Stop acting as though you're announcing the finalists for *The Voice*," she replied. Henley was standing by Anthony's desk at Southwark police station, flanked by Ramouter. The building hummed with activity. She was tired and hungover, and she felt guilty for not going with Rob and Emma—as a family.

"So, as we know, your guy's head has been stuck in a deep freeze somewhere, but by the time it was delivered to you it had obviously been out defrosting somewhere, which accounts for the blood. It wasn't easy, but we managed to prize the jaw open in order to take a dental impression. So, we've got blood and hair samples. I wasn't holding out much hope, but we got a match on Mr. Iceland."

"Who is he, Anthony?" asked Henley.

"I don't know exactly but that isn't the most interesting part in this puzzle. Cast your mind back, Henley, to just over two and a half years ago."

Henley rolled her eyes while Ramouter shuffled uncomfortably next to her.

"We were never able to identify Olivier's last victim," continued Anthony. "No DNA, no prints, no head—"

"Tell me you're joking." Henley was astounded.

"No joke. Olivier's last victim was an Asian male, twenty to thirty-five years of age, but his head was never found—until now."

"Once he realized that we were on to him, he started playing games," Henley explained to Ramouter. "He refused to give us any information about the seventh victim. We didn't know if victim seven was in the army with Olivier or if it was just an unlucky stranger. The only reason we were able to charge Olivier with his murder was because he got sloppy. His hair and carpet fibers from his flat were found on the body. In addition to the symbols that were carved into his back."

"And that's his head?" Ramouter asked. Over the past few days he'd familiarized himself with the old case files. "Victim number seven?"

"Ninety-nine percent sure," said Anthony. "Granted, all I've got is a DNA match on the database, but unless some idiot labeled the exhibits wrong it's pretty much conclusive. If you want to be a hundred percent sure, the samples will have to be extracted from the body."

"That's if they even buried the body," said Henley. "It could have been cremated, for all we know. They're not going to keep a body in the freezer in case it happens to get identified one day."

"Actually, they did," said Anthony. "The body is at Finchley mortuary. You got lucky. This one managed to escape the NCA's push to cremate unidentified bodies in mortuaries across the country. I've called in a favor and I've got a colleague taking samples as we speak. As soon as we get authority, everything is going to Linh."

"You're a star, do you know that?" Henley said.

"You tease," Anthony said with a grin. Then his expression grew serious. "But you know what, in twenty-five years of doing this job, I've never seen anything like this. You've got to admit, Henley, I'm not one for bad language, but this is pretty fucked up."

"Someone has been keeping this man's head in a freezer?" Pellacia chuckled.

"This isn't funny," said Henley.

"It's not… It's just. It's… Shit, I don't know." Pellacia straightened himself. "Sorry. I'm sorry. Do we have any idea who it is and why his head was dumped on your doorstep?"

"We're running his description through Missing Persons right now and an e-fit will go out this afternoon," said Henley. "Why was he dumped on my doorstep? It has to be Olivier's way of showing he's still in control. Wanting to screw with our investigation. Our copycat has to be working with him."

"But there was never any evidence that Olivier worked with anyone. Ryan said he was a loner, and Olivier practically admitted it himself when we saw him," said Ramouter. "It's not as if Olivier had any friends or family to speak of. I read the statements of the officers who searched his flat and the forensics reports. There's no way that anyone would have missed a human head next to a bag of sausages."

Henley gave Pellacia a sharp look, warning him not to start laughing again. Instead, he said, "The trainee has a point."

"Ramouter's right," said Henley. "Then the question is, where has that head been all this time?"

"Speaking of which, Uniform finally spoke to your neighbor Mr. Flores this morning. Turns out that he saw a motorcycle courier on your road when he left his house. He even remembered the company. Velocity Couriers. Stanford's trial is over now, so I've sent him and Eastwood to check it out."

"OK. Well. We may actually start to get somewhere. But I'm going to have to see Olivier again."

Ramouter actually put his hand to the side of his head and started massaging his temples.

"I know that Olivier is working with someone. The symbols cut into the bodies. The head of Olivier's last victim being delivered on my doorstep. You would have to be an idiot to suggest that all of that was just a coincidence."

"But he's in the High Security Unit. His post is monitored. He has no access to a computer or anything like that," said Ramouter.

"Please, you really think that everyone in Belmarsh is sitting there quietly playing Connect 4?"

"So, what's your next step?" asked Pellacia.

"We're going to go back to Belmarsh," said Henley.

Ramouter groaned and put his head in his hands. "Do we have to?"

"Yes, we do. Let's go and pay Olivier another visit."

37

"Back so soon?" Olivier was leaning back in a chair that was not bolted firmly to the floor. "I knew you missed me," he said with a ghost of a smile.

Henley hoped that Olivier couldn't tell that she and Ramouter were reluctant to be there. She had given Ramouter a pep talk as they walked through the prison. They had been escorted through the prison wings and underneath the suicide nets, and had to listen as prisoners called Ramouter a pig and shouted out the things they would like to do to Henley.

"So, what is this, then?" asked Olivier. "Information seeking, a voluntary interview?"

"We want to talk to you about your last victim," said Henley.

Olivier sighed dramatically. "We've already been through this, Inspector. I had no victims."

"His head was delivered to my front door on Sunday morning."

"A head?" Olivier cocked his own head to the side. "A whole head?"

"In a box. Addressed to me."

Olivier laughed, a short bark. "Must have been rather unpleasant. Did you think your husband was getting you flowers? Or was it Pellacia, showing you how much he cares. What do you think, trainee? Your partner caught between two men. It must be so…romantic."

Ramouter didn't answer.

"I don't think the trainee is talking to me today." The smile left his face as quickly as it had appeared. "A head in a box." His voice was hard.

"Your last victim," said Henley. "He's the reason that you're in here. You got sloppy. You didn't take as much care as you did with the others. Someone saw you dumping him outside a community center, you left behind your DNA and you kept his head. I didn't think necrophilia was your thing."

Olivier's right cheek puckered as though he was biting the flesh inside his mouth.

"Ted Bundy decapitated some of his victims, had sex with them and kept their heads," Henley continued. "Is that what you did with victim seven? Did you keep his head in a freezer because you planned to get back to him? Did you have something romantic planned?"

Henley steadied herself and kept eye contact with Olivier. She mentally rode the rhythm of her breath. She wouldn't let Olivier intimidate her.

"Who is it?" she asked. "Who's the person that you've got dropping severed heads at my front door? Doing your dirty work."

Olivier leaned toward her. She could smell his foul breath. "In case you haven't noticed, I've been stuck in here. I can hardly organize a delivery of seafood curry, let alone arrange for someone to find a head and send it to a mid-terraced house in Brockley."

Henley flinched. He knew where she lived. What else did he know about her personal life?

"It would be a very nice house with a blue front door. No, no, blue isn't your color. You have more depth than that. You would like a color to show how resilient you are. Not black. That would be too obvious. Maybe a deep purple."

Henley felt exposed. She mentally counted to ten, trying to regain her composure.

"Your copycat."

"He's. Not. My. Copycat," Olivier replied with crystal-clear irritation.

"It must be hard for you, having no control over him. He's working fast. Far more efficiently than you."

"Three victims and it's only Monday," Ramouter said confidently.

"Maybe you didn't want your copycat to dump the head at my house. Maybe you had other plans, but your copycat is doing things his own way," said Henley.

Olivier's chest rose and fell. He was growing visibly angry.

"What are you afraid of? That your copycat may surpass you?"

The plastic chair that Olivier was sitting in strained and painfully creaked as he leaned back.

"Maybe these new murders are part of his plan and not yours. I know that Detective Ramouter and I are sitting here talking to you, but it's your copycat who's getting all the attention. Are you slowly realizing that it's not all about you?"

"It's always about me," Olivier sneered.

"We have three victims," Henley said, willing her voice to remain steady. "Sean Delaney, Uzomamaka 'Zoe' Darego and Daniel Kennedy."

Henley saw it in his eyes. The names had triggered something. Henley repeated them slowly. There it was again. The flash of recognition in Olivier's eyes.

"How old was she? The girl?" he asked.

"You know how old she was. It's been all over the news."

"Eight, three and four," Olivier said.

"What the hell does that mean?" Henley snapped.

"Not telling," Olivier said in a singsong voice.

"She was twenty-six years old. A nurse," answered Ramouter. "Had her whole life ahead of her until someone cut her up and carved a crescent and a double cross into her skin."

"I always find it odd when people say that of the dead. *They had their whole life ahead of them.* Clearly, they didn't because they're dead. We may not like the method of disposal but when it's your time to go, then it's your time to go." He paused. "Eight, three and four."

Henley got up and walked toward the door. "Come on, Ramouter," she said. "We're wasting time."

"What about your last victim?" asked Ramouter.

Olivier shook his head. "I told you. I didn't kill him, but it's nice that someone is going to put him back together again." He laughed. A deep, crackling laugh that bounced off the walls. "Humpty Dumpty. Except they couldn't put Humpty Dumpty back together again."

38

Eight, three and four. Olivier repeated the numbers in his head like a mantra as the prison officer placed the handcuffs on his wrists. Maximum security. High risk. A danger to everyone, including himself. That was the part that had made Olivier laugh. *A danger to himself?* The possibility that he would ever think to take himself out permanently was ridiculous. Eight. Three. Four. Three murders. Three bodies desecrated and scattered across south London in some pitiful homage to him. He didn't want to be idolized; he wanted to be feared.

Olivier looked down at the officer's neck as the cold metal caught the thin pale skin on his wrist and gathered up the flesh into reddening pleats.

"What exactly do you think you're doing?" Olivier said coldly. The officer flinched as Olivier took a step toward him. There was barely an inch of space between them. The officer's breathing grew rapid as Olivier raised his wrists in front of the officer's face.

"I'm sorry," the officer stuttered. "I'm sorry, they just—"

"Loosen them."

"Of course."

Olivier yawned impatiently as the officer unlocked the handcuffs. He looked down to see the skin on the officer's neck straining as it whitened. This was the best time to attack, when the victim was unaware and distracted by the mundane. It had been easier than he'd imagined it to be—taking off someone's head. Twenty bones in the human head. Only seven bones in the neck. Less muscle to cut through, not as much flesh, but there were still sinew, ligaments and tendons. Sergeant Flynn had been overweight. Fat intertwined between withered muscle and clogged heart valves. Olivier had spat in his face and pissed on his naked body before placing the saw just below his Adam's apple and pressing the blue button. The motor echoed as the metal teeth became coated in blood and flesh, the saw catching and halting at the C3 vertebrae. Olivier laughed as he remembered how quickly the jigsaw blade had dulled. He waited for the officer to ask him what was funny as the handcuffs loosened around his wrists and they made their way back to the secured wing, but he never did.

He moved the image of Flynn's decapitated head from his mind and switched to her. Three. Uzomamaka Darego. Large brown, curious eyes that nervously looked at him directly. He had watched her. Tried to draw her in. He had wanted to see the nerves settle in and for her to break, but she never did. She didn't break for him but someone else broke her.

Olivier picked up a newspaper from the pile that had been left for him on his bed. The article about the body parts in the park had been marked with a green Post-it Note. There was no mention of the symbols being left on the body and there was no mention of the other two victims. Eight, three and four.

"Who the hell *are* you?" Olivier said as he picked up a pen and drew the symbols along the white space on the edge of the newspaper. *His* brand. The paper ripped as he pressed the pen hard against the page. His symbol, which wasn't a double cross. They had been mistaken. It was a double dagger and it belonged to him.

Is there someone trying to get your attention? That was the question that Henley had asked him in her first visit. He had enjoyed the look in her eyes. The urgency, the disgust at being forced to ask him for help. He had seen that struggle between remaining in control and being overwhelmed with hate and anger as Henley had waited for him to answer her question. Henley didn't have a clue. She had wanted his help.

The red-hot anger was churning inside of him, crawling at his skin. He knew that his copycat was not finished and it irritated him.

"You're not up to it, Inspector," Olivier said out loud as he began to pace around his small cell. There wasn't enough space. He needed room to think. He heard a hum outside his cell door as the other eight inmates were let out of their cells for their five hours of association. Olivier walked out of his cell and onto the landing. The High Security Unit was a prison within a prison. *Eight. Three. Four.* He needed to find this fucking imposter for himself. He needed to get out.

39

"I'm not his girlfriend. In fact, I was never his girlfriend and he definitely wasn't with me last Friday night."

Lorelei Fosse picked up her gym bag, threw it into the trunk and slammed it shut. She pulled her designer sunglasses over her eyes and leaned against her car. Ramouter squinted at her in the sunlight. They stood in the car park of a high-priced gym in East Dulwich. Chance Blaine was seriously punching above his weight. Everything about Lorelei screamed potential reality TV star.

"You say that he wasn't your boyfriend?" he asked.

"Never. I didn't even change my relationship status on Facebook. I met him about a month ago in a pub in Borough Market. We saw each for a few weeks and then he blocked me."

"He blocked you?"

"Yep. Can you believe it? I caught him with another woman and *he's* the one who blocks *me*."

"When was this?"

"God, about three weeks ago. I was randomly driving along Lewisham High Street. I was going to see my nan and I stopped at the traffic lights opposite the hospital and there he was with some girl. He was talking to her and then he went down the side road with her. Arm in arm they were."

"Can you describe her? This woman."

Lorelei played with her ponytail as she thought back. "Black. In her twenties, maybe. I didn't see her face clearly. She had long braids."

Ramouter pulled out his phone and brought up a newspaper article. He enlarged the photograph of Zoe Darego. "Was this the woman you saw with Chance Blaine?"

Lorelei took the phone and inspected the photograph for a few seconds, then handed it back. "Sorry. It could be, but to be honest, I didn't really get a close look at her."

"That's fine. Thanks for your help."

"You're welcome. Why are you asking about her anyway?"

"She was murdered."

The color drained from Lorelei's face as she put her hands to her throat. "Did he do it? I wouldn't be surprised. He was into all kinds of kinky shit."

40

Henley was walking back to the SCU from the deli across the road, lunch in hand. She took a sip of green juice, knowing full well that she was making a poor effort to counteract the vodka and fried chicken from her Sunday-night binge.

Ramouter was standing to the side with the phone to his ear. "I've got Stanford on the phone. He wants to talk to you."

Henley and Ramouter did a swap with the bag and phone as they walked back to the SCU.

"Right, good news," said Stanford. "It wasn't a wild-goose chase. The package had been dispatched by Velocity Couriers on Rotherhithe New Road. The booking was made online in the early hours of Sunday morning."

"Where did they pick up the package?" asked Henley.

"Manor Park. Franklin-Jones Cold Storage Facility. Does exactly what it says on the tin. Majority of their customers are businesses, restaurants and medical practices, but they also rent to individuals. Customers are provided with the security code to the front gate and a separate code and key for their rental space. Once you've got your codes, you can access the building whenever you like."

"What about staff?"

"No more than four members of staff, which includes the manager. They work from 8 a.m. to 8 p.m. The place is covered with CCTV and there's security staff at night but that's it."

"What does our courier say about the pickup?"

"Our courier, Vincent Tiegan, says that there was nothing unusual about it. He didn't actually go into the building. The woman—"

"A woman?"

"Yes, he says that the customer was a woman. White. Mid-thirties. Brown or dark blond hair, he wasn't too sure. He says that he wasn't really paying attention. She signed for the collection at the storage place and that was it. He says that was at about 6:30 a.m."

"Why didn't the courier wait and make me sign for the package if this was all legit?"

"Says that he was running late. I've got a copy of the contact sheet. I'm going to email it over."

Henley sat at her desk picking out the onions from her sandwich, while Ramouter read through the contact sheet.

"The rental agreement is in the name of Isaac Felton. He signed it two days after Olivier's last victim was found. He gave an address, phone number and a copy of a phone bill," said Ramouter.

"Have you run a check on the name?" Henley asked.

"Yeah, I did. The only Isaac Felton that I could find died when he was six years old in 1984 and the address is fake. Doesn't exist."

"Great," said Henley. "This storage place is some Mickey Mouse outfit. So, we're back to square one."

"Two and a half years is a long time. You don't keep something like that just in case you may need it someday."

"Olivier clearly had something in mind before we interrupted his plans by arresting him."

"But why now? How is he able to control things to the extent that people are leaving body parts at your front door?"

"I don't know, but he killed seven people. So far our copycat has killed three."

"I may be wrong," said Ramouter, "but I don't think that Olivier has got anything to do with these new murders. Look at how he responded when you said to him 'your copycat.' He seemed irritated by it."

"He wasn't just irritated. He was angry, but the names meant something to him," Henley replied. "He had that look as though he was trying to place them. Especially when he asked about Zoe, but there's nothing in her background or Kennedy's to suggest any links to Olivier. Though she may have a possible link to Blaine."

"Zoe told her friend that she was harassed by a man on her way to work and Lorelei saw Chance near the hospital. I've asked the council for footage from that day."

"We'll bring Blaine in as soon as we've viewed that footage. Until then..." Henley thought back to the description of the woman. The one who had arranged the collection of the head in a box. "We need to find this woman."

41

Jamie Hawkins-Delaney pulled back the chain on the front door and stepped back to let Henley and Ramouter in. He wasn't what Henley had imagined when she had spoken to him on the phone. He had sounded strong, confident, matter-of-fact, but the man in front of her was broken. Not ready to take on the role of a widower. He sniffed and rubbed at his eyes, which were already red-raw. The blinds were not open and the flat had the unmistakable smell of someone who had closed himself off to the world and hadn't left for several days.

"I'm sorry about the mess." Jamie picked up the empty beer cans that were on the floor next to the leather sofa.

"It's fine. Don't worry about it," said Henley. "But perhaps it might be a good idea to open the windows. Let a bit of light and air in."

Jamie busied himself with the task before crumbling.

"I can't believe that he's gone." He put his hands to his face and collapsed on the sofa, among the magazines and crisp packets.

Henley picked up a carrier bag and discarded shirt from an armchair and sat down.

"I am sorry about Sean." Henley reached for the packet of tissues inside her jacket pocket. Jamie took the tissue from Henley's hand, gratefully. "How long had you and Sean been married?"

"Only two years but we met about twenty-five years ago at university and were just friends at first. I always knew that I was gay, but Sean was in denial. Slept with half of the female students, a couple of the lecturers and had two children before he finally came out."

Henley looked at the collection of black-and-white photographs of a young boy and a girl hanging on the wall. Next to them was a wedding photo of Sean and Jamie.

"They're twins," said Jamie. "They live with their mum in Rotterdam. We were going out there to visit them for half term… I spoke to Marie, that's their mum, but she still hasn't told them… I can't even get my head around what's happened."

"I know this is hard. I promise that Detective Ramouter and I won't take long."

"OK, OK." Jamie reached for the bottle of whiskey and poured himself a glass. "I don't usually drink during the day but—"

"It's fine. Was Sean having any problems at work?"

"He was a drug and alcohol worker. He worked in a rehab clinic down in Catford. He's been working there for about eight years. He always wanted to help people. Always thought that people deserved a second chance."

"When was the last time that you saw Sean?"

"I was flying out to Morocco for an assignment. I'm a photographer. I flew out last Thursday. It was a night flight, so Sean dropped me off at the airport. I remember that I texted him to say that I'd arrived. I FaceTimed him on Saturday, as that was his mum's birthday. That was the last time that I saw him. I became worried when I didn't hear from him. His mum hadn't heard from him either and she checked with all of the hospitals.

By the time I got home on Monday afternoon, she had already reported him missing."

"Sean's body was found in Deptford. Can you think of any reason why he would have been in that area? Could he have gone there for work? A client, perhaps?"

Jamie shrugged his shoulders. "Maybe a client, but we didn't have any friends down there. I mean, we've been to the market and we went to a show at the Albany Theatre once, but that was years ago."

"Was there anything that Sean was concerned about?"

"No, honestly there was nothing. Sean loved his job. We used to argue about it because he would always work late. He would even give patients his mobile number." There was an edge to Jamie's tone. Bitterness and resentment taking over the grief. "That was fun. Being woken up at two in the morning by some smackhead desperate for his next hit."

"Is there anything else that you can think of that may have seemed odd, out of place?"

"They wouldn't let me see his body," Jamie said as he stared at the floor. Henley gave Ramouter a look. Jamie was drifting away from them the more he became lost in his grief.

"I'm going to make you a cup of tea. How many sugars, Jamie?" Ramouter asked.

"Oh." Jamie looked at Ramouter as if he'd suddenly remembered that he was in the room. "None. Thank you."

Ramouter returned with the tea a few minutes later and handed it to Jamie. "She couldn't even show me a photograph of his face, just showed me his wedding ring. The policewoman who was here before you said that Sean had been... That his body had been—"

"That's right," Henley said.

"Fucking ironic, isn't it?"

"What is?"

"He did jury service once—"

Henley felt the hairs on the back of her neck prickle. "How long ago was this?"

"About two years ago. He's the only person I've known to get excited about jury service."

"Why was it ironic?"

"Just… The way that Sean was… Died. His case… The trial was similar."

"Did he tell you anything else about the trial?"

"There wasn't much to tell. It ended after a week or so. I'm not sure what happened. It was so long ago."

Henley left her seat and sat down next to Jamie. She put a hand on his shoulder and turned him gently toward her. "Jamie, I know that this is hard, and you've probably got a hundred other things on your mind right now, but did he mention anyone else? Anyone who was on the trial with him? Do the names Zoe Darego and Daniel Kennedy mean anything to you?"

Jamie sat up a little bit straighter and took a deep breath. "No," he finally said. "They don't ring a bell. Who are they? Jamie's clients?"

"No. They're not. I know that I've already asked you and I know that this is a horrible time for you—"

"It's OK. I mean, if it can help you catch whoever did this to my Sean. I just remember him being so pissed off when the judge said that they couldn't continue—" Jamie stopped talking as Ramouter's phone began to ring. Henley shot him a look.

"Sorry," Ramouter said. "I'll take it outside."

"It was that Jigsaw Man," Jamie said suddenly. There was a slight glint of determination in his eyes.

"Excuse me?" asked Henley.

"The trial that Sean was on. He couldn't believe it. It was that Jigsaw Man."

"The trial of Peter Olivier? Sean was on the jury that convicted the Jigsaw Killer?"

"That was it. Sean was so annoyed when the judge ended the trial early..."

Henley had stopped listening. Sean Delaney had been a juror on Olivier's trial. A trial that couldn't continue. Olivier had flinched at Zoe's full name. They were looking for a link between Kennedy, Delaney and Zoe. They had just found it.

"There were two trials," said Henley as they stepped out into the communal area. "The first trial collapsed after a couple of weeks. Olivier flinched when I mentioned Zoe's full name."

"Are you sure?" Ramouter pushed the green exit button.

"Positive. I asked him twice and there was something that triggered him."

"OK. Let's assume that Zoe was on that first trial. How would he even know her name?"

"Have you ever sat in on a Crown Court trial?" Henley asked, pulling out her car keys and opening the door.

"Never," Ramouter replied, getting in from the passenger side. "I've only ever given evidence in a magistrates' court trial."

"The defendant is sitting in the dock when the jury is selected. The defendant will hear their names being called at least twice. Once when they're actually called to sit on the panel and again when they take the jury oath."

"But we checked the jury list to see who was in court when the evidence about the symbols was heard and none of our vics are on there."

"We only checked the list for the trial where Olivier was convicted. We didn't check the list for the trial that collapsed. We need that list and we need to speak to Chance Blaine again. He was convicted of perverting the course of justice. His actions led to the collapse of that trial and he may have been seen with Zoe."

"Why waste time? Why don't we just arrest him now?"

Henley tapped the steering wheel as she thought about it. "Nope. He's smug. Clever, a trained lawyer and a conniving little shit. I need some evidence before I put him in an inter-view room."

"OK. I'll start working on getting that list as soon as we get back to the office."

Henley checked the time on the dashboard: 7:30 p.m. The last thing that she wanted to do was to go back to the office, but she didn't want to go back to an empty house either.

"No, there isn't much point. We won't be able to get hold of the jury list tonight. The Old Bailey jury office will be closed. Why don't I take you home? I'm sure that your wife and little boy would like to see you home at a decent hour for once."

"They're not here. They live in Bradford," Ramouter said sadly.

"Oh. I'm sorry. I didn't realize that you were—"

"No, no. We're not separated or anything like that. It's just... My wife isn't—"

"You don't have to tell me if you don't want to."

"No. I should. My wife isn't too well. She's got early onset dementia. She was diagnosed not that long ago."

Henley pulled the car over to the side and turned on her haz-ard lights. She had been too blind to the fact that something wasn't right with Ramouter. She was pissed off that Olivier had managed to work it out before her. "Why didn't you say some-thing? Why are you here? In London."

"She was supposed to be here with me. All of us. Ethan and his annoying budgie, but it's complicated. Families. They can be... Overbearing."

"Tell me about it. Is that what all the phone calls have been about?"

"Yeah, sorry about that."

"Don't apologize. Now that I know... It's better that I know. OK, so I take it that the only thing waiting for you at home is an episode of *MasterChef* and a ready meal for one."

Ramouter laughed. "Have you been around to my flat?"

"I've got good instincts." Henley smiled, despite the immense sadness she felt at Ramouter's predicament. "As it's already late and we're not going back to the SCU, I'll treat you to a cheeky Nando's."

42

"We can fool ourselves into thinking that this job isn't hard on our families. That they can take it."

Henley wiped away the beads of condensation from the neck of the beer bottle. The rooftop seating area of Nando's wasn't busy and Ramouter and Henley sat in the far corner overlooking the Thames. The sky had already descended into a splash of purple, amber and turquoise while the lights of a growing cityscape flickered in the distance. It was as if the only job of the glass and steel of the city was to provide a distraction from the death and chaos on the streets.

"The thing is, our families tell us that they can handle it and for the first few months, or even a year if you're lucky, they *can* handle it but then something happens. Reality kicks in. You're never home on time, you miss your father-in-law's seventieth birthday party, you refuse to talk about your shit day and then some lunatic tries to kill you," Henley finished, then took a drink.

"I know that it's hard, but I've wanted this for so long. I surprised myself how much I wanted it." Ramouter poured the hottest peri-peri sauce onto his chicken. "And you know that the worse part of this job—for us, I mean—is trying to convince yourself that you're not betraying yourself and your community."

Henley thought back to the red-hot arguments with family and friends over her decision to give up a lucrative job as an investment bank analyst to join the Met's graduate recruitment program.

"My brother, Simon, didn't talk to me for three months," said Henley. Ramouter nodded empathetically. "By the time he was twenty-five he had been stopped thirty-two times by the police for driving because he was black and there I was telling him that I was off to Hendon."

"My mum prays for my soul every time she goes to temple. She said that joining the police was more shameful than my decision to marry a non-Sikh."

Henley relaxed a little as they ate and enjoyed the warmth of the city night. She'd been so pissed about having a trainee that she'd forgotten he was an actual human being.

"I'm sorry about your wife. Haven't you thought about going back?" Henley was acutely aware that she sounded like Rob, asking Ramouter to choose: his job or his family.

"What? And give up rooftop dining at Nando's?" The grin on Ramouter's face disappeared as quickly as it came. "It's what she wanted for me."

"But did *you* want it?" Henley asked.

"I want the job and I want my family. It just seems like I can't have both at the moment."

Ramouter picked up a napkin and dabbed quickly at his eyes.

"Peri-peri sauce get in your eye?"

"Something like that."

Henley knew she could get under people's skin. She had an innate desire to see what made people tick, which buttons to push to make them falter. She wasn't sure if she was inherently manipulative or simply had the gift of persuasion.

"What about you?" Ramouter asked while Henley scooped

rice onto her fork. "You seemed to have managed it. You haven't been forced to choose."

"My husband used to ask me to choose once a day. It became twice a day after Olivier hurt me and I was signed off with PTSD."

"PTSD? I didn't know. I'm sorry."

Henley waved the apology away. "There's nothing for you to be sorry for. You're part of the team and you're working with me. You should know."

"Part of the team." Ramouter grinned. "But you're good now? The PTSD, I mean."

Henley looked up as a couple of Chinook helicopters flew overhead, back to the army base nearby, carrying away her reply.

"It's managed."

43

Henley had had another fretful night and had woken up alone at 4 a.m. covered in sweat and entangled in her bedsheets. She had given up trying to get back to sleep and had arrived at the SCU at 6 a.m.

"Sean Delaney was a juror in Olivier's first murder trial," Ramouter said triumphantly, slamming his hands on his desk, causing Henley to jump. "Daniel Kennedy and Zoe Darego were also jurors on that trial."

"Is that the full jury list?" Henley took a sip of coffee, relying on the caffeine to jolt some life into her.

"This is the list for the first trial. The first jury was selected on September 25, 2017." Ramouter handed over the sheet of paper, which contained the twelve names. "But the jury was discharged in week two because—"

"One of the jurors discovered some information about Olivier, then told the others about it." It was starting to come back to Henley, the cause of the brief hiatus in the trial before the roller coaster of the "Jigsaw Killer Murder Trial" was back on course. "Do we know which juror blabbed?"

"It was *jurors*," replied Ramouter. "Alessandro Naylor, juror

five, and Dominic Pine, juror eleven. I tracked down the prosecutor first thing this morning and from what he can remember Naylor and Pine had somehow found out that Olivier's first
victim, Sergeant Adrian Flynn, had been accused of raping him
when he was nineteen. How come you don't remember this?"

Henley glanced at the clock and then at the dark circles under
Ramouter's eyes and decided to forgive him for the attitude and
irritation in his voice. She was partly to blame for his late night.

"My only involvement in the trial was to give evidence as
one of the investigating officers and as a…as a victim." She felt
a flush of shame. "The first jury was discharged before I gave
evidence. I wasn't even in court. I was technically on maternity
leave. They told us that the jury had been discharged but it's not
uncommon for a trial to collapse because of some kind of jury
problem or a legal issue that none of us understood. The trial
started a few days later with a new jury. I think that they had
me in the witness box in week three for two days."

Henley could remember it clearly. Sitting in the witness box
in court nine at the Old Bailey when she was almost eight
months pregnant with Emma. The prosecutor had asked her if
she wanted special measures. To give her evidence over video-
link, or from behind a curtain, shielded from Olivier. She could
remember declining and being adamant that she wasn't vulner-
able or intimidated and having to squeeze herself into the witness
box. Emma had kicked constantly as though she was protesting
at being in a courtroom.

"Four days later, I gave birth prematurely to my daughter. I
didn't give Olivier or the case another thought until the verdicts
came in," said Henley.

"Hmm. OK, well, Naylor and Pine were both done for contempt, were found guilty in December 2017 and both got a six-
month prison sentence."

"I'm not even going to ask where they got the information
about Olivier from?"

Ramouter smiled. "Joseph McGrath, now known as our favorite estate agent, Chance Blaine. But look again at the juror list. This is where things get even more interesting. Think again about our victims and look at the numbers."

Henley examined the list. "Uzomamaka Darego. That's our Zoe, juror three. Daniel Kennedy is four and Sean Delaney is eight. *Fuck*. Eight, three and four. That's what Olivier said. He repeated those numbers the last time we saw him."

Henley felt sick with the realization that Olivier was one step ahead of them. That he had worked out the connection between the victims before she had.

"But these victims have got nothing to do with Olivier," said Ramouter. "They didn't convict him. That was the second jury. If this was an act of revenge our victims would most likely be from the second jury. It doesn't make any sense."

"As much as it pains me to say it, I think that Olivier was telling us the truth. I don't think he orchestrated these murders." Henley walked over to the whiteboard where there were photographs of Daniel Kennedy, Zoe Darego and Sean Delaney. On the far side of the board was an e-fit, a computer-generated image of the head that was left on Henley's doorstep.

"But our victims might have something to do with Blaine."

"OK, let's say that it definitely is Blaine. You don't start killing for no reason," said Ramouter. "You don't wake up on a Wednesday morning, realize that you're out of milk and decide to chop up the milkman."

"Maybe there was a practice run," Henley said out loud. "What about the other jurors?"

"Two are dead," answered Ramouter as he leaned back in his chair. It occurred to Henley that he had already committed their names to memory. "Albert Kraenish, but that was from natural causes last year. Death certificate says liver cancer."

"And the other?"

"Carole Lewis. Forty-eight years old. She was found stabbed

to death in Highgate Woods back in May. The investigation is still ongoing. The OIC is a DS Lancaster."

Henley's mind was running a million miles a minute, but she couldn't think of anything to say.

"What if Kennedy wasn't the first one?" said Ramouter.

"What do you mean?"

"You just said it. A practice run. What if Daniel Kennedy wasn't the first one? What if it was Carole Lewis?"

Henley checked the wall clock. DS Lancaster was late. Her shift had started sixteen minutes ago. Other officers hovered around the incident room, clearly intrigued as to why two members of the SCU were at their station. Henley had already declined the offer of tea or coffee twice, while Ramouter had been ignored.

A short, heavyset woman walked into the room carrying a thin blue file. She had made no effort with her clothing. Henley could tell that DS Lancaster was the type of police officer who wanted to prove that it wasn't about her, that it was all about the job. She had an edge to her, and Henley didn't like it.

The three of them crammed around her desk. Lancaster placed a hand possessively on the blue file that contained some of her notes, witness statements and forensics reports from the Carole Lewis murder investigation.

Henley tapped the edge of the file. "That case file is a bit thin, isn't it?"

"It's my personal working file," Lancaster replied, instinctively pulling it toward her.

"And that's all you chose to bring with you, even though you were aware that we were coming?"

The noise level in the incident room dropped as Lancaster removed her hand from the file and pushed it over. Henley ignored Lancaster's not-so-subtle tutting as she opened the file.

"We had the husband down as a suspect," said Lancaster.

Henley gave Lancaster a look. A reminder that she was speaking to someone above her rank. Lancaster caught it and corrected herself. "But now that you're here, ma'am…" Lancaster said begrudgingly. "Her body was found by the playing fields on a Saturday morning by a couple of kids on their way to football practice. There were stab wounds to her chest and her throat had been cut. Almost decapitated her. Suspicions naturally turned to the husband because we quickly found out that he was having an affair with their neighbor."

"Charming," said Ramouter.

"Yeah, if you saw the state of him, you'd wonder why anyone would bother," continued Lancaster. She turned her gaze toward Ramouter, wrongly assuming that he would be a natural ally.

Henley watched as Lancaster's gaze went to the ring on Ramouter's left hand before she looked up again.

"Would you like a cup of tea or coffee?" Lancaster asked Ramouter. "We've actually got the good stuff that comes in a capsule."

Henley resisted the urge to roll her eyes or to chastise Lancaster for flirting with Ramouter right in front of her.

Ramouter cleared his throat. "I'm good, thanks."

"Yorkshire, is it?" asked Lancaster.

"Sergeant!" Henley didn't bother to hide her annoyance. "You were saying that you suspected the husband."

"It didn't help that three months before Lewis was killed, the husband had taken out a life insurance policy for the both of them," said Lancaster. "We searched the house and found a pair of his trainers with traces of her blood on them. He says that she had cut herself in the kitchen a few days before and he had stepped in her blood."

"What other evidence did you have?" asked Henley sharply.

"Nothing direct." Lancaster reached for the large bottle of Evian water on her desk. "We called him in to interview and he obviously denied having anything to do with it. He gave us an alibi. Said that he spent the night at a Travelodge with the neighbor, but when we went to see her, she denied it, and when we made inquiries with the Travelodge there were no bookings in his or her name. CPS didn't think that we had enough to charge so we released him under investigation."

"And from the look of this working file, you've left the investigation floundering."

"What? No. I've—"

"Carole Lewis's husband has been RUI for almost six months and you haven't pursued any other possible suspects."

"There *are* no other suspects."

"Are you sure about that?" Henley asked. "According to the forensics report, some of the DNA that was found in Lewis's body was attributed to a Gary Wilkins."

"We spoke to him," Lancaster said defensively. "He made a full admission to having sex with Carole Lewis but that was almost twenty-four hours before she was found dead."

"And you automatically eliminated him as a suspect. There's no evidence here that you even checked out his alibi."

"I'm going to be checking out his alibi," said Lancaster. "This is still an open investigation."

"You're going to check it out after nearly six months," Ramouter said. "Were you even aware that Gary Wilkins was being investigated by the Sapphire Unit at West End Central for his history of sexual assault?"

Lancaster pursed her lips, as though she had tasted something bitter. For some inexplicable reason, she hadn't expected Henley and Ramouter to do their homework.

"I haven't been negligent," Lancaster said defiantly. "Our unit has seventeen murder investigations that are ongoing. We don't have the luxury of being selective with our cases or being left to our own devices to investigate a once-in-a-blue-moon serial crime, ma'am."

Henley bristled at the sharp jab. She was aware of the cluster of detectives to her right who were openly watching the exchange. Lancaster sat smugly in front of her, celebrating her cheaply won point.

"Did you know that Lewis had been a juror on the Olivier murder trial?" Henley asked.

"No, we didn't," said Lancaster, "and even if we had I don't think that it would have been a possible line of inquiry at the time, but it's something that we're going to actively—"

"No, you won't. We're taking this," said Henley.

Lancaster's expression hardened. "But you can't do that. It's my investigation."

"It was, but in my opinion," Henley said loudly for the benefit of every eavesdropping ear in the room, "you've failed to investigate it properly."

"Ma'am, with all due respect. I've been running this investigation—"

"Badly, you've been running it badly."

Henley was aware that the activity in the incident room had slowed down. Conversations had stalled midsentence. Even the phones had stopped ringing.

"You just can't *take* it. You don't have the authority to take—"

"Sergeant Lancaster, don't concern yourself with the admin. I'll have someone from the SCU contact you to arrange the transfer of the case files." Henley scraped back her chair and indicated for Ramouter to follow. "You can keep your working notes."

Lancaster stared back, seething with anger.

"Make yourself available," said Henley.

"Well, I don't think that you're going to be on Lancaster's Christmas card list," Ramouter said as they walked out of the station.

"Couldn't care less," said Henley. "She was trying it on and I don't like it when someone blatantly tries to take me for a mug."

"But she's right though. We don't have authority. We can't just take over like that."

"Don't you think that I know that?" Henley pulled out her phone, which had begun to ring. "Pellacia is going to have to work a bloody miracle and get us authority. God, he's going to kill me for this."

She answered and listened. Her stomach flipped, and the nausea swept over her in waves with every word.

"We need to go. Now." Henley had already begun to run toward her car.

"What is it?" Ramouter quickened his pace to catch up. "What's happened?"

"It's Olivier. We need to get to Queen Elizabeth Hospital, now."

44

Olivier tried for the third time to open his eyes as the voices around him grew louder and more distinct. The back of his head throbbed and there was a strange metallic taste in his mouth.

"Peter. Peter, can you hear me?"

Olivier turned his head in the direction of the voice and managed to barely open his eyes.

"Yes," Olivier replied with a hoarse voice, coughing. "Water."

"Of course. We'll just raise the bed a bit. We removed your breathing tube so your throat will be feeling quite dry and sore for a few hours, but the main thing is that you're alive."

A nurse brought him a cup of water and as he reached for it he noticed the saline drip in his hand. There were no restraints securing him to the guardrail. Olivier turned his head and flinched with pain. Ade, a prison officer, was sitting in the corner with a folded newspaper in his lap. Olivier stopped the smile from spreading across his face when he noticed the view from the window. He'd made it out of Belmarsh prison.

"Don't remove it," warned the doctor as Olivier adjusted the nasal cannula that was pushing oxygen through his nostrils.

"Luckily, it wasn't a heart attack like we thought but we can't discharge you back to the prison just yet."

"Why not?" Olivier asked, running his hand across the sensors on his chest.

"Apparently, Belmarsh is on a lockdown," the doctor replied, and looked at Ade for confirmation.

"If we can't get back into Belmarsh today, then it looks like it's either Brixton or Pentonville, once transportation is sorted out," Ade replied.

"How long have I been here?"

"Since yesterday morning. Do you remember what happened?" asked the doctor.

Olivier inhaled and squinted his eyes. "It's a bit hazy, but I think that I missed out on breakfast. Is there any chance of getting something to eat?" Olivier asked.

The doctor marked off his chart. "Of course. I'll ask the nurse to come in. Also, you might experience some dizziness and nausea when you first try to get up. Don't let it alarm you. It's a perfectly normal reaction. We'll give you some antinausea medication if it's really extreme."

As the doctor left, Olivier caught a glimpse of Karen Bajarami, who was standing guard. She looked at Olivier cautiously before closing the door.

Ade was still sitting in his chair, but his head had lolled back and there was the unmistakable sound of snoring. Olivier had already removed the sensors on his chest, and as he began to extract the saline catheter, blood pooled in his hand. Almost an hour had passed since he'd finished the lunch a nurse hesitantly placed on his tray before racing out of the room. He shifted off the bed and placed his bare feet on the floor. An intense nausea swept over him as he stood up. He sat back down, placed his head between his knees and breathed deeply, waiting for the dizziness and heart palpitations to subside. The lamb stew that he had eaten earlier swirled in his stomach and attempted to make its way back up his throat. A few minutes passed and Olivier pushed himself back up. His prison clothes with his trainers had been placed in a plastic bag that had been dumped in the corner of a room.

Ade jumped up from his chair as Olivier kicked over the metal drip stand and smashed the lunch plate against his head, knocking him out. Olivier grabbed a sharp piece of the broken plate and rammed it into Ade's side. Olivier repeatedly banged his head against the floor until a hospital security guard rushed in and pulled Olivier off Ade. Bajarami spoke into her walkie-talkie.

"Help. We need help!"

Bajarami screamed as Olivier rammed the security guard against the wall. Ade lay gurgling as an alarm went off in the hallway. Olivier loosened his grip as another wave of nausea took hold of him. The guard stumbled toward the door and out into the corridor. Olivier shook his head clear and spotted the food tray and fork by his feet. He picked up the food tray and hit the security guard twice across the face.

"Olivier. Stop. You have to stop," Bajarami cried out as the security guard crawled along the corridor floor.

"Shut the fuck up," Olivier snarled, the nausea bringing him to his knees. From the corner of his eye, he saw Bajarami standing in the doorway. He grabbed the fork, forced himself up and walked up to the guard. There was a sickening crunching sound as Olivier raised his leg and stamped twice on the guard's head. Bajarami threw herself at Olivier and tried to push him away from the guard's convulsing body. Olivier shrugged her off and turned around.

"No. No. Stop!" Bajarami shouted. Olivier lunged at her, plunging the fork deep into her eye. He watched her face freeze in shock before she let out a guttural scream. Olivier covered Bajarami's mouth, then shoved her across the room.

The hospital alarm grew louder as Olivier ran out into the corridor and toward the fire escape.

45

"This is BBC Radio London News. Police are hunting for the notorious prisoner Peter Olivier, who has escaped from Queen Elizabeth Hospital in Woolwich, southeast London. Peter Olivier, also known as 'the Jigsaw Killer,' was jailed for life in 2017, for the murder of seven men.

"Olivier, who is thirty-eight years of age, was at the hospital receiving treatment for a suspected heart attack. He is believed to have assaulted two prison officers in order to make his escape. Olivier is described as white, five foot eleven, with short brown hair and of medium build. He was wearing a blue-and-white hospital gown when he escaped. The police have said that Olivier is highly dangerous and warn the public not to approach him but to call—"

Henley's blood was pumping in her ears. The hospital was swarming with security guards and police. Henley had had to turn on the blue and twos just to push her way in front of the BBC News and Sky satellite vans that had turned up. A helicopter was circling overhead, while the officers on the ground took statements and confirmed updates over their police radios.

Henley checked her watch. Olivier had been on the run for two hours and nineteen minutes. They would have been there sooner if it hadn't been for the accident on the A406 and a car breaking down in the Blackwall Tunnel. All forty-three police forces across the United Kingdom had been briefed and were on alert. The last image of Olivier, taken shortly after his arrest at Lewisham police station nearly three years ago, was posted all over Twitter and the local news. A gaggle of journalists were reporting live from outside Queen Elizabeth Hospital, warning viewers that Olivier was highly dangerous and that he shouldn't be approached.

Henley and Ramouter followed a security officer to a room on the ground floor next to the newsagent's. Henley wondered if there was something that she had missed when she had last visited Olivier. She replayed the conversation between them but there was no coded message, nothing that revealed itself in hindsight. Yet she felt as though she had dropped the ball.

The security control room smelled of antiseptic, burned coffee and stale cigarette smoke. Adam Cole, the head of hospital security, and Lyle Denman, the senior prison officer in charge of transporting Olivier to hospital, stood in front of the bank of security monitors.

"If you think that we're taking the blame for this, you've got another think coming," said Cole as he tapped on the keyboard.

"Are you taking the piss? This ain't on us," said Denman. "We made it perfectly clear that we would need extra assistance with Olivier. Experienced officers. Maybe if you had people who didn't get their security cards out of a cereal box, have been in the country for more than five minutes and could actually speak—"

"Shut it." Henley glared at Denman as he turned around.

Denman put his hands on his hips, revealing yellow deodorant stains under his arms. "Who the—" He stopped when he noticed the lanyard with Henley's warrant card around her neck.

"I haven't got time for this," Henley said as she indicated for Ramouter to pull up a chair.

"How many security cameras are there?" Henley asked.

"There are 186 in the actual hospital building and thirty-two outside, including the car park," said Cole.

"You've got footage from the floor where Olivier was kept?"

"I'm pulling it together now."

Henley tried to ignore Denman, who was making heavy sighs of annoyance in the corner.

"We've increased security around the hospital since the incident," said Cole.

"Shutting the stable door after the horse has bolted, isn't it?" said Henley. "Perhaps you should have increased security *before* Olivier got here?"

"Look, with all due respect, Detective—"

"Inspector." Henley's voice was cold and brittle.

"Sorry. Inspector. It's my responsibility to maintain the security of this hospital and I did my job. We implemented all of our security measures as soon as we were informed that the prisoner was on his way. Once he was in the hospital it was up to the prison officers to keep an eye on him."

"What exactly happened?" Henley turned to Lyle Denman. "Why was Olivier even here? The reports are suggesting that he had a heart attack."

"He collapsed at breakfast yesterday morning. He would have been taken to the health care wing, but he was completely unresponsive, and we thought that he may have had a stroke, so an ambulance was called."

"How many officers escorted him?"

"Two at first." Denman looked down at his feet.

"Just two officers. For *him*," said Ramouter. Henley didn't bother to chastise Ramouter for butting in. He was right.

"I didn't have a choice. Do you know how short-staffed we are? Two officers is the minimum that is required."

"For someone who's nicked a couple of hundred quid from his gran, not for a bloody serial killer." Henley took a step back and folded her arms. She took a deep breath. "I know that Karen Bajarami was here with him, but who was the other officer?"

"Ade Nzibe," said Denman. "He's one of my most experienced officers. Been with me for twenty years."

Denman looked up at Henley as though he was expecting her to award him a gold star.

"Was Olivier restrained?"

"He was at first, but as soon as we arrived, he was taken into the ER and we were told to remove the handcuffs so that they could treat him—"

"Excuse me." Cole actually raised his hand as though he was asking for permission from the teacher. "I've located the footage."

They gathered around the monitor and watched the film.

"Fuck," said Cole. Denman turned away as Olivier, barefooted, stamped on the security guard's head. Bajarami appeared in the doorway and lunged for Olivier.

The screen then switched to the footage from Bajarami's body camera. The footage buffered until it settled on Olivier standing in his hospital gown. Bajarami was shouting at him to stop. The fork could be seen in Olivier's hand. Olivier smiled, then lunged at her. Bajarami's bloodcurdling scream pierced Henley's ears.

"Shit," said Ramouter.

Olivier turned left and disappeared from the shot.

"Where did he go?" asked Ramouter as Henley walked away from the monitors and stood by the door.

"The woman—" said Adam.

"Her name is Karen," Denman said between gritted teeth as he sat down on a nearby chair.

"Sorry, Karen. She managed to press the alarm, but by that time he had already made his way to the stairs. Cameras picked him up again at the emergency exit that leads straight to the car park and, as you know, he carjacked one of the visitors. We've given the details to a colleague of yours. Security made their way to the car park where he tried to run one of my men over."

After a few seconds, Henley let out the breath that she didn't realize she had been holding. The security control room now seemed smaller, claustrophobic. She couldn't breathe.

"Do you know where Karen and Ade are now?" Henley asked Denman.

"I think that they're being treated on the fourth floor," he said.

"Let's go," Henley said to Ramouter. She walked out of the room without offering thanks or saying goodbye.

46

"The car was found about forty minutes ago, dumped in Charlton." Eastwood lifted a large exhibit bag filled with letters onto the table. "Since the alert went out there've been multiple sightings, but I can guarantee a lot of it is bollocks. Over the last hour he's been seen in Hackney, Greenford, a pub in Clapham, Aberdeen and Benidorm."

Henley was standing at the window watching Pellacia as he stood on the steps giving a press conference.

"Is this everything from his cell?" she asked as Eastwood pulled more bags out of the box.

"Yes, this is everything. He has a lot of letters from—I don't know what you want to call them—fans, I suppose. There are a lot of women out there who want to have his babies and men who want to—" Eastwood pulled a face. "Don't understand it myself."

"What about a phone?"

"Hold your horses, guv. I was just getting there."

Eastwood reached into the box and pulled a sealed small exhibit bag. Inside was a mobile phone that was no bigger than a two-finger KitKat.

"It's tiny," said Henley, balancing the phone in her hand. She pressed the on button and waited for the small screen to light up.

"It's as basic as you can get," said Eastwood. "Carphone Warehouse sells them for about eight quid. The only thing that you can do with it is make calls and send texts. There's a SIM card inside and we found the charger."

"Where was it found?"

"The phone and charger were found behind the sink unit in his cell. The SIM card was at the bottom of a box of Coco Pops."

Henley was growing more annoyed with herself. She should have demanded a search of his cell earlier.

"He's been talking to someone." She scrolled through the call log. "The last call was made by him at about 11:45 p.m., the night before he supposedly fell ill. Will you take it downstairs to Ezra?"

"Of course. But that's not all we found." Eastwood handed Henley an A4-sized notebook. On the front page in large black letters were the words *SEARCH RECORD 101*. Henley turned to the first page where Eastwood had drawn a sketch of Olivier's cell. Like everything that Eastwood did, it was neat and precise.

"Tell me what you notice, guv," Eastwood said.

The cell was six feet by eight with a bed, a small table and a wardrobe. On the left-hand side was a toilet and sink. She skipped to the list of items found. Books, PlayStation, television, radio, magazines. Insulin. Syringe.

"What's unusual about this list?" asked Henley.

"Olivier's not diabetic," Eastwood explained. "He'd been complaining of feeling unwell. He'd seen the GP and there had been concerns about low blood pressure and slightly increased glucose levels, but he had not been diagnosed with diabetes. The question is, why would someone who's not a diabetic be taking insulin?"

"Who the hell has been helping him?" Henley slammed her

fist onto the table. "It's not that hard to get a phone into a prison, but insulin? For fuck's sake! We need to find out who gave it to him."

"I would have said Blaine, but there's no way he would've been able to get vials of insulin and syringes through Belmarsh," Eastwood said.

"What about the inside?" Henley handed the search record back to Eastwood. "What if someone inside the prison has been helping him?"

"It's not too much of a stretch," said Eastwood. "I've lost count of the number of dodgy prison officers that have been done for passing on drugs and phones to prisoners. Smuggling in a bit of insulin would be nothing."

"I need you and Stanford to get a list of all of the prison staff who have worked in the High Security Unit since Olivier has been there and arrange interviews with them. The sooner, the better."

Henley turned up the volume on the TV. All of the news channels seemed to have a reporter stationed either outside the Queen Elizabeth Hospital or outside Belmarsh prison. An old photograph flashed across the screen.

"It's misleading," Henley said as Pellacia came out of his office and sat in front of her desk.

"What do you mean?"

"When I last saw Olivier, he looked thin and gaunt. He didn't look like someone capable of escape. The public will be looking for someone like the man in the photograph, someone healthy and strong. Like a different person."

"Well, he's out there. It's all we've got."

"This is madness. Look, Stanford and Eastwood are going to the prison in a bit to interview the officers and I want to arrest Blaine."

"No," Pellacia said determinedly.

"What do you mean, no?"

"Look, I understand why you want to arrest him, but you haven't got enough."

"Stephen, I've got his association with the jurors, he's been visiting Olivier and he harassed Zoe."

"You've got no forensics or direct evidence that he harassed Zoe. All you've got is the word of mouth of a pissed-off ex-girlfriend and a flaky report that Zoe made to hospital security."

"So, you want me to just leave him out there and wait for another body to be chopped up and dumped?" Henley said angrily.

"Calm down. All I'm saying is get some tangible evidence. The last thing I need is for us to be shut down because we've got ahead of ourselves and arrested the wrong person."

Henley didn't reply. She knew that Pellacia was right.

"What about Ramouter? He's doing OK?"

"Yeah, he is, actually, but this investigation—it's a lot. I never had to deal with anything like this when I was a trainee. My first case as a TDC was an armed robbery. Ramouter left his family in Bradford to be here."

"Really? They've broken up?"

"No. Nothing like that." Henley switched the TV off. The office was empty.

"How are you?" Pellacia asked her.

"I'm fine. Tired but OK."

"We've arranged for more protection at Rob's parents' house."

"Don't remind me. His mum wasn't exactly pleased about having a patrol car parked outside her house, but I really couldn't give a shit. She's not my priority."

"And what about you? I'm not happy with the thought of you being home alone."

"I'm not home alone. I've got officers parked outside my house. They've installed panic alarms and CCTV. The chances of Olivier, or anyone else for that matter, coming within ten feet of me are remote."

"Come home with me. Stay with me."

Henley looked down as Pellacia took hold of her hand, letting him intertwine his fingers with hers.

"I want you with me," he said. "Let me—"

"Why do you have to make things so difficult?"

"I'm not. I'm trying to make things easy for you. Uncomplicated."

"Uncomplicated? Why do you act as though I'm not married?"

"Because of the way that you still look at me."

"I'll ask Stanford to stay with me." Henley retracted her hand. "I can't stay with my brother. He's got kids. I can't put that on him."

Henley's head turned toward the door as it swung open and Joanna, the admin manager, walked in.

"Fine. Do what you want," Pellacia said. "What can I do for you, Joanna?"

"I want her, not you," she said.

"Honestly." Pellacia sighed heavily. "I get no respect around this place."

"Perhaps you need to work on your people skills. Go on a course or something."

"What is it, Jo?" asked Henley.

"I need your signature on the transfer request for the Lewis investigation file. And you, DSI Pellacia, have a very irate DSI Chambers from Wood Green CID on line two."

Henley followed Joanna to her desk.

"I see that you've been out causing trouble again," said Joanna, handing her the transfer request.

"I didn't have much of a choice."

"So, this Carole Lewis. Do you really think that she's one of his?"

Henley signed the transfer document and stared up at the photos of Darego, Kennedy and Delaney on the whiteboard. She knew in her gut that a photo of Carole Lewis would soon be joining them.

47

Henley parked in front of Greenwich train station and turned on her hazard lights. She felt a sense of relief when she saw her brother, tall and rangy, exiting the station. Simon spotted her too and had broken into a light jog.

"All right, sis?" Simon got in the car and reached for the lever to push the seat back. "Ah, that's better. I could have met you at Mum and—" He paused. "Sorry. God, it doesn't feel right to just say Dad's house, do you know what I mean?"

"I know exactly what you mean." Henley turned off the hazard lights and pulled away.

"I tried calling him, but he didn't pick up."

"Same here."

"So, little sister. How are you? I heard about the bastard escaping. Thought that you would have told me yourself."

Henley's brother fiddled with the car radio. She knew that he couldn't bring himself to let Olivier's name leave his mouth. She remembered how he had sat at the side of her bed, after leaving his shift as an oncologist at Guy's Hospital and speeding down to Queen Elizabeth's. "You could have come up with a better way of telling me that I was going to be an uncle," he had joked as he surreptitiously checked her blood pressure on the monitor.

"I take it that they haven't caught him yet?" Simon asked.

"Nope. They're looking for him though. Everyone is looking for him."

"He's not coming after you, is he? That business at your house the other day."

"I doubt it." Henley hoped that she sounded reassuring as she drove toward Bellingham. "I can't think of any good reason for him to hang around."

"I hope that they find the bastard at the bottom of a cliff somewhere." Simon yawned. "I'm knackered."

"Stop complaining. You're the one who wanted to be a surgeon."

"I thought that it would make me more attractive to the ladies. Speaking of which, how is the lovely Linh?"

"Leave Linh alone." Henley slapped Simon on the arm.

"Ow. I haven't done anything. I'm a married man with three pain-in-the-arse kids. Allow a man a little time to fantasize."

"Fantasize about your wife."

"Please. Even in my fantasies Mia tells me that she's got a headache."

"You joker," Henley said, laughing. "Simon, you're a surgeon, right?"

"Last time I checked."

"How easy would it be to get hold of atri… Oh for God's sake. Atracium—"

"Atracurium besilate." Simon lowered the volume on the radio. "Why would you want that?"

"I don't want it. It's linked to an investigation. How easy would it be to get hold of?" Henley stopped the car outside their parents' house and they got out.

"Well, you can't pick it up over the counter in Boots, I can tell you that much. It's only ever used for surgical procedures.

It's literally under lock and key. Even I can't just walk into the storeroom and pick up a couple of vials. That's not to say that someone couldn't find a way to get access to it if they wanted it badly enough. Doctors and nurses stealing drugs from the hospital is nothing new."

Henley and Simon stopped at the front door. A set of keys had been left in the lock.

"That's not like Dad." Simon turned the key and opened the door.

Henley felt as though she was walking through a stranger's house. The sideboard where her mum used to keep a vase of fresh flowers was now covered with unopened mail. The gold gilded mirror above it was smeared with fingerprints. The house smelled of cigarette smoke and the souring scent of a kitchen bin that needed emptying.

"Oh, Dad," said Henley as she and Simon walked into the living room. Elijah was sitting in an armchair watching the news; or the news was watching him as he stared into space. An overflowing ashtray was balancing precariously on his lap. A dirty plate lay on the ground next to a can of Guinness. The living room was in disarray. Their dad was a crumpled mess.

"What are you doing here? Why are you in my house?" Elijah stood up. Cigarette butts and ash scattered across the carpet.

"Dad. Dad. Calm down," said Henley.

"You shouldn't be here. I told you that I didn't want you here. I should call the police."

Henley laughed, more out of despair than actual humor, as she took her dad's arm. "Dad, please."

"You shouldn't be here." Elijah pulled his arm away. "She isn't here anymore, so why are you here?"

Henley swallowed hard, resisting the urge to cry.

"We just want to help you, Dad," Simon said, putting an arm around his shoulders. "We know that you're hurting."

"Stop it," said Elijah.

"We're all missing Mum."

"Stop it, stop it." Elijah recoiled and slumped back into his chair.

Henley looked across at Simon. When they were younger, they had never known what to call the moments when their dad had slipped away from them. He would move into the spare bedroom and stay there for weeks. The curtains would be drawn, the room shrouded in darkness as he lay on the bed, staring at the ceiling. Their mum would tell them to leave him alone, let him rest. Henley would sit on the edge of his bed after school anyway, telling her dad about her school day and asking him when he would get up and take her to gymnastics. She was fifteen years old when she'd overheard her mum mention the word *depression* to her aunt Cecile.

"Let Simon and I clean up and maybe—"

"Maybe you should come and spend some time with me, Mia and the kids," Simon said, picking up the dirty plate from the floor. "I can book some time off work."

"I can't let them see me like this," said Elijah. "I didn't want you to see me like this."

Henley's legs felt weak and she allowed herself to drop onto the three-piece sofa. She put her hands to her face. They became hot with tears as she heard her dad say, "I'm broken. I never wanted you to see me broken."

48

Henley sat at her kitchen table in her pajamas, facing the French doors, watching the rain fall. Exhaustion was sweeping through her body in waves. It had taken almost an hour to convince their dad to pack a bag and relocate to Simon's. Stanford had already let himself in and had fallen asleep on the sofa when she had finally arrived home at midnight. It was quiet without Emma singing along to her programs on the TV, Luna barking and Rob moaning about the state of the financial markets as he worked on his laptop. The cup of tea Stanford had made for her had long gone cold. The Indian summer had taken a swift departure and the sky outside was as gray and heavy as her mood. She'd managed just three hours' sleep.

Henley stiffened when she heard the key in the front door.

"That is definitely my cue to go," said Stanford, picking up a banana from the fruit bowl.

"Thanks for staying over."

"It was nothing. It's not as if I was on a promise last night, but, Anj, take my advice."

"I know what you're going to say." Henley got up and poured the cold tea down the sink.

"I'm sure that you do. I know what you're like. You want to take it all on, on your own, but you can't, so go easy on him. All of this, it ain't easy."

The door opened and closed. Henley had about a minute's grace as Rob took off his trainers and wet hoodie. All his text message had said was: We need to talk. Four words that had never, in the history of preempting a conversation, led to a happy ending or agreeable conclusion.

"I bought you a latte." Rob placed the drink on the breakfast bar. "Paul? I didn't realize that you were here."

"Morning, mate." Stanford shook hands with Rob. "Didn't want Anjelica here on her own. Right, I'm off. Tell Emma that Uncle Paul said hello."

"I will." Rob passed her the white cup, which had Anjelica, spelled, again, incorrectly in black ink on the side.

"Thanks," Henley said. The hot brown liquid escaped from the ill-fitting cap and ran down her hands. She didn't want it, but she took a sip anyway. "How's Ems? I was going to Face-Time, but I got caught up with Dad last night."

"Yeah, she's fine. A couple of the kids are off with a stomach bug so don't be surprised when Ems comes down with it. Mum loves having her. Spoiling her to pieces, but she isn't pleased."

Henley rolled her eyes. "Of course she isn't."

"You can't blame her. It was bad enough having the police checking up on us every five minutes but now that they're parked permanently outside the front door..."

"She does know that it's for her granddaughter's safety? If she wants to risk that—"

"You know that she doesn't. Are you not going into work today?"

"No, I'm going in later. Just got a few things to do this morning."

"I've been doing a lot of thinking"—he paused, and then— "This situation isn't working for me."

"What do you mean 'this situation'?" Henley held on tightly to the coffee cup. "What situation do you think that we're in?" Henley stared at Rob with the same blank *I think you're talking shit* look she usually reserved for the suspects she was interviewing.

"I never wanted you to go back after what happened. I still think it was a mistake, but I suppose it wasn't so bad when you were working cases in the office, but now that you're back out there everything has changed. You're putting us in danger."

"Rob—"

"You've put Emma in danger."

Checkmate. Henley got up and poured her latte down the sink. She watched the brown liquid begin its clockwise descent down the drain.

"I have never put Emma or you in danger. If I'd had the slightest idea that someone would... Do you *really* think I want to live like this?"

"Of course you don't, but what have you actually done to change it? You could have walked away. You could still walk away, and now that Olivier has escaped, you *should* walk away. I may not be a bloody detective but even I know that he could turn up here. He nearly killed you. You conveniently forget about that."

"Oh, stop exaggerating. It was a couple of stab wounds. I wasn't at death's door." Even as she said it, her pulse quickened. They both knew it had been more than that.

"Less than a week ago some psychopath left a head on our doorstep. What if it hadn't been just a head? What if someone had come into the house and hurt Emma?"

"I would never have let that happen, Rob. You're acting like all of this is my fault. Why do you want to punish me for doing my job? Don't you think that I feel guilty? Don't you think that I have the same concerns that you do?" Henley's throat tightened. She sat back down on the chair. "I would die if anything happened to Emma," she said. "She's my life. Do you think that

I'm happy about you taking her halfway across London to live with your parents?"

Rob's face hardened. "Your job comes first, always has, and you put what Stephen Pellacia wants before the needs of me and our child. You've done it before and you're doing it again." Rob was shouting now. He stood up and placed his hands on his head. Henley could see the little vein in his neck pulsating with anger. Her right hand began to shake.

"This has nothing to do with Stephen," she finally said. It had occurred to her that Rob suspected that she had slept with Pellacia after her mum had died, but that he couldn't prove it.

"Doesn't it? It was his decision to put you back out there and to keep you out there even after last week."

"You make it sound like he's controlling me on strings."

"Well, if he can't get you in the bedroom he might as well pull your strings some other way."

Henley didn't stop to think. She picked up the closest thing, his beloved Arsenal mug, and threw it at him. He ducked as the mug flew by and shattered against the wall.

"How fucking dare you? You stand there and act all sanctimonious, going on about how I'm putting my daughter in danger, when this is really all about you and your precious ego. Would it make you feel better if I told you that instead of looking for not just one but two killers, I was spending my nights screwing Stephen on his office floor? Is that what you really want to hear, Rob?"

"Are you?"

"For God's sake, no, I'm not. What *is* it? Don't you trust me?"

Rob didn't say anything. The silence was broken by the sound of the post being shoved through the letterbox. Heavy rain fell like stones on the skylight overhead.

"Stop beating around the bush and tell me what you want," Henley said.

"I've already told you. It's us or the job. It's as simple as that."

"You and your bloody ultimatums."

Rob shrugged. "Call it what you like. I'm going upstairs to pick up some more clothes for Emma and me."

"You can't keep her from me. I'm her mum." Henley bit the inside of her cheek to stop herself from crying. She swallowed the blood that had pooled in her mouth.

Rob shrugged. "If you want to see her, you know what you need to do."

Henley got up and opened the back door. She needed to breathe. The wind blew cold rain into her face, but there was nothing that could help ease the palpitations in her chest.

"There's something else," said Rob.

"What is it?" Henley kept her focus on the white starlike flowers on the jasmine bushes at the bottom of the garden. She didn't want to look at Rob.

"Our marriage. It's changed. You've changed. You don't treat me like your husband. I can't even remember the last time we had sex. I feel like we're broken."

There was that word again. *Broken.* Henley felt as though a leaden weight had been dropped into her stomach. Female intuition or a detective's instinct, she knew that a third person was now involved in her marriage.

"The other night, when I left, I bumped into one of the mums from Emma's nursery."

"Which one?"

"You wouldn't know her."

"Where?"

"It doesn't matter."

"Did you sleep with her?" Henley turned around and tried to read the expression on Rob's face. "Well? Did you?"

"I went back to her flat and we had a couple of drinks. I was angry at you."

"Did you sleep with her?"

"I came home."

"That doesn't answer the question. Did you sleep with her?"

"No. I didn't."

"But you wanted to? Otherwise what would be the point in telling me?"

"Not really. I can't explain it, but I didn't. I couldn't. In case you've forgotten…" Rob held up his left hand, tapping his ring finger with his thumb. "I like her, but I didn't want her. But then you and I are… I don't know what we are anymore."

"Don't say broken." Henley walked out of the kitchen. She couldn't be in the same room as him.

"Where are you going?" said Rob as he followed Henley out in the hallway and took hold of her arm.

"Don't touch me." Henley pulled her arm away. "You can make all the threats you want. You can fuck every single mum in that bloody nursery if that's what floats your boat, but this is the last time that you *ever* ask me to choose."

49

Henley had walked out of the room and left the house, Rob's voice following her as he called her a selfish bitch. Now, she was driving along the A12 on her way to Snaresbrook Crown Court where Carole Lewis's husband worked as a security guard.

"I know your husband can be a knob, but…" Linh's voice was loud over the car speakers. "I mean, *seriously*? Who the hell does he think he is to make a threat like that? And why did he even tell you about the skanky nursery mum?"

"I can't even… He had the audacity to accuse me of being unreasonable."

Linh was silent for a moment. "I guess… Someone did dump a head at his front door. No one could blame him for wanting to be somewhere safe with Emma."

"You're on his side?" Henley was incredulous.

"I'm not. I'm just trying to be objective. Look, Anj, you know that I'm more than happy to bitch about him over a couple of bottles of wine, but right now, you need to listen to common sense. Especially while you're driving. As hard as it may be for you and me to believe, I am the voice of reason."

"That's a first. Linh, I do understand. I'm not a monster, but he wants me to give up my job and—I don't care how objective you are—that is not fair."

"No, it's not fair," Linh said firmly. "What exactly does he want you to do? Go and get a nice job in the city? It's not as if he expects you to stay at home and play Suzy Homemaker. Rob just wants you away from *him*."

"Not everything is about Stephen," Henley muttered as she indicated left and came off the dual carriageway.

"It's not, but you can't deny that sometimes he's like an annoying fly that won't get out of your kitchen."

"Linh," Henley snapped. "Is there a reason why you called?"

Linh sighed. "Yes. I've received the original autopsy report for Carole Lewis, but I need to see her for myself."

"What do you mean, 'see her' for yourself?"

"You're going to have to dig her up."

Henley hit the brakes as the traffic lights turned red. "What? Why?" she asked.

"The report mentions some markings that look like a series of scratches. If we dig her up, hopefully the body won't be too badly decomposed, I can take a proper look, then I can be sure if it was our copycat or the husband."

"It wasn't the husband."

"Well, that's your area of expertise. I need to check the actual marks."

"And you need to exhume her body to do that?" Henley asked. She had no problem working with the dead, but she did have a problem with disturbing someone who had already been laid to rest. "Can't you just make the determination from the autopsy file?"

"No. The first pathologist was working from the hypothesis that the husband did it. They would have examined the body differently. I'm working from the hypothesis that we have a serial killer who panicked on his first kill. I need to see her body."

50

Four months earlier…

Carole Lewis sat up straighter, spat out her chewing gum and ran her fingers through her hair. She wondered if he would be able to tell that she'd just been with someone else. She hoped he wouldn't pick up the scent of the other men on her skin. She took out a tissue and dabbed away the sweat on her forehead. The unexpected heat wave had left the night air muggy and stifling. She blew out a breath of frustration as the streetlamp illuminated the figure in front of her.

"Not your usual spot," he said.

Carole slumped back against the bench, crossed her legs and folded her arms. "I'm waiting for someone," she said. "He shouldn't be too long."

"Been waiting awhile?" The man looked back at the route that he had just taken. "Right," he said when Carole failed to answer him. "Well, you know where to find me if your date is a no-show."

Carole pulled out her phone as the man left. It was 10:35 p.m.

She'd been there for twenty minutes. She read back the last message he'd sent her. I'm on my way. x.

Yes. He did want to see her. She hadn't imagined any of it, but she wasn't going to hang around in the middle of the park all night waiting for him.

"Five more minutes and that's it," Carole muttered under her breath. She put the phone back, then stood up quickly as she noticed a man jogging toward her. "Shit!" The edge of her dress caught on the splintered wood of the bench. She pulled at it and swore again as the dress ripped.

"Carole," he said. "Are you all right?"

"Yeah, I'm fine. I just…you know what, never mind. Glad that you finally made it."

"I'm so sorry. I finished work late. I would have called when I was out of the station, but my phone died."

"That's fine. Don't worry about it. Did you want to go for a drink first? You must be a bit parched running up that hill in this weather."

The man pulled the collar of his shirt before taking a step toward Carole and kissing her lips. "Sounds like a good idea. A quick one before, I don't know, we head back to yours?"

"Definitely. The Harp pub is on the other side of the park, but I know a shortcut."

The man pushed himself against Carole. He bit the side of her neck and slid his hand up her dress and between her legs.

"I knew that you weren't wearing any knickers," he said.

"I never do. Are you all right doing it here?"

"You said that it was a good spot."

Carol unbuttoned his trousers. "No one ever comes down to this part of the park. I've got condoms."

"Good."

"Oh my God," said Carole, caught off guard when he put his hand around her throat and squeezed. She closed her eyes while he rubbed her breast and kissed her neck. She felt a wave of excitement and a build-up of nervous energy as he pushed his fingers inside of her. She moved her right hand across his back and toward his waist. It was then that she felt the cold metal handle of a knife.

It all happened so fast. He swiftly pulled the knife from his back pocket and raised it above his head.

"No!" Carole screamed. She crossed her arms in front of her face and cried out in pain as the blade sliced the flesh of her forearm. He grabbed Carole's arm and pulled her toward him. Blow after blow came as he repeatedly plunged the knife into her stomach, sending shock waves across her body. A strangulated scream escaped from her mouth and an intense and painful heat radiated through her body.

The light from the full moon streamed through the thick leaves and glinted against the knife as he pulled it out of her stomach. The blood-soaked material of her dress clung to the serrated knife's edge. She grabbed the blade, in an effort to stop him stabbing her again, but he was too strong. He slashed downward and her right hand fell limply to her side as the blade severed tendons and nerves. She tried to speak but the word *Help* was lost in the pool of blood hemorrhaging from her mouth.

Carole covered one of the wounds on her stomach with her shaking hand. Stumbling, she looked up at him. He wasn't moving. His face was frozen with concentration and interest. He lunged forward, stabbing her again. Carole could feel her body convulse as her legs collapsed under her. She tried to crawl away but the hot blade of the knife stopped her as it pierced her back, chipping away at the bone of her shoulder blade.

The knife came down again, tearing through her lung. He twisted the blade viciously and then pulled it out, breaking the knife tip off in the process. He turned her over and the sound of foxes scuttering through the park echoed in Carole's ears.

Let me die. Let me die.

The words registered in her flickering brain, but her body ignored her, even when the knife tore through her chest again. Her eyes fluttered opened, but her vision was blurred by the blood. She didn't see him raise the knife above her head. Death still hadn't arrived when he slit her throat, with a final violent flourish.

51

Henley fidgeted in her seat and checked the time on the car dashboard. It was almost quarter to eleven. Ramouter was back at the SCU arranging appointments with the jury from Olivier's first murder trial. She had arrived at Snaresbrook Crown Court earlier than planned and had been sitting in the car park browsing through the Carole Lewis murder investigation file. Henley felt an odd sense of detachment as she scanned the witness statements and CRIS reports on her iPad. She missed the feel of paper between her fingers. There were times where she was convinced that she could almost smell a victim's blood through an officer's notebook.

Henley didn't flinch when the crime scene photographs appeared on the screen. Carole had made no attempt to run. Her handbag, clasped shut and splattered with blood, was no more than a few inches from her head. The blue floral dress that she was wearing was hitched up around her waist. She was wearing no knickers and the blood from the stab wounds to her stomach had run like a river and congealed in her pubic hair.

There had been evidence of sexual intercourse. Spermicide and lubricant were found in her vagina and there were traces of semen in her throat. DNA from three different men had been recovered from her body.

Henley understood why Lancaster's attention had quickly switched to the husband. Jealousy, adultery, younger woman and an older husband. Ramouter had also discovered that the location where Carole Lewis was found was popular for dogging. All of the boxes were ticked for a crime of passion and for defense lawyers to jump on the "loss of control" defense on behalf of her husband, but none of that sat right with Henley. Four condoms and Carole's wedding and engagement rings were found in her bag, but her mobile phone was missing. An eyewitness had given a statement that a woman matching Carole's description had bumped into him and his wife as they were leaving the park. The wife had said that the woman had run into them as though she was late for something, not running away from someone.

Henley was sure of two things when she closed down the file. Carole Lewis had known her killer and she had arranged to meet him.

Alan Lewis wasn't much of a looker. His thinning gray hair was pulled back tightly into a ponytail. The skin on his scalp was red and flaky. His brown eyes, which sat uncomfortably on folds of pale white skin, darted up from Henley's warrant card to her face. He licked his thin lips before he answered.

"I'm busy. Can't this wait?"

"Well, I'm more than happy to chat to you here," replied Henley, sitting on the white, crackled Formica-covered table.

The security gate beeped manically in unison with Alan's irritated puffs as he walked through them and headed toward the door.

"So, it's not enough that I've got to put up with you lot fronting up at my house whenever you feel like it and turning the place upside down, but I've got to put up with you turning up at my place of work as well," said Alan as he walked in the direction of the large pond that was flanked with Canada geese. He stopped at a bench and pulled out a bag of tobacco and cigarette papers. "Where's that other one? The brunette. Sergeant Lancaster."

"I'm not with Wood Green CID." Henley walked around Alan and sat down on the bench. The view of the pond was more enticing than a court building that had once housed unwanted children.

"Who are you with, then?"

"The Serial Crime Unit."

Alan stopped rolling up his cigarette and flakes of tobacco floated down onto the grass. "Why on earth would you lot want to speak to me?"

"Because I don't think that I'm sitting here talking to Carole's murderer, that's why. I've got a few questions for you and a request." Henley kept her eyes focused on the geese making their way into the water.

"You believe me. You believe that I didn't kill her?"

Henley turned to look at Alan just in time to see his shoulders sink with relief.

"They had me in that police station for over two days. Do you know what it's like to sit in a cold cell where you can smell your own piss and shit and then they have the bloody cheek to ask you if you want breakfast?"

Henley waited until Alan had regained his composure. "Your wife. How long were you married for?"

"Six years." Alan pulled a lighter out of his back pocket and sat down on the other end of the bench. "I met her… I met her in the park."

Henley noticed the hesitation in his voice. "What were you doing in the park when you met her?"

"The sort of activities that don't involve an actual dog, if you get my meaning, Inspector."

Henley didn't ask him to elaborate.

"We met up a few times. I asked her out for a drink. She was nice, we liked the same things and the rest is history."

"Her body was found in the park in Highgate Woods."

"I know. We agreed that when we got married that we would stop the dogging and we did for about five months, but then she wanted to go back. It's like she needed the attention. I didn't want to share her but she's...was stubborn. I wasn't enough for her. I just wanted her to be careful. I would take her, not to watch because I'm not into that now, but I knew that there were times when she went on her own."

"So, when she didn't come home you weren't surprised."

"No, I was. She always came home. She was good like that. I have a second job. I work security at a club in Kings Cross. I would get home from there about 4 a.m. and she was always home by four-thirty. That was the time the buses would start running again. The morning she didn't come home, I knew something was wrong. I called her phone, but it kept ringing. I went to the park to look for her, but she wasn't in the usual place. I called the police and told them that she was missing but they just shrugged it off. And then later in the afternoon that bloody DS Lancaster was at my front door." Alan took a long drag of his cigarette.

"You told DS Lancaster that you were with Dawn Bradley the night your wife was killed but your alibi didn't check out."

"Have you met Dawn's husband? I'm not surprised that she denied it. Knowing Dawn, she must have used a different name."

"Did Carole ever talk to you about being a juror on the Peter Olivier murder trial?"

"Did she talk about it? She wouldn't shut up about it. She thought that she was so important traipsing up to the Old Bailey every day."

"What did she tell you about it?"

"I told you. Everything. That she was a juror on the Jigsaw Killer case. How he cut up the bodies. How attractive she thought that Olivier guy was, that he was—" He grimaced. "Charming? Can you imagine? There were times that I actually thought she was sick in the head."

"What about the other jurors? Did she ever talk about them?"

"A couple. She talked about a girl called Zoe. They used to meet up for drinks sometimes."

"Anyone else?" Henley scribbled the information down in her notebook.

Alan rubbed at the graying bristle on his chin. "There was some woman that she couldn't stand. Called her Agatha Christie on cocaine. Then there was *him*."

Henley stopped writing. "Him?"

"I can't remember his name. But he used to phone her all the time. I took a look at her phone and I saw the text messages from him."

"Was she sleeping with him?"

"She denied it, but the things that he was saying. You don't talk that way unless you've been intimate. Do you know what I mean?"

"Can you remember his name?"

Alan shook his head. "Nah." He glanced down at his watch. "How much longer is this going to take?"

"I'm nearly done. I just need your permission."

"Permission for what?"

"To exhume your wife's body."

Alan's face paled. "What the fuck for?"

"We believe that her murder might be connected to a series of murders that the SCU is currently investigating."

"You want to dig her up?" He shook his head in disbelief, the cigarette smoldering away between his fingers. "And you think that this same person killed my Carole?"

"It's a possibility, but we can't be sure until we—"

"Dig her up?"

Henley nodded. "I'm sorry."

"What you apologizing for? You didn't kill her." Alan stamped out the cigarette on the bench and flicked the butt toward the pond. He breathed out so sharply that it sounded like a whistle. "Fine. Do it. Do what you need to do. As long as it puts me in the clear, you can dig her up."

52

"Surprised to see me?" Olivier leaned against the doorframe and pushed the hood off his head.

"I…er…what the…" Blaine was in shock. He looked past Olivier to see if there was anyone in the hallway. "How did you get into the block?" he asked. He turned off the light in his flat, hopeful that might just make the man standing in front of him…disappear.

"The security in this building is lax. Any ol' Tom, Dick or Harry could walk in off the street." Quick as a flash, Olivier pushed past Blaine and entered the flat, turning the light back on.

"I told you that the police have already been to see me," Blaine said. He followed Olivier but hesitated in the doorway, reluctant to be in the same room as him. "They've been calling me, checking up on me. They could have someone watching me right now, you don't—"

"Calm. The. Fuck. Down," Olivier said. He opened the fridge, took out a can of beer and opened it. "You're giving me a headache."

"You shouldn't be here."

Olivier eyed him over the can. "I'm not staying. I just need something from you."

Blaine couldn't think what Olivier could possibly want from him when the police already had their eyes on him. "Like what?" he finally asked. Olivier stepped forward quickly, causing Blaine to jump back.

"Why so jumpy?" he laughed. "You had no problem with me when you were coming to see me inside. Look"—Olivier held up his hands—"no handcuffs this time."

Blaine finally mustered up the courage to turn his back on Olivier. He walked into his small living room and checked that the curtains were tightly closed. Olivier sat down and stretched out on the sofa. Blaine stood by the window, unsure what to do.

"Everyone's looking for you." Blaine moved across the room and sat down in his armchair, as far away from Olivier as he could get.

"I'm aware of that," said Olivier. "But one thing I've learned is that the police never look in the most obvious places."

"What do you want from me?" Blaine couldn't hide the tremor in his voice.

Olivier sighed heavily and dropped his head back onto the cushions. "Have you got a decent Indian around here?" he asked.

"What?"

"Indian. Food. Takeaway. A little man on a moped who will deliver it to your house."

"Yeah, there is, but—"

Olivier jumped to his feet, took hold of Blaine's neck and pushed him hard against the wall.

"You're probably thinking that you should have left," Olivier whispered into Blaine's ear and squeezed his fingers around his throat. "You should have packed your little wheelie bag and disappeared the second you heard I was out."

Olivier released his grip. Blaine coughed, the sharp intake of air rattling his chest.

"They're going to think I helped," Blaine said weakly as he slid to the floor. "I can't go back inside."

"I don't think you have much of a choice. They'll pin something on you." Olivier walked over to the sofa and picked up a laptop. "How do you think this copycat feels about me being out? Will he be pleased, or will he be pissing his pants like you? It might even turn him on."

"I don't... I have no idea," Blaine said. He coughed again and touched his bruised neck gingerly.

"My original case files, your notes from my trial. The papers from your own trial. Are they here? You said you kept everything," asked Olivier.

Blaine nodded and pointed at the files and folders held together by elastic bands on the bottom shelf of his bookcase.

"All of them?"

"Everything," Blaine replied, his voice hoarse.

"Good." Olivier opened the laptop and pressed a button. "Password, please. Hurry up, I won't bite."

Blaine hesitantly stood up, walked over and entered his password.

"Thank you kindly."

"What are you doing?" Blaine asked.

Olivier didn't answer. He continued to type away and drink his beer. After a couple of minutes, he looked Blaine square in the eye and said, "I am helping the police with their inquiries."

53

Daniel Kennedy. Zoe Darego. Sean Delaney and Carole Lewis. The names were written in red removable ink on the whiteboard.

"You're absolutely sure that Lewis needs to be on the board?" asked Pellacia. Henley glanced over at Ramouter, who was staring at their boss, his eyes wide with disbelief.

"Of course she's sure," Joanna said before walking past and dumping a pile of papers on Ramouter's desk.

"I'm just playing devil's advocate," Pellacia continued. "We've got a gap of four months between Lewis's murder and Kennedy and Darego being found. Then we have *how* they were killed. Kennedy, Darego and Delaney were all dismembered. Lewis wasn't—her throat was cut."

"It was a bit more than her throat being cut." Henley pulled a large evidence bag filled with letters toward her. "Whoever it was almost cut her head off. It may have been a more opportunistic killing but there was still a degree of planning involved. My gut tells me that she went to that park expecting to meet somebody specific, someone she knew. I just don't know who."

"Your gut isn't enough, I'm afraid. What about the DNA that was found on her?" asked Pellacia. "Any matches?"

"There were two, her husband and Gary Wilkins. Stanford arrested and interviewed Wilkins last night. He admitted to having sex with Carole earlier that night. He says it wasn't the first time and that she was one of the regulars who met in Highgate Woods. He says that he was already at work at the time Carole was murdered but he's changed jobs since then and Stanford is having trouble finding his old site manager. The third was unidentified."

"Is it possible that our killer is one of the other men she slept with?"

Henley shook her head. "We can't rule it out, but the DNA from the unidentified match was found under Lewis's fingernails and from the dried semen on her legs. It wasn't found inside of her. I don't think that our killer had penetrative sex with her."

"I know that we're looking at Blaine and now this Gary Wilkins as viable suspects, but what about the other two jurors who were done for contempt? They're part of the reason why the original trial fell apart. Have you spoken to them?" Pellacia asked Ramouter.

"Pine works full-time as a paramedic, so it's been a bit tricky arranging to meet him because of his shift times, but we're seeing Naylor later—not that he was pleased about it."

"How far did you get with tracing the other jurors?" Pellacia asked.

"It took most of the morning, but I found them," Ramouter said. "There's a couple that we don't have to worry about for the time being. Naomi Spencer is in Vietnam on honeymoon. She left about a month ago and is not due back for another two and a half weeks. Kushal Bollasingham is serving a sentence at High Down. Eighteen months for benefit fraud. He's scheduled for early release next April. Then we've got Hamilton Bryce. He moved to Manchester last year. I asked him if he had been in touch with any of the jurors after the trial and he confirmed that he hasn't."

"Hopefully, we don't have to worry about Bryce. With the exception of Lewis, our copycat seems to be confining his movements to south London, but we should still ask Greater Manchester Police to keep an eye on him," Henley suggested.

Pellacia nodded his agreement.

"That just leaves Alessandro Naylor, Jessica Talbot, Dominic Pine and Michael Kirkpatrick," said Ramouter, folding his list in half. "What do we do now? We can't just rock up at their front doors and tell them that they're possible targets for a serial killer."

"We're going to have to."

"What did the UKPPS say about protecting the remaining jurors?" asked Pellacia.

Henley groaned as she recalled her infuriating conversation with Gia Mapess, the London director of the UK Protected Person Services.

"She was more concerned about policy and procedure than applying her common sense," said Henley. "They need to review the case in order for them to assess the level of threat against our jurors."

"A serial killer running around London isn't enough of a threat?" asked Pellacia.

"Not until they say so and then it's up to the jurors to give their consent as to what sort of protection they want…personal alarms, police patrols—"

Henley was interrupted as the phone on her desk began to ring. She recognized the number on the display; it was Anthony's direct line.

"What's happened to your mobile?" said Anthony. "You weren't picking up, so I thought I'd try to get you the old-fashioned way."

Henley cradled the phone into her neck, reached into her bag and pulled out her mobile. There were five missed calls from

Anthony, but the phone was on silent mode. "Sorry about that. So what's the urgency?"

"Your head."

"Excuse me?"

"Your head. The one that was unceremoniously dumped at your house. I've got an ID for you. Check your email."

Henley woke up her computer and opened the attachment in Anthony's email. The man looking back at her was smiling. The curls of his thick black hair fell onto his forehead. He looked like he was in mid-twenties.

"His name is Elliot Shen Cheung. Twenty-four years old when he disappeared." Henley enlarged the photo on the smart-board. "The e-fit was circulated and went live on the Missing Persons Unit website last week. About two hours ago the unit received an alert that there was a possible identification."

"So who is he?" asked Ramouter. "And what did he do to Olivier?"

"Originally from Hong Kong," Henley continued. "Came over when he was eighteen to go to university in Cardiff. He moved to London when he graduated and was working for an advertising firm in Hoxton Square. He was reported missing by a friend a week before his body, minus his head, was discovered, but apparently no one had seen him for at least two weeks prior to that."

"What about his employers? They didn't think that it was odd that he hadn't turned up for work?" asked Pellacia.

"They said it wasn't the first time that a junior member of staff hadn't bothered to turn up," said Henley.

"Who made the identification?" asked Ramouter.

"The MPU received two alerts. The first alert came from a Tanya Dunnett. She was Elliot's girlfriend, but they broke up about a week before he disappeared."

"And the second?"

Henley could feel the scars on her stomach tightening as she examined the photograph of a smiling Elliot Cheung, who was now lying in six separate parts in the mortuary.

"It was Peter Olivier."

"Excuse me?" said Pellacia. "Peter Olivier contacted the MPU?"

"He didn't call them. It was done yesterday afternoon, via the website. I've already spoken to Ezra and he's trying to track the IP address that Olivier used."

"If it *was* Olivier," said Pellacia. "There are some strange people out there. For all we know, it could be someone claiming to be him."

"It's a possibility," Henley agreed. "But I wouldn't put anything past Olivier. The most important thing is that we've got an identification."

"So, who the hell is Elliot Cheung?" asked Pellacia. "I don't remember coming across that name when we were looking at the rape allegations that Olivier made."

"And he's too young," said Henley. "Cheung was twenty-four when he went missing. There's a reason why Olivier went for him. To pick some random? It doesn't fit his pattern."

Pellacia's forehead crinkled with concentration. Henley didn't need to ask him what he was thinking. She knew.

"You're worried that this case is getting out of hand?" she said.

"We're running this copycat murder investigation; Olivier is on the run and we're effectively looking at reopening a murder case."

"We're not reopening a murder case. All we need to do is find out how Olivier is connected to this Elliot Cheung."

"And why he arranged for Cheung's head to be delivered to your house."

"I already know the answer to that," said Henley. "It's because he's a sick fuck."

54

Despite his best efforts, in the end, Blaine had pissed himself. Olivier smirked at the memory. Blaine had whimpered while Olivier held a kitchen knife to his throat, telling him where his body parts would wash up if he called the police. The whimpering failed to cover up the sound of Blaine's piss running down his bare legs. He thought that Blaine would have shown a bit more appreciation for leaving him alive, but thinking about it now, maybe he should have put Blaine out of his misery.

Olivier leaned over the wrought iron railings and looked down into the dirty waters. He watched as two swans navigated their way around floating plastic bottles. The tide was high. He felt fine drops of river water splash up toward his hands as the Thames broke against the river wall. Scraps of blue-and-white police tape were wrapped around the railings, fluttering against his knees. A nearby yellow sign appealed for witnesses to a murder.

Olivier looked across the river at Docklands. There were new buildings now and an abundance of cranes, with bright red lights on them, stretching into the sky.

He should have kept running. He could have jumped on

the back of a truck, heading the other way, toward Calais. He reached into his jacket pocket and pulled out a folded piece of newspaper that he found on the floor of the car he had stolen. Page seven of the *Evening Standard* from the other day. He ran a calloused thumb across the story on the top of the page. Victim identified. Daniel Kennedy. The first one.

"Fucking amateur," Olivier muttered as he reread how Daniel Kennedy's body was found at the bottom of the Watergate Steps, a mere four feet from where he now stood.

It had all started here. In some way, he should have been grateful for the copycat. The murder of Kennedy had acted as a catalyst. The ignition for Olivier to finally put his escape plan into action.

Olivier breathed in the scent of the river and wondered briefly if the copycat had stood in this same spot and if he had smelled the blood of murder on his skin. Olivier smiled to himself, but there was no humor in it. Henley had been right. This person, this copycat, was a poor imitation of him. Olivier had no intention of sitting back while the copycat took liberties. He ripped up the article and watched the wind carry away the shreds. He would not be reading in a paper that Henley had caught the copycat. No. The paper was going to report that Henley had found the pieces of the copycat that Olivier was going to leave behind.

55

"Is this a windup? It has to be a windup?" Jessica Talbot stood in the middle of her messy living room with her eight-month-old son on her hip and her two-year-old son on the floor surrounded by puzzle pieces and toy cars.

"I'm afraid this isn't a windup," said Henley. The two-year-old waddled over to Ramouter and handed him a Lego.

Jessica Talbot's face grew ashen. She stumbled backward and fell onto the sofa. Her son giggled in her arms as though it was just another game his mum was playing with him.

"I don't even remember them. The others. Why would anyone kill them?"

"That's what we're trying to find out. We've already arranged for police protection for you. The two officers who are going to be looking after you will be here to introduce themselves in a few minutes."

"Protection? I've got three kids. My mum's gone and broken her bloody leg… I've got… I can't. My husband won't like this one bit. This is too much."

"I'm really sorry, but the safety of you and your family is paramount," Henley said firmly.

"What about my daughter? She's eight, she's in school. What are we supposed to do? How can you protect us? You couldn't protect those three other jurors." Jessica's voice grew more frantic.

"Jessica, please calm down."

"How am I supposed to calm down when there's a serial killer after me?"

"We're not going to let anything happen to you. You have my word."

"You can promise me that, can you?" Jessica tried to stop her son from grabbing handfuls of her hair. Her voice dropped to a violent whisper. "You can promise my kids that their mum isn't going to be cut up into pieces and dumped in the middle of a gas station?"

The reaction from Michael Kirkpatrick, juror number ten, wasn't much different.

"I never wanted to do jury service in the bloody first place." Michael closed the door to the conference room on the twenty-fourth floor of TL Global Banking in the city. His heavy arrogance matched the thick dark rain clouds that had obscured the top of the Gherkin and the Shard. He seemed like the sort of man who advocated antihomeless spikes outside his office building.

"Do you know how much it cost me to sit on that jury for two weeks? I would have been better off paying the court for me not to be there. As if a fiver a day, for lunch, and paying for my Oyster card would cover it."

"You do understand what we're telling you?" Ramouter asked.

Michael made himself an espresso and grabbed a Danish from a stack of baked goods.

"I doubt very much that anyone would be coming after me," he said with a full mouth.

Henley couldn't suppress a fit of sardonic laughter.

"Michael, I'm not standing here wasting your time. This is serious."

"How am I supposed to work? I've got meetings with some very important people and I've got to be in New York next month. Are the Old Bill going to be following me to every meeting?"

"If it means that you don't end up cut into—how many pieces was it, Detective Ramouter? Five?" Henley asked, her head cocked to one side.

"Six," Ramouter answered, his face impassive.

"That's right. He cut off their heads," Henley continued. For the first time since they had been talking, Michael looked concerned.

"You may not see New York if we don't catch this killer, but if you're happy to take the risk, then I'm sure I can redirect the resources elsewhere," Henley said, knowing full well that Michael would now be taking as much protection as possible.

Dominic Pine looked unimpressed when he opened the front door and Henley held up her warrant card. "Is this about last night?" he asked.

"What happened last night?" asked Henley.

"My neighbors upstairs kicking off."

"No, it's not about that. You spoke to my colleague this morning." She stepped aside so that Dominic could see Ramouter.

"Afternoon. TDC Ramouter," he said.

"Oh, sorry," said Dominic. "It completely slipped my mind. Long shift last night."

The door pushed back against Henley's face and there was the sound of metal against metal as the security chain was pulled back.

"Thank you," Henley said, stepping into the hallway. Ramouter closed the door behind them.

Henley sniffed. The flat smelled as though the windows had

never been opened and the hallway was in a desperate need of a makeover. The pattern in the carpet was obscured by caked-in dirt and the wallpaper was faded and peeling, but there was something else about the flat that she couldn't identify.

"Do you mind if I put something on? I feel a bit funny standing here talking to you in my boxers?"

Dominic Pine came back in tracksuit bottoms and a blue T-shirt that was inside out. He invited them to sit in the living room.

"So, if you're not here about those nutcases upstairs, what is this about?"

"As I said, Detective Ramouter and I are from the Serial Crime Unit."

"Why does that ring a bell?"

"In 2017, you were a juror on the Peter Olivier murder trial."

"I heard that he's escaped. It's all over the news. Have they caught him yet?"

Henley ignored the question. "We're investigating a series of murders that are linked to the original trial."

"What's that got to do with me? You know that I was kicked off that trial, don't you? I spent three months in prison because of it. Am I at risk? Is that why you're both here?"

Dominic laughed. Henley glanced at his bookshelves, filled with DVDs and an ancient set of red bound encyclopedias. She let the silence linger as the faint voices of the arguing couple trickled in from upstairs.

"It's possible that you may be a target," said Henley. "Three of the jurors that you sat with on the original Jigsaw Killer murder trials have been murdered. Last week the bodies of the jurors Daniel Kennedy, Zoe Dar—"

"Jesus Christ. I think that I'm going to be sick," Dominic said as he got up and walked out of the living room.

Henley followed him to the small galley kitchen where he was throwing up into the sink. She rubbed his back. The countertop was covered with grains of brown sugar and coffee granules. The neglect and the sense of abandonment reminded Henley of her dad's house. Henley looked out of the kitchen window and felt a pang of guilt as a marked police car made its way into the estate. How much protection could they actually give Dominic Pine and the others?

"Does it have to be a marked police car?" Alessandro Naylor had told Henley and Ramouter that he lived with his aunt and uncle and had refused to let them inside the house. "You may be in plainclothes, but you have the look of feds. They're not too keen on you lot around here, so the last thing I need is for the neighbors to see me inviting you in."

"It's a marked car for a reason," said Henley.

"So, this is all legit. I saw that Olivier had done a runner, but I didn't think that had anything to do with me."

"But you saw the news about the others?"

"Two months ago, the geezer across the road was found with a bullet in his head in the middle of his kitchen. Last Tuesday, two gangs of kids decided to have themselves a little knife fight in the park. So, to be quite honest, those three people you mentioned wouldn't have been a blip on my radar."

"Fair enough." Henley didn't have the energy to push the matter any further. "I wanted to meet you to see if you could think of any reason why anyone would be targeting you and the others?"

Alessandro shook his head as he flicked the cigarette butt into the gutter. "None. I told you. After that trial, my life went to shit for a while. I made a mistake. I just got carried away, I suppose, and I paid for it. I came out of prison and I've kept my head down. I took a job with my uncle's plumbing company, not that I like cleaning up people's shit, but it is what it is."

"Did you ever keep in touch with the other jurors?"

"What for? Like I said, I've tried not to think about it. We

were just twelve people randomly thrown together. I didn't really know them and to be honest I forgot about them as soon as
I got carted off to Pentonville prison."

"Over the last couple of weeks has there been anything to
cause you concern? Suspicious behavior? Nuisance calls?"

"Other than the usual 'Do you want to change your energy
supplier?' calls, nothing at all. Do you think Olivier killed the
others?"

"No. They died before Olivier escaped."

"Can't you put me in witness protection or something? You
already know that I'm not keen on you lot being parked up
outside, and if I'm honest, I wouldn't mind a bit of a holiday."

56

A police officer was standing guard outside Karen Bajarami's room. Henley recognized him from Plumstead police station. He was efficient enough as an officer, but it was times like this that Henley wished that the Met had never got rid of the minimum height requirements for new recruits.

"Has she had any visitors?" Henley asked.

The officer stood up a little bit straighter. "Not since I took over, ma'am. She was last seen by the nurse about forty minutes ago, but that's been it. There's been no personal visitors. I'm not sure if she's awake though."

"Thanks," replied Henley before turning to Ramouter. "How about you take the lead? I honestly don't have the brain capacity to deal with this."

Ramouter looked knackered after spending most of the day driving around London but he was able to find some enthusiasm. Still keen to impress.

"Really? That would be great." Ramouter pulled out his notebook and pen.

The officer stepped aside and opened the door. Karen had been moved to a room that was usually reserved for patients who were able to pay privately. The curtains were a warm sunshine yellow and a painting of the Embankment at night hung on the wall above an actual armchair. The TV was on but Karen wasn't watching. She was facing the window.

Ramouter cleared his throat. "Excuse me, Ms. Bajarami."

Karen turned and Henley stifled a gasp. Her left eye was bandaged and the bruises on her face had turned various shades of purple. Her jaw was swollen and a cannula in her left arm connected to a pump on the side of the bed. Henley wondered what state Ade Nzibe and the security guard were in if Olivier had done this much damage to Karen.

"Oh God. Is it that bad?" Karen gingerly raised a hand to her forehead. "I haven't looked. You know what, don't tell me."

Ramouter glanced at Henley before he answered. "We've met before. At the prison."

Karen nodded as she eased herself up. "They took away my morphine first thing this morning. Kermit the frog was sitting in that chair last night and it all seemed perfectly normal."

"Morphine will do that to you," said Ramouter. "We're not going to keep you long. We just want to get a better picture about what happened here yesterday."

Karen closed her one good eye for a moment before she began talking. "The doctors had said that they were happy with Olivier's progress. He would have gone straight to the health wing once we got back to Belmarsh. We told the doctors that Olivier should be restrained but they didn't listen. Anyway, I was sitting outside his room and all of sudden I heard a crash and Ade—" Karen winced and took a breath. "Could I get some water, please?"

"I'll get it." Henley walked to the bedside cabinet, poured a glass of tepid water into the plastic cup and handed it to her. "That will be the morphine. It makes you thirsty."

Karen took a couple of painful sips before handing it back. She leaned her head back on the pillow.

"Thank you," said Karen. "The bastard might have blinded me. I didn't sign up for this crap. Sorry."

"You don't have to apologize," said Ramouter. "So, you heard Ade?"

"Yeah. When I came in. Ade was… He was on the floor by the bed. There was blood coming from his head. I'm not sure what Olivier hit him with. Next thing I knew he'd grabbed me and pushed me to the ground…and… I didn't see the fork in his hand." Karen started to cry.

"Here." Henley pulled out the tissues from the box on top of the cabinet and handed it to Karen.

"Thank you. It was… The pain." Karen dabbed at her right eye. "I'm not sure what happened next. I must have passed out because the next thing I remember is waking up here. I don't understand how Peter could… How's Ade? Every time I close my eyes I can see him lying there."

"He's in surgery right now. He suffered blunt-force trauma to the head and has a clot on his brain."

Tears started to leak from Karen's eye. "And the security guard? They told me that Peter attacked him."

"Fractured collarbone, cheekbone and jaw. Broken nose and cuts to his face. It was more than an attack. Olivier looked like he enjoyed it."

"Jesus, I'm starting to think that I got off lightly. God, I'm so tired and my head is killing me."

"Is there anything else that you can think of? Did Olivier say anything once he came out of his coma?"

"He said something about finally having a view but that was—" Bajarami's head fell forward and she screamed out in pain.

"Ramouter, get a nurse. Now."

Henley put her arms around Bajarami and tried to comfort her as Ramouter ran out of the room.

"Don't worry. Help is coming," Henley said. Bajarami screamed out again and buried herself against Henley's chest. "We've got you."

★ ★ ★

"Olivier could have killed her," Ramouter said.

"I don't think that was his intention. She was just in his way."

"We should go," said Henley. "Let's hope that Ezra has found out where Olivier's been hiding."

Mark would call this the "cooling-off period," Henley thought to herself as she walked down Greenwich High Street. He had explained to Henley more than once that it was something that all serial killers would do. Taking a moment to enjoy the silence as they went back, temporarily, to their normal life. Henley wondered how long her killer's cooling-off period would be. Days, weeks, months.

Henley's stomach growled as she approached the chicken shop. She had been drinking overpriced coffee for most of the day, but hadn't eaten a thing. As she placed a hand on the shop door, her phone began to vibrate.

UNKNOWN CALLER flashed across the phone screen. Henley pressed the green button.

"Hello, Anjelica."

A shiver ran down Henley's back as Olivier's voice rang in her ears.

57

"How did you get my number?"

"Good afternoon to you too. Busy day?" asked Olivier.

"You could say that. I guess it's unlikely you'll tell me where you are?" Henley's voice was steady but inside she wanted to scream.

There was no reply from Olivier. Henley waited, listening to Olivier breathing until he broke the silence.

"I've been catching up on the news. You've been busy. How's the family?" he asked.

"Why don't you hand yourself in?"

"Why would I do that? I can feel the sun on my face, the wind in my hair."

"I wouldn't get used to it."

Olivier laughed. A deep, sarcastic, pitying laugh.

"Why are you hiding?" Henley asked, her stomach in painful knots.

Olivier whistled softly down the phone, saying nothing.

"Are you keeping an eye on me? I don't think I'm the one you should be worried about." Henley prayed that Olivier didn't pick up on the quaver in her voice.

"Meaning?" Olivier asked, bored.

"There's someone out there pretending to be you, taking credit for your particular…brand of killing. Who would do that? Who have you been talking to?"

"You keep asking me these questions. All I wanted was to hear your voice. You've got me all caught up in my feelings."

A deliveryman came out of the chicken shop, so Henley walked back onto the main street.

"I thought you would be grateful to hear from me. Life must be pretty lonely for you now that your husband and little girl have left."

Henley stopped dead in her tracks. The deliveryman hit the brakes on his moped, there was the screech of tires and a car horn beeped.

"Oi, you stupid cow!" shouted the deliveryman, swerving around Henley. "Watch where you're going!"

"How do you know that—" Henley said, sprinting across the road.

"Don't play stupid."

Henley stopped at the stairs leading up to the police station. She felt her throat tighten and the muscles in her legs weaken. She placed a hand on the rusty railings.

"You were at my house?"

Silence from Olivier.

"You were at my house?" Henley repeated, her voice louder this time.

Olivier laughed. "I've been in prison, Inspector." There was a pause that seemed to last a lifetime. "But maybe someone sent me a gift. A little video. Maybe."

Henley couldn't breathe.

"And maybe I saw your lovely house. You opening the door, your husband coming up the path. He's not how I imagined he would be. You told him not to move, but men. They never listen."

"Someone sent you a video?"

Olivier was silent.

"What do you want?" Henley was bordering on panic now. "What do you want from me?"

Olivier ignored the question. Instead, he said, "A word of advice, Anjelica. Be careful crossing the road next time. That moped nearly took you out."

Henley looked down at the phone, but the call had ended. She looked around wildly and then sat down on the steps heavily. Panic was sweeping over her in waves. When Olivier had stabbed her, the fear had been centralized. Now, she was trying to defend herself against something, someone, she couldn't see. There was a slight chill in the air, but Henley was sweating. And even though she hadn't eaten since last night, Henley threw up in the middle of the street.

58

He had been watching her.

When every police force in the United Kingdom had been watching the airports and train stations, chasing every wild goose, no one had thought that he would come for her.

"How did Olivier get your number?"

Henley looked up at the NCA agent who had asked her the question. He used to be DS Bailey, based in CID, at Charing Cross. He usually worked on serious fraud cases. She wondered who he had pissed off to end up on a babysitting case where no one knew where the baby was.

"Chance Blaine, maybe? I gave him my card. But Olivier is resourceful. He always has been. Someone could have just transferred him directly to me. Have you checked with the central switchboard?" said Henley, inching herself closer to the window. They were all squeezed inside Pellacia's office.

"We'll get someone on it. Are you sure that he was out there watching you?"

"If she said that he was there, then he was out there," Pellacia said defensively from behind his desk.

"He told me to be careful crossing the road. He wouldn't

have said that if he hadn't seen my near miss with an idiot on a moped," said Henley.

"And you didn't notice anything out of the ordinary when you left the hospital?"

"No. As I told you, Ramouter and I came back from the hospital. I parked the car. Ramouter went into the station and I went across the road to get something to eat. My phone rang. It was an unknown number. I had no reason to suspect that Olivier was even in the area until he told me to be careful."

"That's good news," said Agent Bailey. "It means that he's got no intention of going anywhere. He's staying in the area. Sorry, I know that's not good news for you."

"Great. He's been in our neck of the woods all this time. What exactly has the NCA been doing?" asked Pellacia.

"You saw Olivier three times before he escaped?" Agent Bailey asked, ignoring Pellacia's question.

"Are you seriously suggesting his escape is Henley's fault?" Pellacia shouted.

Agent Bailey didn't flinch as he kept his attention on Henley. "Of course not, but he called you, Anjelica. He's trying to get close to you. You've got a kid, haven't you?"

Henley nodded.

"Your colleague DS Stanford said that your husband and daughter are in Kensal Green. We've sent our own officers to them. Just as a precaution. I'm sure that everything is OK. What about the head that was delivered to your home on Sunday? Have you got any further with that investigation?"

"We've tracked down the storage company and we've recovered the CCTV and the rental agreement. The details were fake," said Henley.

"And what about the leak to the press about these recent murders? Have you discovered who was responsible?"

"Is there a point that you're trying to make?" Pellacia snapped.

"Stephen. It's a small unit, you've got leaks," said Agent Bai-

ley. "This case is mutating into something else and your senior
investigating officer appears to be a potential target for a convicted murderer. You don't need me to tell you that things aren't
looking that great for you."

Henley could sense Pellacia bristling next to her. These men
were in his space, addressing him by his first name as if they
were peers, as though they would walk out of the SCU in a
couple of hours and sit around the table in the pub.

"What do you think he wants?" Agent Bailey asked Henley.

"I have no idea," Henley said, exhausted.

She was pissed at herself because it was one of the questions
that she should have asked him. *What do you want? How long
have you been watching me? Are you working with the copycat? Who
is he? Why me?*

Henley couldn't understand why Olivier was clinging on to
her like a leech. It was as if he knew that she was broken—easy
prey. Or maybe he could tell that she couldn't let him go.

Pellacia handed Henley a shot of brandy.

"I should be at home." She took a sip. "I need to speak to
Rob."

"Is that wise?"

"How can I not speak to Rob about what's going on?" Henley said wearily. "He's been watching my house. But why?"

Henley squeezed her eyes shut. She wanted to block out the
world. To disappear. She now understood what it meant when
someone said that they had been shaken to their core. She opened
her eyes to see Pellacia staring at her.

"It's not the same for him, is it?" Pellacia said.

"What do you mean?"

"The attention. If he calls the paper or he puts out a random
tweet, it's temporary. People will talk about him, but they're
not engaging with him. Olivier will only be a hot topic for as

long as it takes for another Z–list celebrity to start trending, but with you, he's always got your undivided attention."

"I don't like how this investigation is going," Henley said, changing the subject. "Our copycat goes to ground and Olivier rises up."

"Let's assume that they're not working together," said Pellacia. "What do you think Olivier will do next?"

"I don't bloody know," Henley snapped. "Maybe he'll come for you, finish what he started with me or try to find the copycat himself."

There was a knock on the door and Ramouter walked in without waiting for a response. Henley was about to tell him off, and then she saw the look on his face.

"What's wrong?" she asked.

"I didn't want to say anything in front of the agents, but we've got a problem." Ramouter handed Henley his phone.

Henley read the headline at the top of the *Evening Standard*. "Shit."

COPYCAT SERIAL KILLER TARGETING JIGSAW JURORS

"Shit, shit, *shit*!"

59

Two years earlier...

"The prosecution will be applying to discharge the jury and under the circumstances we have no reasonable grounds to object," Olivier's barrister, Brendan Turnmill QC, said.

The sound of Olivier tapping his fingers rhythmically against his case files filled the small consultation room.

"We're on day twelve," Olivier finally replied. "They haven't even finished their case yet and they want to get rid of my jury."

"That's correct," said Brendan.

"And we're not objecting?" Olivier pulled out a notepad and flicked through the pages. He stopped at *Tuesday. Day Two. Jury Panel.* He ran his index finger along the twelve names he had written down.

"No. We—"

"Which means that you lot have made a mistake." Olivier leaned back and looked across at his solicitor, David Samuels, who had been sitting silently next to Brendan doing everything he could to avoid Olivier's gaze.

"What have you done, Mr. Samuels?" Olivier's tone was hard

and demanding. "I doubt very much that it was our learned friend, Mr. Turnmill QC, who did something so monumentally stupid that it led to my jury being let go. He's the monkey. You're the organ grinder."

David swallowed hard and ran a finger around the collar of his shirt. The sound of a woman crying in the consultation room next door filtered through the cracks in the wall.

"What have you done?" Olivier asked again.

"Mr. Olivier," David said. "It's…well—"

"And where's Joseph?" Olivier asked. "You usually send that little shit to sit in on these conferences."

"That's the problem, Mr. Olivier," Brendan said, glancing over at David with an unmistakable look of disgust.

"I don't want to hear from you," said Olivier without taking his eyes off David.

David spoke softly as though his voice was being suffocated. "Joseph was—"

"Speak up," Olivier commanded.

"Last night Joseph was arrested and charged with perverting the course of justice by tampering with the jury. Your jury," David explained.

Olivier didn't respond as he looked down again at the jurors' names.

"He's allegedly passed on information to one juror and may have tried to bribe another," David continued. "He's being produced at Westminster Magistrates' Court today."

"Which ones?" Olivier asked.

"What ones?" David queried.

"Jurors. Mr. Olivier is asking which jurors!" Brendan replied exasperatedly.

"Oh, I don't think we need to concern ourselves with that right now. It's more important for us to focus on next steps."

"I asked you which ones did your idiotic little colleague tamper with?" Olivier shouted, lunging forward and grabbing David's tie. Brendan scrambled out of his chair and ran out of the room. David's iPad fell out of his hands and onto the concrete floor.

"Which ones?" Olivier asked again over the sound of a piercing alarm.

"The young black girl and…and—"

Olivier suddenly let go as two burly dock officers burst into the room.

"No harm done," said Olivier as he stepped back into the corner and held his hands up. "I was just letting my solicitor know that he was sacked."

Present day

"This all started with you," Olivier said. He pulled out a long piece of kebab meat from a grease-stained container and pushed it into his mouth.

"I shouldn't be here," Blaine said, moving closer to the church wall.

Olivier carried on walking. "They found number three right here." He stamped his foot on the concrete staircase where Sean Delaney's body had been found. The night sky encased the churchyard like a shroud. The minimal light came from the windows of a few flats overhead.

"Why would he dump Delaney down here?" Olivier walked over to Blaine.

"I told you before, they've been watching me," Blaine whispered as he tried in vain to back away from Olivier.

"Four bodies." He pulled out a large green chile from his kebab and threw it down the staircase.

"They've already spoken to Lorelei about me. They've been to my workplace. I can't do this anymore."

"Too bad for you I'm afraid, son."

"I know how the police think. That woman. Henley."

"Show some respect. She's Detective Inspector Henley." Olivier sat down on a nearby bench, patting the seat next to him.

Blaine dragged himself with resignation to the bench. "They think I did it. Killed those jurors."

Olivier laughed through a mouthful of chile-sauce-covered chips. "They probably think you're next," Olivier said.

"What do you mean?"

Even in the dimly lit church grounds, Blaine's face had visibly paled. Olivier enjoyed the slow, pleasurable thrill of taunting him. "Detective Inspector Henley probably wants to use you as bait," he continued. "She's cold like that. A bit like me."

"Is that what you're doing?" Blaine replied, his voice shaking. "Are you using me for—"

Olivier said nothing as he crushed up his takeaway box and threw it into the bushes.

"Do you think whoever is doing this will come for me?" Blaine's voice almost disappeared amid the siren of a passing ambulance and a couple screaming at each other from a nearby flat.

"I told you, this all started with you," said Olivier. "You and I have spent a lot of time talking and I remember everything you told me about Joseph McGrath."

"That's not my name anymore."

"That's not the point, boy. Now, let's think about this logically."

"Is that why you've made me come out here in the middle of the night—to be your sounding board?"

"Or maybe *I* am using you as bait." Olivier's words cut through the air like a blade. "All four of those dead jurors gave evidence in your trial," he continued. "Lewis, Kennedy, poor little Zoe and Delaney."

"But I didn't kill them," Blaine almost whined.

"For fuck's sake, shut up and listen. There were two more jurors who gave evidence against you."

"I... I... I don't remember."

"Of course you do. Two more jurors who got themselves in just as much trouble as you. Now, I need you to remember who you spoke to. Who seemed most eager to want to help you out? Who would want to please me, impress me?"

"I don't know."

"Your stupidity made my copycat. It's all cause and effect. You are going to help me track down those jurors."

"What if I say no?" Blaine replied unconvincingly. "I can go to the police right now and tell Henley that I need protection."

"You could do that, but then I would have no choice but to visit your girlfriend, Lorelei, cut off her head, put it in a box and leave another present on my girl's doorstep."

"You wouldn't. We're not even together anymore."

"Doesn't matter. Actually, maybe I'll go and do that right now as it looks like you need an incentive."

Blaine grabbed hold of Olivier's arm. "No, don't. Please."

"Let go," Olivier said, looking down at Blaine's hand.

"I'm sorry," Blaine stuttered as he stepped away.

"I'm going to find this copycat and you're going to help me."

"But what if he kills me? He could kill me."

Olivier smiled and tapped the side of Blaine's face. "If you die, then you die. Cause and effect, Mr. Blaine. Cause and effect."

60

Henley had woken up in a strange bed that morning, with an intense desire to just stay there. She hadn't had the energy the previous evening to fight Stanford when he had told her to go home, pack some things and stay at his house. She was mentally exhausted and in no mood to be taking part in a press conference.

Henley sat at the end of the table with Pellacia on her left and Chief Superintendent Larsen next to him. Pellacia had planned to read out a bog-standard statement: *We are not prepared to make any further comments in regard to the investigation.* But Chief Superintendent Larsen had other ideas. There were some people who relished the media spotlight, and the borough commander was one of them.

The media room was packed and stifling. Henley felt herself stiffen and focused on making sure that she looked as though she was in control. That she was someone who was in authority. The last thing that she needed was for Olivier to be out there watching her on TV, knowing that he'd got to her.

"Callum O'Brien. *Evening Standard.*"

Henley turned her gaze to the tall, skinny man in the front

row. It had been years since she'd last seen him. He hadn't changed.

"Inspector Henley, how can you be sure that Peter Olivier is not involved in the current spate of murders?"

"As you are aware," the Chief Superintendant said loudly, before Henley had even had a chance to open her mouth, "Peter Olivier escaped from custody nine days after the first three victims were found—"

First. It was only a small word but what it implied didn't bode well. From the corner of her eye she could see that familiar muscle in Pellacia's jaw start to tense with frustration. Callum took the bait.

"You mean there are more? Are you saying, Chief Superintendant, that you expect there to be more body parts being scattered on the streets of London?"

"That is not what I said." Larsen's words almost tripped over each other.

"'The first three bodies' is what you just said. Which means that there have been more than three victims."

"That is no more than speculation."

"Chief Superintendant, how can you call it speculation when, by your own words, less than a minute ago you confirmed that this copycat has killed more than three people?"

"As I was saying—"

"The victims were members of the jury from Peter Olivier's trial in 2017," Callum said loudly. "The trial of the Jigsaw Killer."

The cameras flashed viciously and the hum from the reporters grew louder. This is a shark pool, Henley thought.

"But isn't it correct that Carole Lewis is the fourth victim to be identified, and that the murder investigation has now been transferred from the Murder Squad at Wood Green police station to the Serial Crime Unit?" Callum sounded triumphant.

DS Lancaster. That bitch, Henley thought as she locked eyes

with Callum. She knew that Lancaster had been angry, but she hadn't expected her to go mouthing off to the press.

"I'm not prepared to comment on individual murder investigations," said Larsen.

"Tessa Botchway from the *Guardian*. Are you able to tell us why these jurors were targeted?"

Pellacia leaned toward the bank of microphones. "As the commissioner said, all lines of investigation are being pursued."

"This is a shitstorm," Henley muttered under her breath. Just then, Larsen's assistant appeared from the wings and whispered something into his ear.

"I'm sorry, but something has arisen and I'm going to have to leave. DSI Stephen Pellacia and DI Anjelica Henley, who are leading the investigation, can answer any remaining questions. I will leave you in their capable hands."

Henley and Pellacia exchanged a glance as Larsen practically ran through a side door.

"Inspector Henley? Oi, are you not going to talk to me?"

"Haven't you had enough, Callum?" Henley stopped in the middle of the car park. She could see Ramouter waiting for her next to the car.

"Long time no see, innit. You're looking well," said Callum.

"What do you want?"

"I was wondering why you were so quiet up there. I thought that you would have more to say, especially after your boss cocked it up."

"You know that I'm not one for the spotlight. Anyway, you got all your questions answered."

"Not the point though, is it? It would have been interesting, you being the senior investigating officer and being involved in the original investigations, to know your thoughts."

Henley shrugged and turned her back.

"I've just a quick question," Callum said.

"You had your opportunity to ask questions back inside."

"I know, but I wanted to talk to you. You're the one with all of the information."

"And there are rules—"

"When do you lot ever play by the rules? It's one question, that's all."

"Fine."

"Carole Lewis wasn't dismembered, was she?"

"No, she wasn't."

"So why have you taken over the investigation?"

"That's two questions, Callum."

"There wasn't something on the bodies, was there? I don't know… Like a mark or symbol?"

It wasn't just a random thought. Henley sensed that Callum was working off a credible leak and not a pie in the sky theory that had come to him while he stuffed his face with another sausage roll. There was only one person that Henley could think of who could have passed on that information about the symbols. DS Lancaster, bitter that Henley had ridiculed her by pointing out her ineptitude.

"You've got the notes from the press conference," said Henley. She clicked the unlock button on the key fob and indicated for Ramouter to get into the car. She walked toward the vehicle, Callum calling after her.

"But I wanted something from you. You are the great Jigsaw slayer aren't you, Inspector?"

Henley climbed into the car and slammed the door shut. "That stupid bitch," she said, starting the engine and waiting for the security gates to open.

"What's happened?" Ramouter asked as he reached for his seat belt.

"DS Lancaster has been leaking information to the press. I knew that she was pissed off, but this is… I don't understand how she thinks that she can get away with this?" Henley glanced at the rearview mirror and saw Callum standing in the same spot adjusting his laptop bag and smirking.

"What are you going to do? Grass her up? That will ruin her."

"That's exactly what I'm going to do. She can't fuck around with my investigation and get away with it."

61

As Henley had anticipated, the press conference had resulted in an influx of phone calls to the SCU. Pellacia had managed to convince someone on the upper floors of New Scotland Yard to transfer some experienced bodies to their team. Eastwood had been dispatched back to Belmarsh and Stanford was standing with two detective constables who she recognized from Peckham CID.

"I saw that car crash of a conference," said Stanford, walking over to Henley.

"I don't even want to talk about it," she replied. "Have you seen Ramouter?"

"I think he's downstairs with Ezra, but don't disappear on me. I've got some info for you."

"What is it?"

"Pellacia asked me to look into how Olivier got hold of the insulin. It came from the hospital wing. They finally did a stock check and discovered that three vials of insulin were missing and the insulin that was found in Olivier's cell has the same batch number."

"It has to be a prison officer that was helping him," said Henley as her mind flashed back to Karen Bajarami and Ade Nzibe.

"Wouldn't surprise me. Prison officers are just as corrupt as some of our police."

Henley walked into Ezra's room and looked around. "Where's the Boy Wonder?" she asked Ramouter.

"He's gone to get lunch. He should be back in a bit. There is good news though. We've finally got the enhanced footage from the storage facility."

"Have you had a chance to take a look?"

"I would have, but the files were password-protected." Ramouter turned the laptop in her direction. "But there is something else."

"What is it?" Henley pulled up a chair and sat down.

"Well, the appeal for witnesses might have produced a hit."

"For which victim?"

"Sean Delaney. Remember that his manager confirmed that he had been at work late on the Sunday night before he went missing. According to their records, he left the building at 9:42 p.m. His mobile phone showed that he got a call from… I'm not sure what to call them, clients, patients? Anyway, his name is Leon Merrick. I've been chasing him for the last couple of days and I managed to speak to him a little while ago."

"Get to the point." Henley immediately regretted her tone. "Sorry. I didn't mean to snap."

"Don't worry about it." Ramouter continued: "He says that the night Sean disappeared, he had been calling him for most of the day. He's a heroin addict, had been withdrawing and was desperate to talk to Sean. He couldn't get hold of him and ended up using. Says that it must have been a bad batch because it was the first time that he thought he was going to die. So, he goes to the center on the off chance that Sean or someone might be there. The front door is closed so he tries the back where the staff car park is. He's not too sure about the time but reckons that it was about Eight-ish."

"What did he see?"

"He thinks that he saw Sean passed out in the back of a car."

"You're joking?"

"No, he remembers seeing a car. He hesitated at first because for some reason he thought that it was a police car, but then he realized that it wasn't. He saw a white male standing next to the car and that the door was open. He thought that the man might have been a dealer, so he approached him and asked him for drugs, but the man told him to fuck off."

"Shit," said Henley. "Was there anything else that he remembered? A better description of the man with Sean?"

"Not really."

"Go on," said Henley, suddenly remembering that despite the chaos in her life at the moment she was supposed to be mentoring the trainee detective.

"Only that he remembers tapping on the window, but the man pushed him out of the way. After that, it's all a blur to him."

"It might still be an idea to get him in front of a sketch artist. You never know what could happen. We might finally get a break."

Henley turned around as Ezra came into the room. "You took your sweet time," she said.

"Good afternoon to you too," said Ezra as he dumped a greasy bag onto the table. "Burger and chips. Do you want some?"

"No thanks. We have work to do," Henley said, pointing to his computer.

"Sorry, boss, I'm on it." Ezra sat down at his desk and mirrored his laptop's screen to the television.

"Doesn't seem very exciting," Ezra said as CCTV footage of the front office of the storage facility filled the screen. "It's not long. Only three minutes."

"This is much better," said Henley as the video revealed an

assistant sitting at the desk. About thirty seconds later a woman came into view. With the enhanced footage Henley could clearly see that the woman was wearing a brunette wig that covered the sides of her face, obscuring her profile. She was wearing a denim jacket and black capri trousers. Dark glasses. Nothing memorable about her. Until the woman raised her right hand.

"Ez, pause it there." Henley stepped toward the screen. "Can you zoom in?"

"I can but not too much, otherwise you will just be looking at a bunch of pixels."

"What are we looking at?" asked Ramouter.

"Her right wrist. She has a tattoo. Does that look like stars to you?"

Ramouter squinted at the screen. "Yeah, it does, three of them. It would be better if she took off her glasses."

"Karen Bajarami has tattoos on her right wrist. Shooting stars that run from her arm to the back her hand. I noticed them when we were at Belmarsh."

"Do you think that it's her?" Ramouter asked.

Henley continued to watch the footage in silence. The woman took off her glasses and leaned over the counter as she signed some paperwork. For a brief moment, she gazed toward the camera, then turned to the door.

"Pause it, Ezra. It's her. That's Karen Bajarami."

62

Henley took the Carole Lewis investigation file to one of the empty offices on the third floor, away from the bustle of the incident room. She reviewed the list of twelve jurors. Twelve people thrown together by chance. Even after their names were selected there was no guarantee that they'd sit on an actual jury. They could have easily spent two weeks in a holding pen with 150 others, but again, randomly their names had been pulled out of an envelope and their fates had been sealed.

Five of the jurors were dead. One from natural causes, the other four by the hands of the copycat. The only question that was evading Henley was "Why?" What made these people such a target? It wasn't as if they were the ones who had found Olivier guilty after six days of deliberations.

Henley tapped the case file with her pen. She didn't even have a list of suspects. She had no idea how many people had been in that courtroom each day, watching those twelve jurors before they were discharged. The only thing that Henley knew for sure was that her killer wanted to be famous. He wanted to make a name for himself, place himself atop the headlines. At the end of the day that's what every serial killer or serial rapist wanted. Not anonymity.

Carole Lewis was the first juror. The test case. The lucky one in the sense that she hadn't ended up in pieces at the bottom of a stairwell or dumped in the bushes. Henley opened the file to the CRIS report. All 259 pages of it so far. The entire investigation had initially focused on the husband, even though no evidence pointed in that direction.

Henley frowned as she came across an entry dated two days after Carole Lewis's husband had been invited in for a voluntary interview.

05/03/2019 21:39

ADS 205276 DS THOMPSON

Susp has been arrested and interviewed in regard to the primary offence of MURDER.

Disc seat: D08765783H interviewed and arrested. Exhibit: JPH/1

Susp, Alan Lewis, stated that VIW1 had been harassed and complained about a stalker. Cannot recall the name but says that the VIW1 knew him but was not a friend. Recalls that VIW1 had reported the harassment to Muswell Hill Police Stn.

==========

MIT SUPERVISOR'S UPDATE
OIC actions seen and noted. CPU at Muswell Hill to be contacted—inquiries made re: any possible harassment allegations made by VIW1.

A sharp rapping at the door pulled Henley out of her thoughts. She was surprised to see Dr. Mark Ryan at the door.

"I was in the area and I thought I would see how you're doing," he said.

"You were in the area?" Henley stared hard at Mark.

"OK, I wasn't just in the area. Stephen called me."

Henley rolled her eyes.

"Don't be like that. I brought food. From that restaurant you were telling me about."

Henley looked down at the brown paper bags with the familiar logo of the Caribbean restaurant on Deptford High Street.

"That's guilty-conscience food."

"Of course it is."

"Did you get fried plantain?"

"Two portions and the Guinness punch."

"So, he told you about the delivery to my house?" Henley took the bags from Mark.

"Reason why I'm here, and I wasn't lying about being in the area. I was lecturing at the university. I left you messages."

"It's been manic. I should have called you back."

"How's Rob?"

"Over the moon. At his parents'," Henley replied, opening the containers. "No one cares that I'm upset. They're too busy applauding Rob for doing the right thing." Henley thought of Emma as she picked up a slice of plantain and put it in her mouth. "Emma would eat plantain all day if I let her. In fact, she just loves food. God knows what Rob's mum is making her eat. I shouldn't be blaming him for taking her somewhere safe. I know that I've gone about things the wrong way, but she's my child."

"We all do what feels right to us at the time. No one can blame you for being upset."

"But he took the choice out of my hands, Mark. I miss my baby. If I was coming home and reading *The Very Hungry*

Caterpillar to her for the millionth time, then it would be worth it, but I'm not."

"You're being too hard on yourself. You can't control everything."

"I can't control crazy people dumping severed heads on my doorstep or cutting up young girls into pieces and dumping them in the park like rubbish or even a delusional judge releasing a rapist and a kidnapper out into the streets, but I should be able to control what goes on inside my home. What use am I if I can't even do that?"

"Would you have preferred to have been the one to tell Rob to go instead of the other way around?"

"Don't psychoanalyze me, Mark."

Mark held his hands up in surrender. "Sorry, sorry. Force of habit. I'm here as a friend. Nothing else. So, the investigation?"

"Which one? Olivier being on the run or our copycat?"

"Copycat." Mark put his fork down and picked up his drink.

Henley nodded. "We think he may have killed someone back in May."

"There was a case in the States, about ten years ago. Two serial killers in Arizona who were competing with each other. Between the pair of them they must have killed about twelve people."

"You think that Olivier and the copycat are in competition with each other?"

"It's a theory. There has to be some explanation for why the copycat is using Olivier's exact method of killing his victims—"

"Not exactly the same. He induces some form of paralysis first, so we're assuming they can see what's being done to them." Henley mindlessly dissected the chicken on her plate.

"But if you put that to one side, the MO is exactly the same. They're both cutting up the bodies and discarding them."

"Olivier didn't keep trophies, but my copycat is."

"*My?*"

Henley ignored the look in Mark's eye. "Don't read too much into it. I just mean that it's my case. The point is that this copycat has taken Zoe's eyes, Kennedy's tongue and Delaney's ears."

"And you're sure that he's keeping them?" asked Mark.

"What else is he going to do with them? You're the expert."

"I don't think DS Stanford would agree with you, but you want to know why a killer would keep trophies?"

Henley nodded as she sipped on her Guinness punch.

"Human nature. People like to keep mementos from the big moments in their life. Once your copycat has got rid of the body, what proof does he have of his achievement? What better way for your copycat to impress Olivier and say to him, 'Look at me. Look at what I did for you.' Olivier didn't need any trophies. His agenda with his six attackers was simple. 'You violated and ridiculed me. I'll kill you.'"

"What about Elliot Cheung? He didn't attack Olivier or offend him in any way. There's no evidence that their paths crossed prior to Cheung's murder."

"I'll admit, I'm struggling with the motivation for Cheung's murder, but remember what I said the other day? Copycats want attention, but there has to be something about Olivier that the copycat has connected with as well and he wants to please Olivier."

Henley thought back to the word *impress*. "No." She shook the thought from her head. "Olivier wouldn't be impressed. It would piss him off. In fact, he was pissed off when I told him about the copycat. He wouldn't want to share the limelight. You called him a narcissist, remember?"

"I do. He *is* a narcissist." Mark wiped his hands with a napkin before pulling out a clear plastic folder from his rucksack. "I've been working on the copycat's profile. I suspect that there's some history of mental health problems, which may manifest as a result of being a victim himself."

"A victim of what?"

"Sexual violence. Like Olivier."

"But our copycat would have to be aware that Olivier was raped if that is something he's connected with."

"I think that's most likely. I've concluded that your copycat is a white male, thirty-five to forty years of age. Single, unable to form social attachments but intelligent and able to navigate himself in the working world without bringing attention to himself. Your copycat is being motivated by something that was done to him by your three, sorry, four victims."

"Is that why he's taken trophies?" Henley asked.

"I would definitely say that removing their eyes, ears and tongues and keeping them would be a reward for your copycat and it's also the final act of degradation," said Mark. "He's smart, organized and able to function. I also did some more research into the symbols. Olivier's brand."

"The crescent and double cross? I suppose it makes sense that the copycat would adopt them if he's trying to impress Olivier."

"But it's more than that. It's about duality. The crescent is the moon. It can be illuminating or dark and mysterious. Life and death."

"And the double cross?"

"Not a cross, but a double dagger. It literally means betrayal and revenge."

"Do you really think Olivier gave it that much thought?"

"Who knows." Mark shrugged. "For all I know he could just like it, but for your copycat, it's his way of saying, 'I'm you and you're me.'"

"I've got seven jurors who are still alive," said Henley. "Our copycat can't have issues with all of them?"

"If you ask me, it wouldn't make a difference if it was one person or all twelve who had offended your copycat in some way. He's identified them as a collective. All of your jurors are at risk until he is caught."

63

"I've got him," Ramouter shouted out, his Yorkshire accent coming out stronger than ever. "Guv, I've got the shitty little bastard. He's here. He's right there with her."

Henley ran over to Ramouter's desk.

"Look," Ramouter said as he rewound the footage.

A wave of sadness hit her as she watched Zoe Darego get off the 136 bus. She paused briefly and looked inside her bag before walking toward the zebra crossing. A man appeared at Zoe's side. Henley couldn't see his face, only the back of him. The man pulled Zoe to the side. Henley saw Zoe's lips moving but had no idea what she was saying. After seven seconds the man took hold of Zoe's arm and pulled her around the corner, just as a man and woman walked past. Henley watched, her anger rising, as the couple simply pointed at Zoe, and then turned and carried on walking.

"Don't worry. You'll see him," Ramouter said gently.

The camera switched angles. And there he was. Henley watched the footage showing Chance Blaine pushing Zoe against a tree, his face contorted in anger. The last thing the CCTV had picked up was Zoe hitting him in the face, before she ran out of view, leaving Blaine on the ground.

Henley parked her car on Burnt Ash Hill. A marked police car pulled up beside her, right behind a dark blue BMW 1 Series, with the estate agent's logo on the passenger side door. The lights were on at number 87. Blaine's house-viewing was due to finish in fifteen minutes.

Henley checked that she had her cuffs. Her head began to throb. The last time she had attempted to arrest someone she had ended up on her back, clasping her hands to her stomach, trying to stop the blood from flowing.

"Radio PC Downing and tell them to head to the back," said Henley. "The last thing we need is for Blaine to do a runner."

Ramouter pulled out his radio as Henley hit the doorbell. She pushed open the letterbox. She couldn't see anything, but she could hear voices. Henley banged on the door while PC Downing and his partner PC Raleigh jogged over.

Henley heard Blaine say: "That might be a sign from the universe. You're already getting visitors."

The door opened and the smile on Blaine's face disappeared. He turned around and looked at his clients.

"Chance Blaine, I'm arresting you for—"

Henley didn't get the chance to finish. Blaine spun around and sprinted down the corridor. Ramouter pushed past Henley and chased after him. The woman screamed as her boyfriend pulled her to the side.

"He's running!" Henley yelled into her radio. "Toward the back!"

Ramouter could hear Henley shouting as he chased after Blaine. Blaine pushed over a tall plant as he ran. The teal ceramic pot broke in half and sent clumps of compost across the floor. Ramouter skidded and braced himself against the wall as he tried to grab hold of the tails of Blaine's jacket. The material slipped through Ramouter's fingers as Blaine pushed through the kitchen door.

"Shit," said Ramouter as the kitchen door slammed in his face and the frosted-glass panels cracked. Blaine was on the other side of the kitchen island. He had his back turned to Ramouter as he frantically rummaged through the drawers.

"Blaine. Stop!" Ramouter shouted as Blaine turned around holding a large knife. "Put the knife down. You don't want to do anything stupid."

Ramouter moved cautiously around the island. He spotted a flicker of hesitation in Blaine's eyes, and lunged. Blaine cried out as he fell onto his back. Ramouter kicked away the knife that had fallen out of Blaine's hand. He stood back and watched as Blaine scrambled to his feet and pushed open the back door. But there was nowhere for Blaine to go as PCs Downing and Raleigh were already waiting for him.

64

"I'm not comfortable. I'm in pain," said Blaine as he picked up his cup of water.

"Tough." Henley entered her details onto the computer. "What's your warrant number, Detective Ramouter?"

Ramouter turned on his laptop. "2873PY."

"Thank you." Henley paused as she reached the box for the solicitors' details. "Mr. Blaine, I'm going to ask you again. Are you sure that you don't want a solicitor?"

"Fat lot of good it did me last time." Blaine crumpled the empty plastic cup and threw it onto the floor. He had the look of a spoiled child who believed that he'd been cheated.

Henley could feel Blaine staring at her as she completed the admin part of the interview and then pressed record.

"Do you have any mental health issues, Mr. Blaine?" Henley asked after she had run through the standard introductions and caution.

"Excuse me?"

"Mental health issues," Henley said slowly, trying to keep a hold of her temper. "Depression? Psychosis? Are you on medication?"

"No. I'm not on anything."

"And you understand exactly what the caution means?"

"You're joking, aren't you? I'm a...was a criminal solicitor. I have the right to remain silent. If I choose to talk, anything that I say can be used in evidence against me. If I don't talk now and this matter goes to trial, which it won't by the way, and I give an account in court, the jury could assume that I've made the whole thing up."

"You've been arrested for the murders of Uzomamaka Darego and Daniel Kennedy."

Blaine looked up at the camera in the corner and shook his head. "I had nothing to do with that. I don't even know them."

"Well, now. That's not true, is it?" said Henley.

"Zoe Darego gave evidence against you that resulted in your conviction for perverting the course of justice," said Ramouter.

"That doesn't mean that I knew her, and that was years ago."

"Zoe Darego was reported missing on Friday, September 6, and her body was found last Tuesday," Ramouter continued.

"I've already told you that I was with my girlfriend, Lorelei, on that night," said Blaine.

"Lorelei confirmed that she was never your girlfriend and that she wasn't with you on the night in question." Henley's voice was matter-of-fact, but she was seething. Had Blaine hurt Zoe?

Blaine opened his mouth and closed it again. After a few seconds, he said, "She must have made a mistake with the dates."

"There's no mistake, Blaine. Your alibi is nonsense," said Henley. "Two weeks before Zoe disappeared you were seen with her on Lewisham High Street opposite her place of work."

"That's a lie. I haven't seen her since that the last day in court. I may have been on Lewisham High Street, but not anywhere near the hospital."

"TDC Ramouter." Henley tapped the edge of the laptop.

"This is CCTV footage taken from Lewisham High Street

opposite the hospital." Ramouter pressed play. "This is Zoe Darego. Can you identify yourself on the CCTV?"

Blaine sat back and folded his arms. "You can only see the back of that man. It could be anybody."

"Keep watching." Henley's gaze stayed trained on Blaine.

Blaine's went ashen as Ramouter paused the video and the man's face came into view.

"I'll ask you again," Henley said, her voice hard. "Can you identify yourself on this footage?"

Henley's phone began to vibrate. She pulled it out of her jacket, and saw that she had a message from Ezra. She opened the message, and sat up straighter.

OLIVIER!!! Stupid IP address was hidden behind a VPN; that's why it's taken so long to find it. PO logged onto Missing Persons at 1:38 p.m. on Wednesday via IP address. 76.174.2.5. ISP: Athena Media. Account Holder: Chance Blaine.

"That's you on the footage, harassing Zoe Darego." Henley passed the phone to Ramouter, who to his credit didn't flinch when he read the message. "What did you say to her to make her slap you?"

"It's not what it looks like."

"Oh, isn't it? Why don't you tell me what it looks like?"

"You wouldn't understand."

"Why don't you *make* us understand," said Henley. "What did you say to Zoe?"

"It was nothing." Blaine cast his eyes downward. "It was a coincidence, that's all. I had no idea that she worked at the hospital."

"So, you weren't waiting for her?"

"Of course not. I was just passing."

"Even though the CCTV clearly shows your car pulling up

and parking around the corner on Lewisham Park Road twenty minutes before Zoe's bus arrived."

"I had a viewing," Blaine said quickly. "The guy that I was showing the flat to didn't turn up."

"Right," said Ramouter. "So, you'll be able to show us confirmation of that viewing in the office diary? The same office diary that we asked you to send us but didn't?"

"It…it wasn't booked in. The guy walked in and asked about the flat. I was free so I offered to show it to him."

"So, you weren't sitting in your car waiting for Zoe to turn up?" asked Ramouter.

"No." Blaine sat up straighter in his chair. "As I said, it was a coincidence. I was walking back to my car and I saw her… Zoe. I recognized her and I just wanted to talk. I wanted closure."

"Closure?" Henley didn't bother to cloak her disbelief. "You wanted closure?"

"I went to prison because of what she'd done. I wanted to ask her why she'd lied to the judge about me. I never followed her that day. It was sheer coincidence that we were on the same street that day and I also wanted to tell her that I'd moved on. That there were no hard feelings."

"So why did she slap you?" Henley asked.

Blaine shook his head as though he were genuinely perplexed. "I honestly have no idea," he said.

"OK, I'll ask you another question." Henley leaned forward conspiratorially. "Let's talk about Peter Olivier."

"What about him? You already know that I visited him in Belmarsh."

"You changed your name to Chance Blaine after the prison blocked your visit to see Olivier."

"That's not true. I changed my name because I wanted a fresh start."

"You changed your name because you were desperate to see Olivier."

"He asked me to visit." Blaine's voice rose with panic. "I don't know how he found me, but he sent me a visiting order. I didn't want anything to do with him."

"Oh, please. We're not idiots," said Henley as Ramouter pulled out several sheets of paper.

"That is a list of all the visits that you made to see Olivier," said Ramouter. "Thursday mornings and Sunday afternoons. You never missed a visit."

"That reminds me," said Henley. "Chance Blaine, I'm also arresting you for fraud by false representation. You provided fraudulent information to Belmarsh prison—a fake passport and driving license—in order to pass their security clearance."

"You can't do that. I didn't do anything wrong," Blaine said woefully.

"Olivier told you how to cut up a body, didn't he?" Henley asked.

"What are you talking about? No."

"Two days after you saw Zoe, you visited Olivier and you told him about your plan to carry out his work."

"No."

"You had a plan to get your own back on Zoe and the others for putting you in prison."

"You really are reaching."

"Olivier told you about his plan to escape."

"I had no idea that he was going to do it."

"You knew, all right, which is why you didn't do the right thing and call the police when Olivier turned up at your house on Wednesday afternoon and used your computer to log onto the Missing Persons website."

"We've got officers carrying out a Section 18 search at your flat right now," said Ramouter.

"Olivier was never at my flat," said Blaine.

"We've got an eyewitness who saw a man matching Olivier's

description leaving your building at 3:17 p.m. Nearly ninety minutes after he logged on to the Missing Persons website."

Blaine didn't reply. The only sound came from his foot nervously tapping the table leg.

"He was never at my flat," Blaine finally said. "I wasn't even at home on Wednesday afternoon. I was at a—"

"Let me guess," said Henley. "You were at a viewing."

"I had an appointment."

"You're lying, Mr. Blaine. From the minute I pressed record, you've been lying to me and TDC Ramouter. In fact, you've been lying from the day we met you. You lied to us about knowing any of the victims."

"I didn't kill anyone," Blaine said as his eyes welled with tears.

Henley indicated for Ramouter to take over as Blaine leaned back in his chair and hugged himself.

"Exhibit SR/1. A Samsung Galaxy mobile phone," said Ramouter, pushing the exhibit bag containing the phone toward Blaine. "Can you confirm that this phone belongs to you?"

Blaine picked up the bag and nodded.

"You have to speak," Ramouter said gently, as though he was coaxing a small child out from under the bed.

"That's my phone," said Blaine.

"This is exhibit SR/2. A SIM card that was removed from your wallet. Does this SIM card belong to you?"

"Yes," Blaine whispered.

"Have you been using this card to send text messages and make phone calls to Peter Olivier?"

Blaine's face crumpled.

"No. No. No. I'm not doing this anymore," Blaine finally said. "I want a solicitor. I'm not saying another word to you until I speak to a solicitor."

65

"It's not going to be enough, is it?" Ramouter asked when Henley had booked Blaine back into his cell.

"I can't see the CPS authorizing a charge of murder on what we've got," she admitted. "But we've got enough to have him charged with assisting and harboring an offender."

"Something doesn't make sense," Ramouter said.

They made their way out of the police station. "What's that?"

"Why are Blaine and Olivier still here? What is the point in hanging around? I would have done a runner a long time ago."

Henley's phone pinged with the arrival of an email. "God, it's been nonstop today," she said as she scrolled through.

"Anything important?"

"Not—"

Henley stopped in her tracks and she reread the email from PS Harris at the Community Safety Unit in Muswell Hill.

Thursday, September 17, 2019, at 16:24
Re: URGENT: Carole Lewis Investigation
From: Tony Harris, Met Police
To: Anjelica Henley, Met Police

DI Henley,

Apologies for the delay. PC Morris 875YK is currently on leave but I've spoken to him and he's confirmed that Carole Lewis attended the station and reported four incidents of harassment from February to April 2019 (CRIS No: 87456624/19). I cannot find a copy of the harassment warning on the system, but I've asked PC Morris to forward a copy of the harassment warning which was issued to Alessandro Naylor DOB 06/17/83 to you ASAP.

Regards,

PS Tony Harris

66

Henley and Ramouter had returned straight to the SCU. Henley's head was spinning with the latest developments.

"Is there anything in the CRIS report to show that they even followed up with our juror, Alessandro Naylor, as a possible line of inquiry?" asked Ramouter, handing Henley a cup of tea.

"There's nothing, as far as I can see," said Henley. "They didn't make any attempt to get in contact with him. It's as if DS Lancaster didn't bother looking at any other possibilities once she'd set her sights on the husband."

Ramouter rubbed his eyes.

"It's ridiculous and incompetent. They should have spoken to him. Carole Lewis made four reports of harassment to the police and they took her seriously enough to issue Naylor with a harassment warning," said Henley. She checked her watch: 6 p.m. She had been hoping that she would have been able to leave on time to see Emma, but that wasn't going to happen now.

"What about PC Morris?"

"He's on a rest day but that doesn't matter."

Henley flipped through the report to the harassment allegations. Carole Lewis had visited the police station three times, first on February 18, 2019. She'd reported seeing Naylor standing outside her house on two separate occasions. Almost a month later she'd returned and met PC Morris. According to his entry, Naylor had been seen again outside her house and had sent her text messages. On April 4, 2019, PC Morris called Naylor and left a message that there had been an allegation of harassment made against him. Naylor didn't return the call. Six days later, PC Morris posted to Naylor, by second-class mail, a harassment warning. As far as Henley could tell, Naylor hadn't responded, not that he was under an obligation to respond, and there had been no other reports of harassment. A month later, Carole Lewis was dead.

"Let's go," said Henley, standing up.

"Where?" Ramouter was already putting his jacket on.

"To pay Alessandro Naylor a visit."

"Has someone else been killed?" Alessandro said as he picked up the kettle and poured boiling water into a cup. "PC Welsh the officer who's keeping an eye on me, didn't say anything to me this morning." There was a sense of panic in his voice and hot coffee spilled from the cup as his hand shook slightly.

"No. It's nothing like that," said Henley. "We wanted to talk to you about Carole Lewis and the harassment warning that you received in April."

"A harassment warning. What harassment warning?" Alessandro sat back with a quizzical look on his face. "Me? Harass Carole? Nah, you've made a mistake."

"Carole made a report to the police that you had been seen outside her house and had been texting her. We asked you if you'd had any contact with any of the jurors and you said no. You knew exactly what was going on, the danger that you were in, and you lied to my face."

Alessandro's cheeks reddened. "I just didn't think that it was important. I bumped into her randomly when I was out with a friend for drinks at some pub in Chalk Farm. It was ages ago. She was a bit flirty, but she was like that when I met her on jury service. She flirted with everybody. She insisted on swapping numbers. I only took it to get rid of her."

"Were you two in a relationship?" asked Henley.

"God, no. Look, if I'm honest—"

"Oh, *now* you're being honest."

"I felt a bit sorry for her. She seemed lonely."

"I'm not being funny but you don't strike me as the sympathetic type."

"That's a bit of a cheek, innit," said Alessandro as he sat down at the kitchen table. "Fine. I met her in the pub, and we had a drink and that was it."

"Were you ever at her house?" Henley asked.

Alessandro shook his head, determinedly. "Never. I knew that she lived in Muswell Hill, but there was no way that I was traipsing up there just to get my leg over."

Henley didn't laugh.

"Sorry, but no. I never went to her house. I met her once and that was it."

"What about texting and calling her?"

"She texted me and I replied a few times, but when she told me that she and her husband were into dogging…" Alessandro turned toward Ramouter. "Could you imagine sharing your missus with half of north London? No thanks."

"The harassment warning," Henley asked. "She said that you had been harassing her. Turning up at her house, calling her—"

"That's not true. She called me and texted me. I told her that I wasn't interested in anything more than just friends. I mean, she is—or was—a married woman. That's more trouble than it's worth. And that letter. The harassment warning. I never got it. The police never spoke to me about it. I was never interviewed or arrested. She never contacted me again and I didn't bother her."

"So, when was the last time that you saw or spoke to her?"

Alessandro huffed and took a sip of coffee. "Sometime in March. That was the last time I spoke to her. The next time I heard about her was when you lot turned up at my front door."

"During the time you spoke to her, did she ever mention Joseph McGrath? He calls himself Chance Blaine now?"

Alessandro shook his head.

"Did she express any concern for her safety?" Henley asked.

"She went on and on about her husband. Said that she was thinking of leaving him. I do remember asking her if he had ever hurt her, but she didn't like that question."

"Why did you even ask the question?"

Alessandro shrugged. "Force of habit. I've got sisters, and a little cousin who sat in front of me with a black eye and swore blind that her boyfriend didn't touch her. What can I say? I'm overprotective. I'm sure that you've seen it in your job."

"I've seen a lot in this job," said Henley as she picked up her bag and put it on her lap. "I've had men sit in front of me and swear on their kid's life that they didn't strangle their wife to death."

"I didn't kill her," Alessandro said.

"So you say, but I'm going to need your DNA to prove or disprove that." Henley pulled out an empty exhibit bag and two plastic tubes each containing a cotton swab. She jumped back as Alessandro knocked over his coffee.

"Shit," Alessandro said as he got up and grabbed a sponge from the sink. "OK, OK, it was one time," he said as he wiped up the mess.

"Five minutes ago you said that it was just a drink," said Ramouter.

"I slept with her once," Alessandro replied as he threw the sponge into the sink. He had a pained expression on his face as he realized that he'd backed himself into a corner. "I'm sorry, but I swear down. We had sex in the back of my van and that was it."

"Your van?" asked Ramouter.

Alessandro nodded. "I didn't see her again."

"So you say." Henley pulled on a latex glove. "But I'm still going to need a sample. We can either do it here or at the station. It's up to you."

Alessandro looked defeatedly at Ramouter and Henley and then opened his mouth for the swab.

Ramouter and Henley walked in the drizzling rain toward their car.

"He's lying," Henley said.

"What about? Seeing her again, being in a relationship?"

"Carole's husband said that she was getting calls and texts from one of the jurors all of the time. He thought they were sleeping together."

"OK, let's say that Alessandro Naylor lied about being in a relationship with Carole Lewis. It doesn't mean that he's involved in her murder, and if he was, what about the other victims? Zoe, Daniel and Sean would still be alive if it was just a case of a jealous stalker killing the object of his affection. There's also the timings. Lewis was murdered four months ago. It's possible that Lewis's murder isn't linked to the others."

Henley was quiet, mulling over what Ramouter had said.

"I hate to say it," he continued, "but all roads are leading to Chance Blaine."

"I know," Henley said with frustration. "But we need something more concrete to pin the murders on him."

67

Olivier leaned back and let the sun warm his face. He was less than half a mile from the SCU and surrounded by tourists taking photographs of anything that moved. Olivier pulled out his mobile phone and took a photograph of himself. There were only three numbers saved in his contact list. He began to walk away from the lunchtime crowds as he sent the photograph to DI Henley and then pressed call. She picked up on the fourth ring.

"Where are you?" Henley asked. "I couldn't tell from your photograph."

Olivier kept silent, listening to the background noise on the phone. He could hear the warning sound of a van reversing.

"Olivier. Are you still there?"

"You didn't even say hello."

"What do you want?"

"I wanted to check in."

"You could surrender to a local police station. That would be a nice way for you to check in."

"We both know that isn't going to happen. I was watching you the other day," he said. He smiled as he heard Henley's sharp intake of breath. "The press conference."

"What do you want?" she asked again.

"It was nice to see Pellacia after all this time. I could see how much it thrilled him, sitting so close to you. What was he doing? Touching you up under the table?"

"I don't have time for your games, Olivier."

"In case you failed to notice, I'm not the one playing games. Your copycat is the one walking around and dropping body parts like he owns the place."

"Is that why you're still hanging around?" Henley asked. "You want to find him yourself, don't you?"

"Let's be honest, Inspector, at the rate you're going, you're not going to be winning any prizes for effective police work."

"Is that your plan? To find him, chop him up and scatter him outside my front door?"

Olivier smiled. He was enjoying hearing the frustration and the passion in Henley's voice.

"I was thinking that we could share information?" Olivier said. "You help me. I help you. A trade."

Silence. Olivier couldn't even hear Henley breathing.

"It must be burning you up, trying to tie up all these loose ends," said Olivier. "You've got me out here and Mr. Blaine feeling sorry for himself in Lewisham police station."

"Blaine has been talking," Henley said slowly. "A lot. About you and him working together."

"I know what you're doing. You're trying to make me bite. You're trying to put all of those little pieces of circumstantial evidence together like a jigsaw, but you and I both know that those pieces just don't fit." Olivier laughed as he heard Henley kiss her teeth. "It must be a horrible feeling, knowing that I'm out here and that I'm going to find him before you do."

"That's not going to happen."

"It will—that I promise you. It doesn't matter how hard you try, Inspector, you're always going to be two steps behind me."

68

Henley told no one about the phone call. All she cared about now was her daughter. She had decided to risk the wrath of her mother-in-law and visit Emma. Henley didn't have a problem with Rob's dad—they had always got on like a house on fire—but his mother, Natasha, was sharp, pretentious and thought that her son could have done better.

The house was across the road from Kensal Green tube station and a stream of people were already making their way out. Not for the first time, Henley wished that Rob's dad would make good on his promise to cash in on the ridiculous market price of his house and retire to St. Lucia with his wife in tow.

As she waited at the front door, Henley wondered if she should have put the tattered Met Police sign on her dashboard. Anything that would wind Natasha up would have been a small victory, but Henley was sure that the police car parked two doors down was doing a good enough job.

"Oh," said Natasha, opening the door. She pulled her gray cashmere cardigan tighter as though she was protecting herself from the cold front that was Henley. "I wasn't expecting you. It's late."

"It was a last-minute thing." Henley stepped into the house. Natasha huffed and smoothed back a strand of dyed black hair behind her ear.

"It's not right, you know," Natasha said as they walked down the hallway. The walls were covered with family photographs. Henley wrinkled her nose at the smell of fresh paint. As long as Henley had known Rob, she had never known his mother to work. Instead, she ordered renovation after renovation of the house and booked cruises, while Rob's dad continued to work as a partner in a corporate law firm.

"What's not right?" Henley asked.

Natasha stopped abruptly. "Kiss me neck back. You've put Robert's father and me in danger." The Jamaican accent that Natasha kept so hard to keep at bay on a daily basis crept through. "I have a police car outside my home, as if I'm the criminal. Do you know how embarrassing it is, Anjelica? Cha! I don't feel safe in my own home. It's not right that you put my son and granddaughter through this."

"What would you prefer? That I give up my job, become a stay-at-home mum, spend my time pureeing carrots and choosing kitchen cabinets?"

"Would that be such a bad thing? Or maybe you could just make this"—Natasha waved a perfectly manicured hand toward the kitchen, where Rob and Emma were presumably behind the closed door—"permanent."

Henley resisted, not for the first time, the urge to slap Rob's mum. Instead, she pushed past her and opened the door to the kitchen.

Emma jumped up from her chair, spilling her bowl of pasta and chicken onto the floor.

"Hello, baby girl. What are you doing up so late?" Henley fell to her knees and pulled her daughter toward her. She smelled her hair and paused. It wasn't the same. She was used to the smell of coconut and jojoba. Now Emma smelled of vanilla and honey.

"You changed her shampoo?" Henley said to Rob, who was on the floor picking up the food.

"Mum recommended it." He reached under the table for a stray piece of chicken.

"I brought some more of Emma's things. Including her shampoo." Henley covered Emma's face in kisses. "Oh, I've missed you, my angel."

"I miss you. I love you." Emma planted a wet kiss on Henley's forehead.

Henley felt her heart break and her eyes sting with tears as she kissed Emma back.

"Where's Luna?" Henley asked, looking around.

"In the conservatory," Natasha said. She switched on the kettle and busied herself with the pretense of making tea. "Robert knows that I'm allergic. I honestly don't know why he couldn't have left the dog with you, but I forgot that you're never home."

Just ignore her, Henley said to herself. She could withstand the sarcastic jabs from Natasha if it meant spending precious time with her daughter.

Henley stood up with Emma in her arms. "Shall we go and say hello to Luna?"

"Yes. I want Luna," replied Emma.

"Me too. And then I'll give you a bath and wash your hair."

Luna started to bark before Henley had even placed a hand on the double-glazed door to the conservatory. She was getting a better reception from the dog than she did from Rob and his anally retentive mother.

"You should have told me you were coming." Rob stood in the doorway of what used to be his old bedroom.

"Why? So, you could tell me that you wouldn't be in?" Henley replied, stroking Emma's hair as she slept in her lap.

"I wouldn't have done that."

"You really can't use that rubbish that your mum gave you in Emma's hair. It's drying it out."

"Come on. Mum could have been giving me the most expensive shampoo on the shelf and you still wouldn't be happy."

Rob stepped into the room and closed the door. Henley looked at him properly for the first time since she had walked into the house. She knew that it wouldn't have been easy for him to seek refuge with his parents and be subjected to his mother's controlling and manipulative antics.

"Have they caught the person who did it?" Rob sat down on the other end of the bed. "You know. The box."

"We're still making inquiries but there is a suspect," Henley replied.

"A suspect? Have you arrested them yet?"

"I can't talk about it, Rob."

"What do you mean, you can't talk about it? It was our house."

"OK, OK. There is someone. A suspect, but she's in the hospital. We'll arrest her as soon as she is fit to be discharged."

"A woman? Why would she do something as sick as dumping a—"

"I have no idea. Did you tell your parents why you came? The exact details."

"You're having a laugh, aren't you? I doubt Mum would have let you through the front door if she knew, but she's not an idiot. She watches the news and knows that it's got something to do with the investigation that you're on."

"I miss my daughter, Rob."

Rob's face fell. "What about me? Do...do you miss me?"

"Of course I do," Henley lied as she gently lifted Emma off her lap and rested her on the bed. She kissed her and felt a sense of satisfaction, now that Emma smelled like Emma. "I miss my family."

"But you're not exactly doing anything to get us back. Anj, I haven't lived with my parents since I was twenty-one. This isn't easy for me. Emma cries for you every night."

"Rob, you're the one who gave me an ultimatum. My job or you. You're the one who nearly had it off with some…" Henley paused as Emma stirred. She got up and walked out of the bedroom and indicated for Rob to follow her.

"Come on," Rob said. "Luna needs a walk."

"I don't want to be like this. This isn't me. I'm not a nag. We've never been that sort of couple," Rob said, aware that his mother was watching them from behind the net curtains.

"No, you're not. We're not and I don't blame you for leaving," said Henley. They turned left onto Holland Road, feeling the chill of the evening air. "I just didn't like the position that you put me in. Asking me to choose, Rob, that's not right. If it was the other way around, I would never have put you in that position."

"I know that you wouldn't, but the fact is, Anj, it's not the other way around and this isn't the first time."

"I'm not at risk this time. *We're* not at risk." Henley could see that Rob wasn't buying her bullshit. "I'm not asking you to come home," she said and took the dog leash from his hand.

"You don't want me back?"

"That's not what I said. Of course I want you back. I just don't want you to come back until we've caught who's doing this."

"But you said that you have a suspect."

"It's a bit more complicated than that. Sweetheart, I know that I can be hard-headed at times."

"Hard-headed is an understatement."

"Rob, come on. I'm trying."

"So, you agree with me? It was right for me to leave?"

"Yes. It was, and if I'm honest with myself, it's probably better that we're not together right now, not while Olivier is still out there."

"I don't like it that you're on your own. Are they looking after you?"

Henley could hear the apprehensiveness in her husband's voice. She knew what he really meant. If there was someone else sleeping in the place where he should have been.

"I stayed with Stanford the other night. You know what he's like. He's a hard man to say no to. They've got surveillance on the house and there hasn't been anything to worry about. Trust me. I'm fine."

"I'm glad that you stayed with Stanford. At least I know that you're going to be in safe hands with him and Gene looking after you, but fine isn't good enough," Rob said. "I do love you. I know that I'm not the easiest but it's—"

"I know that you do." Henley reached out and hugged him. She felt his body stiffen and then relax a bit as she kissed him.

"You could stay tonight," Rob said as they pulled apart.

"God, no. Your mum would put a pillow over my face in my sleep."

Rob laughed. "Come on, she ain't that bad."

"Isn't she?" Henley pulled gently on Luna's leash and they continued to walk.

"It hasn't been a picnic for me, you know," Rob replied.

"Your mum waiting on you hand and foot, please."

"She asked me if we were getting divorced."

"I'm surprised that she didn't download the application forms for you. What did you say?"

"I told her that it was just your work."

She ran through the logistics of staying the night in west London and then getting back to the SCU in the morning. They were running a distant second to actually spending the night and seeing her daughter in the morning.

"OK, I'll stay," she said.

69

"I didn't know that we were doing flexi hours." Stanford held the door open for Henley. "It's almost nine-thirty."

"I got stuck in traffic," she replied.

"From Brockley?"

"Kensal Green."

"Ah," replied Stanford, the realization of where Henley had been dawning on him. "How's my little Ems?"

"She's good. She asked about you and she drew you this." Henley handed him a piece of paper etched in orange, purple, blue and green crayon. "Apparently, it's you and her in your car."

Stanford smirked as he turned the drawing around. "She really caught the blue in my eyes."

"Where's Stephen?" Henley looked toward the empty office.

Stanford shrugged. "Haven't seen him since yesterday afternoon. Why?"

"I need to tell him that I've put in an official complaint against DS Lancaster."

"Shit, Henley. You know what's going to happen when people find out that you grassed up another detective?"

"She could have jeopardized this investigation by giving sensitive information to the press. Who does she think she is?" Henley said angrily.

"Hey, don't have a go at me. I think that you did the right thing. I just want you to be ready for the backlash."

"I know. I'm sorry."

"Accepted." Stanford entered the kitchen and switched on the kettle. "Anyway, I got that information you asked for. So, your boys, Blaine, Pine and Naylor... Tea or coffee?" he said as he held up a mug.

"Tea," said Henley, reaching for the sugar.

"All three were absolutely as clean as a whistle until the contempt of court and perverting the course of justice thing. Did you know that you can get two years for contempt of court?"

"I did actually."

"Course you did. The judge made an example of all of them. Blaine got whacked with two years; being a lawyer he should have known better. Pine and Naylor got six months. Doesn't matter that they only had to do half of their sentences. Prison is prison. Naylor got sent to Pentonville, but you'll never guess where Pine and Blaine ended up?" Stanford handed Henley her cup of tea as they walked back to her desk.

"I honestly have no idea."

"You didn't even try. They were both sent to Belmarsh."

"Really? That's a bit harsh. They should have gone to a Cat C prison, but Olivier was in the High Security Unit. He wouldn't have had any contact with them."

Henley spotted a brown archive box on her desk. Ramouter sat at the desk opposite, head down, phone in the crook of his neck as he wrote furiously on the notepad in front of him. "What is that?" she asked, pointing at the archive box.

"I told you. I got the information that you asked for. That is the original investigation file for the contempt of court case." Stanford wheeled over a chair and sat down next to Henley's desk. "Custody records are on top."

Henley put down her cup of tea and pulled out a yellow folder. Inside were the custody records for Naylor, Pine and Blaine. She pulled out four small pale blue notebooks tied together with an elastic band.

"So, as we know, two weeks into the trial, the jury that our dead jurors were on was discharged," said Stanford. "According to the court transcripts, the judge only went as far as to say that one of the jurors was in contempt of court and that's the end of that. Three days later the trial starts again."

"What exactly did Blaine tell Naylor and Pine?" Henley flicked through Naylor's custody record, the document that detailed almost every moment of his brief stay at Snow Hill police station.

"He told Naylor and Pine that Olivier's first two victims had raped him when he was in the army, which makes no sense to me. Surely that would give them a reason to find him guilty of murder?"

"There's only one reason why Blaine would have done that," said Henley. "He wanted the jury discharged. Ideal scenario would be if Naylor, Pine and Zoe convinced the rest of the jurors to find Olivier not guilty of murder and guilty of manslaughter or—as mad it sounds—acquit him, or worst-case scenario, it's three against nine and that's enough for a hung jury."

"Madness," said Stanford. "Maybe there's something in that dusty box that will shed more light on this."

"The prosecution in that trial were in a dilemma. They wanted to show Olivier's motive for the murders but they couldn't risk the jurors losing sympathy for the victims. Not that it mattered," Henley mused. "Remember, he sat in that witness boss for three days and denied everything. His defense team never submitted that he was a rape victim or was suffering from PTSD because as far as he was concerned it was all a setup and he never did it. So, Blaine tells Naylor and Pine, then what?"

"According to Naylor's evidence, he discussed it with Pine

and they agreed to keep the information to themselves. But Pine had other ideas and according to the witness statements, during one of their breaks—"

"Who was the witness?" asked Henley.

"Carole Lewis. She says that she was smoking a cigarette with Daniel Kennedy and Michael Kirkpatrick when Pine told them what he had found out."

"Carole Lewis told the judge?" Henley asked as she put down Naylor's custody record and picked up Pine's file.

"No, she didn't. Zoe Darego did. Michael Kirkpatrick didn't see what all the fuss was about."

"How did Zoe find out?"

"Kennedy told her what Pine had said, but Zoe didn't do anything until Blaine followed her onto the bus and threatened her. Zoe, then being a very dutiful juror, wrote a note to the judge. It was all downhill from there."

Henley reached over to the pot of pens on her desk and pulled out a yellow highlighter and began to mark the pages of a custody record.

"Shit, no one ever took swabs?" Henley said, picking up Naylor's custody record for a second time and flicking through the pages again, just to make sure that she hadn't missed anything.

"What are you talking about?"

"Pine was arrested at 9:57 a.m. by DC Leissner and Naylor was arrested at 9:44 a.m. by DC Connor. They both arrived at Snow Hill police station at 10:42 a.m. Pine's detention was authorized at 10:45 a.m. and Naylor at 10:50 a.m. by Custody Sergeant Dixon. Pine requested the duty solicitor but Naylor doesn't, and he's interviewed at 11:30 a.m. Pine's placed into a cell at 11:25 a.m. and then he's taken out at 12:38 p.m. for a consultation with his solicitor. He's interviewed at 1:25 p.m. and he's not charged until 3:57 p.m. Naylor was charged at 3:35 p.m. They're both in the station all day and no one has taken any samples of their DNA and they weren't livescanned."

Stanford sat up straighter in his chair. "Are you sure?"

"I've been through both their custody records three times and there's no entry for anyone either taking Naylor's and Pine's prints or any samples."

"How could someone not take their prints or DNA?" Ramouter asked incredulously. "It's the first thing that they would have done after they were booked in. That's standard procedure."

Henley could feel all eyes on her as she tried to process what this meant. Human error would be the simple answer. A busy custody station with overworked civilian staff, someone may have just forgotten or thought that someone else had completed the mundane task of checking that your suspect was who he said he was and wasn't a career criminal. All they had to do was make sure that the detainee kept their hand firmly on the glass while a scan was taken of their fingerprints and palm and kept their mouth open while his cheeks were swabbed.

"What about Chance Blaine? He's still sitting in Lewisham waiting to find out if he's going to be charged with murder."

"I've only got him bang to rights for helping Olivier, not for murder," said Henley. "But Naylor? He lied about knowing Carole Lewis."

"You don't seriously think that it's him, do you? Naylor, I mean," Stanford asked. "Someone not doing their job properly is not evidence. No offense, Henley, in terms of physical evidence, there's nothing linking Naylor to the murders of Lewis, Kennedy and Darego."

"But we can't write Naylor off," Ramouter interjected. "He did lie about his association with Carole Lewis and we have unidentified DNA on Carole's body; it could be his."

"And according to the court transcripts, all of this started with Zoe writing a letter to the judge." Henley picked up a marker from her desk and went up to the whiteboard.

"So, what do we do? Arrest Naylor?" asked Ramouter.

"Not yet," said Henley. "Stanford's right, we need something physical. Ramouter, I'm going to need you to chase up the results of the DNA swabs that I took off Naylor. We can't be pushed to the back of the queue on this," she said before adding Naylor's name to the suspect list.

70

"Hold on. Let me get this straight." Pellacia placed his hands in a steeple under his chin. "Karen Bajarami is the woman who arranged for the delivery of Cheung's head to your front door?"

"It's her on the CCTV," said Henley. "I've met her, Ramouter's met her and I can confidently say that's her."

"OK. Is there any footage of her actually going to the storage unit and physically handling the box?"

"No," Henley conceded.

"At best, the footage is circumstantial. Like a lot of your evidence in these investigations."

It was all Henley could do not to throw something in Pellacia's face.

"We've got a statement from the courier, Vincent Tiegan," said Ramouter, who was sitting next to Henley. "We get him in for a VIPER ID viewing and if he identifies the woman who handed him the package as Bajarami—"

"It's still not enough," said Pellacia. "What about any of the prints from the box? Forensics?"

"Anthony recovered four sets of fingerprints," said Henley. "Mine, Rob's and the courier's were eliminated, but the fourth came back unmatched to any on the system. Olivier's DNA was found in Elliot Cheung's hair."

Pellacia loosened his tie. "If we can get Bajarami's prints, and it's a match, that will be better. Any reason why we can't bring her in now?"

"She's not fit to be discharged and her being linked to the delivery of Cheung's head is one thing. The problem is that we don't have any evidence that she was involved with Olivier's escape," said Ramouter.

"It's not exactly a leap to think that she's involved, in some way, with Olivier's escape if she's arranged for the delivery of the head of Olivier's last victim."

Henley thought back to when she had first met Karen Bajarami. She was professional, courteous and didn't give the slightest hint of any favoritism toward Olivier. Whereas the governor had almost fallen over himself with his adoration for Olivier.

"What about Blaine?"

Henley sighed wearily. "Blaine gave a 'no comment' interview once he got a solicitor in. The CPS are now advising that we charge him with obstruction of a police officer and bail him for everything else. Which is absolute bollocks. We've got more than enough evidence to charge Blaine with assisting Olivier and with fraud."

"They want us to release him. Christ."

"I'd prefer it if he was remanded into custody, but Blaine could lead us to Olivier if we keep an eye on him."

"Is there anything else?" Pellacia said.

"One more thing. Ramouter?" said Henley.

Ramouter cleared his throat. "We have someone who may be the last person to have seen Sean Delaney alive. The problem is that he's a drug addict and was under the influence at the time."

"Any half-decent defense barrister would rip his evidence to pieces," said Pellacia.

"Aye, most likely, but what he now says is that he saw someone who he *thinks* was Delaney being placed into what he *believes* was an ambulance. Not the van version, but a station wagon. There is no record of Delaney being admitted to any of the local hospitals, but it got me thinking. Dominic Pine, one of the jurors, is a paramedic. Zoe and Kennedy were involved in grassing Pine and Naylor up to the judge. The last person that Delaney was seen with may have been a—"

"All of this according to a drug addict," interrupted Pellacia.

"It can't be ignored, guv. If you let me finish."

"I'm not ignoring anything. I don't like speculation and that's a lot of speculation. Is Pine up on your suspect board?"

"No, he isn't," Henley conceded. "But you shouldn't dismiss what Ramouter has to say."

"All our appeals for witnesses have resulted in nowt," Ramouter said stubbornly.

"And it could be that your drug addict may have just made a mistake," said Pellacia, "but it's something that you're going to have to follow up. Where was Pine when Delaney went missing?"

"That's the thing," said Henley. "Pine has an alibi. He was working when Delaney, Zoe and Kennedy went missing."

"OK," said Pellacia. "The next step has to be to talk to Bajarami. Olivier is out there and she's the closest—"

There was a sharp knock on the door before Joanna poked her head through.

"Sorry to interrupt," said Joanna. "Thought you should know. The exhumation license has come through. They're going to be digging Carole Lewis up on Sunday night."

71

It was almost ten and Henley thought about the times she would
have welcomed walking into a quiet house, but that was before
Rob, Emma and Luna had left. She spotted Emma's stuffed rabbit
under the kitchen table and tried to push back the tears that were
burning her eyes. She turned around and got back in the car.

She knew that it was a bad idea going to Pellacia's house.
When she got there she sat outside with the engine running.
She watched the front window for a few minutes. Television
light flashed through the gap in the curtains. She jumped when
someone tapped loudly on the window.

"How much longer are you going to spend sitting in your
car?" asked Pellacia.

Henley rolled down the window.

"Rob's gone, Emma's with him. Even Luna has gone," she
said, turning off the car engine. "I can't stay in an empty house.
It's too quiet."

"Well, you'd better come in, then."

"Why didn't you go back to your in-laws?" Pellacia asked, closing the front door behind him.

She pretended that she hadn't heard him. She walked into the living room, aware that Pellacia was watching her every move. There had been some additions to the photographs on the mantelpiece above the empty fireplace. A smiling baby boy. Another of a woman who had the same eyes as Pellacia, but who had now forgotten he was her son.

"How is she?" Henley asked.

"No better, no worse. Last week she thought that I was Uncle Tony. He died when I was twelve."

Henley's mind went to Ramouter and his wife. She couldn't imagine what it must feel like to watch your wife or your mother slowly lose their capacity to remember you.

"Losing again, are you?" Henley picked up the Xbox control pad from the sofa. She knew Pellacia wouldn't want to talk anymore about his mum.

"Yeah. Playing against my nephew in Melbourne," Pellacia said. He was still standing in the doorway. "The jammy little bastard."

I shouldn't be here. We're acting like kids, Henley thought to herself. She tried to think of something to fill the awkward silence.

"I'm not staying," she said, unpausing the game.

"Course you're not."

"He's going to know it wasn't me that beat him." Laughing, Pellacia turned off the Xbox and switched the TV to the news.

"You can give him my username if he wants to play a proper gamer again."

They said nothing for a while, just watched the news with the subtitles on. No one but close family and friends knew that Pellacia had only partial hearing in his left ear. They were sitting close together, but not too close. There was still space between them, but not enough space to stop his arm from occasionally brushing against Henley's.

"Why are you here, Anj?" Pellacia asked.

"Because I'm pissed off and my house is too quiet."

"You didn't have to come *here*."

"I know that I didn't, but you get it. This job, what it does to you."

"But isn't that why you married Rob? You wanted someone outside of the job. Someone who didn't know what the job did to you. That's the reason you gave me."

Henley didn't answer. That was what she had told herself when she had made her decision to finally end her relationship with Pellacia and be with Rob.

"You could have just called. Sent a text."

"Wow. Anyone would think you didn't want me here."

Henley knew she was taunting him. From the second Pellacia had seen her car parked outside his house, it was inevitable what was going to happen. Henley wasn't sure whether Pellacia had pulled her toward him or whether she had pulled Pellacia toward her. She just felt his mouth on hers.

"I've missed you," he murmured. Henley slipped her top over her head and he began to kiss her neck, his hand pushing its way into her jeans.

"I know," Henley replied, her breath catching in her throat. She missed him too, but she couldn't say that aloud. Right now, all she needed was for Pellacia to take her away from all of the loss, violence and self-doubt that was drowning her.

72

"Lauren, baby. Everything all right in there?"

"Everything is fine. I'll be out in a bit."

Lauren checked her reflection in the three-way mirror. She had done everything to make sure that he would be happy. He had told her that yellow was his favorite color. The summer clearance sales were over, and the shops were filled to the brim with the colors of autumn. She'd had to hunt high and low to find the yellow silk camisole among the blacks, plums and charcoals. She turned sideways and adjusted the straps on her shoulders.

"Lauren, I'm going to open another bottle of red. Is that all right?"

"That's fine, darling."

She reapplied the red-carpet lipstick and spritzed herself with perfume and straightened the silver chain around her neck. He had told her that he liked long hair; she had grown it. He had told her that roast lamb was his favorite. She had taken herself to Smithfield's at 7 a.m. and spent an exorbitant amount on an organic leg of lamb. He had wanted their first night to be special. She had pushed the self-help books under her bed and lit sticks of fire of love incense. She looked back at the double bed. The brand-new John Lewis duvet set was now a crumpled mess. She looked down at her wrists. The marks across both wrists were starting to fade. She hadn't told him that the restraints were too tight.

"Here you go."

"Thank you." Lauren took the glass of wine from him. She felt a flutter of nerves in her stomach.

"Are you OK, sweetheart?" he asked, sitting down on the sofa and patting the seat next to him.

"I'm fine. I was just thinking. This may sound strange, but I don't want to waste any time. Do you know what I mean?"

"I know exactly what you mean." He took a sip of wine. "Hmm. This is really good. You have such great taste."

Lauren felt her cheeks growing hot as she leaned back against him. "We could have gone out to dinner, but I wanted you to have a nice home-cooked meal."

"And it's appreciated. Lauren?"

"Really? I'm glad."

"Don't act surprised. You've made this evening so special. I wouldn't normally want to rush into a relationship, but with you…"

He slipped a finger under the strap of her camisole. She gasped as he moved his hand downward and under the material. He cupped her breast and squeezed tighter than he had before.

"Do you like that? Do you want me to fuck you again?"

"Yes, I do."

Lauren placed her glass on the table. She didn't notice when she knocked it over. Red wine pooled on the table and water-falled over the side. She leaned in and kissed him. There was the sweet taste of blood as he bit her lip, breaking the thin skin.

"Let's go back to the bedroom," he said.

"OK. Just give me a minute and I'll meet you in there."

Lauren walked into the bathroom, breathless. The excitement of what she was going to do again was causing her lungs to close up. She opened the bathroom cabinet and reached for her asthma inhaler. She closed it and jumped, startled to see his reflection in the mirror staring back at her. Then the light went out. His hands were around her neck in an instant.

"Sorry about that," he hissed. "Didn't mean to scare you."

Lauren opened her mouth to speak, but no sound escaped. She tried to say his name, but the force of her head connecting with the glass mirror lodged the word in her throat. He threw her onto the floor, knocking the wind out of her. She put a hand to her chest and listened to the scream that was penetrating the soft membrane of her eardrums. It took her a second to realize that the agonized sound was coming from her.

I can't breathe, Lauren tried to say, turning onto her stomach and crawling toward the door. He grabbed her hair and pulled, hard. She felt pressure on her back and pain in her right shoulder as he turned her over.

Confusion and blood-tainted terror clouded Lauren's brain as she looked up at the man who was supposed to love her. She didn't recognize him. This wasn't the man whose eyes had sparkled with desire and tenderness when he'd stroked her face before kissing her. Every muscle in this man's face had stiffened with steely determination. His eyes were dead. Lauren's brain told her to run but her body was locked with fear.

"Please don't do this."

"Don't beg."

She could feel his bony kneecaps squeezing into her rib cage as he straddled her. The orange glow from the streetlamps outside had seeped through the gaps in the blinds. The silver blade of the knife flickered like cheap fairy lights. She tried to kick out as he covered her face with his rough palm, squeezing shut her nose and mouth. The knife came down quickly. Her neck felt warm. She was choking. She felt as though she was drowning, but how could she be drowning when she wasn't underwater? Then all went black.

He'd had to wait. Wait for the chill to settle in the early morning air and for the last house on the street to switch off their bedroom light. He'd had to kick away a cat who had been sniffing at the bags at his feet. He had thought carefully about where he would put them to make sure that they would be found, but this time it had to be different. Something special. Ten more minutes and then he would go. He closed his eyes. He could see her. He had memorized every contortion that her face had made. The cat came back. It hadn't learned its lesson. There was a pond not far from where he was standing. He thought about drowning it.

He kicked the cat harder this time and had to stop himself from laughing as it bounced against the brick wall. He picked up the rucksack that had been resting next to the large duffel bag on the ground.

The bag was lighter now.

He held the rough canvas material to his face. The bottom of the bag was damp with blood. Dirt and gravel clung to the bloodied flesh where the plastic had unraveled. The limbs had rubbed against the stained canvas. He rubbed the damp spot with his fingers. He put his fingers to his nose and sniffed. The coppery scent seeped into his nostrils. He stroked the long strand of brown hair that was caught in the zip, and smiled. He placed the strap across his shoulders and then pulled up the handle of the duffel bag.

He smiled because he already knew that *he* had done a better job than *him*.

73

The bedside clock ticked forward to 5 a.m. Henley lay awake in a familiar bed staring at the ceiling and listening to the early morning chatter of starlings outside. Pellacia was on his side, facing her, eyes closed but with his arm around her. Guilt filled Henley's chest.

She gently pushed Pellacia's arm aside.

"Where are you going?" Pellacia mumbled.

"Bathroom." Henley shifted over to the right side of the bed. She stepped, naked, onto the carpet.

"Make sure you come back." Pellacia moved himself into the place that Henley had just left and pulled the duvet up to his chest. She didn't answer. Instead, she picked up her clothes and left the bedroom. She quickly washed her face with cold water to take away the dried sleep from her eyes and the pillow marks on her face. Henley walked down the staircase, avoiding the step that she knew always creaked. Before she reached the last step the sharp ringtone from her mobile phone broke the silence. She walked into the living room and saw the screen of her phone glowing among the cushions that were now scattered on the floor. Henley pulled a face. Why was Ramouter calling her at 5:04 a.m.?

"I've been trying to get hold of you for ages. There's been another one."

"What?" Henley whispered. She placed the phone in the crook of her neck and picked up her trainers by the sofa.

"Uniform found another body, cut up like the others—"

"Where?" Henley stood up as she heard a creak on the staircase.

"Isle of Dogs?"

"How did you know about this?"

"I'm on the rota for emergency calls. CID from Limehouse called the SCU and it got diverted to me."

"Where are you now?"

"I'm at the SCU. I wasn't sure whether to make my way to the Isle of Dogs or wait for you."

Henley turned around to see Pellacia standing in the doorway watching her. He ran a hand through his bed-raddled hair. Henley pressed the mute button and, as extra security, put the phone to her chest.

"You said that you were just going to the bathroom," Pellacia said.

"I have to go," Henley said quickly. She walked past him and grabbed her bag and jacket from the banister.

"Anj—" Pellacia pleaded.

"I can't... Not now." She unmuted the phone.

"Hello... Are you—" said Ramouter.

"You just can't—" said Pellacia.

"Head straight to the Isle of Dogs. I'll be with you in about twenty minutes. Thirty at the most." Henley ended the call. "Stephen, you don't understand. This isn't about us. There's been another one."

74

"Do we have any idea who it is?" asked Henley as she looked for somewhere to park.

"I only know that the victim is possibly female. I thought that the copycat had stopped." Ramouter's voice was loud over the car speakers. "Ran out of steam."

"They never stop. They may go quiet for a while—"

"A while? It wasn't even a week."

"The press conference must have prompted him. Suddenly, he's getting attention. He's on the front of papers and the first thing being spoken about on the news. Do we know who discovered the body?"

"Douglas Gill," Ramouter repeated from memory. "Forty-eight years old. He's a builder. Kitchen, bathrooms, that sort of thing. He left his tools in the van overnight, went to get them this morning and that's when he found her."

"I'm parking up. I'll see you in a sec," said Henley.

A crowd had formed behind the blue-and-white police tape that fluttered in the breeze. Callander Drive on the Isle of Dogs was a new addition to the *London A-Z*. The road was bordered by identical new-build terraced houses, each the color of rice pudding. A makeshift forensics tent covered the driveway of number 39.

"Oi, stop," shouted an officer as Henley placed her hand on the tape.

"DI Anjelica Henley from the SCU." She reached inside her pocket for her warrant card and then swore. "I've left my—"

"Sorry, I didn't realize. TDC Ramouter said that you were coming," the officer replied sheepishly, lifting the police tape. Henley thanked him as she ducked under and made her way toward Ramouter. Along the way she caught a glimpse of the stocky white man sitting on the doorstep of the house next door. Through the open door behind him, Henley could see a petite woman dressed in shorts and a nightshirt, talking to a female officer. The man looked up at Henley almost apologetically.

"From the sound of things, it's not looking good," Ramouter said to Henley.

"I take it that's Douglas Gill." Henley indicated at the man who had stood up and gone back into the house.

"Yep, that's him. He thought that someone must have broken into the van, but it doesn't look like entry's been forced."

The van had been parked haphazardly and was covered with the decaying grime of the city. Someone had helpfully written on the driver's side of the van: I WISH THAT MY GIRL WAS THIS DIRTY. A streak of exposed metal glinted under the mobile number, and a large dent pocked the door.

Henley examined the lock. Except for the usual grime and a smudge of dried paint, Ramouter was right. The lock was almost pristine.

"The van has never been reported stolen?"

Ramouter shook his head.

"It's either that he forgot to lock up or whoever it was had a key," said Henley.

"Or he could have programmed a key fob. It's easy enough to

do." Ramouter handed Henley a pair of gloves. "That's a lot of planning but it would explain why the van's alarm didn't go off."

"It takes a lot of effort though. To target this particular van, to copy the keys, only to make sure that there weren't any prints. Why not just take the van and dump it somewhere?"

Ramouter shrugged as they both stood looking at the van doors.

"What time did Gill arrive home last night?" asked Henley.

"He said that he was finishing a job in Leytonstone and arrived home at 9 p.m. He went out again at ten but didn't take the van. Says that he met his girlfriend at the Fox and Crown pub and they stayed until eleven. The pub is around the corner and he got home around five past. He didn't come out again until four-thirty this morning."

"That gives us only a four-and-a-half-hour window," Henley said as she pulled at the door. "Our victim may be local."

The stench of dead flesh choked their nostrils.

"Jesus Christ." Henley covered her nose and mouth with her palm. Next to a large dented toolbox was an arm that had been neatly cut off at the shoulder. The fake diamonds on a rose-gold watch, still on the wrist, sparkled in the stream of sunlight. The second arm rested on a pair of dirty overalls. Two bloodstained legs were pointing in the direction of the door, while the torso, wearing a blood-spattered yellow camisole, was propped up at the end of the van, next to a large bucket of plaster. A woman's head was hanging on the van wall. Her long brown hair had been tied around a hook. Her mouth was open, her tongue hanging out. Two dead eyes stared back at Henley.

"What. The. Fuck?" Ramouter stepped back and placed his hands on his thighs. There was a rustle of plastic as Anthony stepped into the tent and Ramouter walked quickly out.

"Sorry, I should have warned you," Anthony said.

Henley was unable to take her eyes off the dead girl's head. "This is different to the others. It smells… Fresh."

"Looks fresh too," said Anthony, clasping his hands behind his back. "It's a horrible way to go."

Henley focused her attention on the bloodied limbs. "They're all there."

"What are?"

"The body parts. Our copycat has been keeping parts. Trophies. Everything is here. I can see her ears."

Henley looked again at the hanging head. The woman's dead brown eyes stared back at her. Her lips were covered with bright red lipstick and dried blood and it was at that moment that Henley knew. This one was different. All of the copycat's victims had been dumped within a two-mile radius. South of the river. The freshness of the body made Henley suspect that this woman had been killed nearby. The opposite side of the river to where Daniel Kennedy's torso had been found.

"This is Olivier," Henley said. "He's sending us a message."

75

As the police went door-to-door, appealing for witnesses, Henley and Ramouter walked up the garden path of number 40. The front door opened before Henley had a chance to even place her hand on the brass knocker, and she found herself face-to-face with a man who looked to be in his late sixties with white unkempt hair, wearing a faded Leyton Orient football shirt and *Star Wars* pajama bottoms. A bull terrier appeared at his side. Henley felt her nose twitch. The smell of cannabis was overwhelming.

"Don't worry about her. She's harmless," he said, grabbing the dog by the collar. "I saw you two from across the road."

"I'm Inspector Henley and this is my colleague, Detective Ramouter."

"Inspector? Can't be many of you lot in the force," he said.

"You lot?" Henley said, making no effort to hide the disdain and irritation in her voice.

"Women inspectors, I meant. Young ones too."

Ramouter tutted and folded his arms across the chest.

"Is it a body? I didn't think that Doug was the type, but then again if I had her as my girlfriend…"

"Mr….?"

"Bellamy. Ian Bellamy."

"Mr. Bellamy, we don't want to take up your time, but we noticed that you have CCTV cameras set up outside your house."

"Yeah, had them put up when I was getting some work done. Got fed up with people trying to dump stuff in my skip. Then there were a couple of break-ins last summer. All about security."

"They're not just for show?"

"Definitely not. Top-of-the-range. My grandson used to work in Maplin. Got me a staff discount."

"Do you mind if we come in and take a look at the footage?"

"What, now?" Bellamy looked nervously into his house.

"We don't care about the cannabis. We're only interested in the footage. This is a murder investigation." Henley bent down and stroked the top of the dog's head.

On the living-room coffee table was an ashtray with the remains of a spliff, a couple of empty snap bags and an open bag of tobacco.

"It's for medicinal purposes," Ian said. "For my back. Sciatica. Herniated disc. Haven't been able to work for years."

"The footage," Henley said, ignoring him and his small collection of Class B drugs.

"Over here. It's hooked up to my computer. I've even got an app on my phone. I've got four cameras. One over my driveway, two focused on the street and the back garden."

Ian walked, almost dragging his leg, over to the large iMac in the corner of the room and pulled out a battered office chair. Henley pretended not to notice the porn site that Ian quickly shut down.

"I usually delete the footage at the end of the week."

"We just need to see the footage from last night," said Henley.

"From about 10 p.m." Ramouter pulled a chair from the dining table nearby and placed it next to Ian. Henley remained standing.

"That's Doug and that's his girlfriend," Ian said as the footage filled the screen.

"It's really good quality," Ramouter said to Henley.

"Top-of-the-range, 1080p camera, two-way audio, night vision. It's like Blu-ray."

Henley watched as Doug and his girlfriend walked past the van and up the street. "OK, can you speed it up a bit?"

Ian nodded and increased the speed. A couple of kids rode by on mopeds at 10:30 p.m. and the front door to number 37 opened at 11 p.m. A woman stood on the step smoking a cigarette. At 11:15 p.m. Doug and his girlfriend came back and then the street was quiet for one, two, four hours.

"Stop," Henley said. The clock in the top right-hand corner of the screen showed 3:18 a.m. She looked closer. A man in a black hoodie and jeans stopped at number 39. He wore a rucksack on his back and pulled a large wheeled duffel bag.

"Who's that?" asked Ian as he looked across at Henley.

"Let it play," was all Henley said. She gave Ramouter a knowing look. Even though the man was wearing a hoodie, they had both seen enough of his side profile to know that Henley had been right. It was Olivier.

The man walked up to the back of the van and placed a large duffel bag and rucksack on the ground. He opened the car door without issue.

"It wasn't locked." Ramouter shook his head. They continued to watch as the man checked both ends of the street before taking off his rucksack. Henley felt her shoulders tighten as, with some effort, he threw the rucksack and duffel bag into the van. It didn't take a genius to work out what was in there.

"Do you know what, that's enough. Thank you. I'm going to be sending another officer around to take a copy of the footage and a statement from you. Is that OK?"

"Yeah, I mean… That's fine. Will you tell them about the

weed?" Ian looked over Henley's shoulder and toward the coffee table.

"Just the footage and a statement, Mr. Bellamy. You don't
have to worry about anything else."

"I need coffee," said Henley as they walked back toward the car.
The activity in front of number 39 was still ongoing. Henley
saw Linh walking into the forensics tent.

"How can you want anything after being in there?" Ramouter
nodded toward the forensics tent.

"I've seen worse," Henley replied, pulling out her car keys.

"Have you? Because I haven't," said Ramouter.

Anthony's trainee approached with a camera in his hand. "Inspector Henley."

"It's Samuel, isn't it?"

He nodded. "Anthony asked me to find you."

"Is something wrong?" she asked.

"No, everything is fine. Well, as good as it can be. Dr. Choi is
in there now, but it will be a while before they move the body.
Anthony wanted me to show you this."

Samuel turned the camera screen toward Henley. "They found
it in her—" Samuel looked away. "It was in her vagina."

Henley zoomed in on the pink driving license. "We've got
ID." Henley handed the camera to Ramouter. She watched as
Ramouter's expression darkened. "What's wrong?" she asked
as Ramouter handed the camera back.

"I recognize the name," Ramouter said. "I'm sure that I've
seen it before,"

"Where?"

"I think she's one of the women who's been writing to Olivier."

76

Henley had sent Ramouter straight to the address on Lauren Varma's driver's license. He should have been feeling pleased that Henley was trusting him to go off on his own, to check out Lauren Varma's flat, but he couldn't help but feel that he was being sold a dud. That Henley had just found the perfect opportunity to get him out from under her feet. Disgruntled, he turned the volume up on the radio. He bopped his head as grime artist Giggs rapped about "talkin' da hardest" on the streets of Peckham. The Rotherhithe Tunnel was closed, causing the traffic to build up in east London.

He turned on the sirens. His stomach flipped with nervous excitement as the cars in front of him began to maneuver out of his way. His phone beeped. He looked down to see a message from DC Swanson from the local nick. Henley didn't trust him enough to go poking around Lauren's flat without some kind of backup, or before the family members formally identified the body, though they hadn't found any family members yet.

Ramouter met DC Swanson in the parking bay.

"Sorry, I'm a bit late. Not used to London traffic. Satnav said fifteen minutes," Ramouter said in an effort to break the ice.

"This is London, mate. You need to add another twenty minutes to whatever those things tell you."

"Will bear that in mind," Ramouter replied.

"Tell Henley that she owes me one for doing babysitting duty."

"It's not like that. Just making a few inquiries and I drew the short straw," Ramouter said.

"Course it ain't, mate."

The communal doors to the Kingfisher building had been propped open by a plastic crate. They took the elevator to the fourth floor. Ramouter was surprised that it didn't smell of urine.

"This is quite a nice block of flats," he said as they stepped out and walked along the carpeted corridor.

"One of the better ones. Still wouldn't live here though."

They stopped outside flat 4F.

"So, what are we doing?" said Swanson. "We're not breaking the door down, are we? Because, in case you haven't noticed, I haven't got a battering ram on me."

Ramouter didn't answer as he knocked on the door of 4F. Just to check. He pressed his ear to the door but couldn't hear anything. He pulled out the small bunch of keys that were in an exhibit bag and one of the few items not covered in Lauren's blood.

"Are you looking for Lauren?"

Behind Ramouter a slim white man in his early forties stood in the doorway of 4G. "I think that she's gone away for a couple of days."

"Is that what she told you?" Ramouter asked.

"Yeah, I'm Gio. We've been neighbors for about five years. About time she got a boyfriend, if you ask me. She certainly looked a lot happier. Funny thing is, I always thought that she was a lesbian and then I thought she might be asexual."

"Right," said Ramouter as he and DC Swanson shared a look. "We'll arrange for an officer to take a statement from you, but when was the last time you saw her?"

"Hmm, I think it was Wednesday night. Yeah, it was definitely Wednesday, because it was Champions League and I popped out to get some beers. When I came back there was a man outside her door. I remember thinking, *Good for her.* And then about an hour later, I could hear them... You know... Doing it. These walls aren't exactly soundproof, you know."

Probably had his ear to the wall more like, Ramouter thought to himself as he put the key in the lock.

It was odd that the overaccommodating neighbor hadn't even asked if Lauren was OK, if anything had happened to her. From the looks of things, once she was formally identified, Gio would be the first one standing in front of the camera telling the world how shocked he was, how this was a quiet area and that she kept to herself.

The flat was small. The corridor was tiny. On the wall was a key rack with no keys next to a framed poster promising that GOOD THINGS ARE GOING TO HAPPEN. Ramouter shook his head at the tragic irony. He walked into the small open-plan living room and kitchen. Dirty dishes filled the sink. On the small dining table were two bottles of wine—one empty, the other a third full—and a tipped-over wineglass, a large red stain on the floor beneath it. Ramouter jumped as the automatic air freshener squirted the overpowering vanilla aroma in his direction. The bookcase was a mixture of chick lit, true-crime paperbacks, CDs and DVDs all covered with dust.

Ramouter looked around for family photographs or anything to show that there was more to Lauren Varma than secondhand books and cheap air freshener, but found nothing. He examined the bedroom, which was warm and stuffy. A blue duvet lay in a crumpled heap on the floor. An empty red condom box rested on the chipped bedside table, its wrappers on the floor. Ramouter checked the wardrobe and pulled open the drawers. In the second drawer he found Lauren's diary. The last entry was dated Tuesday night.

I know that it's a risk, but you have to take a risk in life, don't you? I can't believe that after all this time I'm finally going to meet my Peter. Once we're together, properly together, in each other's arms, everything will be better. We all make mistakes...

"Not as big as this," Ramouter muttered, putting the journal back.

"What was that, mate?" Swanson was hovering by the doorway.

"Nothing, nothing," said Ramouter as he picked up a pile of letters that had been hidden beneath her underwear. They were all the same standard envelopes kindly provided by Her Majesty's Prison Service. Ramouter opened the first one, silently impressed by Olivier's penmanship. He was a sadistic monster but you wouldn't guess that from these pages. Olivier quoted Shakespeare's sonnets. He wrote about his devoted love for Lauren and how the crumbling justice system had made a terrible, tragic mistake.

As Ramouter pushed the bathroom door open, he was struck by the pungent scent of rotten meat. Stale and coppery. The fumes soaked into the grooves of his throat. Blood, mixed with flesh, and bone covered the floor and stained the grout. The white porcelain bathtub was covered in dark streaks of blood and congealed hair.

A bloodbath. That was the term people used, without really thinking about what it meant, but now Ramouter was seeing it for himself, for the first time.

77

Karen Bajarami pushed the food tray away. She'd managed to eat a couple of spoonfuls of mashed potato and some kind of meat pie before giving up. The painkillers had stolen her sense of taste, but only slightly dulled the throbbing pain around her right eye. She put her hand to her still swollen cheek and wiped away the infected discharge that had soaked through the bandage. This wasn't the plan. She thought back to their conversations. She thought about Ade, how his head had been crushed into the ground, and how no one would tell her how he was doing. The nurses thought that it was the pain that kept her awake at night, but it was the sound of his breaking bones that gave her nightmares. She was changing the channel to the news when her door creaked open.

"What are you doing here?" Karen whispered as Olivier walked into the room. Her eyes filled with tears again as Olivier walked over and kissed her forehead.

"You shouldn't be here. They're looking for you. Everyone is looking for you," she said.

"Shh. I brought you a present," Olivier replied. "Close your eyes…sorry, I meant eye."

Karen did as she was told. She trembled as Olivier put his hand around her neck. She felt the coolness of a necklace, a metal chain, rest against her skin.

"Can I look?" Karen asked, fingering the pendant.

"Not until I've gone, but you can look at me."

Karen tensed. The tenderness in Olivier's voice had gone jagged.

"I thought that there was a policeman outside," Karen said. "I was supposed to have security."

"Are you scared," Olivier asked, "of me?"

Karen's heart beat faster as Olivier brushed away a strand of hair that had fallen across her forehead.

"No. Of course not… I just. What if someone finds you here? I don't want anything to happen to you. We have plans."

"If it makes you feel better, I'm not staying. I just wanted something from you. I'm running low on cash. I thought that you could give me your cash card. It's not like you're going anywhere for a while."

"You want…money? Is that why you came here?" Karen asked.

"Among other things." Olivier walked to the cabinet. "Is it in here? Your purse?"

"It's next to my phone."

"I need your pin number." He removed the card and placed it in his back pocket.

"Four-eight-seven-three."

"Right, I'm going to leave but before I do I need to ask you something else."

Karen froze as Olivier placed his calloused hand on her chin and lifted her head up. No emotion in his gaze, only a steely determination.

"You've already spoken to Detective Inspector Henley," Olivier said as he squeezed Karen's cheek.

"She…she came by but I didn't say anything to her."

Olivier squeezed harder. "She's going to come again to talk to you. She's not stupid. She's probably already worked out that you've been helping me."

"But I was careful and you…you hurt me when—"

Olivier pushed his hand against Karen's mouth, trapping the breath in her throat.

"You will tell her nothing. You promised me that you would always be loyal. Do you remember that?"

Karen tried to turn away from him, to escape his terrible gaze.

"I'm not sure if I believe you," Olivier said as he jammed his fingers into Karen's bandaged eye, the other hand covering her mouth, suffocating her screams.

Karen grabbed handfuls of the blue blanket as red-hot shock waves of pain coursed through her body.

"What are you going to tell Inspector Henley when she comes?"

Karen coughed and gasped for breath as Olivier released his hands. She tried to speak as her damaged eye bled. "Nothing," she finally said. "I promise."

Olivier stood up with satisfaction. "Loyal," he said.

"Loyal," Karen whispered back.

78

"I was right. Lauren Varma," said Ramouter.

Henley and Ramouter were back at the SCU with hundreds of letters to Olivier spread across a desk.

"I just don't get it. How could anyone in their right mind want to be in a relationship with Olivier?"

"You met him," Henley replied, unwrapping her bacon roll. "He has a way about him."

"But he's a murderer. Surely at some point something would click in your brain and tell you that writing to him and agreeing to meet him may not be a good idea."

"What did Mark call it again?" Henley flipped through the notes from her conversation with Mark earlier when he had been stuck in traffic on the M6. "Hybristophilia. People who are sexually aroused and attracted to people who have committed cruel, gruesome crimes, for example, murder and rape."

Ramouter pulled a face.

"Maybe she thought that she could fix him," Henley said solemnly. "People get into relationships with all sorts of strange people. Some people like a project. Turn them into something different. For all we know Olivier could have persuaded Lauren to help him."

"You think that Varma, Bajarami and maybe Blaine were working together?"

"Right now, nothing would surprise me."

"Ah, I found it. Her last letter to him."

Ramouter handed the letter over to Henley. It was dated a few months ago and there was a slight whiff of perfume on the lined pages. The letter was written in purple ink with hearts instead of a dot above the letter *i*. It reminded Henley of letters written by lovestruck teenage girls in the back of their school notebooks. She began to read out loud.

"My darling, I was so happy when I received your letter and it was even better to hear your voice. That was the best surprise and really made my day. I wish that I had recorded our telephone call. I love you so much. I miss hearing your voice. It would be nice if I could actually see you and touch you. It upsets me that I may never be able to hold you in my arms. I've been shopping and I've bought you a tracksuit and a pair of trainers. I've booked a few days off work next week, so I will come down to the prison…"

"God, this is nauseating," Henley said. "How many more are there?"

"From her? Another eight that I've found. She's been writing to him for about a year."

"Poor delusional cow," Henley said as she picked up the ringing phone on her desk. "DI Henley,"

"Hey, it's Linh. Didn't get a chance to speak to you earlier."

"How's it going down there?"

"They're about to move the body. I'm heading back to the mortuary, but I just wanted to give you a heads-up. I'm estimating time of death to be within the last twenty-four hours."

Henley nodded. If the CCTV wasn't enough to convince her that Olivier was responsible, the fact that Lauren Varma had been killed recently went against the copycat's entire MO. "Are there any parts missing?"

"No, as you saw for yourself, two arms, two legs, no missing fingers or toes, but what I can tell you is that there are ligature marks on the wrists and ankles and bruising on the neck and the back of her head. Can't say yet if the bruising was caused post-mortem. Other than the driver's license being put inside her, I can't see any external signs of sexual activity, but I will let you know. Haven't got much on today so I can pretty much start as soon as she gets here. There's something else."

"What is it?"

"She's been branded. But this is different."

"How is it different?"

"It's a series of letters and numbers across both her breasts. I'm not sure what it means. I've got pictures, which I can email to you now."

"Thanks, Linh."

Henley put the phone down and repeated to Ramouter what Linh had just told her. A couple of minutes later her computer pinged with an email alert. Henley opened the email from Linh. It was a close-up of Lauren Varma's breasts. Beneath the blood, five numbers and two letters had been cut across the skin.

"What do you think it means?" said Ramouter. "A postcode? A password, maybe?"

"No. No." Henley copied out the sequence on a piece of paper. "A0743TP. Can't you see it?" she asked.

"No. What am I looking at?"

"Doesn't that look like a prisoner number to you?" Henley turned toward her computer and pulled up the email that Pellacia had sent confirming her visit to Belmarsh prison the previous week.

"The bastard." Henley turned the laptop around to show Ramouter.

"You've got to be joking," said Ramouter. "Peter Francis Olivier. Date of birth November 8, 1975. Prison number A0743TP. Why would he do that?"

"He doesn't care. He really doesn't care. This is just a game to him now," Henley said, furiously pacing around the room.

"So, what now?" asked Ramouter.

"What do you mean?" Henley stopped pacing and tried to calm down.

"Well, we've got two investigations running alongside each other. Our copycat and now Olivier's gone and killed again. Do you think that they're working together?"

Henley shook her head. "No, Olivier is too egotistical for that, but we can't rule anything out. We can ask Mark what he thinks. But cutting his prison number into her breasts—he's making sure we know it's all about him. I doubt that he would want to share his handiwork with anyone. In his head, he probably thinks that the copycat is substandard. Probably wants to show him how it's done."

Just then Pellacia walked through the door, carrying a box of doughnuts.

"You had an early start. It's not exactly healthy, but it's something," said Pellacia, putting the doughnuts down onto Stanford's desk.

Ramouter's face paled. "I don't think that I can eat anything right now," he said.

"That bad, was it?"

"Go ahead, Ramouter. Update him," said Henley as she distracted herself with the letters on her desk. Ramouter ran through the investigation so far.

"Any sightings of Olivier?" asked Pellacia when Ramouter had finished.

"No, there's been nothing. It's like he's disappeared into the wind again."

"And I've got more bad news for you. Chance Blaine was released twenty minutes ago."

"Fuck." Henley put her hands to her head. "I didn't want him out. I thought that you were going to speak to the CPS?"

"I did but they weren't having it. At least he's got bail conditions. To live and sleep at his home address and no contact with the rest of the jurors. Stanford and Eastwood are carrying out surveillance on him for the next twenty-four hours. That should make you happy?"

"No," said Henley, storming out of the office. "That does not make me happy."

Henley looked at her face in the bathroom mirror and grimaced. Not that she was one to spend hours doing her makeup, but she usually did a good job of hiding the dark circles under her eyes and the small scar on her cheek. She finished brushing her teeth and sprayed herself with deodorant. It wasn't even midday, but she just wanted to go home, lie in bed and cry a bit. The bathroom door opened. It was Pellacia.

"What are you doing in here?" Henley asked.

"Why did you come to me last night?" Pellacia closed the door behind him.

"Now is not the time."

"So, when would be a good time? You were going to walk out of my house without saying a word."

"You know full well that it wasn't like that. Ramouter called and—"

"You were almost out the door before he called you."

Henley picked up her bag from the edge of the sink. "I shouldn't have come. It shouldn't have happened."

"I don't understand why you keep fighting me on this."

"Because I have a husband and we have a child. What do you want from me? I made a mistake."

"Is that what I am to you, then? A mistake."

"No, of course you're not. I'm sorry, that was the wrong word… I was… Lonely. *I* made the mistake."

Pellacia looked down at the old, cracked tiles on the floor while Henley tried to avoid her reflection in the mirror.

"You know how I feel about you," Pellacia finally said.

"Stop. Stephen, please."

Pellacia placed his hands on his lips, composing himself. Preparing himself. "I didn't plan to follow you in here. I'm sorry."

"It's OK. *I'm* sorry." Henley wanted to reach out, to hold him, but she held back.

"It's not easy. Seeing you every day, worrying about you… Anyway, I thought that you would want to know. DS Lancaster has been formally suspended, pending an investigation. Still doesn't answer the question as to who leaked the initial story to the press, but hopefully we'll…" Pellacia's voice trailed off. "You do realize that you're involved in three separate active investigations?"

"Technically, Olivier's escape hasn't been allocated to us. The NCA have that one." Henley opened her bag and rummaged around for the hand cream.

"Doesn't really matter what the job sheet says. You're involved in all of this. I just want you to be careful. I'm worried about you." And with that, he walked out.

Henley went into one of the stalls, pulled down the toilet seat and sat down. Her mouth felt dry and her breath was coming through in rapid gasps. She wanted to strip naked and throw herself into a pool of water, to shock her body into normality. She kicked the toilet door, leaving behind a dent.

"Oh my God." Henley pushed her hands against her temples, anything to stop the pulse in her head. She squeezed her eyes closed, but the images of Zoe Darego, Lauren Varma, Daniel

Kennedy and Sean Delaney's bloodied and dismembered bodies kept flashing in her head. It was all too much. She had thought that she could control it. Keep the PTSD locked away.

"Henley, are you in here? There's a call for you."

Henley tried to respond to Joanna, but her words were swallowed up in tear-filled chokes.

"Henley?" The tone in Joanna's voice switched.

Henley stiffened as Joanna gently tapped on the door.

"Anjelica, love. Open the door."

"I can't."

"Come on. Yes, you can."

Henley took a deep breath, stood up and opened the door.

"Oh, sweetheart, come here."

Henley fell into Joanna's arms. Joanna held her tighter and rubbed her back.

"I thought that I could do this, Jo," said Henley. "But it's all falling apart."

"You put too much pressure on yourself. You don't have to do this to yourself."

Henley pulled herself away, walked toward the sink and ran the cold tap. Her eyes were red and puffy. Her face pale and strained.

"I should have seen it coming," said Joanna as she pulled sheets of tissue paper from the dispenser.

"I thought that I was ready," Henley said as Joanna soaked the paper and gently wiped away the streaked mascara from under her eyes. The cool tissue felt soothing. "That first day by the river. I had nerves but I did the job. I went to the mortuary. I looked at Kennedy's body cut into pieces and I thought…" Henley didn't try to stop herself from crying again.

"Is that when it started?" Joanna handed Henley more tissues.

There was no point hiding it from Joanna or herself. Henley saw herself sitting naked on the edge of her bed, watching her right-hand tremble. She had gone to bed that night convinced that she was dying.

"I wish that you'd said something to me," said Joanna. "You've been through so much, poppet. If Rhimes was here…" Her voice trailed off. "I wish that he hadn't…well. You know."

"I miss him," said Henley. "I miss him and hate him at the same time. Rhimes wasn't just my boss. He knew me. He was family and he killed himself. He brought all of us together and he didn't even try and let us help him. I hate that I'm weak right now. Look at me, Jo. I'm losing everything. I'm losing myself."

"I've got some diazepam in my desk drawer," said Joanna. "Don't look at me like that. They're probably out of date. I found them when I was clearing out Rhimes's desk."

"I shouldn't." Henley checked her reflection in the mirror. "God, I look like shit."

"They're low dosage. Just a little something to calm you down. If you don't want it, then I can go across the road to the bookies and ask one of those lads who hang around outside for a couple of ounces of weed."

"You don't have to do that."

"Well, at least take half of the pill."

"Just half."

"Promise. Go downstairs to the old cells. I'll bring you down a cup of tea and have a kip for an hour. I'll cover for you. They've got enough to keep them busy for a while."

"Thanks, Jo."

"Anytime. Someone's got to keep a lookout for you."

The diazepam had calmed her, slowed down her heartbeat, but it couldn't stop the voices in her head. Closing her eyes didn't erase the images of bloodied body parts. Henley sat up and looked at the wall where a previous occupant had written the word *wanker*. Henley wanted to lock the door and hide in the cells forever, to insulate herself from the chaos outside. She banged her hand against the wall as the image of Olivier, lying on top of her, licking her face, plunging the knife into her, lingered in her mind's eye, a video on pause. She could hear him repeating his promise to kill her. She had thought she was ready, that she was strong enough, but right now she was convinced that this case was going to kill her.

79

Queen Elizabeth Hospital had grown calmer. The enhanced security had disbanded, and the journalists and camera crews had finally moved on. Henley took the lift up to the third floor. No one paid any attention as she walked past the nurses' station and made her way to Karen's room. An unimpressive security guard sat outside the door playing a game on his phone. Henley followed the instructions on the safety poster, pressed the dispenser on the wall and rubbed her hands vigorously with the antibacterial liquid. The TV above Karen's head was restricted to the nonpremium channels. As far as Henley could tell, she was watching another episode of *Judge Rinder* even though her right eye was covered with a bandage. The bedside cabinet was filled with flowers and the requisite bunch of grapes and a large bottle of Lucozade.

"Hello, Karen," Henley said.

"Oh, Inspector. Sorry, I've forgotten your name," Karen replied, pushing herself up on the bed. Her face was still heavily bruised and swollen.

"Inspector Henley. They were still going heavy on the painkillers the last time I was here."

"I needed them, but they've taken away my drip now. This is just antibiotics." Karen tapped at the cannula in her hand. "I caught an infection yesterday."

"How much longer are you staying in, then?"

Henley forced herself to put a smile on her face. To show that she genuinely cared.

"I should be going home on Sunday. The doctors are just waiting for this infection to clear up."

"And the eye? I hope that there's no permanent damage?" said Henley. She pulled a chair from the corner and sat down.

"They're still not sure." Karen put a hand to her bandaged eye and winced. "I had the dressing changed yesterday but everything is still swollen. They're not sure if the damage is going to be..." She put a hand to her chest and took a breath. "They're not sure if the damage is going to be permanent."

"Have you managed to see your colleague, Ade?" Henley asked. Would there be any acknowledgment that she was partially responsible for his condition?

"Oh...er... I haven't been able to see him. How is he?"

"He's still in a coma. He has a fractured skull and there's swelling in his brain."

Karen looked down at the hospital-issued blanket. "I... Will he recover?"

"They're not sure."

Karen looked up at Henley with her good eye before turning away. "I didn't think..."

"You didn't think what?"

"Nothing, nothing. Ade didn't deserve that. It all happened so quickly."

"You spent a lot of time with Olivier, didn't you?"

Henley noticed the subtle spark in Karen's good eye at the mention of his name.

"It wasn't by choice. It was just part of my job. I wasn't with him all of the time."

"But you were short-staffed. Not enough prison officers? It's the same as the force. It's the same everywhere." Henley leaned forward in her chair. "You're overstretched, so probably ended up doing more than your fair share?"

Karen nodded. "The pay is rubbish. The hours are rubbish and there aren't enough of us."

"Did you know that Olivier had access to a mobile phone?"

Karen didn't answer.

"Do you have any idea how he would have got a phone?"

"Another prisoner? Or one of the guards. It wouldn't be the first time."

"Even in the High Security Unit? I thought that they would have been a bit more vigilant about that sort of thing."

"I didn't know that he had a phone." Karen shifted uncomfortably in her bed. "It's not as if he was kept in isolation. There were other prisoners that he could talk to. They could have easily given him a phone."

"Did he tell you that he was feeling ill?" Henley picked up the jug of water on the table and poured a glass for Karen.

"Not at all." Karen gratefully took the cup. "He didn't ask to see the doctor unless he mentioned something to another guard before I started my shift."

"You weren't with him when he collapsed, were you?"

"No, I was doing checks on the wing. Is this an interview?"

"No, no. I just wanted to see how you were doing and to ask you a few questions about when Olivier escaped. You're an important witness. We still haven't caught him yet, so any information you can give us about that day is vital."

"I told those other officers everything I knew when they came this morning." Karen sounded almost petulant.

"They were agents from the NCA and there's been another murder since then and we have evidence that leads us to Olivier being a suspect."

"Peter wouldn't... I mean... Why would he?"

It wasn't lost on Henley that Bajarami always called Olivier by his first name.

"He's a killer. It's what he does. There's a possible attempted murder charge for what he did to Ade and of course the GBH with intent charges against you and the security guard."

Henley could tell that her questions were making Karen uncomfortable and nervous, as she began to fiddle with the chain around her neck. "It's like I said in my statement. It all happened so quickly. I was outside when I heard the commotion and then when I got in the room, he... I didn't even know that he had the fork in his hand."

She looked as though she was about to cry but Henley wasn't convinced the tears were genuine.

"Was there anything else that you wanted to ask me?" Karen asked.

"There is actually. Someone provided Olivier with insulin. Turns out that the insulin was taken from the hospital wing of the prison—"

"What are you saying?"

"Well, I don't think that Olivier left his wing, strolled down and got it himself. An officer must have got it for him."

"It wasn't me."

"Do you have any idea who it could be?"

"No, no... I don't... I have no idea why anyone would help him. Look at what he did to me and Ade."

"There is one more thing," said Henley. "The Franklin-Jones Cold Storage Facility. Have you heard of it?"

Karen repeated the name and shook her head. "Why?"

"We've got footage of a woman who looks like you in the reception area of the storage facility last week."

"No, it couldn't have been me. I've never been to Manor Park and I'm pretty sure that I was working last week. It must be someone who looks like me. I've got one of those faces."

Henley's stomach flipped. "I never said that it was in Manor Park."

"I thought that you did. Is there anything else?" Karen asked. "It's just that I'm really tired."

The chain that Karen had been fiddling with had escaped the confines of her hospital gown and was now dangling from her neck.

"No, that's it," Henley said. "Your necklace. My daughter would love that. She's crazy about stars."

"Thank you." Karen sat back in her bed and quickly placed her necklace inside her hospital gown.

"What's the crystal next to it?"

"Oh, I'm not sure. It was a get-well gift."

"Your boyfriend?"

"Something like that." Karen sat back in the bed and held out the chain in front of her. "A good friend."

Henley left Karen in her room and made her way to the nurses' station.

"Excuse me—" Henley held out her warrant card to the nurse sitting at the desk. "I need to ask you a question about your patient Karen Bajarami in room six."

"I'm not allowed to disclose any information about our patients," he said.

"I don't want information about her specifically. I just want to know if she's had any visitors. I'll go downstairs and check with security, but if you were here—"

"She's had a few," said the young nurse who was sitting next to him. Her nametag said Isma. "I think her mum came again yesterday and a couple of her work friends. I had to tell them there were too many in the room."

"Is there anyone else?" asked Henley.

"Oh, there was a man who came first thing this morning. Do you remember, Julien?" said Isma. "He bought her a bunch of

M&S ready meals and asked if there was somewhere we could keep them."

"Oh, yeah, him," said Julien, ignoring the phone ringing on his desk. "I buzzed him through. He wasn't too impressed about the menu. Can't say that I blame him. I wouldn't feed it to my cat and I don't even like my cat."

"Can you remember what he looked like?"

Julien looked across at Isma and shook his head. "Not really. He was white, tall. Maybe in his forties. He was very nice, gave us some chocolates to say thank you. If my gran was here, she would say that he was charming."

"He's clearly got a plan," said Henley. "I doubt very much he's hanging around just because he's concerned about his girlfriend."

"So why even visit her?" Pellacia asked, frowning. "What use is Karen Bajarami to him now? She's helped him escape and she nearly lost an eye for it. Why didn't she scream blue murder when Olivier came to see her?"

"You didn't see the look on her face when I asked her about the necklace. She was pleased."

"We need to bring her in." Pellacia was unequivocal.

"I know that, but I'm stuck until a doctor says that she's fit to be discharged," said Henley.

"PACE guidelines don't actually say that she has to be interviewed at a police station and it doesn't mean that we haven't got grounds to search her flat. For all we know, Olivier could be staying there. Where does she live?"

"Kidbrooke. It's going to take me about an hour to scrape an application together and then I've got to find a judge or magistrate to hear my application."

Pellacia checked his watch. "You've got time. Get the application done and then show yourself at Camberwell Green Magistrates' and get before a judge. As soon as we get the warrant, we're searching Bajarami's flat and then we're arresting her. I don't give a shit if she's declared fit or not."

80

Henley printed off a second copy of the application for a warrant to search Karen Bajarami's flat. She doubted that she would find Olivier sitting in the front room with his feet up, but she was praying she'd discover concrete evidence of Bajarami's involvement in Olivier's escape.

Her phone rumbled. Linh was calling.

"Hey, you," said Henley. "What's up?"

"He used a ripsaw."

"He used a what?"

"A ripsaw. You know, a carpenter's saw. Google it. I bet that your dad probably has one."

Henley's mind flashed back to an image of her uncle Joel holding down the branches of their apple tree while her dad attacked it with a saw.

"Who used a ripsaw?" Henley asked. "Olivier?"

"No, not him. Your copycat," said Linh. "Remember, Olivier's cuts were always clean because he used an electronic saw. A jigsaw. Which is exactly what he used on Varma. This other loon is using a good old-fashioned saw."

"But that would take... Well..." Henley couldn't think of a more delicate way to phrase it. "Isn't that just hard work?"

"Not really. I mean, the middle phalanx is going to be much easier to cut through than the femur, but then again, the simplest place to cut is the joint, like you're jointing a chicken."

"Oh, for God's sake," Henley muttered under her breath as she placed the search warrant application into a folder.

"If you are cutting through bone, then, depending on how fit your victim was, the bone may not even be that hard. God forbid if any of your victims were skiers or climbers—then your copycat would have had one hell of a job. Their bones are as hard as... They're just incredibly hard. Personally, I would have started with a hacksaw instead of a ripsaw, but I can't really determine if he used both."

"And our copycat used the same method on the last three victims?" Henley imagined Kennedy, Zoe and Delaney sitting motionless, unable to close their eyes as a man, his face darkened by shadows, sawed off their limbs.

"I've got a wound expert preparing a full report for you," said Linh.

"Thank you, Linh. I appreciate it."

"Not a problem and come over to mine if you're at a loss tonight. It's been ages since we got drunk, had a good old bitch about life and danced to the classics of '95."

"Why '95?" Henley laughed for the first time in days.

"I don't know. I've lost count of the number of posters that I've seen advertising a 'Back to '95' club night. So I'll see you later?"

"You will." Henley ended the call with immense gratitude for her friend.

"It's a bit savage, isn't it?" said Ramouter after Henley had told him how the copycat had been dismembering his victims.

"I think that's an understatement," she said.

"I mean, his whole MO is savage. Our copycat paralyzes them, makes them watch as he cuts off their limbs and, even after they're dead, he stabs them," said Ramouter.

"You're not suggesting that Olivier is more humane, are you?" Henley asked with surprise.

"No, not humane," Ramouter mused. "He's just a bit more clinical about it, isn't he? Efficient."

"Lauren Varma wasn't about efficiency," Henley said sadly. "He doesn't care, which is why he made such a display of her."

"But he made such a big deal about this being a miscarriage of justice."

"To him it probably is. The miscarriage to him is that he was caught."

Henley had seen the photographs of Lauren Varma's flat that the forensics team had emailed over to her. Even though Ramouter had worked CID back in Bradford, she doubted that he had ever come across scenes like the one Lauren Varma had been killed in and the one in which she had been found.

It had only been two weeks, but she could already see the pressures of working in the SCU on his face. They had no real support. It was just them. A unit that had been positioned as a reward, but was really a way to keep their old boss out of trouble. Now Rhimes was dead, and even though she had absolute faith in Pellacia to run the SCU, Henley worried the department was running on fumes.

"Salim."

He looked up, aware that this was the first time Henley had used his first name.

"Talk to Mark Ryan. Believe me. You don't want to get too deep inside the head of these psychopaths. This sort of work will screw with your brain and it will hit you when you least expect it. Mark's good to talk to."

"I don't want anyone to think that I can't hack it."

"No one would ever think that."

"OK. I'll give him a call."

"Good. It won't hurt. What was your plan for the rest of the day?"

"Just to go over the statements, see if we've missed anything and then home."

"Fancy a trip to the seaside?"

"What?"

"The witness who said that he saw Sean Delaney being put into an ambulance."

"Leon Merrick?"

"He's in a rehab facility in Hove, isn't he?"

"For at least three months."

"Leon is the closest that we've got to a possible identification. I want you to go and see him."

"What? Now? It's almost 5 p.m."

"Yes, now."

"I don't think that my Oyster card will get me as far as Hove."

"Take my car."

Ramouter stared at Henley as though she had temporarily taken leave of her senses. "Are you sure? I've never been to Hove."

"Hove is not the end of the world, Ramouter."

Henley walked back to her desk and flicked through the file until she found what she was looking for. "Take these." It was the custody pictures taken of Alessandro Naylor and Dominic Pine.

"These photographs are a couple of years old," Ramouter said as he grabbed his jacket from the back of his chair.

"They'll have to do. We haven't got any recent pictures of Pine and Naylor, and they haven't changed that much," Henley replied. "Either the photo will trigger something in Leon, or it won't."

81

The journey down to Hove was quite straightforward, and if he was honest, Ramouter was glad to get out of the office. The intense feeling of the SCU, and Henley, were making him feel claustrophobic.

As he stepped out of the car in front of the Elysium Clinic, he had to admit that the coastal air felt different. For the first time since he'd left Bradford and the pressures of looking after a wife amid her denial of early onset dementia, he could breathe.

The reception area looked as though it belonged to a spa hotel, with expensive-looking white sofas and armchairs in front of a large bay window that looked out to the sea. It was a far cry from the public rehab center where Sean Delaney had worked.

"Good afternoon. Can I help you?" said the woman behind the reception desk.

"Hi. I'm Detective Ramouter." He didn't feel the need to tell her that he was still a few months away from being signed off as a fully-fledged detective. "I'm here to see one of your patients."

The red-lipsticked smile on the receptionist's face quickly disappeared as she looked at Ramouter's warrant card.

"Do you have an appointment? We pride ourselves on confidentiality. We just can't have anyone walking in."

Ramouter straightened himself up. Maybe he hadn't said the word *detective* loud enough. Henley wouldn't have this, he said to himself. She never had to say much to get what she wanted. She had an authoritative presence about her, something that they didn't teach you in police training.

"As I said, I'm Detective Ramouter and I want to speak to Leon Merrick."

"We get a lot of journalists coming in here, pretending to be family, friends and—"

"Look, do you want my boss to call your boss? Believe me, I doubt that would be a good thing for either of us. I've shown you my warrant card. I've told you who I am. I know that Leon Merrick is here. I want to see him now."

The receptionist looked down at her computer. After what seemed like the longest minute in Ramouter's life, she said, "He has a group therapy session which is finishing in about fifteen minutes. I'll have someone take to you to one of the visitors' lounges. Would you like a tea or coffee while you wait?"

Ramouter had to stop himself from asking if he should take off his shoes when he was led into the visitors' lounge by another member of staff. He had just eaten his second shortbread biscuit when a tall dark-haired man walked into the room. His collarbone stuck out sharply as he extended his hand.

"I'm Leon," he said with a smile, revealing teeth that had been chipped and stained by a crack pipe.

"How are you?" Ramouter asked, his eyes following the track marks and yellowing bruises on Leon's arm.

"Doing OK." Leon sank into an armchair.

"Anyway, Leon, I'm not going to take up a lot of your time."

"Nah, it's fine, mate. My options this afternoon are yoga, mindfulness or Reiki." Leon screwed up his face. "Not even a trip down to the pier. Apparently, I'm not ready for that yet. Have you caught him, the person who killed Sean?"

Ramouter shook his head.

"He was nice, you know. Decent. Not patronizing like a lot of them. He actually cared. He didn't deserve to die like that."

"I wanted to ask you some more questions about that night. I thought that things might be a bit clearer now that you're…"

"Not as high as a NASA spaceship. What do you want to know?"

Ramouter took out his notebook and flicked through the pages. "You said that you got to the center about eight."

"It might have been later than that because I remembered that I sat in the pub for a bit and the football was on. Sunday night. It must have been Spanish footie. Seven-thirty kickoff and I left when it finished, so it must have been around 9:30 p.m."

"And you went straight to the center?"

"Yeah. I was clucking and when that happens you get one thought in your head and you just focus on that. I remembered thinking that I needed to see Sean because he would help me. Sometimes… I mean… He's not supposed to, but if he had it, he would have given me some methadone, to take the edge off. Calm me down."

"What time does the center usually close?"

"Officially, nine."

"Even on a Sunday?"

"They have group therapy sessions. If you're really lucky you might get a Jammie Dodger and a cup of tea. Not like this place. Every posh herbal tea known to man and pastries that no one eats."

Ramouter looked down at his own cup of tea next to the bone china teapot.

"Anyway," Leon continued as he picked up a biscuit from the plate. "I remember walking past and the light was still on."

"How do you get into the center?"

"You have to be buzzed in. They've got one of those inter-coms with the security camera on the front and then there's an emergency exit at the back. I think that it's supposed to be the fire escape."

"Were you buzzed in?"

Leon leaned back as he chewed on his biscuit. "Couldn't have been, otherwise I wouldn't have gone around the back."

"What made you go to the back?"

"Sean smokes. Usually out the back by the car park. I went to the back, saw his motorbike was there and then I saw the ambulance car thing."

"And it was definitely an ambulance?"

"Yeah. Not a big one, but like I told you on the phone, one of those car ones."

"Too much to ask if you could remember the number plate?"

"Ha, chance would be a fine thing. The car door was open and my crazy head thought that someone might help me or that there might be drugs in there."

"You said last time that you saw a man in the back of the car?"

"Yeah, I did. He was slumped down. I couldn't see his face. He was at a funny angle and the man was putting his legs in."

"Is there anything that you can remember about the man in the back seat?"

"Like I said, I think that it was Sean, but I couldn't be a hun-dred percent sure."

"What about the man? You spoke to him?"

"Yeah, but he shoved me out of the way."

"Can you describe him?"

There was silence, occasionally filled by the sounds of seagulls flying by and Leon munching on a biscuit.

"White. A little bit shorter than me, and I'm six foot three, so he was at least six feet. He was wearing dark clothes. Could have been green. Trainers, I remember that. Dark hair, short. He was bigger than me but not as big as you."

"I didn't think that I was that big," Ramouter said with a grin.

"No, you're not. He was just between the two of us. Put it this way, if he was a boxer, he would be a light middleweight."

"Anything else?"

"Broken nose. Well, it looked disjointed to me. Stubble."

"I want you to take a look at these photographs," said Ramouter. "Can you see the man who was in the car park of the drug center on September 8, 2019, at around 9:30 p.m.?" He pushed aside the bone china tea set and the plate of posh biscuits and fanned the photographs across the table. He had printed off photographs of twelve other men who had volunteered to have their images taken and used in an ID parade and had mixed them up with the photos that Henley had given him. "Take your time."

Leon kneeled down and inspected the pictures.

"Not him, not him, not him." Leon picked up three of the photographs and put them on the floor.

"This one," Leon said, picking up a photograph and handing it to Ramouter.

"Are you sure?" Ramouter took the photograph of Dominic Pine from Leon's shaking hand.

"I'd put money on it. Definitely."

"That's the man you saw in the car park?"

"A hundred percent."

Ramouter had been thinking about getting fish and chips and eating it on the pier before heading back to London, but as he put the photographs in his pocket, he found he had lost his appetite.

82

"Where's Ramouter now?" asked Pellacia.

"Somewhere on the M23." Henley pulled out her phone to check if there had been any more messages from Ramouter.

"Well, at least we've got an ID on Pine."

"At best it's someone who *looks* like Pine who was possibly putting someone who *looked* like Delaney into an ambulance."

"No CCTV of the car park?"

"Nothing there. I don't think the council are that interested in the security of a bunch of recycling bins outside a drug center."

"What about the ambulance service?"

"I've been chasing them, asking them to confirm if there were any paramedics dispatched to the drug center or surrounding streets on the night that Delaney disappeared. It's like you said. The evidence is flaky at best. An eyewitness who's a drug addict is not enough to wipe Naylor's and Blaine's names off the board."

"Take a step back," said Pellacia as he walked up to the white-board. "What happens if we use all of our resources on putting together a case against Pine?"

It was the same tactic that Rhimes had used when he could see that his team were at the breaking point.

"If we focus on Pine, then we have no eyes on Naylor and Blaine. Naylor has already slipped away from the officers protecting him and he has access to commercial and private properties because of his work," said Henley. "And Blaine? Well, he's Olivier's little helper. I'd have to be an idiot to think that he doesn't know how to contact him or vice versa."

"Don't forget Bajarami," said Pellacia. "She's your loose thread."

Henley screwed up her face in concentration. She had to find a way to tighten the noose around her three suspects without jeopardizing the lives of her jurors.

"I'm going to head off to Bajarami's place," said Henley. "Eastwood is already on her way."

There was a sharp rapping on the door. Henley turned around to see Ezra standing outside.

"Everything all right?" asked Henley, concerned. The first time that Ezra had come to the incident room he'd stumbled across A3-sized autopsy pictures on the wall. He hadn't been back since.

"Yeah, I just need to show you something," Ezra said. "In private."

Henley looked at Ezra quizzically. "What is it?" She followed him out into the corridor.

"You need to promise, right, that you won't get mad," said Ezra, leaning against the wall and tapping his passcode into his iPad.

"Why would I get mad?" Henley knew full well that whatever Ezra had done would not be admissible as evidence in any court in the world.

"In my defense, all I've done—"

"What have you done?" Henley snapped.

"Take a look." Ezra handed the iPad to Henley.

"It's subscriber information," said Henley as she scrolled

through the list of phone numbers. "From Olivier's mobile phone."

"Yeah. I've been waiting for the phone company to do a subscriber check, but they've been saying for the past few days that their systems have been unavailable."

"So, what did you do?"

"It's best for all of us if I don't answer that. So, Olivier's phone is pay-as-you-go. Someone has been paying for the credit, which means that they've either been buying top-up vouchers, or they've been using their debit card online."

"Please tell me that they've used a debit card."

Ezra smiled. "That will be the inadmissible-in-court bit. All you need to know right now is that I've got the registered card details."

"Karen Bajarami couldn't be that stupid," said Henley.

"She tried not to be. It was registered to one of those cards that you can load up with money and use like a credit card, but she loaded it up using her own NatWest debit card, which was registered to K. L. Bajarami."

"Are you sure?"

"A hundred percent, but there's more. Now, this stuff will be admissible as soon as I get the authorization application processed."

"What is it?"

"OK. There are private numbers that were calling his phone. So, I've unmasked them. The first number is Chance Blaine and the second number—"

"Please tell me that it's her phone."

"Full two-year contract that expires next March. She pays her bill by direct debit and is always running out of data."

For the first time since Kennedy's body was found, Henley felt that she was getting somewhere. The panic was still there in the middle of her chest, but it wasn't debilitating. She called Eastwood and told her to start the search of Karen Bajarami's flat without her. She picked up the file containing Pine's failed attempt to appeal against his sentence. The request for the court transcripts had taken some time, and after arguments of who was going to pay for it, Joanna had made a call to someone. Stanford was taking bets over whether Joanna had offered a bribe, made a threat or gone with good old-fashioned blackmail.

Henley read through the transcript. Pine's barrister had ultimately failed to convince three Court of Appeal judges that Pine's sentence should be suspended. Pine had been beaten up and raped on his second day in prison. His attacker had then injected him with heroin. Two days later, Pine had suffered a drug-induced psychotic break. Pine was ticking another box in Mark's profile of the copycat. A victim of a traumatic sexual attack. The problem was that Pine had a clear alibi that ruled him out as a suspect. Henley's phone rang. It was Eastwood.

"Hi, Eastie. How did it go?"

"For starters, Karen Bajarami lives with her mum, who was not best pleased about us rocking up at her front door while she was watching *Bargain Hunt*."

"What did her mum say?"

"She watches too much telly if you ask me. Started mouthing off that she knew her rights and that she didn't have to talk to us. I showed her a photograph of Olivier, asked if she had seen him. She said no."

"Did you find anything in the flat?"

"We hit the jackpot. In Bajarami's bedroom we found the mobile phone box for the same make and model that was found in Olivier's cell. We also found an itinerary for an EasyJet flight to Málaga for two, scheduled for yesterday. Passengers names: Karen Bajarami and Raymond McFarlane. In the wardrobe we found a duffel bag filled with men's clothes, underwear, all brand-new, five grand in cash and passports. Legit passport for

Bajarami, fake one for Olivier. If you ask me, I don't think Olivier putting a fork in her eye was part of Bajarami's plan."

Henley looked at the phone number she had scribbled onto a Post-it Note. When she had visited Karen earlier, she had seen her mobile phone on the cabinet, among the flowers and get-well cards. Henley dialed.

As the phone rang, Ramouter walked through the door looking disheveled. Henley put a finger to her lips as he opened his mouth to talk.

"Hello." It was Karen's voice. "Hello," she said again.

Henley waited for a couple of seconds.

"Peter. Baby, is that you?"

Henley put the phone down, knowing that soon she would be placing her handcuffs on Karen Bajarami's wrists. Unless Bajarami had realized it hadn't been Olivier on the phone and tried to make a run for it instead.

83

"I've got news," said Anthony.

"Is it news that I'm going to be happy about?" Henley had decided that the least she could do was treat Ramouter and Ezra to dinner as a thank-you for coming in on a Saturday. Linh had readily agreed to join them.

"I would be happy with it. I've got prints. A couple of partials taken from the plastic wrapping that Sean Delaney's body was in. I've also got blood that doesn't belong to him."

"Are you serious?"

"Absolutely. The only problem is—"

"It's not a match for anyone in the database," said Henley.

"Nothing, and I ran it through three times. The only thing that I can confirm is that the blood that was found on Delaney's body is a DNA match for one of the semen samples that were taken from Carole Lewis's body."

"Thanks, Anthony. I know that you've been swamped. I appreciate it."

"Hey, anytime. Just sorry that it's taken so long and, before you ask, I've been chasing down Naylor's DNA results. I'm hoping for Monday morning at the latest."

"Was that good news?" Ramouter asked.

Henley repeated what Anthony had just told her. It was good news, but right now it had no value.

"This is beyond frustrating," Ramouter said as they walked along the riverfront and toward the restaurant on Greenwich Pier.

"Leon's statement is not enough, and the ID isn't enough either," said Henley.

"But it gives us a date to work with. We can pinpoint when Sean Delaney was taken."

"That helps. I'm just wondering why he kept Delaney that much longer than the others."

"You saw the state of Delaney's body," said Ramouter. "According to Linh he'd been dead at least four days before his body was dumped. It just makes me wonder, where had our copycat been keeping them? Pine lives on the fourth floor and you saw his flat—it's small. And Naylor lives with his aunt and uncle. What if our copycat is keeping them somewhere else? Somewhere local."

He's keeping them somewhere else. Henley thought back to the first time that they had met Dominic Pine at his flat. He had welcomed them in, but there had been something at the time that she couldn't put her finger on. There had been a staleness to the flat. The dust, the old calendar on the wall. It had brought back memories of a fake identity case that she had worked on back when she was a trainee detective. Frederick Jankowski. A fifty-eight-year-old man had been using the identities of dead children in order to claim nearly a million pounds in benefits. When she had first visited his flat in Stockwell, it had smelled like an old suit that had been dumped in a charity shop. Musty, as if the windows had never been opened. It turned out that

Jankowski never lived in the flat. His real home was a large Victorian terrace in Kensington.

"First thing tomorrow, let's pay Pine another visit," Henley said to Ramouter.

84

The depot for the Deptford London Ambulance Service was tucked between a row of terraced houses and a cash-and-carry, and set back behind gates.

"How many ambulance services depots are there in London?" Ramouter asked as Henley flashed her warrant card at the security camera.

"Seventy. If I'm honest, I must have driven past this place a million times and never clocked it."

"There's a lot to London," said Ramouter as he turned his attention to his side of the road where a young black girl with wild multicolored hair sat on the ground. She was looking in Ramouter's direction but straight through him. "Some poor sods think that the city will save them. How old do you reckon she is? Twenty-five?"

Henley took a quick glance as she drove through the open gates. She couldn't allow herself to feel any sympathy for a girl sitting in dirty shorts on a damp pavement.

"We make our choices." Henley thought of the decisions she'd made that hadn't benefited her or her family. "The world can age you."

★ ★ ★

"We thought that Dominic Pine would have been here," said Henley.

"Why do you want to talk to Dom?" asked the deputy station manager, Lisa, as they followed her through the control room, noisy with the sound of ringing phones and sirens.

"We're not at liberty to say, but it's nothing for you to be concerned about it."

"He's not in trouble, then?"

"No. He isn't."

"Hmm, and it's too much wishful thinking that you're here to tell us that you finally caught the bastards that broke in here last month and ransacked a couple of our ambulances?"

"No, it's nothing to do with that."

"He's one of our best," Lisa volunteered as she stopped at the lifts and pressed the button. The doors opened immediately. "That's why I fought so hard for him to come back after all that nonsense."

"What nonsense would that be?" Ramouter asked as he waited for Henley to step into the ancient lift.

"All that prison stuff." Lisa had to raise her voice to be heard as the lift made a jaunty ascent. "He's a good man. Works hard, and if you ask me, what he did wasn't wrong."

"But he broke the rules," Henley said. "The rules are in place for a reason."

Lisa tutted and rolled her eyes. Henley had the feeling that Lisa was going to launch into a well-worn rant.

"Should he have done it? Should he have broken the court rules and told the other jurors about what he'd found out about the Jigsaw Killer?" Lisa continued as the doors opened and they stepped out into an almost serene corridor. "Probably not. Was it worth putting him in prison for six months? Absolutely not. System is a joke. They were going to strike him off."

Henley tried to resist the urge to tell Lisa to shut up, but she doubted that anything would have stopped her so instead she asked, "Who was going to strike him off?"

"Our ridiculous disciplinary board. Bunch of hypocrites. Otis, a guy who worked with me for fifteen years and Dom's old partner, had been tampering with the MDT in the ambulance—"

"MDT?" said Ramouter.

Who the fuck is Otis? Henley thought to herself.

"Mobile Data Tracking." Lisa stopped at the last office at the end of the corridor and knocked loudly. "It's like GPS," she continued. "We use it to track our ambulances, see who is closest to the latest emergency. Otis used to turn it off and reset it so we could never get hold of him. Do you know what the board did when they found out? Suspended him for eight weeks, but with—"

Lisa stopped talking as an Asian man in his mid-fifties opened the door. He extended a hand, which Henley shook.

"You must be DI Henley. I'm Ken Devi. The station manager. Thank you, Lisa, that will be all."

Ken led them into his office, which stood in complete contrast to the rest of the station. His desk was impeccably clean. Even Ramouter was starting to shift uncomfortably, as though he had just been called into the headmaster's office.

"Please take a seat. Do you want a cup of tea or coffee?"

"No, we're fine." Henley sat down in the chair in front of her.

"OK, so. I've taken the liberty of printing out the information that you've requested. I must say that this has caused me a bit of embarrassment as I like to think that I've kept on top of these things, considering the problems that we've had in the past."

Henley could see that whatever Ken had discovered was causing him a lot of discontent. Ramouter raised an eyebrow at her.

He handed a sheet of paper to Henley. "That is a list of all of the ambulances and fast-response units that were dispatched from our station on September 4 between 6 p.m. and 6 a.m. on September 7. As you can see, we received a high number of emergency calls the evening of the sixth, which in itself isn't unusual for a Friday night but—"

"No vehicles were dispatched to the drug and alcohol center on Comet Street in Catford?" Henley handed the piece of paper to Ramouter.

"None."

"Was Dominic Pine working that day?" asked Henley.

Ken nodded, causing his glasses to slide down his nose. He pushed them back up. "He was on a 6 p.m. to 6 a.m. shift."

"Who was his partner?" Ramouter asked. Henley smiled to herself; she was about to ask the same question.

"Dominic is one of our most experienced crew members, so he had been allocated to an FRU, that's a Fast Response Unit. It makes sense as we've been short-staffed, and we can attend to more emergencies, so he didn't have a partner, so to speak," Ken replied.

"He was solo?" Henley asked.

"With the exception of when we've had him out training the new recruits, he's been solo."

"You said Pine worked the six to six shift," said Henley.

"Yes." Ken handed over another sheet of paper. "This a list of all the emergencies that Dominic was dispatched to. We track our ambulances and FRU with the MDT. Mobile Data Tracking. That way we can dispatch the nearest ambulance to the emergency. Dominic's MDT was switched off between 9:22 p.m. and 11:37 p.m."

"On our way up here, Lisa was telling us about someone called Otis," said Ramouter.

"I'm sure that Lisa enjoyed telling you that Otis was suspended for switching off his MDT," said Ken. "The one thing that Lisa and I can both agree on is that Otis should have been suspended."

"How long were Otis and Dominic partners?"

"More than three years. I wouldn't be surprised if Otis was the one who taught Dominic how to switch off the MDT."

"Pine had the MDT switched off for over two hours," said Henley. A two-hour window would have been enough time for Pine to attend the detox center and take Delaney. "Are you alerted when the MDT is switched off?"

"No. All the person in the control room knows is that they can't contact a particular ambulance. It's imperative that we respond to an emergency within eight minutes, so they would have just moved on to the next one."

"In the past six months, how many times has Pine switched off the MDT?"

"Seven times. The first couple of times were switched off for about three to five minutes before his shift ended back in June and July. But in the past six weeks, he's turned it off four times. The last time was yesterday morning at 5:37 a.m. Just before his shift ended."

"Where is Pine now?" asked Henley.

"I'm assuming he would be at home. He swapped shifts with another colleague. Today is his day off."

85

"There must be some mistake," said the sergeant who had been allocated the job of protecting Pine. He sounded as though he was half asleep. "Pine is working the 6 p.m. to 6 a.m. shift. I dropped him off at the depot myself at quarter past five."

"We've just come back from the depot and his manager said that today is his day off," said Henley as she stood outside Pine's front door. The door knocker was missing and the doorbell didn't ring when Henley pressed it.

"That doesn't make any sense. I've got a copy of his rota and he's working today and Monday."

Henley ended the call and dialed Pine's number. She wasn't surprised to hear the automated female voice tell her that the person she was trying to reach was unavailable. Ramouter's face was against the window, peering through the yellowing net curtains, while Henley banged on the door with her fist.

"Anything?" she said to Ramouter, slamming the letterbox a few times.

"Not that I can see," Ramouter replied. Henley kneeled down, and peered through the letterbox. All she could see was old carpet and an empty hallway that led to the kitchen.

NADINE MATHESON

"Well, he's not at work and he's not here." Ramouter leaned back against the balcony. "Why don't the UKPPS have eyes on him?"

"Because they're idiots and don't have a clue," said Henley as she banged the front door with her fist again, more out of frustration than a misguided belief that Pine was sleeping in his bedroom. "They thought that he was at work."

The neighbor's door swung open.

"Why are you making so much damn noise—what dey arse is wrong with you?"

An elderly black woman stepped out, her head wrapped in a dark blue headscarf; her face was almost lineless, but her body was showing the signs of age. "Big Sunday morning and you're banging that door like mad people for the past fifteen minutes. I should call the police," she said, her words tinted with a Trinidadian lilt.

"I'm sorry for disturbing you. I'm—" Henley said.

"Disturbing me? My husband has high blood pressure and you're out making noise like—"

"I'm Inspector Henley and this is TDC Ramouter."

"You're an inspector?" The woman's voice dripped with skepticism.

"Yes, we're from Greenwich police station. I was just wondering if you could help us."

The woman's eyes darted around nervously.

"What is it?" she said, once she was satisfied that there was no one out there to accuse her of being a grass.

Henley didn't ask to be let in, knowing that this woman's hospitality would only extend as far as the doorstep. "How long have you lived here?" asked Henley.

"Oh Lord, since 1978."

"You must have seen a lot of changes around here?"

"And not for the better, if you ask me. If my husband could have traveled, I would have gone back home long time ago."

"How long has your neighbor at number 45 lived here?"

"He came here after us. I'm not sure the exact date but it was eighty-someting."

"And he had children? A son?" asked Henley.

"Bertrand? No, no. Never married. Never seen him with a woman," she whispered. "Ever."

"And what happened to Bertrand?"

"Oh, he dead."

Henley didn't bother to hide her surprise. She rubbed her right temple. "And when did he die?"

"Lord, must be seven months now. Cancer. He went into hospital and he never came back. He was a nice man."

"So, who's living there now?"

"Well, no one. His nephew, Dom, Don, someting like that. He still comes now and again. I don't know what for, but if you asked me, I'm surprised the council haven't taken the flat back yet. They quick to run you down for the damn council tax—"

"How often do you see his nephew?" asked Henley.

"Well, I used to see him once a month or so, but the last time I saw him was a few days ago. I could hear the washing machine going but he don't live there. No sah. Never lived here."

Henley's mind was racing as she drove back to the station.

"He was always able to escape under the radar," she said. "He works for the LAS twelve hours out of the day, sometimes more, and the minute protection was authorized, our copycat went quiet, over a week of absolute quiet."

"Because Pine knew that we were watching him."

"But they weren't following him," said Henley.

The traffic lights turned red and the warning lights began to flash rapidly, signaling that Creek Road Bridge was about to be raised. Henley pulled up the handbrake and turned off the engine. She could see a couple of barges making their way down the creek.

"I was just thinking," Ramouter said, "a harassment warning letter was sent to Naylor in April. A few weeks later, Lewis is dead. She wouldn't have agreed to meet up with Naylor if she was that fed up of him."

"No, she wouldn't," Henley agreed. "I want you to check the electoral registers when we get back to the SCU. Naylor and Pine had to be on the register when they were both picked for jury service. That would give us an address, whether it's still his current address is another story."

As Henley turned onto Greenwich High Street, the phone rang. It was a blocked number, which meant that it was most probably a call from the SCU or Olivier. She felt herself growing hot.

"Hello, Anjelica. It's Ezra."

"Everything OK?" Henley asked as her pulse rate lowered. "Why are you in the office on a Sunday?"

"This case is important, innit, and I wanted to make sure that I updated you. We got the authorization and subscriber information back for Olivier's phone and it confirms everything that I've already told you."

"What about the bank account details? The card that was used to top up," asked Henley as she turned into the station.

"All there. She actually registered the pay-as-you-go account using her own debit card before she started using a money card. I've printed everything out and left it on your desk."

"The mobile phone, debit card, CCTV. It's enough to arrest and charge her, isn't it?" asked Ramouter as Henley pulled into the station.

"More than enough."

86

Olivier leaned against the wall of the darkened alleyway that separated numbers 27 and 29 Callander Drive. He fondled the heart-shaped key ring that was attached to Lauren's car keys as he looked out into the street. He had been waiting for almost three hours. The white van where he had dumped Lauren's body had been taken away almost seven hours ago and the last of the news reporters had gone. There was nothing to gawp at now. Olivier chuckled to himself as he lit a cigarette and then checked the time on the mobile phone that Lauren had given him: 1:07 a.m. He was wondering how much longer he should give it when he saw him.

As the man walked slowly up the driveway, Olivier peeled away from the wall and circled around him. The knife, still stained with Lauren's blood, was in his pocket.

"Dominic. Hello, boy."

Dominic Pine turned around. Olivier smiled when he registered the look of surprise on the man's face. Dominic sidestepped, but Olivier blocked him.

"I... I... Don't—" Dominic cried out as Olivier placed his

hand on his left shoulder and squeezed down on the pressure point.

"Dominic Pine," said Olivier. "Juror eleven."

"No, no, I'm not," Dominic replied unconvincingly through gritted teeth. "Please, I won't—"

"You won't what?"

"I won't say anything. Please let me go."

"Shh." Olivier pressed a finger to Dominic's lips. Olivier watched with bemusement as Dominic squeezed his eyes shut and then slowly opened them again. Olivier laughed sardonically when Dominic began to cry.

"Were you hoping that I'd disappeared?" Olivier asked. "They say you should never meet your heroes, but I thought you would be more enthusiastic than this."

Olivier grabbed Dominic by the collar and grinned when he felt Dominic's body grow tense.

"Come on, Dominic. Say something. This is getting embarrassing."

"How do you know who I am?" Dominic's voice was a strained whisper.

"I never forget a face, and it doesn't take a genius to work out what's been going on here. I should be flattered, but I'm not."

"I don't know what you're talking about. I haven't done anything."

"Yeah, right. They always come back, you know," Olivier said.

"Who comes back?"

"Men like you. The weak. The insecure. The emotionally stunted. They always come back to the scene of the crime, but you, being the sort of man who lacks imagination, came to mine. It's pathetic, really."

Olivier released his grip on Dominic and patted him on his shoulder with mock affection before he reached into his pocket, pulled out the knife and placed the blade against Dominic's throat.

"What the fuck?"

Olivier released the pressure slightly. He wanted to see what Pine would do. Fight or flight? The dim light from the crescent moon illuminated Dominic's face, giving Olivier his answer. Dominic was frightened but there was a hint of unstable, self-sacrificing determination in his eyes.

Dominic grabbed Olivier's wrist and tried to move the knife away from him. He flinched as the tip of the blade scratched his skin and blood began to seep.

"You're feisty, aren't you?" Olivier said, lowering the knife. "But you don't have the upper hand here, son."

"What do you want?"

Olivier stood up straight when he heard the challenge in Dominic's tone. Olivier had seen it before, seven times in fact, that fleeting moment when the victim felt emboldened.

"You're asking the question as if you have options," said Olivier.

Dominic stepped toward Olivier and raised his head so that he could meet his eyes. "You're the one who came for me," he said defiantly. "You call me pathetic, but you're the weak one, the suggestible one. You killed some poor cow because you wanted to flush me out. It must have been eating you up inside knowing that I was out here, making your precious detective inspector chase me."

"There you are." Olivier tapped the knife against Dominic's cheek. "I knew you were in there somewhere. It's not me that you wanted to impress, it was her."

Dominic stayed silent.

"What's wrong?" Olivier asked. "You couldn't afford to buy the inspector flowers so you thought she'd be more amenable to body parts instead?"

"Fuck you," Dominic spat back.

Olivier scraped away the phlegm that had landed on his cheek, just under the rim of his lower eyelid, with the edge of his knife. He put the blade to Dominic's chest and wiped it clean.

"You're not an idiot," Olivier said. "You knew I would come for you."

"You're predictable," Dominic said with forced confidence.

Olivier let out a vengeful laugh.

"I can't believe I actually thought you and I were the same," Dominic said disgustedly.

"You and I are nothing alike."

"You should have understood. I did it for you. If those jurors hadn't been so gutless you would have been free and I would never have ended up inside."

"Jesus Christ. Are you on something, boy?"

Rage flickered in Dominic's eyes. "We were both betrayed by people we trusted," he shouted. "But we showed them who was really in control. I thought you'd appreciate what I did for you. That you would respect my work. *Our* work."

"You're looking for respect?" Olivier asked scornfully.

"Not anymore. I don't need anything from you."

"Let's go." Olivier grabbed hold of Dominic's elbow and dragged him toward the alley that led to a small car park. He pulled harder, ignoring the sound of Dominic's trainers trying to gain traction against the pavement as he resisted. Dominic twisted his body, kicking over a recycling bin. Glass bottles rattled across the concrete. Olivier pushed Dominic against the bonnet of a black Mini and pressed the knife against his stomach. Olivier pulled out a set of keys and opened the car door.

"I'm not going with you," Dominic hissed. He jerked away and fell forward onto his hands and knees. Olivier sighed heavily with boredom and grabbed Dominic by the collar. The cheap material began to tear.

"I'm not going—"

"Did I say you could talk?" Olivier let go of Pine. "Your work is a fucking embarrassment, boy. Now get in the car."

Olivier shoved Dominic forward and he fell onto the passenger seat.

"Where are we going?" Dominic asked.

Olivier ignored him, started the car and headed toward the Rotherhithe Tunnel.

Fifteen minutes later, Olivier drove into the sprawling Pepys Estate in Deptford. Three of London's tallest tower blocks loomed like unofficial guardians overhead. The River Thames bordered the back of the once notorious council estate.

"What are we doing here?" Dominic asked as Olivier parked the car.

"I thought that we would go for a nice moonlight stroll."

Olivier stepped out and indicated with the knife for him to get out.

Olivier clutched Dominic's arm as they walked along the river. He shoved him hard against the safety railing, knifepoint pressed to his chest.

"You're out of your depth, son."

Olivier grabbed hold of Dominic's neck and squeezed. The more Dominic clawed at his hands, the tighter he squeezed. The high tide waters of the river slapped against the wall. The dim lights from the flats nearby shone across Dominic's face. Dominic's eyes widened and turned glassy, and his face reddened. Olivier smiled.

"You didn't even try and do better than me."

Olivier let go and pulled out a wad of newspaper articles from his back pocket as Dominic fell to the ground coughing and gasping for breath.

"This is amateur hour," said Olivier. He threw the well-read pages at Pine's head. "You just chopped them up and dumped them all over my manor. You didn't even show them off first."

"You scattered one of your victims all over the A2," Dominic shot back.

"It was a puzzle; I had a system. You're just shit. You didn't even try and do better than me," he repeated.

"I don't know what you're talking about."

"You don't have the brains to do anything original. You took my brand. My symbols. They belonged to me." Each word that Olivier spat out was followed by a hard kick to Pine's ribs. "I don't need you putting my tag onto your shitty work, you sniveling little shit."

Olivier kneeled down, placed his hand on the back of Dominic's neck and squeezed. "What did they do to you? Did that pretty little black girl turn you down or something? Was your dick too small?"

Dominic scratched away at Olivier's hand.

"Your little ego couldn't handle the fact that she grassed you up. Pathetic."

"Fuck off," Dominic gurgled.

Olivier squeezed harder, his fingers pushing down against Dominic's jugular vein. He squeezed until he saw tiny blood vessels bursting in the whites of Dominic's watering eyes. He held on as Dominic's pulse slowed and the flesh under his chin began to swell.

Olivier released his grip.

Dominic vomited until there was nothing left. He gasped for air as he grabbed hold of the rusty railing and pulled himself up. "They have no idea…it's me," he said. Each word was expressed with pained exhaustion. "I'm a target. A potential victim. You're the one who's escaped. They're looking for you. Not me."

Olivier's laugh echoed through the still night air. "Is that what you think? *I* found you. The inspector will find you too, if I let her."

"You're nothing." Dominic gasped for air. "*I'm* making you relevant again."

Olivier placed his hands to the top of his head and leaned back. "And they said I was the delusional one. Well, good luck with it all." Olivier extended his hand.

"What are you doing?" Dominic asked in surprise.

"I'm wishing you luck."

"But…but…" Dominic spluttered.

Olivier cocked his head as the sound of the police sirens in the distance grew louder. "Suit yourself," he said.

"I won't be spending the rest of my life in a prison cell after I'm done." Dominic's voice was faint and unconvincing.

"Be careful what you wish for, son," Olivier said as he pressed his forehead against Dominic's head. "This is not over; I am not over. I know my next move. I'm not doing this out of some misguided Notion to be recognized. This isn't a means to an end for me. I can stop you but nobody can stop me."

87

11 a.m. DC Eastwood fanned herself with the Sunday supplement as she watched the block of flats from the car. Chance Blaine had returned here almost thirteen hours ago after being released from custody. With the exception of the flicker of lights from the fourth-floor bedroom window there had been no movement from Blaine's flat since Eastwood had taken over from Stanford four hours ago.

Just as she was about to pick up her bag of popcorn, she saw him.

Blaine pushed through the communal doors and pulled out his phone. He kept his head bowed and walked briskly. After he rounded a corner, Eastwood turned on the engine and followed him. She stopped at the traffic lights and watched Blaine begin to jog in the direction of Woolwich Arsenal train station. Eastwood took a side road to the station's entrance. She got out as Blaine went inside.

Eastwood followed him until she was obstructed by a couple of Jehovah's Witnesses who were setting up their magazine stall by the entrance. Then she was swallowed up by a group of hungover teenagers. She pulled out her Oyster card and pushed through the barriers.

Across the platform, he was talking to another man. They looked like they were arguing, and a woman who was standing nearby took a few steps back. The train horn blared louder as the tannoy announced the arrival of the 11:24 to Gravesend.

Eastwood could hear the woman's ear-piercing scream long before the train's brakes screeched harshly through the air.

"What do you mean he's dead?"

Henley stopped walking while Emma ran off ahead with Luna at her side and into the park.

"What's wrong?" Rob asked.

Henley mouthed, *It's work*, waving him away. She listened to the sound of sirens on the other end of the phone.

"Eastwood, what's happened?" Henley asked again.

"Chance Blaine is dead," Eastwood repeated. "He left his flat and I followed him to the train station."

"He jumped?" Henley walked slowly in the direction of her family. She could sense that Eastwood was trying to cover up her shock with a forced professionalism.

"I'm not sure. I didn't see what happened."

Henley could hear the quaver in Eastwood's voice. "Eastie. Breathe. Take a moment."

"I should have been quicker."

"It's not your fault. Tell me what you know."

"There are witnesses. The problem is that they're all saying different things," Eastwood continued. "A couple of witnesses are saying that a man pushed Blaine in front of a train, but another witness and the train driver are saying that he jumped."

Henley listened to the muffled sound of Eastwood talking to someone and a door being slammed. "Where are you right now?" she asked.

"Still here. In the station manager's office," said Eastwood.

"He's pulling up the CCTV footage from the platform. Listen. Give me a minute. I'll call you back."

A few minutes later, Henley's phone pinged. Emma was tugging at her bag, looking for her drink. "Go and find Daddy," Henley said to her daughter, opening up the WhatsApp message from Eastwood and seeing that it was a video of a computer monitor. Her message read:

I know it's a bit crap, but this is the footage from the platform.

Henley pressed play.

"Chance Blaine is here. Pause the video, please. Zoom in. Right. Guv, take a look at the man in front of him."

Henley felt her legs give way and she dropped onto the grass as she saw Olivier push Chance Blaine off the platform, and into the path of an oncoming train.

88

Henley walked into the SCU on Monday morning with a banging headache. She had planned to spend Sunday with Rob and Emma, going to the park and having lunch like a normal family—that was until she had seen Olivier kill Blaine. Henley's plan to arrest Karen Bajarami had also been thwarted. Bajarami had developed sepsis. The most that Henley could do was to convince the powers that be to put a police officer outside Bajarami's room. No visitors allowed.

Henley took off her jacket and placed it on the back of the chair. "How was the rest of your weekend?" she asked Ramouter.

"Good. Went up to Bradford." Ramouter smiled. "My little boy… It was good. Knackered though. Missed the last train… Shit." Ramouter looked at Henley in disbelief. "I can't believe Blaine is dead. Are we sure he didn't jump?"

"What difference would it have made if he'd taken his own life?" said Henley. "He's gone." She didn't tell Ramouter the rest, that she blamed herself and that some sod wouldn't have spent their morning scraping Blaine off the train tracks if she had fought harder with the CPS.

"By the way, Linh called." Ramouter reached for the Post-it Note on his computer. "Lauren Varma's sister will be arriving at 10 a.m. for the viewing and Carole Lewis's body arrived at 6 a.m. She's started the autopsy and removed some fibers from the neck wound which came back as cat hairs, grass hairs and a dark green material made up of polyester and cotton. Paramedic uniforms are usually dark green made up of sixty-seven percent polyester and thirty-three percent cotton."

"Cross-contamination?" asked Henley.

"Unlikely. Paramedics never attended the scene. It's a bit of a stretch but maybe it wasn't his intention to kill her in the park. If Pine was in uniform, maybe he planned to incapacitate her and kill her elsewhere. I mean, who would take any notice of a paramedic attending to someone?"

"It still doesn't make much of a difference. Without evidence putting Pine at the scene of her murder or a positive identification of him we're no closer to finding out who's responsible than when we first found Kennedy's body parts on the river."

"Well, I've got the CCTV from the park where Carole Lewis's body was found. I'll go through it. Maybe I'll pick something up."

Henley walked to the window. From the fourth floor her view was limited to a Greenwich High Street obscured by mid-September rain. It was only a few days ago that Olivier had called her, taunting her. She had no idea what his game was or why he was determined to hang around. It made her wonder if Mark was right when he said that Olivier and his copycat were in some kind of sick competition.

Henley left Linh and walked the short distance to the waiting room where she greeted Lauren Varma's sister, Katherine.

"Good morning, I'm Detective Inspector…" The rest of the words were stuck in a loop inside Henley's head as she found herself staring at Lauren Varma's face. "I'm sorry," Henley said.

"Ah," the woman said. "You didn't know that we were twins. I'm Katherine Masters."

"DI Henley."

Katherine was identical to her sister except for her hair, which had been cut into a chin-length bob. She was dressed in an expensive suit more fitting for a job interview than the viewing of the dismembered body of her twin.

"How long will this take because I have an appointment in the city?"

"It shouldn't take long."

As Katherine followed Henley down the corridor, her facade, carefully constructed with expensive makeup and designer clothes, seemed to crack. Katherine's knuckles tightened as she clutched the metal chain of her bag.

"It's just through here." Henley stopped at the viewing room. Katherine halted too and looked down at the door handle.

"Er...will...will I be—"

Henley gently placed a hand on her arm. It was the same question that they all wanted to know, the family of the dead. How close will they be? Will they have to touch her? Will she look the same?

"You'll be behind a viewing glass and I'll be with you."

There was nothing inviting about the viewing room. A bottle of water and some plastic cups sat on the small table. Henley had lost count of the times that a family had picked up the nearest object and thrown it against the window. She could still trace the almost invisible scar where shards of the glass tumbler thrown by a grieving father had caught her cheek.

"Are you ready?" Henley asked.

"Not really." Katherine shrugged. "But I might as well get on with it."

Henley tapped on the glass, where Linh's assistant, Theresa, was waiting. Katherine didn't move as the curtains drew back.

She was still for a minute and then her head started shaking, followed by an almost silent, "No."

Lauren Varma looked whole beneath the white sheet. There were no signs that she had been disjointed and displayed like a macabre art installation.

Henley could feel Katherine's anguish as she finally stepped up to the window and placed a hand on the glass. "Can I be with her?"

"I'm sorry," Henley said. "I have to ask—"

"That's my sister. That's my La-La."

As Katherine began to cry, Henley took her arm and led her gently out of the room.

Henley guided her outside to the car park to escape the claustrophobia of the mortuary and to wait for the Uber that was three minutes away. The rain had stopped but the sky was still a misty gray.

"She said that she had met someone but..." Katherine's voice drifted off as she began to fiddle with the chain around her neck. "Someone that she had met at work. Where's her stuff?"

"Excuse me?" said Henley.

"She wouldn't want anyone touching her things. She was funny like that. She would want me to have her chain."

"What chain?"

"Like this one." Katherine pulled out the silver chain that she had been fiddling with. At the end of it was a silver star and a silvery gray pendant. "We got them when we were fifteen. It's a moonstone. Lauren's into crystals and things like that. Was it with her when she was found?"

"I will have to check," Henley lied. She didn't have to check. The last time that she had seen Lauren's chain was around Karen Bajarami's neck.

"OK," Katherine said softly. "She didn't deserve this, you know. Not my La-La."

"No one ever does," said Henley as Katherine's phone began to beep.

"My cab is here. Is there anything else that you need from me?"

Henley shook her head. "Not for the moment."

"Right. Well, thank you." Katherine clutched her bag and began to walk toward the gate.

"Oh, there was one thing," said Henley.

"What was it?"

"Did your sister have any friends?"

"Not really. She was always a bit of a loner, but she did mention that she belonged to a group. I thought that it was a book club. There was a woman that she got on with."

"Did she tell you her name?"

Katherine paused. "Karen. Her name was Karen."

Henley called Ezra as she watched Katherine's cab drive away.

"Ezra, I need you to do something for me," she said.

"What is it?"

"We seized Karen Bajarami's laptop and phone. Go through it."

"What am I looking for?"

"Anything that links Karen Bajarami to Lauren Varma. They belonged to some kind of group and I'm thinking that the group had something to do with Olivier."

"Not a problem. One more thing before you go. I've left something for you on your desk."

"What is it?"

"Er... Just come up and see me when you get in. I need to explain it to you in person."

Henley ended the call and walked back into the mortuary. She pushed aside the question of why Ezra needed to see her in person and instead prepared herself to finally see Carole Lewis, in the flesh.

89

Carole Lewis had been buried in a cheap coffin in a family plot, beside her maternal grandparents. Henley held the green mask tightly against her face. Carole was Jewish and hadn't been embalmed. She had spent four months in the freezer and her family had wanted her buried as soon as the body was released. Despite the late heat wave the grave had been waterlogged. Carole's skin had blackened, and her face was barely recognizable. Her fingernails had fallen off and there was leakage escaping from her stab wounds.

"I thought that you would have been done by now. I timed it wrong," said Henley.

"Sorry. It took a little bit longer than I thought. How's the investigation going?" asked Linh as she peeled off her gloves and threw them into the clinical waste bin.

"Two steps forward, one step back." Henley looked down at Carole Lewis's naked body. Whoever Carole used to be only remained in the memories of those who loved her, or resented her, in equal measure. "It's like Olivier and this copycat have just gone to ground. Disappeared into the ether."

"It would have been better for me if they had embalmed

her," Linh muttered, picking up a file, and flicked through her notes. "Right, I've managed to get some samples for toxicological screening."

"Couldn't you use the original samples?"

"I would have done, but they lost them. Another reason to have her here. Anyway, I want to do a full toxicological screening to check for the presence of atracurium besilate in her system."

"Wouldn't that have been picked up in his initial autopsy?"

"Not necessarily. She also had cocaine in her system, but the purity was only twenty-two percent, which is actually pretty good considering the usual crap we see. The rest of it was made up of the usual stuff—benzocaine, codeine, paracetamol and one percent unknown."

"Do you think that she was high when she went to the park?"

"Considering the amounts in her system, yes, but she would have been able to comprehend what was happening to her."

"But she's got defensive wounds," said Henley.

"Yes, on her palms and arms, suggesting that she tried to grab the knife and she put her arms in front of her face, like this." Linh crossed her arms in front of her face.

"Her attacker approaches her," Henley said as she picked up a water bottle in substitute of a real knife. "And comes at her?"

"She may have been under the influence, but her reflexes would have kicked in. She raises her arm, he attacks. She grabs the knife. She stumbles back. There was swelling in the tissues around her right ankle. She falls to the ground, and her killer comes at her again, this time to the chest, but those cuts barely break through the subcutaneous fat."

"He goes for the throat," said Henley.

"Right to left."

"Excuse me."

"Your copycat is left-handed. Cuts to the left side of the chest. I'm thinking that once she falls to the ground, he takes her from behind and the cut to the throat was made from right to left. He would have been covered in blood. I've extracted fibers from the wound in her neck. A mixture of grass, dirt and some material. They will have to be sent off. Don't take your gloves off. Take a look at her left calf."

Henley bent down. The wound was hard to miss. It wasn't as deep as the cuts on the other bodies, but half of the symbol was there. It was incomplete, but Henley could see the double cross. "Your copycat obviously didn't have enough time to finish the marking. He must have been disturbed. Does this make Carole Lewis victim number four?" asked Linh as Henley stepped away from the body.

"No, that would make her number one."

90

"You can come upstairs, you know. We don't bite," said Henley.

She watched Ezra rip the brown tape of a cardboard box.

"I'm still emotionally scarred," he said, before registering Henley's stricken face. "Oh, shit. Sorry. I didn't click. It's just a pair of trainers."

"It's fine." Henley felt her shoulders drop a little as she looked at the pair of black trainers Ezra was holding up.

"These are a pair of classic Air Jordans straight from the States. You can't get them anywhere in the UK. So, you got the map that I left on your desk. I know that you like things ol' skool."

"Says the man who just spent a small fortune on a pair of vintage Air Jordans that I owned when I was fourteen."

"Actually, my uncle sent them to me from New York. Early birthday present."

"You're something else. So, this cell site map?"

"Yep, for Kennedy's phone. The one that you haven't found yet. Here, let me make some room." Ezra picked up his laptop, placed it on the windowsill and cleared the desk of his keyboard, Xbox controller and his new trainers. "As you know, Kennedy's phone was alive and kicking until last Tuesday and his tag went dead in Ladywell Fields on the previous Friday. So, I've focused on that time period, between Friday night and Tuesday morning."

"Did Pellacia ask you to do this?" Henley couldn't hide the fact that she was impressed.

"Nah, I thought that it would give me something to do and, to be honest, I'm nosy. Right, you know how mobile phones work."

"Ezra! Of course I know."

"Just checking. So, mobile phones connect to the nearest cell site mast when you turn them on. Now Kennedy's phone is a bit basic and has no location tracking, but his phone still connects to a cell site mast, and the ones in London have a range of a little over half a mile."

"The blue dot here." Henley pointed to a blue dot in the middle of Ladywell Fields. "That's Kennedy's phone?"

"Yeah, and it connects to the cell site mast on top of Lewisham Hospital and then it starts to travel. Remember, this isn't the exact location—"

"But it's within a mile of where Kennedy is?"

"Exactly, so follow the blue dots."

Henley traced her finger along the map, thorough Lewisham, Brockley, Nunhead and Peckham. Her finger stopped on the last blue dot. A cell site mast on top of the Peabody Estate in Camberwell, across the road from the Magistrates' Court.

"Whoever took Kennedy and Zoe avoided the main roads," said Henley. "This is to scale, isn't it?"

"Yeah, two centimeters is a mile, and a mile isn't hitting Lewisham High Street, Lewisham Way or New Cross Road. All of these masts are on the roofs of blocks of flats in the back streets."

"What's this green dot?"

"That's Zoe's phone and it follows the same route. Sometimes, her phone connects to a different cell site mast, like here." Ezra pointed to a green dot on a road next to Morrison's supermarket in Peckham. "She's on a different network, so that would make sense."

"That's further evidence that Zoe was with Kennedy."

"Except her phone stops connecting to any masts after the Morrison's; which means that her battery must have died."

"But Kennedy's phone carries on into Camberwell?"

"And then it bounces off three masts in the area."

"Why would it do that?"

"Most likely the signal is weak and it's trying to connect to the nearest mast," Ezra explained. "These three dots here are the last three masts that Kennedy's phone connects to on Tuesday morning."

Henley peered down at the map. The red dots were on top of Picton Street, not too far from the court. Another was on top of the Camberwell College of Arts and the last dot was on Wilson Road.

"You know how triangulation works, don't you?" Ezra stared at Henley quizzically.

Henley thought back to the boring cell site analysis lecture that she, Stanford and Pellacia had been sent to almost nine years ago. They had sneaked out halfway through and headed to the pub.

"If a phone is picked up by three cell site masts, you can calculate the distance to the phone from each point."

"You get a B for effort." Ezra picked up a black Sharpie from his desk and drew a circle, two centimeters in diameter, around each red dot. "You see this area where all three circles overlap? Kennedy's phone is somewhere in that area."

Henley traced her finger across the small oval area on the map. Gables Close, Hanover Street, Peckham Road and Stanswood Gardens. An area populated by blocks of flats, council offices, doctors' surgeries, long roads of Victorian terraces and building sites. Somewhere in that space of just over half a mile was where Sean Delaney, Daniel Kennedy and Zoe Darego had been murdered.

91

It was late. Eastwood was out on a date, Ezra had gone home early and Stanford was trying to make the most of his beloved Arsenal season ticket. Ramouter was slumped at his desk, watching CCTV footage in a trancelike state. Henley had sent a couple of police officers to Pine's uncle's flat to see if there were any signs of life. They had reported back that the flat was in absolute darkness, and according to his neighbor, Pine hadn't been back since the last time she was asked.

"Why don't you go home?" Henley said to Ramouter. "There's only so much CCTV that you can go through before you drive yourself mad."

Ramouter didn't try to suppress the yawn. He had definitely lost the enthusiastic glow he'd had when she first met him on Watergate Street. "Are you sure?" he said.

"Go home, call your little boy, read him a bedtime story. Eat something healthy."

"Healthy? Have you seen my fridge?" Ramouter paused to answer a call on his phone.

"Yes... I see... When?" Ramouter sat back. "OK. Any visitors… How long until she's fit… Right… Call me if anything changes. Thank you."

"That was the hospital," Ramouter said. "Ade died fifteen minutes ago."

Henley leaned back in her chair and put her hands to her head.

"Also, Karen came out of surgery an hour ago. They couldn't save her eye."

"You're looking at me as if you expect me to feel sorry her," Henley said.

"No, not for her. For Ade," Ramouter snapped. He stared at Henley as though he couldn't believe the absurdity of her words. "It's him that I feel sorry for. He didn't deserve this. Karen is just as much to blame for his death as she is for Lauren Varma lying in pieces in a fridge down the road." He kicked over the wastepaper bin in anger. He swore as rubbish scattered across the floor.

"Take a moment," Henley said. "Breathe."

Ramouter composed himself. "I'm sorry. I shouldn't have done that. That was wrong."

"It's OK. What did they say about visitors?" Henley asked.

"Her mum and one of the officers from the prison tried to visit in the morning. There hasn't been anyone since she came out of surgery. No one else even resembling Olivier has been near the hospital."

Henley put her phone down and pushed her chair back. Every bone in her body was crying out for a hot bath, half a sleeping tablet and bed.

"They tried to bring him out of the induced coma," Ramouter said. "But he suffered a brain bleed. He worked for the prison service for twenty years."

"Go home," Henley said firmly. "I'll see you in the morning."

She watched as he walked out of the office. His shoulders were low, the air around him defeated.

Henley pushed her keyboard away in frustration. It slammed

against the mug, sending the last dregs of her coffee spilling out across her desk. She scrambled to mop up the mess with tissues.

"You OK?"

Henley hadn't noticed that Pellacia had left his office. She didn't have the energy to lie to him.

"No. The other prison officer, Ade, died. Pine has disappeared into the wind, and even if he was sitting in front of us right now, it wouldn't make a difference. All I've got is an identification from a drug addict who was off his face, partial prints that I can't match to anyone—"

Pellacia sat watching Henley even though her face was turned away looking out the window.

"Come home with me," Pellacia said as he leaned forward and put his hand on Henley's leg.

She didn't push it aside. "I can't," she said. "After everything that's happened, I don't think that it's a good idea and I'm knackered."

"Which one is the excuse?"

Henley turned. "Neither of them."

Pellacia looked down at the ground.

"You and I are straightforward, you know," he said. "Out of all this. You and I are the only thing that actually makes sense. Whether it's as friends or as more. We're straightforward, Anj. It's only everything else around us that is complicated."

Henley didn't get a chance to answer because at that moment her mobile phone began to ring. She pulled a face when she saw the name that was flashing on the screen. It was Agent Chris Snyder from the National Crime Agency. She had known Chris back when he had been a DC at Lewisham police station, but it was gone 10 p.m. It was unlikely that he was calling for a chat. She showed the screen to Pellacia, just as his own phone began to ring.

"Hello, Chris—what is it?" Henley asked.

"All right, Anjelica. I know that it's a bit late in the day…" said Chris.

"That's an understatement."

"We've got a problem. Michael Kirkpatrick has gone missing."

92

Michael Kirkpatrick, juror ten, had been annoying and uncoop-
erative, but at no point did Henley want him to be the copycat's
fifth victim. When she arrived at Michael Kirkpatrick's home
in Streatham, there were a group of officers passing the baton of
blame between them. Ramouter had just taken his dinner out of
the microwave when Henley had called with the update. It had
taken a lot of convincing before he agreed to stay where he was.

Chris Snyder walked up to Henley. "Didn't mean to drag
you out."

"What happened?" she asked.

"I got a message on Friday morning from the UKPPS that
Kirkpatrick was no longer consenting to personal protection.
I made my position clear that I was not authorizing the with-
drawal of his protection, but I don't know… There were crossed
wires somewhere."

"Crossed wires? Chris, this was a fuckup. Plain and simple.
You lot were supposed to be keeping an eye on him," said Henley.

"I know," said Chris sullenly. "Is there any news on the others?"

"Naomi Spencer is still in Vietnam. Hamilton Bryce is safe

but they've relocated him as a precaution. Officers are with Naylor at his home, and Jessica Talbot and her family are in a safe house; only Dominic Pine is unaccounted for." Henley stopped and took a breath. She could feel the enormity of the case on her shoulders.

"Talk me through what happened," Henley said as they stopped at the door.

"No one has seen Michael Kirkpatrick since he left Leadenhall Market on Friday night at around 8:45 p.m.," explained Chris. "According to his colleague, Scott Boxtree, they both left work at around quarter to six and went for just the one. He thinks that they had had about three pints and then they both walked to London Bridge. Boxtree got the tube to Walthamstow and he assumed that Michael went home."

The house consisted of six flats spread over three floors. Michael Kirkpatrick lived in flat B on the ground floor. The door was wide open and there were officers inside. At the other end of the corridor an officer was talking to a Chinese woman who looked angry.

"That's his girlfriend, Anna. She was away on a business trip and says that she spoke to him two nights ago. She tried to call him yesterday, but he didn't pick up, so she called him at work—"

"And he wasn't there?" Henley took the plastic gloves from one of the uniformed officers standing by the door.

"No. She called Scott and he said that Michael hadn't turned up. We've checked with his line manager and he didn't call in sick. She got home after nine and saw this." Chris pointed toward Michael's flat.

Henley checked the front door. There were no signs of forced entry. A pile of letters and takeaway menus were stacked neatly on a side table, but that was the only sign of order in the flat. There was a large green stain on the floor with broken glass nearby. The framed Liverpool football shirt had a large crack in the glass and the coffee table was at an odd angle in the center of the room as though it had been roughly pushed aside.

"Where's CSI?" Henley asked.

"I've been chasing. It's been one of those mad nights. But we should be getting someone down here within the hour."

"Did any neighbors report a disturbance?"

Chris shook his head. "Nothing reported. The couple in the flat opposite said that they only really saw Michael on the weekend. Passing ships and all that."

In her mind's eye Henley could see what had happened. Someone had surprised Michael at the door and pushed him through. Judging by the shattered flowerpot and soil spread across the floor, there had been a struggle. From what Henley remembered, Michael Kirkpatrick looked as though he could handle himself. He had definitely fought back. As she examined the dirt on the floor, two things caught her eye. A footmark and an orange cap, about two inches long. It looked like the cover for a syringe.

"Do me a favor. You remember Anthony? Our senior forensic investigator," Henley said to Chris.

"How could I forget. We still use him. First on my list. Want me to call him?"

"If we can't get the locals to pull their fingers out, then call Anthony. I'm sure that the NCA must have some influence."

"Miss working with you," Chris said as he pulled out his phone.

Henley looked back at the scene. Michael Kirkpatrick had definitely been taken from home. If he was going out for his run at around 6 a.m., then that would have fitted with the time that Pine had turned his MDT off. In seven hours, Michael Kirkpatrick would have been gone for forty-eight hours. If Henley had to guess, it would be another twenty-four hours before he was found in pieces somewhere in southeast London.

A light drizzle had begun to fall outside. A woman was smoking on the doorstep of the house next door. There were others, even at this hour, looking out from windows at the commotion. Henley walked over to a young PC. He straightened himself as they all did when he noticed her police ID.

"Can I help you, ma'am?" he said.

"Yeah, you can. Have you spoken to any of the neighbors?" Henley asked.

"Yes, we did. PC Ogbanna and I spoke to the neighbors. No one saw anything or provided anything useful, but Ms. Landry—"

He pointed to the woman standing on the doorstep smoking. She looked directly at Henley before throwing the cigarette butt onto the ground and going back inside.

"She said that she knew Michael Kirkpatrick, but only in passing. He had helped her with her buggy a few times. She says that yesterday morning after 6 a.m. she had stepped out to have a cigarette. Her husband doesn't like her smoking in the house and the baby was sleeping."

"What did she see?" asked Henley.

"An ambulance. Not a big one but the one that's like—"

"Like a car."

"Yeah, a station wagon. She said that she didn't take much notice. She saw it pull in next door but then the baby woke up and she went back in."

"Anything else?"

"Not really. Just said that she thought it was odd because she didn't hear any sirens."

93

The CSI team hadn't arrived by the time Henley had left Michael Kirkpatrick's home. Anthony was en route to a shooting on the Kingsland Road, but had promised to dispatch two of his team with unrealistic promises of paid overtime. Henley could feel the anger overwhelming her as she walked back to her car. Someone had dropped the ball and no one was taking responsibility. She was doing everything that she was trained to do, to the best of her ability, but it didn't feel as though it was enough. As if *she* wasn't enough.

Henley drove back toward Greenwich. The electoral roll register checks had produced negative results. Pine hadn't bothered to register at all, once he was released from prison.

"There must be something?" Henley said to herself. She drove down Brixton Hill, heading toward Greenwich. She picked up the phone and called Ezra.

"Ezra, I'm really sorry to bother you so late," Henley said while stopped at the traffic lights outside Brixton prison.

"That's all right. But I might have you talk to my girl; she nearly accused me of having a side chick."

"I'll speak to her afterward if you like. I need to know if you can do something for me. It's urgent but—"

"Say no more. What do you need?"

"An address. I can give you a name and date of birth, but we keep hitting a brick wall when it comes to where he may be living now. I just thought that maybe bank accounts, phone, council tax—"

"OK, OK. I've got you," said Ezra.

"I owe you, Ez," said Henley. As she gave him the only personal information that she had on Dominic Pine, it wasn't lost on her what she was asking Ezra to do. It was no different to what he had been sent to prison for, but at this point she couldn't see another way. Michael Kirkpatrick had gone from a "missing person" to "kidnapped" and there was every possibility that in twenty-four hours he would be dead.

"What are you doing here?" Henley asked as she walked into the kitchenette of the SCU.

Ramouter was dressed in jeans and a hoodie, waiting for the kettle to boil.

"It didn't feel right to be sitting at home watching football highlights when he's taken another one. Tea?"

"Thank you. That would be great."

Henley gave Ramouter a summary of what she had seen at Michael Kirkpatrick's flat and what the neighbor had seen. Ramouter shook his head and swore in the right places.

"So, what do you think?" Ramouter asked as he pushed over the packet of Jammie Dodgers toward Henley. "Is he just sticking with his plan or do you reckon that we've escalated things?"

"If anyone has escalated things, it's Olivier by killing Lauren Varma. This is not our fault." Henley dunked her biscuit in her tea. "Our copycat's cooling-off period is over. That's all. If we were going to look for the positive…" Henley rolled her eyes at the absurdity of looking for the positive in this situation. "He's on the move and he's not being careful. He's never taken anyone from their home before. My theory is that he's watching all of the jurors. He knows their work patterns, where they live. He's taken them out in the open. I mean, who in their right mind will be suspicious about an ambulance? If you were out on the street, whether in your car or walking, what's your natural instinct?"

Ramouter leaned back. "Once you hear those bloody sirens, you stop. If you're driving, you'll always pull to the side."

"But you never think that it's suspicious, do you? You may be curious, but you definitely don't think that it's dodgy. Unless it turns up at someone's house with no sirens, no blue lights and it disappears just as quietly."

"Pine is using the ambulance to pick up his victims. Taking them somewhere and then he has to return it back to—"

"Back to the station. He uses the same FRU every time. There has to be DNA from at least one of the victims. I don't care how good or careful you are, I doubt that Pine could clean a vehicle that well to remove every trace of evidence."

"But we can't just march down to the station and ask if we can borrow their FRU. At the moment we're running our investigation on hypotheses and assumptions."

Henley didn't disagree. They sat in silence, drinking their tea, both wishing that it was something stronger.

"So, what's the plan?" Ramouter asked.

Henley was about to tell him that the tea and the chat had been a welcome distraction, but it was almost 1 a.m. and that maybe he should go home—then the phone rang.

"Ez," said Henley. She hadn't been expecting to hear from him this quickly.

"Grab a pen," Ezra said. "I've got two addresses. The first is 76 Beech Avenue in Bexleyheath. He's got a bank account registered to that address and there's also an Eileen and Ivan living there. Have you got that?"

"Yeah, I have." Henley scribbled the address down on the back of an envelope. "Next one."

"158 Hanover Street, Camberwell. Electricity, gas, water and mobile phone contract."

Henley thanked Ezra and told him to take the morning off and that she would clear it with Pellacia.

"Boss, before you go," said Ezra, "remember the cell site map. Have you still got it?"

"Hold on a sec." Henley reached for the folded sheet of paper that was underneath a copy of yesterday's *Metro*. "Got it."

"Can you see it?"

"Shit," she said as she placed her finger in the space where the three circles that Ezra had drawn overlapped. In the middle of that space was Hanover Street. If there was any hope of finding Michael Kirkpatrick in one piece, then she needed to get to Camberwell, now.

94

158 Hanover Street was the last house in a long row of terraces. The front was obscured by overgrown rosebushes and Japanese knotweed. Like a couple of the other houses on the street, there was a skip in the small front garden filled with broken pieces of plasterboard and wood. To the left-hand side was a wooden door with peeling black paint which Henley guessed led to the back garden. Even though it was now the early hours of the morning, the street was not silent.

"What do you think?" Ramouter looked up at the house.

"Let's take a quick look around," said Henley.

"You don't want to wait for backup?"

"They're fifteen minutes away. We're just looking," Henley repeated, not sure if Ramouter believed a word of it.

The garden wall was at least six feet high and there was no way that she could see over it, but she noticed an alley running behind it. Ramouter followed her as she walked through the alley, disturbing a fox who stared at them for a few seconds before running off. She stopped at the wooden gate. The back garden wasn't as overgrown as the front. She peered through the slats and could see the rear of the house. The kitchen window and back door were covered in sheets of newspaper. To the right she could see the roof of a shed. She tried the handle on the gate again and could hear a metal padlock on the other side, knocking against the wood. As she did so, she thought that she heard the sound of banging.

"Did you hear that?" Henley whispered to Ramouter. He shook his head.

She pulled at the handle again and this time they both heard it. The sound of banging and then a dull thud coming from the shed. Just then a light switched on inside the house. Henley could see the faint outline of a figure in a frosted first-floor window.

"Someone's in," Henley said to Ramouter. "Knock on the door and see if he lets you in."

"But what do I say to him. If it *is* him?"

"Tell him the truth," Henley replied as the light upstairs switched off. "Tell him that Michael Kirkpatrick has gone missing. We're checking up on him, and then lie. Tell him that Olivier has been seen in the area."

Ramouter pressed the doorbell. As he waited, he checked his watch and listened for the telltale signs of backup, but there were no sirens or flashing blue lights in the distance. He felt nervous as he rang the bell again. He hoped that it had been Henley's mind playing tricks on her when she had pointed someone out in the windows. He felt his throat constrict slightly as he placed his hand on the door and it gave way. The hallway was dark and he could hear the sound of a ticking clock. The bare floorboards creaked. The house smelled of damp and sawdust. At the end of the hallway, the light from the kitchen spilled out onto the floor. He thought about turning back. to wait. Instead, he carried on.

The kitchen had been gutted. There was a sink and the walls showed the markings of where the cupboards should have been. The space was empty except for a microwave, which sat on top of a fridge. Ramouter sneezed as the dust from the old plaster that had been ripped from the walls tickled his nose.

There had definitely been someone in the house. But the door had been left open, which meant that someone had obviously left in a hurry. That should have settled Ramouter but he couldn't shake off the feeling that something wasn't right. He spotted shoe prints on the exposed concrete floor that didn't belong to him. He crouched down and tracked the wet bloody swirls left behind from the soles of a pair of trainers that led into the kitchen, circled around and went back out into the hallway, but there were no bloodstained prints leading toward the front door.

Henley found a small table that had been dumped in the alley next to a broken lamp and a rusty barbecue. The gate was secure and there was no way that she would get through it without bringing a lot of attention to herself and alerting Dominic Pine. She carried the table to the gate and steadied herself as she felt the metal legs bend. She placed her right foot on the edge of the wood panel and pulled herself up. She could feel splinters pushing into the palms of her hands as she gripped the top of the gate harder.

The loud engine of a car passed by. Once the car turned a corner and the engine grew quieter, she pulled herself over. She searched blindly with her foot for somewhere to grip and felt thorns from a rosebush attach itself to her jeans. There was nowhere solid for her to place her feet and she dropped onto the hard concrete. She winced and grabbed her elbow as a shooting pain coursed through her arm. She rolled over, stood up and placed a hand against the wall of the shed. It felt solid, not like the flimsy sheds normally used to store lawn mowers and broken vacuums.

She stopped as the light on the ground floor turned on, illuminating the newspapers. While the garden was overgrown with grass and weeds, a trampled path led from the back door directly to the shed. The one window, on the shed, that faced the house was blacked out. Henley kicked the bottom of the door twice and then placed her ear to the door. This time she heard it louder. The sound of something falling to the ground. And muffled screams.

95

Twelve hours earlier…

He had fought back but the killer in front of him was stronger. He felt a fist connect with his jaw and his nose. He heard the sound of bone crunching as his mouth filled with blood and his tongue brushed away pieces of tooth. He thought he'd had the upper hand when he punched, kicked and clamped his mouth around the killer's ear, bitten hard and pulled. He thought he'd won when he heard the killer scream but then something hard had connected with the side of his head. He couldn't remember being dragged across the floor. He didn't remember being stripped naked and propped up against a wall.

"You're awake. It's about time."

He recognized the voice, but he couldn't turn his head. Every muscle in his body was frozen. All he could do was look straight ahead into the dimmed light of the room. There was a window in front of him, but the curtains were closed. He wanted to raise his head. To open his mouth, to tell the killer that he was sorry, that he could leave and he wouldn't say a word to anybody, but he couldn't move.

"You must have wondered. What it would feel like," asked the killer, "to have no control. All you can do is watch and listen to the voices in your head and ask yourself repeatedly, *Why me?*"

He could feel the tiny muscles in his eyes straining as he tried in vain to search for the killer, to find the danger, but then he stopped looking as a pair of legs appeared in front of him. He watched as the killer raised his right leg, but he didn't feel a thing as the foot connected with his chest, knocking him onto his side. He wanted to say, *Don't do it. Please don't do it.* He willed himself to speak or to just move his little finger and then he felt it. Sharp pins and needles prickled his neck and jaw. His body was waking up. He opened his mouth. "No," he whispered as he looked up at the killer. "No," he said again as the killer's hand grabbed his legs and pulled him across the floor.

"Sorry, I can't hear you. You're going to have to speak up," said the killer.

"No," he repeated.

"Hmm, I'm afraid that it's a bit late for that. I can't really deviate from the plan."

He struggled to raise his head and follow the sound of footsteps around the room and then he saw the sharp teeth of the blade.

"No," he said again as the blade waved teasingly in front of him and then he heard laughter.

"I thought that I would start with an arm," the killer stated. "I'll end up cutting a major artery if I start with your leg and the last thing that I want is for you to miss out on all the fun."

"Please. Stop," he begged. He should have been grateful and considered it a blessing that he couldn't feel any pain; but he knew what was being done to him. He bent his head back and closed his eyes, but he couldn't ignore the feeling of the skin on his right arm being gently tugged and the river of vibrations as the saw went back and forth. He couldn't shut out the heavy groaning sound as the saw made its way through bone. Then it stopped. There was no movement, but he could hear heavy breathing and then a loud grunt of satisfaction as the saw was thrown onto the ground.

"Look at that," the killer said calmly.

He recognized the horseshoe-shaped scar on the inside of his detached arm. He had fallen off the shed roof when he was nine. The bone had stuck out from the flesh. He didn't listen when his mum had told him to get down. He never listened. He could see the bone now as his arm hovered in front of his face. He recognized his fingers. He didn't close his eyes as the blood from the severed arm fell onto his face. He let the blood fill his eyes. He wanted the darkness, but he couldn't stop the sound of the saw as it began to make its way through his leg.

96

The door to the shed was padlocked but Henley could see that the bolts securing the lock were old and rusting. The wood had signs of rot. Henley crouched down and searched among the tall grass for anything that she could use to smash it open. Her fingers curled around cold metal and she picked up the broken blade of a lawn mower. She pushed the blade between the wooden door and the flat metal of the lock and pulled. She could feel the blade cutting into the skin on her hand, which was already filled with splinters and dirt. After a couple of minutes, the rusty screws were pried loose and came away from the door. Henley threw the blade onto the grass and pulled the door open.

Henley almost tripped over Michael Kirkpatrick, who lay bound on the ground, his feet facing the door. He looked up at her, his eyes wide with fright. She tried to stop herself from retching. The shed smelled of urine, the coppery smell of blood and rotten flesh.

"Do you remember me? I'm Detective Henley." Henley pulled out her phone and turned on the flashlight app. Michael's mouth was bound with silver duct tape. His face was cut and bruised and covered with dried blood which had settled into the grooves of the tape. His hands were tied behind his back with black cable ties. His wrists were purple and swollen while his fingers were almost white, the blood struggling to circulate.

Henley tried to gently pull the duct tape from Michael's mouth. "It's OK, it's OK. I've got you," Henley said as Michael let out a loud gasp of air and began to choke up with tears.

"Please, please, he's going to fucking kill me," Michael said, his voice hoarse and shaking. "He's promised to kill me."

"No, he's not." Henley pulled out her police radio. She hoped Ramouter would have turned his radio on and would get out of the house.

"This is Detective Inspector Henley. Code Zero. I need immediate emergency assistance to 158 Hanover Street, Camberwell. Sierra. Echo. Five. Four. Charlie. Lima. I repeat I need emergency assistance."

Henley put the radio down and looked around for something to cut the cable ties binding Michael's wrists and feet.

Henley shivered. It had happened in here. The killings. Next to a carpenter's table, a large roll of plastic stood in the corner. Two large saws and a smaller hacksaw lay under the table. The ground was stained with dried blood. The light bounced off something metallic not far from Michael's feet. It was a long black braid with a gold cuff in the middle, similar to the braids and cuffs that had been on Zoe Darego's head.

Flecks of plaster rained down on Ramouter from the ceiling. He stood still and listened to the sounds of the house. The clock in the hallway continued to tick and water from the kitchen tap dripped rhythmically into the ceramic sink. He walked around the bloodied footprints on the floor and up the hallway and toward the stairs. He placed a hand on the rough, stripped banister. His footsteps were muted by the dust-covered carpet on the stairs.

The second floor was narrow and confined. The hallway was

less than five feet long with a bathroom, a bedroom with an unmade bed and a third door that was closed. He pushed open the door and walked in. He started to retch as he breathed in the scent of fresh blood. He turned on the lights.

"Oh God." Ramouter gagged as the blood-soaked carpet squelched under his feet. He found himself staring at Dominic Pine's severed head.

The rest of the body had been arranged on the floor like a macabre jigsaw. It took less than a second for Ramouter to reach for his radio.

Henley's voice requesting emergency assistance crackled over Ramouter's radio.

Ramouter stepped back into something solid. He felt hot breath against his ear.

"TDC Salim Ramouter," said Olivier. "I didn't think we would be seeing each other again so soon."

Ramouter turned and faced Olivier. They were nose to nose. Fear prevented Ramouter from moving away.

Olivier pointed a knife in the direction of Pine's remains. "Did you like what I did? I was trying to get the composition just right. It was a bit of a rush job, but I did my best."

Ramouter said nothing. His brain had shut down with the terror coursing through his veins.

"Cat got your tongue, TDC Ramouter? You really need to work on your people skills."

Ramouter took an unsteady step back and stumbled on Pine's left arm.

"Don't run away." Olivier's voice was soft, almost tender. "That one behind you tried to run and you can see how that turned out for him."

Olivier lunged toward him and Ramouter cried out as the knife pierced his arm. Olivier pulled the knife out and went for him again. Ramouter ignored the pain and the blood darkening his sleeve, and shoved Olivier away. He picked up his police radio and pressed the emergency button.

"Code Zero—" Ramouter shouted before Olivier rammed a shoulder into him. Ramouter grunted out in pain and fell back, banging his head against the wall before falling onto Pine's torso. Disorientated, it took him a moment to realize that his hands were in Pine's intestines.

Olivier punched Ramouter in the face and pushed down on the wound on his arm. "I'm going to give it to you just as good as I gave it to your inspector. Leave you with something to remember me by."

Ramouter could see the open door, behind Olivier, silently beckoning him. He pushed Olivier to the side. Olivier stabbed the knife back into Ramouter's open wound. Ramouter screamed out.

Henley's voice sounded out from the radio. "Ramouter. Ramouter. Answer me!"

Before Ramouter could warn Henley to run, Olivier punched him in the face, hard enough to crack his teeth. He tasted blood and spat out chunks of molar. Olivier snatched the radio.

"Hello, Inspector," Olivier said. "I've got your boy here. Right under me."

Ramouter kicked out, catching Olivier in the groin. The sound of police sirens echoed in the distance. Ramouter turned over and tried to get to his feet, but he felt overwhelmed with dizziness and fell back down. Over the radio he could hear the channel had been switched to a group talk as officers confirmed that they were making their way to Pine's home.

"Olivier?" Henley yelled over the radio.

"Henley!" Ramouter shouted.

Olivier grabbed his leg. Ramouter felt a sharp prick in his ankle and then there was the feeling of ice water running through his veins. He looked down to see Olivier holding a syringe. Olivier reached for a saw that had been charging in the corner, and in that moment Ramouter managed to stand up. He gritted his teeth and threw himself at Olivier, determined to stop him. Olivier shouted out as he fell against the wall, and grabbed on to Ramouter to steady himself. They tumbled down the stairs, breaking the balusters on their way down. Ramouter felt nothing as Olivier fell on top of him. He tried to move his legs. He couldn't. His entire body was turning to concrete. Every joint was locked in place and every muscle had contracted and seized up. He heard a window being broken, but he couldn't open his mouth to scream for help.

"Ramouter," Henley shouted. Her voice was barely audible over the growing sound of sirens.

Ramouter tried to turn his head but couldn't. From his position on the floor he could see the front door opening. Olivier didn't look back as he ran out. A few seconds later he heard brakes screeching and the unmistakable sound of metal hitting bone and flesh.

97

Hanover Street was lit up as if dawn had broken early. The sirens had gone silent but the emergency lights were still flashing. The police had broken through the back gate and the paramedics were now putting Michael Kirkpatrick on the gurney. He was dehydrated and in shock. Henley had had to prize his hand away when she heard the distress call from her partner.

"Where's Ramouter?" Henley asked as officers filled the back garden.

"He's still in the house," said an officer. "He's alive but hurt. The paramedics are with him."

"And Olivier? Peter Olivier was inside that house. I heard him."

"I don't know, ma'am. There haven't been any sightings of him."

"And Dominic Pine?"

The officer shook his head. "No sign of him either, but we haven't searched the house yet."

Henley followed the paramedics as they wheeled Kirkpatrick to the waiting ambulance.

"Where are you taking him?" Henley asked.

"King's College Hospital," said the female paramedic.

"OK, can you make sure you stay with him at all times," Henley said to the police officer who had followed her. "He cannot be left alone. Do you understand me?"

"You're not coming with me?" said Michael. "I need you with me."

"I promise I'll be there, OK," Henley said, squeezing his hand. "I need to check on someone first."

Henley tried to ignore the onslaught of emotions—shock, grief, anxiety and the euphoric rush of adrenaline—as she jogged around to the front of the house. The BMW that they'd seen earlier was parked in front of Pine's house. A large crack spread out like a spider's web across the windscreen. The driver of the car, a young Asian boy, was standing to the side against his car with a police officer. The boy was shaking. "I didn't even see him. He just ran out. I wasn't even going that fast. He just came at me."

"Fam," said the driver's friend, who was leaning against the passenger door. "I thought you killed him."

"What happened?" Henley asked him.

"Mate, all I know is that some crazy white man dashed out into the road. The brudda must be a crackhead or something. One minute we're chilling in the car and the next thing I know this dude was on the bonnet. I thought he was dead. My boy started screaming in the car—"

"I wasn't screaming, Ashton," the driver said.

"What you lying for, bruv?" Ashton said. "Listen, he started screaming and I got out."

Henley wanted to shake the pair of them. "Did you see where he came from?"

"Nah, he came out of nowhere. I got out of the car and tried to help him. Trying to be a good citizen and all that. I told him that I was going to call an ambulance—"

"Where is he, where did he go?"

"That's what I'm trying to tell you. My man was off. You

would have thought that he had just tripped over or something. He got up, and ran toward the block. I filmed him running off. Do you wanna see it?"

"Don't move," Henley said to the friend, spotting Eastwood walking toward her.

"Stanford filled me in. How's Ramouter?" Eastwood asked.

"All I know is that he's alive, thank God. Olivier was here and somehow he got to him."

"What do you mean Olivier was here? I mean…" Eastwood put her hands to her head in exasperation. "What. The. Actual. Fuck."

"I have no idea." Henley looked around. "I need you to go with Kirkpatrick to the hospital. The ambulance hasn't left yet. Once he's calmed down and been checked out, get a statement from him. I need to know everything that he saw and heard before I got here. And, Eastie, don't leave his side. I want someone I know and trust keeping an eye out."

Eastwood nodded and ran over to the ambulance.

Henley's adrenaline was dissipating. She knew that Ramouter was alive, but she was still worried about what she would see, what she was responsible for. She could feel the shame rising up. She had put him in danger. She had almost killed him.

Relief washed over Henley when she saw Ramouter lying on the floor. The only part of him that was moving were his watery eyes. Henley kneeled next to him and wiped away his tears.

"How's he doing?" she asked the paramedic who was treating the knife wound.

"He's been stabbed repeatedly in the arm, but I have no idea how deep the wound is. There's bruising to his chest, so we're looking at the possibility of broken ribs, but he can't move, and he can't speak. He's been beaten up pretty bad. There could be injury to his spinal cord—"

"No," said Henley, spotting the syringe on the floor. "He's been injected with atracurium besilate."

The paramedic shook his head and muttered something that Henley thought sounded like "I've had enough of this shit. I should have called in sick." Two other paramedics appeared at the door with a stretcher.

"Do you have any idea how long he's been like this?" the paramedic asked her.

"Within the last twenty minutes," Henley said. She looked up to see Stanford coming down the stairs. His face was ashen.

"OK. Right. Fuck," said the paramedic. "I've never dealt with anything like this before. I don't even know what atra… atraci—whatever the hell it's called—is."

"It induces paralysis. I'll be at the hospital with you, OK?" Henley said to Ramouter. She squeezed his hand, not even sure if he could feel anything.

Henley moved out of the way as the paramedics maneuvered Ramouter onto the stretcher.

"Are Forensics on their way?" asked Stanford.

"What's up there?" Henley asked, but she didn't need to wait for Stanford to answer. She already knew. "He's dead, isn't he? Dominic Pine."

"He's upstairs in the front bedroom. In pieces. Lots of pieces. I can't go back up there. You shouldn't go up there either. What the hell happened here, Henley?"

"Olivier happened."

"Are you sure it was him?"

"I heard him over the radio… He called my name. It was him. Oh my God, Ramouter. How could I—"

Henley felt a panic rise through her. She bent down and placed her hands on her knees.

"Hey, don't do that," Stanford said. He put his arm around her and gently pulled her up. She allowed Stanford to hold her as they both watched Ramouter being wheeled out. "Don't beat yourself up."

"How could I not? I should have waited for backup. I shouldn't have let Ramouter go in there alone. I fucked up, Stanford. He'll never forgive me for this."

"This is not your fault. You weren't to know," Stanford said determinedly.

"Easier said than done. I can't believe that Pine was right in front of us, mocking us the entire time."

"Pine's the least of our worries right now. The main thing is that we've got Kirkpatrick, and Ramouter is still with us. Do you want to come and take a look in the kitchen before Forensics start their business?"

"How bad is it?"

"Compared to what's upstairs?"

"Tell me."

Stanford rubbed at his stubbled face. "In all my years, never seen anything like it."

Henley pulled on her gloves and walked into the kitchen. The fridge motor was still working nosily away. She opened the door.

On the bottom shelf was a plastic bag of disintegrating zucchinis sitting in a pool of brown slime. Five vials of atracurium besilate were on the top shelf. Henley opened the vegetable drawer and pulled out a Ziploc bag.

"Oh God," she said. Staring up at her from inside the bag were the eyes of Zoe Darego.

98

"I've never been so popular in my life," Ramouter joked as he sat up in the bed. The AB had started to wear off after forty minutes, but the doctors had still conducted an MRI scan to confirm that there was no damage to his spine. Henley, Pellacia and Stanford were in the room. There were also officers stationed outside. It was almost six in the morning and the rising sun was beginning to break through the clouds. Henley had had enough of hospitals to last her a lifetime.

"How are you feeling?" Henley asked as Pellacia prized the last of the coffees out of the tray and handed it over.

"I feel like I've been knocked over by the Hulk," said Ramouter. "It hurts every time I take a breath."

"I'm sorry about that. I should have waited." Henley ripped open three sachets of sugar and poured them into Ramouter's cup. "I shouldn't have let you go into the house."

"How were we to know that Olivier was going to be there? If it makes you feel better, I don't think that he wanted to kill me," Ramouter said unconvincingly.

"No, that doesn't make me feel better."

Ramouter winced as he raised the coffee cup to his lips. He

had three broken ribs, one of which had punctured his lung. The stab wounds to the arm were deep and a nerve had been severed. "Have you spoken to my wife?"

"No, but I did speak to your sister-in-law a little while ago," answered Pellacia. "I told her not to worry, that you're doing OK, but she was quite insistent that she will be coming down to London with your wife today."

"Sounds like her. What about Kirkpatrick?"

"He's here," said Henley. "Being treated for dehydration and shock. He hasn't got any serious injuries. Mentally? I don't know how he's going to cope." Henley couldn't help but think back to her own ordeal. How she had held on to Pellacia for dear life after he had found her. How the antidepressants and therapy sessions did little to keep the flashbacks at bay. Kirkpatrick confirmed that Pine was the one who took him. He had fought back but then he blacked out. He woke up in the shed with Pine leaning over him and telling him that he was going to come back and was going to start by cutting off his left arm, but Pine never came back.

"And Olivier?" Ramouter asked as his eyes flicked to the door.

"He's not here and you've got protection. There're officers on the ward. We've got everyone looking for him. The car that hit him wasn't going that fast, but he has to be injured. I don't know how he managed to walk away."

"He's the bloody devil, that's how," said Stanford.

"So, what happens now?" asked Ramouter. "Pine's dead and Olivier is still out there?"

Henley checked the time on her watch and shook her head. She was exhausted, overwhelmed with guilt and still had work to do. "We're just waiting to get the all clear so that we can arrest and interview Karen Bajarami," she replied. "With Blaine dead, she's the only thing that links us to Olivier."

"I want to be there when you interview her," said Ramouter.

"You're having a laugh, aren't you? That's not going to happen," said Pellacia as his phone began to ring.

"Guv, I have to be there. If it wasn't for her—" Ramouter weakly pleaded.

"That is not happening. You're in here for another few days and you're not coming back to the unit until you're fit. You've got a punctured lung and broken ribs. You're an HR headache that I don't need."

"Yes, guv," Ramouter said sullenly.

"To be honest, you do look like shit," said Stanford after Pellacia had left the room. "I'd rather not be looking at your ugly mug for the next few days."

"Thanks," Ramouter replied. "The love is real."

"For God's sake."

Pellacia leaned against the wall of the SCU building, threw the empty cigarette box toward the bin at the end of the car park and missed. He walked around the back of the building and ran his hands through his hair in frustration. He didn't feel as though he had a handle on anything. His life and his command of the SCU were spiraling out of control. The revelation of Dominic Pine as the copycat and his death should have been his crowning glory. But he had a junior officer laid up in the hospital. Olivier was out there and killing again. And he had broken his own rule by letting Henley back into his life. But he needed her.

"You're looking a bit stressed, mate."

The familiar voice gave him goose bumps. Pellacia's heartbeat quickened as he turned around. Olivier pushed back his sweatshirt hood. There were deep scratches and dried blood on his face. His bottom lip was split open and swollen.

Pellacia reached for the radio in his pocket but Olivier was too quick for him. Olivier struck him in the stomach with a brick and Pellacia doubled over, the air escaping his lungs. Olivier kneeled in front of him and grabbed his hair. Panic gripped Pellacia in his desperation to breathe. Henley had told him that it felt like someone had put a plastic bag over her head when she'd had her first panic attack. Pellacia's last thought before he blacked out was of her.

The rest of the day was filled with letting the remaining jurors know they were no longer targets and that the copycat killer, Dominic Pine, was dead. Henley had given a brief press conference while Anthony's team were still at Pine's place recovering evidence. The image of Zoe's dead eyes kept coming back to Henley. Upstairs they had found photographs of all three mutilated victims pinned to the bedroom wall. For the life of her she couldn't work out why Pine would have kept the photographs on display. The pain that he had caused and for what? To get one over on Olivier? To exact revenge on people who had only been doing the right thing? Petty. Selfish. Egotistical.

A monster.

Henley had managed to go home and shower before the scheduled press conference at 6 p.m., but she was still exhausted. She had been awake for more than twenty-four hours and the day wasn't over yet. She had received the call that Karen Bajarami was fit to be discharged from Queen Elizabeth Hospital, and Stanford and an exhausted Eastwood had arrested her. Stanford had messaged her during the press conference to confirm that Bajarami had been booked in at Lewisham police station, declared fit to be interviewed and was now sitting in the cell.

"You're making me feel like the rebound boyfriend," Stanford said as Henley punched in the security code that would let them into the custody suite.

"Stop being so precious," Henley replied.

"I can't help it. It was me and you for years and then some little upstart appears and takes my place," Stanford said. "How's he doing anyway?"

"I checked in an hour ago. He's doing well. Couple of days and he'll be home."

"I actually feel sorry for him," said Stanford.

The custody suite was busy with detainees being either booked in or charged. Henley knocked on the door of interview room three and let herself in. Karen Bajarami looked at her with her one good eye. The other eye was covered with a bandage and she looked utterly miserable. Henley recognized the duty solicitor as Morgan Tyler. She was one of the best ones.

"Evening, Inspector," said Morgan. "We're ready."

99

The interview room was cold, as always. The sound of the air-conditioning unit whirled in the background. Stanford sat next to Henley, wordlessly opening three blank CDs and placing them in the recorder. Bajarami sat opposite Henley, practically squeezing herself into the corner as though she was trying to make herself disappear. She looked pale and on the verge of passing out.

"Before we start, is it all right if I call you Karen?" Henley finished entering the interview details on the monitor.

"It's fine," Karen replied.

"The FME said that you're fit to be interviewed. I just want to check if you want anything. Water, another cup of tea—"

"I'm fine."

"Good." Henley pressed record. "Right, we'll start. I'm Detective Inspector Anjelica Henley and also present is—"

"Detective Sergeant Paul Stanford."

"We're in interview room three at Lewisham police station. This interview is being audio- and video-recorded. We're interviewing today—could you please confirm your name for the

record," said Henley. Karen Bajarami looked across at her solicitor, who nodded.

"Karen Irina Bajarami," she said.

"Thank you," said Henley. "Also present is your solicitor—"

"Morgan Tyler from Tyler Lawson solicitors, and I'm inform-
ing you now that my client will be answering 'no comment' to
all questions that are put to her."

Henley completed the rest of the introductions and cautions
without taking her eyes off Bajarami. "Karen, you've been arrested for conveying a prohibited article into prison, namely a
mobile phone, assisting a prisoner, Peter Olivier, to escape, obstructing the course of justice, preventing the lawful burial of
a body and conspiracy to commit murder. We've already disclosed this information to your solicitor, and you know that
we have evidence that you provided a mobile phone to Olivier
and also bought the phone credits. What would you like to say
about that?"

Henley and Stanford were prepared for Bajarami to answer
"no comment" to all their questions for the next hour.

"It's not what you think," Karen said.

Stanford tapped Henley's foot under the table.

"Karen, I'm going to remind you of the legal advice that I
gave you in consultation," Tyler said, writing something in her
notebook.

"Sorry, sorry. No comment," Karen said.

"As you can see, the mobile provider has confirmed that the
phone account was set up using a debit card registered to you.
Then you topped up the account on three subsequent occasions."

"No comment."

Henley was already getting tired of the no comments. "You
weren't the only woman that Olivier was in contact with," she
said suddenly.

Karen looked back at her with shock. Henley knew then that
Olivier was her trigger.

"What are you talking about?" Karen asked.

"I'm reminding you again of the legal advice I gave you in consultation and that was to answer 'no comment' to all questions put to you," Tyler said again, but Henley could hear the resignation in her voice—things were not going to go as she had advised.

"You and Olivier were in a relationship, weren't you?" asked Henley.

"Yes, we were," replied Karen.

"Even though this was a complete breach of your duties as a prison officer?"

Tyler looked as though she was going to interrupt again but Bajarami went on before she could say anything.

"You don't understand. He was different with me. He wasn't the man they described."

"He killed seven people before he came to Belmarsh."

"It was a miscarriage of justice. Mistakes were made."

Henley had to give Stanford a kick under the table to stop him from laughing.

"You've been a prison officer for eight years. Has anything like this happened before?" Henley continued.

"No, of course not. I'm good at my job and he saw that. He treated me with respect, not like some of those other prisoners."

"When did it start? The relationship."

"About eighteen months ago, and it wasn't what you think. He just wanted someone to talk to. He was sweet and gentle. Not a monster. He said that I understood him."

This time it was Tyler's turn to suppress her surprise with a cough as she caught Henley's eye.

"He understood you?"

"Yes, he did. He's intelligent and good-humored."

"Whose idea was it to get the phone?"

"Mine."

"Yours?" Henley needed her to reconfirm this for the recording.

"Yes. It was hard. Seeing him every day, not being able to talk to him properly. I mean, I have a job to do, but I just wanted to talk to him all the time."

"How often did you talk to him?"

"Every other night."

"Did you send him videos?"

"No. His phone was basic. I couldn't do that."

"Did you show him videos?"

"Yes. On my phone."

"Did you film me, outside my house, opening a box that contained the head of Elliot Cheung?"

Karen paused as she looked across at her solicitor.

"I don't want to answer that," she said.

"I'm sure that your solicitor has told you that a police interview isn't like selecting sweets at a pick 'n' mix. It's not going to look good on you that you're choosing to answer some questions and be quiet on others."

"I'll thank you not to comment on the advice that Ms. Bajarami has been given in consultation. Either ask her a question or end the interview," Tyler said.

"DS Stanford is going to show you footage from the security cameras that were installed in the reception area of the Franklin-Jones Cold Storage Facility in Manor Park," said Henley.

Stanford pressed play on the laptop and swung it toward Karen. She watched the footage, her face expressionless.

"Is that you walking out with Elliot Cheung's head in a box?" Stanford asked.

Karen put her hands to her forehead, visibly distressed.

"Is that you in the video?" Stanford repeated. "It's not a difficult question." Stanford's tone indicated firmly that there was only one acceptable answer.

"Yes," Karen said quietly. "Yes."

"Were you outside Detective Inspector Henley's house when Elliot Cheung's head was left on her doorstep?" he asked.

"Yes."

"Did Olivier give you instructions to remain outside the inspector's home and to film her?"

Karen's voice was barely a whisper. Her face still hidden behind her hands. "Yes," she said.

"You need to speak up," said Henley.

"I said, yes," Karen shouted. "He wanted to see everything. He wanted to see you."

Henley watched as Karen struggled to keep hold of the dark, poisonous feelings of jealousy that were boiling inside of her.

"Did you know that he was calling other women?" Henley asked, pulling out a photograph of Lauren Varma.

"Who's that?" Karen said, pointing to the photograph.

"That's the woman who also thought that she was in a relationship with Olivier."

"You're lying."

"And once he escaped, after he tried to kill you, he went straight to her."

"No. That's not true. He loved me."

"You knew about Lauren Varma, didn't you?"

"I have no idea who she is."

"That's not true, is it? You and Lauren met online. You were both members of a support group for women who are in relationships with prisoners."

"I don't know what you're talking about."

"And you both realized that you had something in common. You were both in love with Peter Olivier and she later told you that she was in a relationship with Olivier."

"No, no." Karen shook her head.

"You were jealous and that angered you. You thought you were the only one."

"How could I be jealous? I didn't know anything about her. This is all rubbish."

"Right." Henley produced two exhibit bags filled with letters. "This is exhibit RE/3. Letters from Lauren Varma to Peter Olivier. And exhibit SR/4. Letters from Peter Olivier to Lauren Varma. Your fingerprints are on all these letters."

Karen's face turned pale.

"Love letters," said Henley.

"She was obsessed," Karen said quietly.

"You're going to have to speak up for the mic."

Karen shook her head vigorously. "Nothing. I didn't say anything. No comment."

"Karen, part of your job as a prison officer is to check all of the outgoing and incoming letters, isn't it?"

"Yes."

"And you checked all of Olivier's mail. Your prints are all over these exhibits."

Karen didn't reply.

"Do you know what I'm thinking, Karen?" Henley took a sip of water. "I think that there was another woman vying for Olivier's attention and you didn't like it. You read the letters and that made you angry. It was fine when it was just Lauren Varma talking to you online about her feelings for Olivier, but when you found out that she had been writing to him and that he had been writing back—"

"Stop it. Stop it. You have no idea."

"You were checking his letters and you read what he had said to Lauren in those letters. Stanford?"

Stanford cleared his throat and began to read. "'I touch myself when I'm looking at your picture. I've imagined your sweet mouth around my...' He's very explicit. 'There is no other woman that can make me feel the way you do.' Ouch, that must have hurt. Finding out that you were no more than a— what do they call it on the streets, Inspector?"

"Side chick," said Henley. Tyler turned her head and pursed her lips.

"That's it. A side chick. That would hurt. A lot," said Stanford, placing the letter back on the table.

"You told Olivier to get rid of her," said Henley. "Karen, we have copies of the text messages that you sent to Olivier three days before he escaped."

"'If you truly love me, then you will get rid,'" Stanford read from the printout in front of him. "'You said that I was the only one. I want L gone.' And he did what he was told."

Karen put a hand to her mouth, but Henley had already seen it. A smile.

"And because you helped him to escape, Lauren Varma is now lying in six pieces in Greenwich mortuary," said Stanford.

Karen dropped her hand. "What are you talking about?" she asked.

"You provided him with insulin, which put him into hypoglycemic shock and gave him the symptoms of a heart attack," continued Henley. "Once he was in the hospital, you made sure that you would be with him and then you helped him escape."

"That's not true."

"The only thing you didn't plan for was that Olivier would kill Ade."

"He didn't kill him." Karen began to cry. "It was an accident."

"He slammed Ade's head so hard against the floor that he fractured his skull and he stabbed you in the eye with a fork. Somehow, I seriously doubt that losing your eye was part of the plan."

"No, no, that was... He loves me."

"Karen, you've lost your eye. Is that love?" Henley leaned across the table. "What was the plan? For you to leave your job and run off into the sunset with him? Start a new life together?"

Karen didn't answer, sniffing noisily instead.

"We searched your flat and we found the tickets to Málaga. Money and a bag filled with men's clothes. Passports. One of those passports is fake. That's another charge, on top of conspiracy to commit murder."

"Would you like a break? Another consultation?" Tyler asked. She pulled out a packet of tissues from her bag and handed it to Karen.

"No, no, I'm OK," Karen answered.

"He's killed another woman. She wrote to him and he wrote back. He seduced her, slept with her and then he butchered her," said Henley.

"He wouldn't do that. He promised me that he…"

"What did he promise you?"

"Nothing."

"Where is he?"

"I don't know."

"I don't believe you."

Karen laughed. "You would say that. He used to talk about you a lot. Said that you were responsible for ruining his life. He was obsessed with you."

"Where is he, Karen?"

"When you came to see him at the prison, his face…lit up. The way that he looked at you. He never looked at me that way. He wanted to get you back. You and that other officer who put him in that hellhole. Ruined his life."

Stanford and Henley exchanged a look.

"What other officer?" Stanford asked.

"Your boss. The one who was sitting with you at the press conference."

Henley's heart dropped to her stomach. Stephen.

"How would he get him back?" Henley asked, trying to keep her voice steady.

"I don't know. I didn't really pay attention."

"Karen, you're in love with him. You listen to every single word that he says. You've risked your life for him—"

"Inspector, I suggest that you ask Ms. Bajarami a question

instead of making grandiose speeches," said Tyler, sitting up straighter.

"What did Olivier say to you?"

"That he wanted to get him back. That he wanted to make you pay. To scare him a bit. I told him that it wouldn't work, but Peter said that he was just as guilty as you were. That you were responsible for the bodies on the street. Not him."

Stanford whispered into Henley's ear.

"For the benefit of the tape, DS Stanford is leaving the inter-view room at 21:28 hours."

"Where is Peter Olivier?"

"I don't know," Karen replied stubbornly.

"Karen, I know that he visited you while you were in the hospital. A witness positively identified him on the street where you live. You've been in contact with him. Where is he?"

"No comment."

"Karen, the longer that Olivier is out on the street, the more chance there is of someone else being murdered. You've already got the deaths of two innocent people on your hands. Do you really want another?"

"That's not what—"

"Where is he?"

"I can't tell you," Karen cried out. "He made me promise."

"I'm going to ask you again. Where is Peter Olivier?"

Karen started crying.

"I can't," she wept.

"Karen. Please. Where is Olivier?"

"What if he finds out that I told you? He killed Lauren… What if—"

"Where is he?"

Karen heaved as though she'd been punched in the stomach. "Convoys Wharf. In Deptford," she said.

Henley knew Convoys Wharf. She had grown up a stone's throw away from the forty-acre industrial estate. It had been a bustling hub for air freight and transport trucks. Searching for Olivier among the countless disused warehouses would be like looking for a needle in a haystack.

"Where in Convoys Wharf?" Henley asked.

Karen bent her head and whispered softly, "No. I can't."

"What do you mean that you can't? You need to tell me where he is, Karen."

Karen kept her head bowed and remained silent as she twisted the edge of her T-shirt.

"For fuck's sake," Henley said, not caring that it would be picked up by the microphones and would soon be scrutinized by lawyers and judges as they read the transcript. "You do realize what you're doing, right? You're protecting a murderer. A man who will kill you in an instant and have no regrets about doing so. Have you been there?"

"No comment," Karen replied.

"Convoys Wharf is a very big place. Did you arrange to meet Olivier somewhere specific after he escaped from the hospital?"

It was subtle, but Karen nodded.

"For the benefit of the tape, Karen Bajarami is nodding her head. Does that mean yes, Karen?"

"Yes, it does. But I'm not going to tell you where. I can't answer any more of your questions. I'm not doing it. I'm done."

"Karen. This is—"

"I said that I'm done," Karen shouted. "No comment. No comment—"

Henley resisted the overwhelming temptation to slap her across the face. Instead, she said, "I'm going to suspend the interview at 21:43 hours. Don't for one second think that—"

Henley stopped as Stanford opened the door, but he didn't enter the room. He beckoned for her to come with him.

"What's wrong?" Henley asked as Stanford pulled her into another interview room.

"I can't get hold of Pellacia," said Stanford. "We've called his mobile, the office and even his landline at home. No one has seen him since he left the hospital. He was supposed to be at a meeting at the Yard six hours ago. He never arrived."

100

Units had been sent to Pellacia's home and reported that he was not there, and neither was his car. Ezra and Joanna confirmed that he hadn't returned to the SCU and that there was no point asking for any CCTV footage because the security cameras bolted to the wall of the Greenwich police station were disconnected eight months ago. Another Met Police cost-saving measure. All attempts to contact Pellacia by police radio were met with dead noise. The last person to see him was Henley and that had been when he'd left the hospital.

"I don't understand," said Henley as she and Stanford drove to the Convoys Wharf industrial estate. A police van carrying the few available officers that Lewisham police station had to spare had already been dispatched from the station. Henley took a deep breath and checked that her stab vest was securely fastened. "Why has he taken him. Why bother? Olivier hasn't shown any interest in Pellacia. According to Karen it's all about me. I mean, the fact that he's been staying at Convoys Wharf. I grew up across the road from there. It's as if everything he's doing is to—"

"Rub your nose in it?" Stanford finished Henley's sentence.

"To show you how much he knows you? Or maybe he wants revenge. Sorry to be blunt, but if it wasn't for Pellacia stopping him, Olivier would have killed you."

"Take the next right. The other road is no entry," Henley said as Stanford drove through the red traffic lights. "Who really knows what's going through Olivier's mind?"

"You."

"What do you mean?"

"You're on Olivier's mind. Getting to Pine first and killing him. Hurts you. Almost killing Ramouter. Hurts you. Taking the man who loves you. Hurts you."

Henley could feel her eyes burning with tears. Everything that Stanford had said was right.

"So, what's his plan, then?" she asked. "Take him, torture him and leave him in bits across the river?"

"Not that I've ever considered myself to be any kind of optimist, but we don't know that he's got him yet. For the first time in my life, I'm hoping that he's just got knocked over by a bus."

Stanford pulled the car up to the front gates of Convoys Wharf. Over two weeks ago Henley had driven past the same spot after Pellacia called her with news that a body had been found on the Watergate Steps. She shivered and heard her mother telling her, "Someone's walked over your grave."

It was nearly 10:30 p.m. and the locals who had been drinking in the Admiral pub were standing outside, pints in hand, gawking but unsurprised about the police activity on the doorstep. The wharf had stood abandoned for ten years. The surrounding walls were covered with graffiti and posters protesting against further development. The security guard's box stood empty and weeds had pushed through cracks in the ground. For all Henley knew, this could have just been a fool's errand.

It was pitch-black. The only light came from the high-rise buildings of the Docklands and the sweeping flashlights of the officers who had already arrived and were searching for Pellacia and Olivier. Henley and Stanford walked to the side where part of the fencing had been pulled apart. They both squeezed through. The open channel on their radios reported that more units were finally on their way to assist with the search.

"What if Pellacia isn't here?" Henley turned her back to Stanford. She didn't want him to see that she was scared. Scared for herself, Pellacia and Stanford. "It could be Olivier is screwing with us. Screwing with *me*."

"We don't have to go any further. We can wait for the rest of the units to turn up with the search dogs," said Stanford as the sound of police chatter escaped from his radio. "We can wait."

Henley looked out across the wharf. The few officers that were in there—looking for Pellacia—didn't know the area like she did. They were searching blindly.

"You could be right," said Stanford hesitantly. "Olivier and Pellacia may not even be here."

"No," Henley said as she double-checked the battery level on her own radio.

"OK. I've got your back. So where shall we start?" Stanford asked. "This is your manor."

"He could be anywhere," Henley replied. She ran her flashlight against the black wall that bordered the right side of the wharf. "There used to be some old houses at the back, toward the river."

"Do you want to head there?"

Henley nodded.

The sounds of the river crashing against the wall grew louder as Henley and Stanford walked. There were six residential buildings that were still standing but all in various states of dilapidation. Henley and Stanford entered the first house. Used needles, heroin-stained spoons, abandoned condoms and homemade crack pipes were scattered over the ground but there were no other signs of life. Their radios crackled. No sign of Pellacia or

Olivier. Henley and Stanford continued their search through each building.

"This is just a waste of time," Henley said as they left the last building.

"What about that one?" asked Stanford, shining his flashlight up against the Master Shipwright's House on the other side of the wall. It wasn't technically part of Convoys Wharf, but Henley could clearly remember climbing over the large gate with Simon and their friends and playing on the grounds when she'd been a teenager.

For a second, Henley prayed for a panic attack. It would just be her and Stanford if they went to the other side of that wall. She would be placing them both in danger. But if Pellacia was there, they could save him.

"How do you feel about climbing a wall?" Henley asked Stanford.

"You're joking, aren't you?"

"Yeah, I am. Come on. I know a way."

Henley had led Stanford back onto Watergate Street and down the alleyway that led toward the steps where Daniel Kennedy's torso had been found. In the end she had made him scale the wall at the top of the steps. Stanford swore as he landed on the ground and tripped over a discarded bike.

Henley heard the sound of crunching glass and froze. She looked at Stanford and held a finger to her lips. They walked around the house. The windows and most of the doors had been boarded up, except for the door at the back of the house. The security screen that had once covered it had been prized away and was hanging off the edge.

"Maybe they're not here," whispered Stanford as they walked toward the door. There was no fencing or wall at the back of the house. There was a raised platform that dangerously overlooked the river, where someone had left some old deck chairs. Henley entered the house, leaving Stanford outside.

"Stephen, are you here?" Henley said as the light from her flashlight bounced off empty beer bottles and takeaway boxes. The rest of the room was vacant. Henley stepped back outside.

"Anjelica!" Stanford's voice rang out from the darkness. Henley spun around but she couldn't see him.

"Where are you?"

"Over here. Under the awning. He's over—"

Henley ran past the deck chairs, toward the awning, and called out for Stanford after his words cut off abruptly. She tripped and hit the ground. She tried to ignore the hot shooting pain that was spreading across her left shoulder.

"Oh my God," Henley gasped when she saw Stanford's body in front of her. There were broken bricks and parts of a rusted wheelbarrow set on the ground. She prayed that Stanford had simply lost his footing and banged his head. He lay on his side, his mouth slightly open. Blood was trickling down his forehead. Henley crawled over toward him and checked for a pulse. He was out cold but she released a breath when she felt the strong rhythmic pulsating flow of blood under her fingertips. She reached for her radio and pressed the emergency button.

And then she looked up.

Pellacia had been stripped naked and was hanging by his arms from the roof beams of the awning. His bruised skin stretched taut across his chest and a crescent and double cross had been cut into his stomach. A plastic bag had been placed over his head. It softly fluttered in the breeze.

You're too late. Olivier's won, screamed the voice in Henley's head. She looked around, surprised that Olivier was not standing in front of her, gloating and applauding her failure, but there was no one. Stanford remained motionless on the ground and Pellacia's body hung like a sacrifice in front of her.

Henley clutched her stomach, convinced that her guts were

being ripped out. It was her fault that Pellacia was dead. There was no one to blame but herself. A cold wind from the river slapped Henley hard across the face. Should she take Pellacia down? Should she wait? Where was Olivier?

Henley's radio crackled. Other officers were asking her to confirm her location. The radio fell out of her hand as she watched the plastic press against Pellacia's mouth and mold around the contours of his nostrils as if the air was being sucked out. An electric shock ran through Henley's body. Pellacia was suffocating. But he was still alive.

"Stephen!" Henley shouted. She stood on her tiptoes and stretched her hand toward Pellacia's head, her fingers failing to grip firmly onto the bag. She bent down, grabbed an old beer crate that was nearby and stood on it. "Fuck," she said when her foot crashed through the rotten dried-out plastic. She pulled her foot out and balanced herself precariously on the edges of the crate.

"I'm going to get you down." Henley ripped the bag off Pellacia's face and grappled with the rope that had been tied around his wrists. She looked around as the rope became loose around her fingers, but there was no sign of anyone. For all she knew, Olivier could have already made a run for it or was waiting in the darkness to finish off what he had started.

Henley fell off the crate as the rope came loose and Pellacia fell against her. Pellacia groaned as he turned his head toward Henley. His right eye was blackened and swollen shut. There were cuts and bruises across the left side of his face and chin.

"I'm here, Stephen. I'm here," Henley said as she placed him onto his back, took off her jacket and covered him. She heard Stanford groaning behind her as she confirmed their location on the radio.

"They're coming to us. The units are on their…" Henley stopped when she heard Olivier calling her name.

"Inspector Henley," Olivier shouted out.

Henley scanned the area where she thought Olivier was shouting from but she couldn't see him.

Pellacia stretched out his hand toward her. He opened his mouth to speak but his words were lost over the sound of the police helicopter and the rising waves crashing against the river wall.

Henley tried reaching for a broken bottle, but before she could wield it, Olivier was behind her, grabbing her hair, the roots slowly tearing out in his maniacal grip.

"I didn't think you would be stupid enough to come and find him," said Olivier, dragging Henley along the ground. Henley screamed as sharp rocks and pieces of glass cut into the skin on the small section of her back that wasn't protected by her stab vest. "I had something else planned for you."

Henley clawed at Olivier's arms, feeling her nails pierce into his skin. She heard Stanford shout out her name as the searchlight from the police helicopter overhead seeped across them.

"Shit," said Olivier as the light temporarily blinded him. He stumbled back and loosened his grasp. Henley felt the tension release and took her chance to get out of Olivier's grip. She tried to scramble away, but Olivier pulled out his knife and rushed her. She reached for her baton and swung it, catching the side of his face.

Olivier, caught off guard for only a moment, lumbered toward Henley with the knife still in his hand, forcing her to step back toward the river. She tried to swing away but missed, and he pushed the knife into her chest but the blade bent against the Kevlar material. They fell to the ground, and Olivier smashed Henley's head against the edge of the platform. She struck Olivier repeatedly on the back, but not once did he wince in pain. Instead, he raised himself up and pushed down on Henley's wrists. The river was now at high tide and the water was beating loudly against the wall. She wasn't sure where the spray was coming from, whether it was the drops of putrid river water splashing onto her face or the specks of salty sweat dripping from Olivier's forehead. Olivier licked the side of her face. Slowly. His tongue traced the corner of her lips and moved up toward her eye. He pushed his groin harder against Henley's leg.

"Do you like that?" Olivier looked over at Pellacia, who lay unmoving. "I'm going to show you that he's not man enough for you. How do you think it will make him feel to watch me in you?"

Henley tried to raise her knees to get out from under Olivier, and screamed with the effort of it. She felt sick as his weight crushed into her and his hot, rancid breath seeped into the pores of her skin. The helicopter searchlights flooded the area as more water splashed against her face. Henley heard police officers shouting out for her, Pellacia and Stanford over their radios. Blue lights began to break through the cracks of the wall. Henley felt Olivier shift, giving her the room to knee him twice in the groin. He grunted in pain and Henley spotted the jagged edges of a shattered wine bottle. She grabbed the bottle neck and pushed the jagged edge into the side of Olivier's face. The glass sliced his flesh and a shard broke away. Olivier's screams pierced Henley's ears and then were lost among the sounds of sirens. Olivier rolled over as Henley turned onto her hands and knees and stood up. She kicked Olivier as hard as she could in his ribs.

"You fucking bitch," Olivier shouted out as his face contorted, the piece of glass that was stuck in his face glinting in the light.

Henley turned to run, to get back to Pellacia and Stanford, but Olivier grabbed her, spun her toward him and began to pull her toward the edge. She wrestled her right arm free and pushed the glass deeper into Olivier's face. Her hand was hot and red as Olivier's blood ran. Adrenaline coursed through Henley's body and it took all her strength to push Olivier away from her. She felt him lose his footing and loosen his grip. She sensed footsteps approaching, but Henley knew there wasn't enough time to wait for the cavalry to arrive. She pushed him again, hard. Olivier screamed out in the darkness. Henley stood still and held her breath until she heard it. A loud, hard splash as Olivier's body hit the water.

101

Henley was curled up in an armchair in Pellacia's hospital room. It had been thirty-four hours since Olivier had fallen into the river. The River Police had searched for his body, but they hadn't found him. They believed it was unlikely that he had survived the fall and that his body would eventually wash up somewhere over the next couple of days, but Henley wasn't convinced. Stanford had called Olivier the devil and she was sure he was right.

Henley opened her eyes to see Pellacia sitting up in bed, watching her. He had a broken collarbone and dislocated shoulder. He'd suffered internal bleeding from a ruptured spleen and had been rushed into surgery. The symbols that had been cut into his stomach were not deep and did not need stitches, but they would leave a scar.

After he'd woken up from his morphine-induced sleep, Pellacia explained how Olivier had been waiting for him when he arrived at the SCU car park. He remembered being attacked and then waking up in the trunk of a car before Olivier beat him and knocked him out for a second time.

Stanford had suffered a minor concussion and had three

stitches in his head. He had been kept in the hospital for twenty-four hours for observation, before being sent home.

"You should still be sleeping." Henley winced and unfurled from the armchair; the cuts on the small of her back still felt raw as they rubbed against the bandages. She made her way to Pellacia, placed a hand tenderly on the side of his face and kissed his forehead.

"I thought that you had gone home."

"I did, but I came back."

"I'm glad you did," he said softly. He saw the look of concern cross her face. "I think it looks worse than it feels."

"I doubt it," Henley replied. Her eyes ran down to the large dressings on Pellacia's stomach. The wound was seeping and she could see the faint image of a double cross through the bandages.

"What is it?" Pellacia asked as he took hold of Henley's hand.

Henley couldn't bring herself to speak Olivier's name.

"They will find him," he said.

Henley shook her head. "Until someone can show me a body, I'm going to be sleeping with one eye open. I won't be able to—"

"No one could survive that fall, Anjelica, or that water. No one."

Henley didn't answer. She gently kissed Pellacia on the cheek and then pulled her hand away. "I have to go."

There was disappointment on Pellacia's face. He turned away to face the window. After a while he spoke. "I was thinking about Elliot Cheung. Trying to work out why Olivier chose him."

"I wish I knew." Henley stepped back from Pellacia's bed. "Cheung wasn't linked to any of the other victims. Maybe he was just in the wrong place at the wrong time and Olivier killed him because he just…felt like it." That sounded thin and implausible, even to her ears.

"Poor kid. What about Karen Bajarami?"

"She was at court this morning. Eastwood confirmed that

she was refused bail. The case was sent to the Old Bailey. She should be on her way to HMP Bronzefield later this afternoon."

"She's the only one who is actually going to be punished and sent to prison for all this. I'm starting to think that Pine and Olivier got off lightly," Pellacia said bitterly. "Bajarami's life will be a living hell when they realize she's an ex-screw. After what she did, I wouldn't be surprised if someone takes her out."

"You know what? I don't really care," Henley said. "Her being in prison won't be enough but it will be something. Someone has to pay for taking all of those innocent lives."

"I think that Pine has paid," said Pellacia. "Olivier made sure of that."

"That wasn't Olivier's job," Henley said darkly as her emotions wavered between anger and resentment. "I made a promise to Zoe's grandparents and I didn't keep it. I wasn't the one who caught Zoe's killer. Olivier did that. He took that promise from me."

Henley brushed away the tears from her face and walked out of the room, ignoring Pellacia's pleas for her to come back as the voice in her head mockingly repeated the same three words: *Olivier has won. Olivier has won.*

102

Henley stood on the steps of the SCU, trying to work out where Olivier had been standing when he had watched her that afternoon. It was raining heavily, but she didn't try to seek shelter. She couldn't shake off the feeling that Olivier would always be out there watching her. Waiting for her. She pulled out her phone and her finger hovered over Stanford's name. She had an intense desire to run as far away from the SCU as possible. The phone in her hand began to vibrate. She watched Rob's name and picture flash on the screen. She took a deep breath, her thumb hovering over the end call button before pressing accept.

"I saw the news," said Rob. "Is it over, then?"

"Yes, it's over," said Henley. "I'll tell you about it later, but this case is done."

"And Olivier?"

"He's… Dead." Henley knew it was a lie.

"Really? That's it, then? All of this is over?"

"It is. I hope it is." Henley looked down at her heavily bandaged right hand. She had needed four stitches and it was likely that she had suffered permanent nerve damage.

"I can't believe that he's finally gone. Out of our lives. For good," Rob said. "How did he...? Actually, I don't really care. I just want you to come home. So, what are you going to do now?"

"What do you mean?" Henley asked, walking down the steps and toward the High Road. She could have sworn that she had seen someone familiar on the other side of the street, standing in front of the chemist—Olivier's face on the body of the man sheltering from the rain.

"I mean, what's next for us?"

Henley squeezed her eyes closed as she tried to block out an image of Olivier's body hitting the river.

"Rob, can we talk about this when you and Emma get home?"

"Yeah, of course. Where are you now?"

"I'm still at the SCU," Henley said. The raindrops were cold and harsh against her face. She stepped back from the edge of the pavement as the traffic lights turned red and a double-decker bus stopped in front of her, obstructing her view.

"Right...it's safe... We need..." Rob's voice became disjointed as the signal broke up.

"I can't hear you properly," said Henley.

"I was saying that we need you. Emma needs you, but I need to know, Anjelica. Have you decided yet? Is this the last case?"

Henley didn't answer. The lights turned green and the bus moved on. A woman stood at the door of the chemist, struggling with her umbrella. All she could see was Olivier. He was the face on every person she saw. When she closed her eyes, he was there. She could feel Olivier pressing down on her chest. She could smell him. Her heart started to race, and she couldn't catch her breath. The cold rain was doing nothing to cool down the heat spreading across her face. Pins and needles ran up and down her leg, and a wave of fear swept over her.

Olivier was *alive*. She could feel it.

Henley stumbled back to the steps of the SCU and sat down on the wet concrete. The fear of dying, the loss of control, had drained her. She reached into her jacket pocket and pulled out the business card of the therapist that Mark had given her last week. She put the phone back to her ear.

"Rob, I need help."

ACKNOWLEDGMENTS

A heartfelt thank you to the *"Trash Fictioners"* Amber, Esther, Jem, Jonathan, Luke, Patricia, Satu and Steph, who were there at the very beginning when *The Jigsaw Man* began life as a 1000-word assignment on our Creative Writing MA at City, University of London. You've been on every single step of this journey with me and I couldn't ask for a better group of writing friends. I love our friendship and that we continue to support each other. I'm looking forward to seeing you at our next dinner.

A special thank you to Claire McGowan, Laura Wilson and William Ryan, who saw the potential of *The Jigsaw Man*, even when I couldn't, and encouraged me every step of the way. Your guidance and support have been invaluable.

My agent, Oli Munson, knows that I think that this entire journey with *The Jigsaw Man* has been completely "mad," but this novel would not be in your hands if it wasn't for him and the wonderful team at A.M. Heath. You have all been brilliant and working with you has been an absolute joy. Thank you for everything.

To my editor, Manpreet Grewal, who loves Henley and Olivier as much as I do and who was instrumental in pushing me to shape and go that little bit further with *The Jigsaw Man*. I knew that HQ was the perfect home for me and I want to thank every single member of the team who were enthusiastic about *The Jigsaw Man* from the very beginning.

Thank you to John Glynn and the fantastic team at Hanover Square Press, who are looking after my novel in the US and have been equally as enthusiastic. I've loved working with you all.

A special mention to Sarah Hilary, who was my mentor and continues to support me. Thanks to one of my oldest friends, Amanda O'Brien, who entertained my random questions about police procedure.

Lots of love and thank you to my guiding stars: Mum, Dad, Gavin, Jason, Sheulee, Edwin, Gaynor, Harminder, Kirsty and Lavinia, who have supported me through this madness and always picked up the phone to listen to the latest twist and turns of my journey.

Thank you to all of my family and friends for their unwavering love, support and encouragement. Just because I haven't mentioned you doesn't mean that you've been forgotten. I love you all. Always and forever.

And finally, thank you, dear reader, for buying my novel. I hope that you've enjoyed it, and feel free to get in touch. x.